WITHIN PLAIN SIGHT

A DETECTIVE BYRON MYSTERY

WITHIN PLAIN SIGHT

BRUCE ROBERT COFFIN

THORNDIKE PRESS
A part of Gale, a Cengage Company

LIBRARY OF CONGRESS CIP DATA ON FILE.
CATALOGUING IN PUBLICATION FOR THIS BOOK
IS AVAILABLE FROM THE LIBRARY OF CONGRESS

ISBN-13: 978-1-4328-8058-3 (hardcover alk. paper)

Published in 2020 by arrangement with Witness Impulse, an imprint of HarperCollins Publishers

Printed in Mexico
Print Number: 01   Print Year: 2020

For Mom and Dad.

For Mom and Dad

Truth only reveals itself when one
gives up all preconceived ideas.

— GIDO SHOSEKI

CHAPTER 1

Tuesday, 3:07 A.M.,
July 11, 2017

Erwin Glantz sat inside the dumpster, staring wide-eyed into the garbage bag, his heart hammering. He struggled to comprehend what he was seeing. His vision was focused, despite the large quantity of alcohol flowing through his veins. The drinking had gotten bad as of late, and along with it came hallucinations. But he knew that this was no figment of his imagination. The contents of the bag were very real, a nightmare in vignette. After a moment, he cinched both sides of the plastic bag together, closing it, successfully removing the macabre image from his sight, but not from his memory.

The trash receptacle, which had previously afforded him shelter from noise and inclement weather, now seemed much too small. The filthy grease-stained walls felt like they were closing in. The stench of rotting waste he'd previously been oblivious to was suddenly overpowering. His insides were roiling, threatening to revolt. He scrambled out of the dumpster and onto the pavement, careful to avoid the bag and its contents. Dropping to his knees, he retched up the sour contents of his stomach. When he had finished, Glantz rolled onto his backside and leaned against the metal waste receptacle to catch his breath.

Hidden from the alley, in the shadow of the dumpster, he wiped the debris and spittle from his wiry beard with the back of one calloused hand. Despite the warm night air, a shiver ran through him. He pulled his knees up to his chest and wrapped his arms around them, rocking back and forth. He closed his eyes, while his brain struggled to process what it had just witnessed, and why. He could simply leave what he'd found, he reasoned. Place some other garbage on top of it to make sure that nobody else discovered the bag or its contents and then just walk away. *Sure.* His alcohol-muddled brain couldn't find any flaw in that plan.

He stopped rocking and opened his eyes wide. He held both hands up in front of his face as if studying them. *Fingerprints.* His prints were now all over the bag. And not just prints. Probably hair and fibers. He turned to look at the puddle of vomit he'd left on the ground. *DNA.* With his history it was likely the cops would think he'd done this horrible thing. He could hear their questions. *Where have you been? Why did you do it? Tell us where it happened.*

Glantz struggled to get his thoughts together. The sun would be up soon, and he needed a cohesive plan. One that didn't involve his incarceration. He couldn't leave the bag and its awful contents, that much was obvious. But if he took it with him and was stopped by the police, how would he ever explain it? A no-win scenario for old Erwin. He closed his eyes and began to rock again. The rhythmic motion temporarily soothed him, carried him away.

CHAPTER 2

Wednesday, 5:17 A.M.,
July 12, 2017
The flies buzzing around the body were a telltale sign that death had not occurred overnight. *Perhaps a day or two at most,* Portland Police Detective Sergeant John Byron thought as he scribbled onto a fresh notepad. The bound paper tablet, removed from the glove box of his unmarked Taurus moments before, would serve as a case diary of sorts. Times, dates, names, facts, every detail would be documented. As the department's lead homicide investigator, Byron was responsible for overseeing every aspect of the investigation. As always, depending upon case complexity, one notebook might easily become ten, or even twenty. Byron paused a moment to survey the body. A light breeze carried with it the foul note of decay, causing Byron to revise his earlier estimate. *Maybe more,* he wrote.

The corpse was female, partially dressed in matching teal-colored bikini style underwear and bra. She was thin but not scrawny. Athletic. Her tan skin was shifting toward blue/gray. Lividity was clearly present where it shouldn't have been, around the front of her torso and extremities. After death blood pools to the lowest points of the body due to the effect of gravity. Whoever this woman was, she had died facedown. Her fingernails, recently manicured in a French style, were lacquered a bright tangerine color with white tips. A delicate-patterned silver band encircled the ring finger of the right hand. Her left hand was unadorned.

Byron wordlessly studied the scene, the silence broken only by an occasional passing vehicle, the incessant shrill whine of cicadas, and the rhythmic click of Gabriel Pelligrosso's digital camera.

"Any guess on age?" the flat-topped evidence technician inquired.

"Tough to tell," Byron said as he jotted another entry into the book. "Her hands look young."

Pelligrosso nodded in agreement, then returned to his photographic documentation of the scene.

The body had been posed in an almost natural-looking position, seated on the ground among the scrub brush and weeds, legs together, knees up, arms crossed in front of the calves, like one might sit on a beach looking out at the waves. Byron wondered if there was something symbolic about the setup.

Pelligrosso looked up from his camera once again. "Think this might be related to those others, Sarge?"

The question, and what it might mean, was already occupying a large chunk of Byron's thoughts. Impossible not to consider, given the recent media coverage, but also much too early to be jumping to any conclusions.

"Time will tell, Gabe."

Byron turned his head toward the sound of someone slamming a car door. He recognized his boss's voice. Lieutenant Martin LeRoyer was speaking with the young uniformed officer standing post on Maple Street. The freshly minted officer was maintaining a crime scene log, standard procedure in any murder investigation. LeRoyer, commander of the police department's Criminal Investigation Division (CID), would be required to check in just as Byron and Pelligrosso had. Rank had its privileges but compromising a murder scene wasn't one of them.

Byron watched as LeRoyer stepped through a hole in the chain-link fence and approached on foot. He gestured for the lieutenant to keep to his right on the pavement. No need to trample the scene further. Crime scene 101. One route in, one route out.

"Morning, gentlemen," LeRoyer greeted.

"Morning, Lieu," Pelligrosso said.

"Marty," Byron said.

"What do we have he—" LeRoyer stopped cold. Cupping a hand over his mouth, he appeared to be fighting back the urge to vomit. "Oh, sweet Jesus."

"If you're thinking about losing your breakfast, I'd rather you didn't do it inside my crime scene," Byron said.

LeRoyer staggered back a step, his face twisted up in disgust. "Where the hell is the rest of her?"

CHAPTER 3

Wednesday, 5:23 A.M.,
July 12, 2017
The killer, or killers, had chosen an abandoned lumberyard to dispose of the body. Forest City Lumber had been one of the largest building material suppliers in Greater Portland when Byron first donned a uniform as a beat cop for the Portland Police Department in the mid-nineties. Its proximity to the waterfront and rail lines, previously traversing the center of Commercial Street, had made shipping, in or out, quite convenient. But with the rise of the trucking industry the rail lines had been torn up and the family-owned lumber company eventually succumbed to the discount pricing and do-it-yourself branding of mega-stores like Lowe's and Home Depot. Forest City Lumber had become a memory. And a place to discard bodies.

The fenced-in two-and-a-half-acre lot was

bordered by four different thoroughfares, Commercial, Maple, York, and High Street. A long stick-built office building, one large storage barn, and an industrial-sized steel Quonset hut, all vacant, crowded the west side of the property closest to High Street. Scattered about the remainder of the crumbling asphalt were long open-air drying sheds, nothing more than red sloping roofs mounted atop wooden pilings. Byron could still remember driving past and seeing stacks of freshly cut lumber. The victim had been discovered in one of the smallest sheds located at the back of the yard, tucked up against York Street.

Byron continued to monitor his superior for signs that LeRoyer was about to contaminate the scene with breakfast.

"Jesus, John," LeRoyer said after taking a few deep breaths and regaining his composure. "You could have warned me." The lieutenant pointed at the remains. "That might be the sickest thing I've ever seen."

Byron, no longer shocked at the horrors people were capable of inflicting on each other, couldn't argue with his boss's assessment.

"Who found the body?" LeRoyer asked.

"Security guard named Hopkins called it in," Byron said, flipping back a page in his notebook. "Said he was checking the grounds at quarter to five this morning. His dispatcher notified ours."

LeRoyer tore his eyes away from the gruesome scene and scanned the area. "Have we searched for the rest of her?"

"Not yet," Byron said. "We need more help, but I don't want anyone else tramping through here if I can help it. Mike Nugent is on his way in."

"So is Bernie," LeRoyer said. "I pulled him from George's side."

George was Detective Sergeant George Peterson who supervised the Crimes Against Property side of CID. Detective Bernard "Bernie" Robbins was one of Peterson's detectives. One of his least popular detectives.

Pelligrosso stopped what he was doing and exchanged a quick glance with Byron.

"Problem?" LeRoyer asked, directing both his question and an annoyed expression toward both investigators.

Pelligrosso, who had wisely remained silent, returned to his picture taking.

"I had hoped for Luke Gardiner," Byron said, attempting to remain as politically correct as possible.

"Gardiner's unavailable," LeRoyer said. "He's the lead on those West End safe burglaries."

"Property crimes, Marty?" Byron said.

"I'm not pulling Gardiner off that case. Besides, he just had another one. Look, you just said you needed more help and, as it turns out, Bernie's available."

Detective Robbins was available, as Byron knew, for precisely the same reason he was always available. Robbins bitched so frequently, about every case he was assigned, that Sergeant Peterson, due to retire in several weeks, had pretty much given up on him. Robbins's piss-poor attitude had been like a cancer within the Property Crimes Unit of CID, and Byron wasn't keen on having it metastasize in his Violent Crimes Unit.

"Besides," LeRoyer continued, "Nugent is a phone call away from being out on paternity leave anyway."

Unconvinced, Byron continued to stare down the lieutenant, hoping to make him budge on the issue.

"Pair Nuge and Bernie up on this, then when Nuge goes out Bernie will be up to speed. Relax, John. It'll all work out."

As if conjured by LeRoyer's words, Nugent and Robbins arrived in their respective unmarked cars, adding to the number of police vehicles already choking Maple

Street. Byron watched the two detectives check in with the uniformed rookie. Nugent's shaved dome gleamed in sharp contrast to his new and hopefully temporary partner's unkempt coif.

"Sure, it will," Byron said, his words dripping with the intended extra helping of sarcasm.

"Where's Mel?" LeRoyer said, referring to Detective Stevens, in a not-so-subtle attempt at changing the subject.

Byron returned his focus to the body. "At 109, interviewing the guard."

Portland Police Headquarters was located at the northwest corner of Middle and Franklin, at 109 Middle Street, where it had stood since its grand opening in 1972. More commonly referred to by all who worked there as 109, the odd-shaped pile of brick and glass had replaced the original antiquated granite building that once stood on Federal Street between the county courthouse and jail. CID was housed on the top floor, along with a number of other administrative offices, including the chief's.

Detective Melissa Stevens sat at the scarred wooden table directly across from the uniformed security guard in CID Interview Room Three. The guard's name was

Craig Hopkins. He had wavy blond hair, blue eyes, and boyish good looks. According to his driver's license he was twenty-nine years old. And based solely on his accent, Stevens guessed he was from the South.

"Never seen anything like that," Hopkins said, shaking his head to emphasize the point.

Stevens studied the guard's picture ID. "How long have you been employed by Secure Incorporated, Mr. Hopkins?"

"You can call me Craig," he said.

Oh, please, she thought. "How long have you worked for Secure Incorporated, *Craig*?"

"Let's see, I started working for S.I. about a year and a half ago, right after I left the army. Work mostly overnights."

Stevens recorded every detail of their conversation in her notebook, even though the entire conversation was being video-taped by a remote digital system located in the CID conference room. She'd never known a notebook to malfunction. She couldn't say the same about computers.

"And what do you do for the company, specifically?" she asked.

"Respond to alarms. Patrol the various commercial properties that S.I. oversees. I do a little bit of everything. Kinda like a cop."

Wannabe, Stevens thought as she fixed him with a halfhearted grin. "What time did your shift start last night, Craig? Or was it this morning?"

"Last night, at twenty-one hundred hours. My shift ends at zero seven hundred." He checked his watch. "Well, it was supposed to end at zero seven hundred."

"You wanna contact your boss? Let them know you'll be late?"

"Nah, I'm okay for now. They know I'm with you."

He's flirting with me, she thought. *What a tool.* "Tell me again what time you discovered the body."

"0449 hours this morning."

"Exactly 4:49 a.m.?" she said.

"Yes, ma'am. I wrote it on my clipboard and radioed it in to my dispatcher."

"I'll need the document you wrote that note on."

"Sure thing. I'll give it to you when I get back to my patrol car."

"Did you notice anyone else in the area?"

"I didn't."

"How did you happen to check the lot this morning? Were you responding to an alarm?"

"No. The owners of that property contract with S.I. for security. They're in the process of selling. Several out-of-state developers are bidding on it. It's been on the news. I think they're planning to turn it into a hotel or something."

"Is it alarmed?"

"The property? No. The buildings are, but the open-air structures aren't. Neither is the yard."

"Cameras?"

"Nope."

Stevens nodded her understanding. "How often do you check on that particular location? Every night?"

Hopkins's face reddened. "I'm supposed to, but to be totally honest it's been a few days since I last checked."

Byron and Pelligrosso stood sweating near the body as they watched Doctor Ellis amble across the lot toward them. Ellis was whistling. Nugent and Robbins had already begun their visual search of the property looking for the rest of the victim and any of her belongings, with the understanding that if they discovered something they were to make a note of where it was and leave it for Pelligrosso to photograph and bag later.

Ellis was toting his weathered black leather

examination bag in one hand. Sporting Ray-Bans, tan cargo shorts, and an untucked black Iron Maiden T-shirt, he looked like a middle-aged tourist from a bygone era. No bystander would have guessed that this colorful character was the State of Maine's deputy medical examiner.

"Top o' the morning, gentlemen," Ellis said, greeting them in his signature theatrical way.

"Doc," both investigators said simultaneously.

"The office said you had something a bit unusual for me. What have you —" Ellis stopped in his tracks and made a show out of removing his sunglasses.

Neither detective said anything.

"Well, this is a first for the good Doctor E," Ellis said. Placing the leather bag on the pavement, he unzipped it and removed a pair of blue latex gloves. As Ellis worked his hands into the gloves, he turned to the evidence tech. "My boy, have you finished with your photos and all that?"

"I have," Pelligrosso said.

"All right then," Ellis said with an enthusiastic twinkle in his eyes. "Let's have a closer look, shall we?"

"Have you had much of a problem with

trespassers on that property?" Stevens asked Hopkins.

"Every once in a while. Sometimes during bad weather some of the street bums will take shelter in one of the lumber drying sheds."

"Is that what that structure is, where you found the body? A drying shed?"

"Yeah. At first, I thought it was somebody who'd set up camp there. But then I got a closer look. Not a camper."

"Did you touch anything?"

"No, ma'am. I watch those cop shows on TV. As soon as I saw what it was, I stepped out and called my dispatcher."

"Tell me about the damage to the fence on the Maple Street side of the lot. How long has it been like that?"

"Awhile. The owners of the property contract with a maintenance company. They keep repairing it with wire, but it doesn't last. The kids keep cutting through it."

"Kids?"

"Yes, ma'am. Sometimes the teenagers go in there to drink and — fool around."

"Have you caught many kids in there?"

"A few. Only a couple of times, though."

"Can you remember when the last time was?"

"Maybe a month or so. You could call

S.I.," he said, reaching inside his uniform shirt pocket. "Here's my business card. That's the number to the main office in Westbrook. Would you like my cell?"

Stevens ignored the question. "When you found the body had you driven in, or did you walk?"

"I parked on Maple Street then walked in through that damaged section of fencing. Same one you guys came through."

"Do you have a key to the gates?" she asked, knowing that they would need access to remove the body.

"I do." Hopkins pulled up the collection of keys hanging from his belt by a wire retractor and searched until he located the correct one. "Here it is."

"Well, that's interesting," Ellis said, shooing away several flies that had lighted on the body.

"What is, Doc?" Byron asked as he looked up from his notes.

"One of the vertebrae has been cut. Not just the spinal cord, but actual bone."

"Any idea what kind of instrument the killer used?" Pelligrosso asked.

"Wasn't a surgical instrument, I can tell you that. The cut isn't fine enough." He pointed to the skin where the neck had been

severed. "See how ragged the dei.
around the edge here?"

"Then what?" Byron asked.

"Don't know. Not a circular type of saw either. I'm thinking reciprocating. More akin to something you might carve a turkey with."

"Was that the cause of death?" Pelligrosso asked.

"I wouldn't think so. This cut appears to have been made postmortem."

"Any estimate on time of death?" Byron asked.

Ellis stood up and regarded the body. He was about to scratch his nose with his gloved hand when he caught himself and used the back of his forearm instead. "Rigor is long past. There's some minor decomp, along with a bit of skin slippage. Couple of days, at least. But she can't have been here that long."

"What makes you say that?" Byron asked.

"Well, with the heat we've been having . . ." Ellis paused for a moment to survey the general area. "And rodents and birds likely would have been at her, too."

Byron nodded and made a notation in his notebook to have Dustin Tran check recent missing-persons reports. If this woman was local, and had been in the wind for several

one should have been looking for

ss?" Ellis said.

the expert, Doc," Byron said.

will get you everywhere, Sergeant, but as you know time of death is anything but a science. Far too many unknowns and variables, I'm afraid."

Byron grinned. He had heard Ellis deliver the same canned speech numerous times on the stand, particularly whenever some overzealous defense attorney attempted to pin him down in order to benefit his or her client. "Best you can do then."

"I'd say we are probably looking at sometime Sunday morning." Ellis studied the body for a bit. "And I'd also say that the doer of the dastardly deed may have kept the body someplace chilly after dispatching her."

"Like?" Pelligrosso asked.

Ellis turned toward Pelligrosso and gave a Groucho-esque eyebrow wiggle. "Who knows. Might be the same place her head is at."

After completing the interview, Detective Stevens transported Craig Hopkins from 109 Middle Street back to the scene. Byron had decided that they would remove the body via the Maple Street gate, avoiding the more heavily traveled Commercial Street thoroughfare. Drawing attention to the hearse would only garner additional public attention, which would lead to media scrutiny, which of course they didn't need. A freshly waxed black funeral home transport was already backed up to the locked gate as Stevens pulled up and parked.

"I don't understand it," Hopkins said after fumbling about for several moments. "I'm positive that this is the key that opens all of these locks."

Stevens watched Hopkins try several other keys on the ring before returning to the one he claimed should have worked.

"Could someone have installed a new lock?" Stevens asked, trying to be helpful.

"I guess," Hopkins said. "But this key worked the last time I tried it."

"When was that?"

"Beginning of last week."

"What's up?" Nugent said as he and Bernie Robbins approached them on foot from inside the fence.

"We can't get the lock open," Stevens said.

"Well, we gotta get the body out," Nugent said. "Cut the chain."

"I don't have anything to cut it with," Hopkins said.

29

"I do," Stevens said. "Be right back."

Byron, Nugent, Robbins, and Stevens stood watching as Pelligrosso and a pair of funeral home attendants zipped the partial remains into a maroon body bag. The three men then hoisted it onto a rolling stretcher.

Byron couldn't help noticing the strong resemblance the attendants bore to the comedy duo of Stan Laurel and Oliver Hardy, one tall and beanpole thin, the other short and stout. The only thing missing were the black derbies. He didn't mention it.

For now, they would refer to the victim as Jane Doe. Neither the detectives nor Pelligrosso had located the woman's identification anywhere on scene and, aside from the matching underwear, there was no clothing on her person. Byron telephoned Detective Dustin Tran in the department's computer lab, requesting that he check all the local active missing-persons cases for Caucasian women between the ages of twenty and thirty. Byron knew Pelligrosso would be able to obtain the victim's prints following the post, but right now it was more important to bag the hands to try and preserve any evidence that might lead them to the killer. In cases where the victim fought their attacker, skin, blood, fibers, and other foreign materials were often recoverable from under the fingernails. And in the age of DNA trace evidence had become even more important.

"Who would have changed the lock?" Byron asked.

"Hopkins doesn't know," Stevens replied. "Said it worked fine when he opened it a week or so ago."

"How does he seem?" Byron asked, casting a glance toward the open gate where the guard stood talking with the uniformed officer.

"Hopkins? Okay, I guess. Nothing hinky about him. He's just a bit of a flirt."

Nugent laughed. "He flirted with you? Did you tell him he's barking up the wrong tree?"

Stevens slugged Nugent hard on the shoulder. "You jealous?" She readdressed Byron. "Truthfully, he seems harmless. I think finding the body kinda weirded him out."

After securing Jane onto the stretcher, Laurel and Hardy each grabbed an end and lifted, raising the wheeled transport to its full height and locking the stainless-steel legs in place.

"Almost ready to head out, Sarge," Pelligrosso said. "I'm gonna follow the transport up to Augusta."

"Okay, Gabe. Mel and I will head up within the hour."

"What do you want me to do about securing the scene?" Pelligrosso asked.

"Let's get our own locks on all the gates," Byron said. "Do you have enough?"

"I do. But that still leaves one big-ass hole in the fence." They all turned to look at it.

Byron approached the young uniformed officer maintaining the crime scene log. His brand-spanking-new name tag read: E. Gallant. Below that was an equally shiny Serving Since pin engraved with the year 2017, or what Nugent would have referred to as a Serving Since Tuesday pin.

"What does the *E* stand for, officer?" Byron asked.

"It's Evan, sir."

Byron recognized the face, but not the name that accompanied it. "Have we met before, Evan?"

"Yes, sir. I used to work down at DiMillo's."

"The restaurant?"

"No, sir. The marina. You and Detective Joyner interviewed me about the murdered attorney, Paul Ramsey, a couple of years ago. Ramsey kept his boat there."

"You were a dockhand, right?"

"Yes, sir."

"How long have you been working the street?"

"Six months. I just got off probation."

"What time did you start your shift last night?"

"Twenty-one hundred hours, sir."

Byron nodded. "We're gonna need you to guard the scene awhile longer. You up for that? If not, I'll contact the day class shift commander and have them assign someone to relieve you."

"No, sir. I'm here as long as you need me."

"Good. One more thing. The news media will be poking around before too long. They'll likely be asking questions. What are you going to tell them?"

"Nothing. If they want information, they have to speak to you."

Byron grinned. "Better yet, why don't you point them in the direction of Lieutenant Martin LeRoyer."

"Yes, sir, Sergeant."

Byron began to walk away then paused a moment and turned back. "Welcome to the show, Officer Gallant."

Pelligrosso accompanied the attendants as they rolled the remains toward the livery. The detectives followed.

Byron addressed Detective Stevens. "Let's contact the property owners and get them to do another repair on that fence. And find out if they changed the lock for some reason. Maybe they just forgot to tell the security company."

"You got it, boss."

Byron looked down the street where several people were seated at an outside patio connected to the Courtyard Marriott. Each of the hotel's patrons had strategically positioned their chairs so that they were all facing in the same direction, allowing for a better view of the festivities while they enjoyed their lattes. He turned his attention to Nugent and Robbins. "Grab a couple of uniforms and canvass the area. Check for surveillance cameras, witnesses, anything that might help us. With any luck somebody coming or going from the hotel may have seen something."

"We'll take care of it," Nugent said.

"Also, let's record and check every vehicle parked in the area. I want to know if the victim may have initially come here under her own power or if this was only a dump site. There might be some relevance to this particular location."

Robbins turned to look at Commercial Street. "Jesus, Sarge. There must be forty cars parked in front of this property alone."

"And?" Byron said.

"And, I'll take care of it."

CHAPTER 4

Wednesday, 8:00 A.M.,
July 12, 2017

Byron drove directly to 109, hoping to get a quick glimpse at the day's cases before making the trek to Augusta. With any luck he would locate a report of the missing young woman. He found a stack of reports from the overnight left on his desk by property crimes Detective Sergeant Peterson under a handwritten note that read, *I won't miss this. Love, G.* Byron didn't imagine the soon-to-be-retiring sergeant would.

"Chief wants to see you before you head up to Augusta," LeRoyer said without fanfare from the doorway to Byron's office.

Byron looked up, choosing his words carefully. "Really, Marty? She's been here what, a month? And she chooses this very moment to have a sit-down with me? Probably has nothing to do with the case we just caught, right?"

36

LeRoyer frowned. "I'm curious, do you live just to make my life difficult? I get enough of that at home from Jenny and the kids. I don't need it from you, too."

"Bet Lynds doesn't even know my name," Byron said.

"Actually, *Sergeant,* she does." The lieutenant tapped the face of his watch. "And she's expecting you." LeRoyer disappeared down the hallway before Byron could mount a further protest.

"Goddammit," Byron mumbled to himself. "And it's detective sergeant."

As if in answer to his blasphemy, the desk phone rang. The electronic display read: P. Milliken. The P stood for Patricia. Milliken was the chief's executive secretary. During Byron's twenty odd years at 109 the PD's top cops had come and gone, but Milliken had remained.

Byron grabbed the receiver. "Morning, Pat."

"Oh good, you're in," she said with her usual inflection of condescension. "The Queen Mum has requested an audience with you, Detective Sergeant Byron."

Byron laughed out loud at the moniker.

"When should we expect you?" Milliken asked.

"Don't suppose never is an option?"

"I'll let her know you're on the way."

Byron hung up, then pulled his cell from the pocket of his suit coat. He texted Pelligrosso: He and Stevens would be delayed getting to Augusta.

The previous month Pamela Lynds had been named Portland's first female police chief. The announcement followed a nationwide search to permanently replace former Chief Michael Stanton, who had moved on to greener pastures. Much to Byron's delight, former Acting Chief Danny Rumsfeld, or Rumpswab as he was more commonly known by the rank and file, had been passed over, mainly due to his botched handling of a police shooting involving a Portland High School student. Describing it as a debacle would have been a dramatic understatement. Most everyone at 109 assumed that Rumsfeld, now relegated to second banana, was likely on borrowed time.

The door to Lynds's office stood open. She was seated behind her desk, in full uniform, sans duty belt, studying an open file folder.

Byron knocked on the open door. "You wanted to see me, Chief?"

"Sergeant Byron," Lynds said as she removed her reading glasses and rose to greet him. "I appreciate you taking the time to meet with me."

"Not at all," Byron said, unaware that he'd had a choice.

He stepped into the room. Lynds greeted him warmly with a firm dry handshake and good eye contact.

"Have a seat," she said, gesturing toward the half circle of visitor's chairs located in front of her desk.

The office was in disarray. A dozen cardboard boxes stood stacked in a corner farthest away from her desk. The walls were bare, the nail holes filled, and the surfaces repainted pale blue. There were no awards hung nor photos of Lynds glad-handing celebrities, at least not yet.

Byron took a seat in one of the burgundy-colored faux leather chairs closest to the window wall, allowing him to face the office door, which Lynds was closing to give them some privacy. Even within the confines of the chief's office, Byron had learned the prudence of keeping his back to the wall. Or perhaps especially in the chief's office.

Byron estimated Lynds to be in her late fifties, somewhere between five and ten years his senior. She was attractive, wore no jewelry, save for the gold four-star clusters pinned to each side of the collar on her short-sleeved uniform shirt, and only the faintest traces of makeup. Her auburn hair was shoulder length, curled under, and parted in the middle. She was average height, appeared fit, and carried herself in a way that exuded self-confidence. Word from Connecticut, where she had previously held the rank of patrol captain, was that Lynds wasn't afraid to assert herself lest anyone mistakenly think she was a pushover. While Byron hadn't had an actual conversation with the freshly minted chief, he had observed her handling of the Old Guard and was duly impressed. Rumsfeld had dutifully fallen in line in his new role as the assistant chief, at least publicly. Byron was confident that falling in line had more to do with Lynds's expectations than Rumpswab's desire to play nice. Byron wondered how long it would be before she followed the command playbook and cut the Ass Chief loose.

"I apologize for not having made time for this sooner," Lynds said as she settled into a chair across from him.

"No worries, Chief. We both have hectic schedules."

"I know you are in the middle of a murder investigation, so I won't keep you."

Byron nodded but said nothing. Her smile

40

remained pleasant, but her eyes were all business. She, too, was sizing him up.

"I've been reading up on your homicide case history, Sergeant. Impressive clearance rate."

"It's a small city. We don't get as many homicides as you're probably used to."

"Still. I see you're a second-generation badge, too."

"My father worked these streets for many years." He paused. "You said, 'too'."

"My uncle was on the job in Jersey. And both of my brothers are still on in Baltimore."

Byron forced a polite smile, wondering when Lynds might dispense with the pleasantries and move the conversation forward.

"Your investigative skills reflect positively on this department, which of course, assuming they continue, will reflect positively on me."

And there it is, Byron thought. Like every chief he had ever known, Lynds was already angling to take credit.

Her pleasant expression hardened. "Conversely, any negative behavior from my lead homicide investigator would be a poor reflection on my ability to lead."

"Agreed," Byron said, realizing that this wasn't a discussion.

"I want you to know that I am not one of those administrators who micromanage. I believe that you should have the autonomy to conduct your investigations without interference from the Chief's Office."

Byron wondered if Lynds was being sincere or if she was simply quoting scripture from some eight hundred page police command training manual.

"That said, it is important you understand that I will not tolerate any grandstanding or operating outside the rule of law." She paused a beat to let her words sink in. "Not even for the good of a case. I don't believe the end justifies the means. Be honest with me, Sergeant, play by the rules, and you will find in me an ally. Do we understand each other?"

"Perfectly," Byron said.

Lynds maintained eye contact while Byron waited in uncomfortable silence for her to make the next move.

"I understand we have something else in common," Lynds said at last.

Byron cocked his head slightly.

"I, too, am a friend of Bill W."

He was surprised by her candor regarding her alcoholism. Was this a peace offering? Was she giving him a glimpse of her vulnerable side to establish trust, or was this simply an attempt to cozy up to him? He couldn't be sure.

"How long?" It was all he could think of to ask.

"Five years. You?"

"Little over five months."

She nodded. "They say it gets easier."

"Does it?" Byron asked.

She smiled, then moved on without answering his question. "My former police department in Hartford may be larger than Portland's, but I find that police work is still police work. It's pretty much the same wherever you go. I've only been here a short time so I'm still evaluating, but I believe that a team is only as strong as its weakest link."

"I agree," Byron said, wondering if Lynds was in any danger of running out of cliches.

"Excellent." Lynds stood, signaling the end of their meeting. "I look forward to working with you." She extended her hand again.

Byron rose from his chair, gave a quick shake, then headed for the door.

"By the way, Sergeant, I understand your victim was found decapitated."

Byron opened the door then turned back toward her. The urge to frown was overwhelming, but he successfully fought it, maintaining a flat expression. It was obvious that Lieutenant LeRoyer had yet to master the art of compartmentalizing information. "Yes. Of course, we're hoping to keep that in-house as long as we can."

"Of course. I understand completely. Any reason to believe this case might be connected to the recent murders in Massachusetts?" Lynds asked, referring to the two recent unsolved cases in and around the Boston area where female victims had been found decapitated. "The Horseman cases?"

Byron had wondered how long it would be before someone higher up asked about the similarities.

"Too soon to say, Chief. Something we'll be looking at, though."

The meeting with Lynds had gone somewhat differently than Byron had envisioned. He liked her no-nonsense attitude and hoped it wasn't only for his benefit, but experience had taught him that most first-time police chiefs, especially those from larger outside agencies, were simply punching a ticket. They usually stayed a few years to gain some experience at a smaller department like Portland, then it was off to something bigger, better, and far more lucrative. Only time would tell if she would stick around long enough to steer the department in a better direction or just a different one. After nearly a year under the highly political and highly ineffectual leadership of Acting Chief Danny Rumpswab, Lynds might just be a breath of fresh air.

Byron walked through CID toward his office, catching curious glances from several detectives. Evidently his meeting with Chief Lynds hadn't been a secret either.

The inside of *Portland Herald* newspaper reporter Davis Billingslea's Honda Accord was sweltering. He was parked on the waterfront side of Commercial Street, across from the abandoned lumberyard. The air-conditioning, like most everything else in his aging and rusted jalopy, was busted. He'd lowered all four windows, attempting to mitigate the heat from the direct sunlight, but it wasn't helping. Neither was the shrieking gull standing beside his door awaiting a handout.

Billingslea had tried the direct approach, walking up to the young cop standing guard outside the fence and asking what they had, but that hadn't worked. Officer E. Gallant told him he'd have to speak with Lieutenant LeRoyer if he wanted information. In other words, Sergeant Byron had issued a gag order. Billingslea had seen it before. There was no love lost between them. Billingslea didn't know which thing was causing him the most pain, the blind zit growing at the tip of his nose or Detective Sergeant John Byron. At the moment it was a toss-up. The acne would pass, but he didn't imagine Byron was likely to depart anytime soon.

Billingslea had been monitoring the various goings-on between Byron and his investigators for more than an hour by radio. He'd heard them request a funeral home transport, but most everything else had been kept off the air. He figured they were using cellphones to communicate with the dispatcher. Now, apart from Gallant, Detective Mike Nugent, Evidence Technician Gabriel Pelligrosso, and one of the property crime detectives named Robbins, all the other investigators, including Sergeant Byron and Detective Stevens, had departed for parts unknown.

He watched as Pelligrosso and Nugent accompanied a private security guard on foot around the perimeter of the vacant property. They appeared to be checking the gates, possibly even changing the locks, but Billingslea couldn't be sure from his vantage point. Robbins, also on foot, appeared to be recording the registration numbers of every car parked nearby. The death they were investigating might have been nothing more than a vagrant, one of several hundred living in Portland. Maybe another one had died from a drug overdose, or perhaps drank themselves to death, he thought. But then again, it seemed as though Byron and the others were putting a lot of effort into keeping it quiet. No, something bigger was happening here, he was sure of it.

Billingslea waited until after Pelligrosso departed and Nugent and Robbins disappeared inside the Marriott before making his move. He fired up the Accord as the security guard climbed into the marked green-and-white Security Incorporated patrol car. The guard drove down Maple then turned south onto Commercial Street. Billingslea followed.

Detective Bernie Robbins had barely climbed inside the car before Nugent slid the transmission into Drive and punched the accelerator. Partnering with the CID troublemaker had already put Nugent in a foul mood, but being forced to wait while Robbins stood outside the car conducting what was most likely personal business on his cellphone really pissed him off.

"Jeez, what's the rush?" Robbins asked. "Mind if I close the door first?"

"You do know we're supposed to be working a case here, right?" Nugent said.

"Relax, partner. I am working. It's not my fault the piece of shit they assigned me won't start."

"You copy all the registrations like the sarge asked?"

"Yup. I'll get someone to run them when we get back to 109."

"Or you could run them yourself. Did you canvass all the York Street businesses?"

"Yeah, ma, I did. They're all closed Sunday night. No witnesses. Thanks for checking on me, though."

Nugent gave Robbins the stink eye. It was a toss-up which of the veteran detective's traits he hated most, the condescension or the laziness. Both set a bad example for the younger detectives to follow, and Nugent knew from experience that some of them undoubtedly would.

"So, who do you think's gonna get Peterson's seat in CID?" Robbins asked.

"Don't know," Nugent said. "Hadn't really given it a lot of thought."

"Well, I have. Word is Crosby is right for this one. Kenny's five-year stint with the Drug Unit is about up, so they'll be pulling him back to the PD anyway. I think he'd be great upstairs."

Nugent didn't, but kept it to himself. In addition to being tight with Crosby, Robbins had a reputation for getting people to talk out of school about someone then running out and telling that person what was said. Nugent tried to conjure up the word that described someone like Robbins but couldn't. He guessed he'd have to settle for *asshole.* He looked at Robbins and shook his head. Yeah, he thought, *asshole* would do.

"What?" Robbins asked.

"Nothing."

Fifteen minutes later, Byron and Stevens were cruising north on I-295 toward Augusta. They both knew Ellis would wait until they arrived before proceeding with the autopsy, but Byron was still annoyed at having been delayed. Chief Lynds could just as easily have given him her "toe the line" speech some other time. Like perhaps when he wasn't up against a ticking clock. The way Byron figured it, if Ellis was right about the time of death, the killer had at least two days on them already, maybe three.

They were passing the Augusta toll when Stevens's cell rang with a call from Mike

Nugent.

"Hey, Nuge," Stevens said, placing her phone into the dash holder and punching the speaker button, allowing Byron to be a part of their conversation. "You're on speaker. How's your new partner?"

"That's cute," Nugent said. "Couple things. First, Bernie and I finished canvassing the area. We got the registrations for everything parked nearby, and I got the Marriott to give me a list of guests back to Sunday night and their contact info. I spoke to a few already. There's a shitload of people we'll need to contact here, Sarge."

"Drop Bernie off at 109 and have him start on it," Byron said. "He can work with Dustin if he needs anything checked."

"Already done," Nugent said.

Stevens grinned at Byron. Nugent wasn't stupid. They both knew he'd find a way to distance himself from Robbins as soon as possible.

"You said you had a couple of things," Byron said. "What's the other?"

"I might have a lead on our Jane Doe," Nugent said.

"Go with it," Stevens said as she flipped open her notebook and uncapped her pen.

"Dispatch just received a call from a woman named Destiny Collins," Nugent

50

said. "She hasn't heard from her former roommate, woman by the name of Danica Faherty, and she's worried."

"What makes you think our Jane could be Faherty, Nuge?" Byron asked, aware that Nugent wasn't prone to jumping to conclusions.

"Faherty works at a restaurant as a maître d'. Fits the general physical description of our Jane. Collins hasn't had any contact with her since this past weekend. Said they had a lunch date scheduled for Monday, but Faherty never showed. Not like her, at least according to Collins."

"Did she provide an address or cellphone?" Byron asked.

"For Faherty? Yeah, she did. Said she's been leaving messages and texting but Faherty's voicemail is now full. According to the reporting officer, they used to share an apartment on Brackett Street. Collins went by to check, but the place is locked up and nobody answers. I'm headed to Collins's place now. I've got Faherty's cell number and the landlord's information."

"Okay," Byron said. "Let me know if you get anything further, and I'll have Gabe check Jane Doe's prints against Faherty's. Any word from the security company?"

"About the locks? No. I haven't had time

to contact them yet. But I had the security guard check the other gates as Gabe was installing our locks. The Maple Street gate was the only one his key wouldn't open."

"Tell me you seized the lock," Stevens said.

"Tagged it in myself."

"Anything else?" Byron asked.

"Yeah. Davis Billingslea came sniffing around right after you left."

CHAPTER 5

Wednesday, 10:15 A.M.,
July 12, 2017

It took Byron and Stevens another twenty minutes after exiting the highway at the Augusta exit to reach the medical examiner's office due to a three-car accident at the rotary where Routes 202, 201, and 11 converged, the first of two roundabouts through which they had to pass and the one closest to the copper-domed state capital building. Using the delay to his advantage, Byron telephoned Detective Dustin Tran in the PPD's computer lab.

"Morning, D.S. Byron," Tran said.

"D.S.?" Byron said.

"Yeah, you know. Like how they say detective sergeant on all those British mystery shows on Amazon Prime."

Byron and Stevens exchanged a glance.

"I don't have cable, Dustin," Byron said.

"You don't need it. Just internet. You gotta

get it, Sarge. It's totally cool."

Stevens rolled her eyes.

Byron continued. "Dustin, I need you to drop whatever you're doing and find everything you can on a Destiny Collins and a Danica Faherty."

Stevens spelled out the names phonetically and provided Tran with the information Nugent had given them.

"Is this connected to our Jane Doe?" Tran asked excitedly.

"Maybe," Byron said. "Call me back as soon as you have something."

"I'm on it, Inspector."

Byron's next call was to the Boston Police Department's Homicide Unit. He removed the phone from its dash cradle, switched it off speaker mode, and held it up to his ear.

The telephone at the other end rang so many times Byron was expecting the call to go to voicemail when at last someone picked up.

"Homicide, Sergeant Murray speaking."

"Pete. John Byron."

"John? Holy shit! How's it hanging?"

"Same as always," Byron said, casting a glance in Stevens's direction to see if she'd picked up on his cousin's inappropriate sense of humor. Judging by the smirk on her face, she had.

Murray continued. "Hey, I heard you were down here for Molly's funeral service. Sorry we never caught up. And I'm sorry for your loss, cuz."

Byron's mother, Molly Donnelly, had passed away in January following a long battle with Alzheimer's. They hadn't been close.

"I wasn't in Boston long," Byron said. "You know how it is."

"Yeah, guess I do. So, what can I do for you, Johnny?"

Byron despised the schoolboy nickname but, not wanting to encourage his cousin further, he let it pass. "I'm calling about a body we just recovered."

Murray laughed out loud. "News flash, we've got all the bodies we can handle down here already."

"This one might interest you, though."

"Why's that?"

"It's missing its head."

"No shit?"

Byron spent the next several minutes bringing Murray up to speed. Amid the "uh-huhs" and "no shits" Byron heard the scribble of pen on paper as his cousin recorded the details. Finally, traffic began to move. Byron and Murray agreed to connect again after Byron had uncovered more information.

Billingslea had been following the Security Incorporated patrol vehicle for the better part of twenty minutes. He was trying to figure out how he would approach the guard and what he would say when his cell buzzed with an incoming call. The ID displayed on the screen was Flatfoot. It was the contact name he had created to hide the identity of Portland Police Detective Sergeant Kenny Crosby should the phone ever fall into the wrong hands. Crosby, on loan to the Maine Drug Enforcement Agency, was one of Billingslea's go-to sources for the inside scoop at 109.

"Got something I think you'll be interested in," Crosby said.

"Have anything to do with the body on Commercial?" Billingslea asked.

"Not over the phone, dickhead. Where are you?"

"Scarborough. Route 1 bypass."

"Meet me in the lot of the Egg and I. Fifteen minutes."

Billingslea stared at the phone. Crosby had already disconnected. He hated how small Crosby made him feel. Like Crosby was tossing a bone to a stray dog. Only Kenny Crosby wouldn't toss the bone, he'd hurl it as hard as he could, hoping to injure the animal. But when information was hard to come by, as it always was with Byron, Crosby usually came through. The only question was, at what price?

Mike Nugent sat on the edge of the couch in Destiny Collins's living room, watching as she paced back and forth in front of him. He was sure that at any moment she would work her way through the oriental carpet to the hardwood floor beneath. Across the room, a uniformed patrol officer stood, waiting patiently, clipboard in hand, trying to piece together enough information to complete a missing-persons report.

Nugent cleared his throat. "Ms. Collins, tell us again when the last time was that you spoke with Danica."

"Dani," Collins said absently as she searched her memory. "I think the last time was Saturday morning. I'd just gotten home from work at the hospital. Worked a double shift at Maine Med. Dani called just as I was walking in the door. We chatted for a few minutes, then I went to bed."

"What time was that?"

"Around ten, I guess."

"Do you remember what you talked about?"

"Not really. I was dead on my feet."

"Did you talk again after you slept?"

"No. By the time I got up Saturday afternoon Dani had already left for work."

"And you said she works at Alessandro's, correct?"

"Yeah, down in the Old Port."

"And you were supposed to meet up for lunch?"

"On Monday, my day off. We had agreed to meet for lunch at Noble. It's that barbecue place, out near Riverton School, but Dani never showed."

"Did she call to cancel?"

"No. Nothing. And it's not like her."

"Does Dani have a boyfriend?"

"Not really."

"Not really?"

"Well, she had been going out with this guy named Morgan Bates. But they kinda broke it off about six months ago."

"Kinda?"

"Well, actually Dani broke it off. I don't think Morgan was ready for it to end."

Nugent exchanged a quick glance with the officer to make sure he had picked up on that information. He had. Nugent watched him make a note.

"What makes you say that, Destiny?" Nugent asked.

" 'Cause he started coming around all the time. To the apartment we shared on Brackett Street."

"To see Dani?"

"Yeah. Bothering her. Acting really weird. To tell you the truth, I never really cared for the guy."

"Do you have any recent photos of Dani or Morgan?"

"Yeah, sure. Hang on and I'll pull up my Facebook page."

The Egg and I was a small chain restaurant located at the end of a L-shaped mini strip mall on Route 1 in the town of Scarborough. Billingslea had backed into a parking space in the corner of the lot, farthest from the entrance, facing the building so that he'd see Crosby drive in. He checked his watch. Crosby was ten minutes late. He was contemplating calling him back when somebody violently slapped the roof of his car.

Crosby opened the door and jumped into the passenger seat.

"Ha. Scared you, didn't I?"

"You nearly gave me a heart attack."

"Sorry I'm late, honey."

"Where's your car?"

"Next lot over. You didn't expect me to just drive up next to you so we could swap spit, did ya?"

Billingslea despised this man. "You said you had something for me."

"Yup. But first, you know the drill."

"Lunch?"

"Of course."

"Where to?"

"Subway. I feel like eating good in the neighborhood. Get it?"

Billingslea started the car and drove through the lot. He thought about correcting Mr. Full of Himself by explaining that he was using the Applebee's motto, but kept it to himself.

Crosby leered at him. "So, you want to know all about the mysterious body, huh?"

Byron and Stevens found Gabriel Pelligrosso standing beside the nude body of their victim on the opposite side of the table from Ellis and Nicky, the doctor's peculiar lab assistant. Pelligrosso and Ellis were chatting. Nicky, who wasn't much of a conversationalist, stood silently brooding.

"Top o' the afternoon, detectives," Ellis said. "We were beginning to wonder if we'd have to undertake the procedure without you. I trust your meeting with the new chief was a smashing success, Sergeant?"

Byron glared at Pelligrosso accusingly. The

flat-topped evidence tech was unsuccessful in his attempt to suppress a grin.

"We got stuck behind a traffic accident," Stevens said.

"A far sight better than being a part of it," Ellis said.

Byron and Stevens removed their blazers and donned the same disposable Tyvek garments Pelligrosso was wearing, required clothing whenever they intended to be up close and personal during an autopsy.

"This is the first time I've ever performed a post without need of the neck stand," Ellis said proudly as he surveyed Jane Doe's remains. "Should go quicker."

Postmortem examinations are a key aspect of every homicide investigation. Establishing the cause and manner of death is paramount to proving that death was the direct result of the actions of another and not by natural or self-inflicted means. Byron accepted this. What he'd never been able to accept was the science behind finding that truth. In this case, the victim had already suffered the ultimate indignity, having been murdered, decapitated, then put on display for all the world to see. The process of being systematically disassembled by Ellis, like some college biology experiment, only seemed to compound the disrespect.

The victim's body was toned and tanned. No cuts, abrasions, or bruises. As a matter of procedure, Pelligrosso swabbed under the fingernails, but there were no obvious signs that she had put up any kind of struggle.

"It looks like our Jane engaged in sexual intercourse sometime shortly before death," Ellis said after he swabbed the vaginal cavity.

"Forced?" Byron asked.

Ellis shook his head. "Doesn't look like it. No signs of trauma. Unless she was drugged, it was most likely consensual." Ellis waited while Pelligrosso snapped photos of the pubic region.

Byron made a mental note to check with Murray regarding any semen or DNA samples that might have been collected from the Boston victims.

Ellis bent down to re-examine the neck wound. "Have a look at this," he said.

"You find something?" Byron asked.

"Nicky, hand me the tweezers," Ellis said. Nicky did.

Using a hemostat to grasp the loose skin near the edge of the cut, Ellis pulled the flap away from the neck. He probed inside with the tweezers, carefully removing a tiny dark-colored triangle shaped object.

"What is it?" Pelligrosso asked.

Ellis gently placed the object on a stainless-steel tray then rinsed it with saline. He twisted the high intensity magnifying light attached to the tray stand until the object was illuminated properly. "Looks like a tooth."

"A tooth?" Pelligrosso said.

"From a saw blade," Ellis said as he poked at it then turned it over with the tweezers. "There's shiny flecks attached to it as well."

"Diamond?" Byron asked.

"Looks like," Ellis said. "I'll double down on my original guess and say that whoever removed her head used a reciprocating saw with a diamond tipped blade. The ultimate turkey carver. Certainly would explain the rough uneven cut and the saw marks on C4 and C5."

"Like they couldn't decide where to make the cut?" Stevens asked.

"Or the blade was bouncing around on them," Ellis said. "Not exactly a precision instrument." He continued his search, locating three additional teeth, each smaller than the first, handing them to Pelligrosso.

Over the next hour the detectives watched as Ellis methodically went about his work, painstakingly removing, examining, and weighing each vital organ. The only thing Ellis couldn't examine was the missing head.

When he had finished, Ellis removed his gloves and protective gear, a signal to Nicky that he could begin closing. Byron studied Ellis's face. The doctor looked troubled.

"What gives, Doc?" Byron asked. "Can you give us a cause of death?"

"No."

"Pending tox?" Pelligrosso asked.

"Goes without saying, my boy. But if it comes back negative, I will be forced to list cause of death as unknown."

"You're serious?" Byron had never known Ellis to arrive at an unknown conclusion.

"I am. Decapitation was not the cause of death. My initial assessment about the head being removed postmortem was correct. The victim was a healthy active woman in her twenties. Good heart, lungs, everything. I couldn't find any evidence to support illegal drug use. In short, there's no obvious medical reason she's dead."

They all watched as Nicky made quick and silent work of sewing up the chest cavity.

"Something stopped this girl's heart from beating," Ellis continued. "But I'll be damned if I know what it was."

CHAPTER 6

*Wednesday, 11:45 A.M.,
July 12, 2017*
Byron and Stevens pulled out of the parking lot onto Hospital Street and headed toward Gardiner. Byron's mind was racing. The bright sunshine of the day had all but been washed away by the macabre hand they had been dealt. Ellis's words still echoed inside his head. *Decapitation wasn't the cause of death.*

Who was this girl? Could she be Danica Faherty? Pelligrosso had scanned the victim's fingerprints and, assuming there was a record in the AFIS, Automated Fingerprint Identification System, database, they would quickly locate a match. But if not, well, they'd jump off that bridge when they came to it.

Byron's stomach grumbled, a not-so-subtle reminder that he hadn't eaten. Up before the dawn call-ins meant coffee only and Byron was confident that caffeine didn't qualify as a food group. He looked over at Stevens. "You hungry?"

"As weird as that is, yeah, I could eat. Whatcha thinking?"

"Something greasy?"

She grinned. "After what we just saw? Of course."

"Jimmy's it is."

Davis Billingslea felt his excitement building as he drove back toward Portland. His meeting with Kenny Crosby had yielded some great information, though the drug sergeant ate like a horse. Their trip to Subway had cost Billingslea nearly twenty-five dollars. Even worse was watching him talk with a mouthful of food, spraying lettuce onto the passenger seat and floor of the Honda.

"The body was decapitated," Crosby had said, wiping chipotle sauce from his chin with the back of his hand.

"Decapitated? As in — ?"

"Yeah, numb nuts, as in no head."

Billingslea took the Franklin Street off-ramp from 295. As usual, the ramp was backed up due to the Marginal Way traffic light. While sitting in traffic, sucking the diesel exhaust from the seafood delivery truck

66

idling in front of him, he read over his notes again. He uncapped his pen and repeatedly underlined the last two words he'd written on the page. *The Horseman.*

Jimmy's Diner was basically an oversized shed. Situated in the center of a dusty hardpan lot on the side of Route 126 in Gardiner, several miles from the highway, the clapboard-sided building with its multi-colored layers of peeling paint, the outer-most of which was supposed to have been white, wasn't much to look at, but the food served inside was always fresh and hot. A faded and grease-stained cardboard sign tacked to the wall proclaimed Jimmy's hand-cut fries to be the best in the state. Although their French fries were excellent, Byron had always wondered who decided such things. And what would Jimmy's have to do to be stripped of such a lofty title?

The detectives placed their orders at the counter, then carried their soft drinks to an empty corner booth and sat down. As usual, Byron commandeered the bench that faced the door.

"You used to come here with Ray Humphrey, didn't you, Sarge?" Stevens said.

"Yup. After every autopsy."

"Must bring back a few memories, huh?"

"Not really," Byron lied. "There's only so much nostalgia you can connect to a place like this."

It wasn't true, of course. Byron thought about his old mentor a lot. Jimmy's Diner only worsened the ache. The surroundings and scent of fried food dredged up memories and pushed them to the forefront. And the violent way Humphrey's life had ended had notched a deep and painful mark in Byron's life. Like an indent marks a paragraph, losing Humphrey had been like losing a father for the second time.

"Why do you think he cuts the heads off?" Stevens asked absently as she thumbed away at her cell.

Byron considered her question a moment before answering. "You're asking if I think it's the same person responsible for the Boston murders?"

Stevens nodded and sipped from her straw. "From what I've seen on the news, they're all female victims, dumped in the lots of abandoned businesses, and beheaded. And we don't get too many of those."

Byron couldn't deny the obvious similarities, but it was way too soon to jump to the conclusion that the person responsible for

Jane Doe's death was connected to the others.

"Suppose you're right," Byron said. "What makes you think it's a *he*?"

"Would've taken a lot of strength to carry the body to where we recovered it," she said.

"Or more than one person," he countered.

He pictured himself seated here with Diane Joyner doing the exact same dance. Diane had been his partner on several homicide investigations, before her promotion to sergeant placed her in her current public relations position. Byron considered the PR job a waste of manpower at the best of times, but particularly in Diane's case. Diane was a born investigator. But now here he sat with Melissa Stevens who, if he thought about it, displayed many of the same traits as Diane. Tenacious, inquisitive, and relentless, Mel had all the makings of a career homicide detective.

"Or someone with a vehicle," Stevens said after a moment, making his point. "Maybe they drove in with the body. Maybe that was what the effed-up padlock was all about."

He sipped from his soda as he considered it. Aside from the obvious case similarities, and the unusual nature of decapitating one's victims, if this was the same killer, he, or she, seemed to have broken their modus operandi by moving north into Maine. Murray had said that the profile they were working from suggested the killer may have known the victims. Perhaps even studied their schedules. Suddenly migrating to Maine didn't square with that. If it was the same murderer, and not some one-off, or copycat, clearly something had changed. Byron hoped this wasn't the beginning of a serial nightmare for the Pine Tree State or, for that matter, New England.

Stevens looked up from her phone. "The *Portland Herald* already has the body recovery story online."

"Tell me there aren't any details, at least," Byron said hopefully.

"Nope. Just says the police recovered a body from an abandoned waterfront business. Then it just goes on about the pending sale of the property and the possibility of a hotel being constructed."

"Food's up," the woman behind the counter said just as Byron's cell chimed with an incoming call.

"I'll get the food, Sarge," Stevens said, jumping up.

"Thanks. Grab some extra napkins, would you?" He pulled the phone out of his pocket and checked the caller ID. It was Nugent.

"Sarge, you headed back?" Nugent asked.

"Mel and I are grabbing a quick bite. What's up?"

"Just got a look at a photo Danica Faherty texted to Destiny Collins last week."

"And?"

"It's a picture of Faherty's manicure. Pretty sure it's her, boss. Right down to the lacy silver band on her right ring finger."

Byron and Stevens took their lunches to go. Nugent provided them with the Brackett Street address for the apartment that Faherty and Collins had once shared. While en route to the potential victim's residence they each made phone calls. Stevens contacted the victim/witness advocate and asked her to be on standby while Byron tasked Tran with digging up contact information specific to Danica Faherty's next of kin.

Byron pulled to the curb in front of a three-story unit on Brackett. Nugent was standing on the sidewalk talking with a deeply tanned middle-aged man wearing blue jeans, a khaki-colored T-shirt, and a Boston Red Sox baseball cap.

As Byron and Stevens climbed out of the unmarked Nugent approached them, leaving the other man alone.

"That the landlord?" Byron asked.

"It is. Name's Wescott."

"He knows why we're here?" Stevens asked.

"Missing-person case is all I told him." Nugent pulled out his phone and brought up a photo, holding it out for Byron and Stevens. "The picture I told you about. Faherty sent this to Collins after getting a manicure on Friday."

It was a photo of freshly manicured hands, hands that looked a lot like the ones belonging to the corpse lying in the M.E.'s examination room in Augusta, right down to the tangerine-colored nails with white tips. Also depicted was an intricate silver band encircling the right ring finger.

Byron nodded. "Where's Destiny Collins?"

"Back at her condo. I figured having her here wouldn't help anything. Especially if we locate a scene."

"Good thinking," Stevens said.

"Does she know about the body?" Byron asked.

"Haven't told her yet. Figured you'd want to be the one to do that. By the way, that's Faherty's car parked over there," Nugent said, pointing to a silver Nissan Sentra parked in the driveway. "Wescott identified it. I ran the tags, it's hers."

"Anything visible?" Stevens asked.

"Nothing obvious through the windows or on the exterior, it's locked up tight."

Byron paused a moment as he ran several scenarios through his head. The car being in the driveway increased the probability that whatever had happened to Danica Faherty might well have occurred inside her residence.

The three detectives approached Wescott. "You must be the landlord," Byron said.

"I must be," he said, offering up his hand. "Earl Wescott."

"Sergeant Byron and this is Detective Stevens. Thanks for your help. You have keys?"

"Right here. Miss Faherty lives in the second-floor apartment," Wescott said.

"How many units in the building?" Byron asked, noting Wescott's use of the present tense.

"There's actually three, counting the attic, but the second floor is the only one currently occupied. My first-floor tenants moved out last week."

"Mr. Wescott, I'm gonna need you to wait out here with Detective Nugent while we check the apartment," Byron said. "May I borrow your key?"

"Sure thing."

After entering the building, out of Wescott's sight, Byron and Stevens both donned latex gloves. They still had to clear the apartment but doing it without contaminating a potential scene was always preferable. Slowly and methodically they trudged up the stairway to the second floor, eyeing everything carefully as they went, searching for visual evidence of foul play. They found nothing out of the ordinary.

Upon reaching the landing, Byron activated the flashlight on his cellphone and inspected the exterior jamb of the apartment door casing for signs of a break-in. Seeing none, he tried the knob. Locked. Stevens stepped back to allow Byron to unlock the door using Wescott's key.

Byron and Stevens unholstered their weapons and stood on either side of the doorway. They exchanged silent nods then entered the apartment, Byron first followed by Stevens.

The door opened directly into a furnished living room.

The first thing Byron noticed was the thick stuffy smell of a closed-up space. No lights were burning. The apartment was illuminated only by the diffused daylight spilling in through the sheer curtains. The air was still and hot. They passed through the living room to the kitchen, where an unpleasant odor hung in the air. Something had spoiled. Garbage perhaps. The sink was clean save for a single bowl and spoon that had been left to soak. On the counter beside the stove stood a green-and-red canvas shopping bag full of dry goods. Byron made a quick mental note to find out where and when Faherty had shopped for groceries.

After clearing the main living area, they continued down a hallway that ran the length of the apartment. The first door on the right was the bathroom. Empty. At the far end of the hall were two doors opposite each other. The door on the left was closed, the other stood open. Byron stepped into the room on the right while Stevens remained in the hall, her gun trained on the closed door. Byron could tell that room had most likely been Collins's bedroom, now relegated to a storage/workout room following her departure. A silver-and-black elliptical machine stood in front of a small flat-screen television. After clearing both the room and the closet, Byron returned to the hallway. Training his gun on the closed door, he gave a silent nod to Stevens. She reached out and turned the knob then shoved the door open. The door banged loudly against the wall. Byron did a quick peek into the darkened bedroom. The shades were drawn, and the air was cool. The dull whir of a window-mounted air conditioner was the only sound. They entered, checking the closet and under the bed before securing their weapons. Byron used his phone's flashlight to make a slow sweep of the room. The bed was unmade, and standing beside it was an ironing board, from which several items of women's clothing hung. On the opposite side of the bed was a painted wooden bureau. Several drawers stood open with clothes spilling out. On top of the bureau sat a laptop computer, plugged in and charging.

"Looks like my place," Stevens said, breaking the silent tension.

Byron killed the flashlight app then punched up the speed dial. "Nuge, we're clear in here."

"You got a scene?" Nugent asked.

"No," Byron said. "I don't think it happened here."

Byron was on the phone with Pelligrosso as the two detectives exited the apartment building. "You back at the lumberyard yet?"

"Just heading there from 109 now," Pelligrosso said. "You need me for something else?"

"We just searched Faherty's Brackett Street apartment. There are no obvious signs of foul play here. I'm gonna need you to confirm her prints before we go any further."

"Give me the address, and I'll be right there."

It took another half hour for Pelligrosso to photograph everything inside the apartment and to lift prints that matched the ones he'd taken from the corpse.

"We're positive that the body we recovered this morning is Danica Faherty?" Byron asked Pelligrosso.

"We are. I lifted matching prints from the kitchen counter and from the hairbrush in the bathroom."

Byron frowned, knowing that Pelligrosso's confirmation meant he was now left with the unenviable task of notifying Destiny Collins of her friend's death.

Byron turned to Nugent. "Did Collins say anything that might shine a light on what happened to Faherty? Like who we should be looking at?"

"You mean besides the Horseman?"

"Yeah."

"Maybe," Nugent said.

"Maybe?" Byron asked.

"Ex-boyfriend," Nugent said, pausing to

flip open his notebook. "Name's Morgan Bates. Collins said Faherty broke up with him about six months ago."

"She say why?" Stevens asked.

"No. But she did say that Bates continued hanging around even after the breakup."

"Like a stalker?" Stevens said.

"Like maybe he didn't get the message," Nugent said.

Byron cut in. "Nuge, I want you to stay here and give Gabe a hand. When you've finished with the apartment let's tow her car to the basement of 109. I want it impounded until we know for sure whether it was used as part of the crime."

"You got it."

"Anything else you want us to take?" Pelligrosso said.

"Yeah, grab the laptop from the bureau in her bedroom. I want Tran to go through it. And let's install our own padlocks on the front and rear doors to this apartment. I want the option of coming back."

"I used up our supply of padlocks at the lumberyard this morning," Pelligrosso said. "Murph should be in the lab by now. I'll have him swing out and buy some if you're okay with that."

"Do it," Byron said. He turned to Stevens. "You ready?"

"Not really. But I guess someone's gotta do it."

They were halfway to the door when Byron stopped and turned back to Nugent. "Do a knock and talk with some of the neighbors before you go, too. Maybe we'll get lucky."

"I'll take care of it, boss."

"One more thing, Nuge. Get on the horn and find out where the hell your new partner is. He can help with the canvass."

Byron sat at the kitchen table with Destiny Collins, while Stevens kept the advocate occupied in the next room. Collins was staring blankly at a framed color photograph of Faherty and weeping. The smiling blue-eyed woman depicted in the photo was vibrant and full of life, nothing like the abandoned corpse they had recovered only hours earlier.

"When was that picture taken?" Byron asked, speaking as gently as he could, hoping to establish a bit of rapport.

"Last summer," Collins said. "We spent the day in Cape Elizabeth, at Two Lights State Park. Just the two of us. Dani was — so happy."

"Destiny, I know this is hard for you," Byron said. "But it's important that we gather as much information as possible. The more we know about Dani and her routine the better. Do you understand?"

She nodded and grabbed another tissue from the large box on the table and blew her nose loudly. "Can you tell me how she died?"

"I'm sorry. I can't share the details with you."

Byron was only too happy to spare Ms. Collins the horror, at least for now.

"Had Dani been seeing anyone?" Byron asked.

"I think so."

"Do you know who?"

"She wouldn't tell me."

Byron lifted a brow. "I'd have thought that was something she'd share with you. The two of you being so close."

"I think she had her reasons for not telling me."

"Any idea what those reasons might have been?"

"No, not really. Whoever it was, I think she started seeing him about five or six months ago, right after she broke up with Morgan."

"Morgan?"

"Morgan Bates, her previous boyfriend. I told the other detective about him."

Byron wondered if maybe the mystery relationship hadn't begun after the breakup, but before. "And Dani broke up with him?"

"Yeah, but Morgan never really went away. I don't think he could accept that it was over."

"How long were they together?"

"About a year, I guess. Morgan used to tend bar at Alessandro's, the restaurant she works at —" Her voice hitched in mid-sentence. "Worked at."

"He used to tend bar there?"

"I think he was fired."

"Any idea why?"

She shook her head. "I'm not sure. I think he might have gotten into it with one of his bosses."

"Do you know why Dani and Morgan split up?"

Destiny paused a moment before answering. She appeared to be choosing her words carefully. "Let's just say Morgan has a temper."

"Was he ever violent with Dani? Or threatening?"

Collins hesitated before answering. "Only once."

CHAPTER 7

Byron spent the next twenty minutes gathering additional information on Faherty and Bates. He excused himself after receiving an urgent text from Diane Joyner and stepped outside to call her.

Sergeant Diane Joyner had been the Portland Police Department's public relations spokesperson for nearly a year. Previously, she had been a part of Byron's Crimes Against Persons Unit in CID and a valuable partner on homicide cases. Tall, beautiful, and tough talking, she had moved to Maine from New York after being hired by the Portland Police Department, quickly rising to the rank of detective. The attraction between Byron and Diane had been mutual, but neither had acted on it, at least not until Byron's ex-wife, Kay, officially served him with divorce papers. And like most workplace romances, theirs had been one of 109's worst-kept secrets.

Byron pressed the speed dial for Diane's number on his cell. She answered on the first ring.

"Let me guess," Byron said before she could speak. "Billingslea has been sniffing around our body."

"Worse," Diane said. "He knows about the decapitation."

"Goddammit."

Byron had known that it would only be a matter of time before someone leaked the information to the press, but he hadn't expected it to happen so soon. He only hoped the leak hadn't come from inside 109.

"So much for keeping a lid on this," he said. "Tell me he doesn't know her identity at least."

"If he does, he didn't let on. He's still referring to her as Jane Doe."

Davis Billingslea, while technically the *Portland Herald*'s police beat reporter, spent most of his time snooping around and generally mucking up CID's investigations. Delusions of grandeur trumped whatever common sense the young reporter possessed. Byron knew what Billingslea would do with the headless angle, and it wouldn't be good. If he reported on the crime's similarity to the Boston cases, public pressure would mount quickly, an invitation for all the crazies to come crawling from the woodwork. The false leads would increase CID's workload exponentially. The last thing any of them needed was for the meddling reporter to control the direction of their investigation. Byron had to slow Billingslea down.

"Any chance you can get him to back off?" Byron said. "At least until after we notify her family?" Byron asked.

"So, you *have* positively identified her?"

"Yeah. Danica Faherty. I'm speaking with her former roommate now."

Byron's cell chimed with an incoming text message from Pelligrosso. "Hang on a sec. I got a text from Gabe."

The message read: Finished at apartment, locks in place, car secured, heading to lumberyard with Murph.

"Anything new?" Diane asked, pulling him back into the conversation.

"No, just an update. Can you get Mr. Fourth Estate to back off, or not?"

"I'll do my best, but you should know Chief Lynds is planning to hold a press conference tomorrow morning."

"Of course she is."

Byron knew that the chief would want to get out in front of this case. Lynds's career aspirations, whatever they might be, might be irrevocably damaged if she remained silent and this case did turn out to be connected to the Horseman killings.

"Okay," Byron said. "Thanks for the heads-up."

"Talk later?"

"Yup."

Before Byron could return the phone to his coat, it rang with an incoming call from Lieutenant LeRoyer. No doubt seeking an update. Byron pressed Ignore, pocketed the phone, and stepped back inside.

Diane had just finished the call with Byron and was about to check voicemail when someone rapped on the open door to her office. Chief Pamela Lynds stood in the doorway.

"Chief," Diane said.

"Got a second?" Lynds asked.

"Of course." Diane returned the handset to its cradle and rose from her chair. "Your office?"

Lynds gestured with her hand for Diane to remain seated. "Thought we might speak here."

"All right," Diane said, returning to her seat.

Lynds entered the room and closed the door. "A bit less formal than my office." She slid the visitor's chair away from the wall and spun it to face Diane's desk then sat down. "It sounds as though the media circus has begun."

Diane cocked her head to one side, not completely understanding the comment.

Lynds grinned. "Couldn't help but overhear part of your phone conversation."

"Ah. One of the local reporters knows about the missing head."

"Billingslea?"

"The one and only."

"At a minimum, if he goes public with the headless angle, I'll be forced to mention the unusual nature of this case at tomorrow's press briefing."

"Of course."

"Well, I don't want to keep you, so I'll come straight to the point. Sergeant Peterson's impending retirement has caught us all by surprise. A large hole to fill in CID."

Diane nodded. "He's held that position quite a while."

"I couldn't help notice that you haven't submitted your name for consideration. You are aware that the deadline is next Monday, right?"

"I am."

"May I ask why you haven't thrown your hat into the ring?" Lynds asked.

"Well —"

"Does this have anything to do with your personal relationship with Sergeant Byron?"

Diane hesitated a moment before answering. Was she hearing the chief correctly? Was this an offer to return to CID as a sergeant? If so, it was precisely what she wanted. What she had dreamed of in fact. The detective sergeant position was the only reason she had accepted the stripes in the first place. But was she ready? She hated the constant feeling of instability that came with promotions, yet somehow she had arrived at another career crossroad. Leaving NYPD to come to Maine had been difficult but necessary. And her personal involvement with John had bordered on irresponsible, at least while she had worked directly under him. But now they were equals, at least insofar as the command staff was concerned.

"That may be one of the reasons," Diane said at last. "Personal relationships within the same unit have always been frowned upon."

"And yet they still occur, don't they?"

Lynds said. "They certainly happened in Hartford."

Diane said nothing, waiting to see where the chief was headed and wondering if Lynds spoke from personal experience.

"Diane, I'm not one to stand on principle simply for tradition's sake. Hell, if law enforcement stayed true to its traditions neither of us would even be working here, would we? The good ole' boys club would still be open for business."

"I guess that's true," Diane said.

"You know it is."

Diane nodded her agreement.

Lynds leaned forward and lowered her voice, as if someone else was present. "I'll let you in on a little secret. I'm far too progressive to let a little thing like a personal relationship stand in the way of promoting my most qualified candidate for detective sergeant."

Diane paused. She had to tread carefully here. Was this a test? She didn't know the chief well enough to hazard a guess as to what angle she was working. But one thing was obvious, Lynds didn't give much thought to the chain of command, at least not in the downward direction.

"Who says I'm the most qualified?" Diane asked.

Lynds sat back in her chair. "Lieutenant Marty LeRoyer for one. Your investigative experience for another. Both here and in New York."

Lynds had been checking up on her. "But this isn't just a detective's position," Diane countered. "It's a detective supervisor. I haven't supervised anyone yet."

"So, what you're actually saying is that you're worried others will say you haven't paid your dues."

Diane hated to admit it, but that's exactly what she was afraid of. As the department's public relations sergeant, she hadn't supervised a thing. No one answered to her. Her job was to simply try and control the flow of information to the media. Most days she barely felt like a police officer, much less a sergeant.

Lynds continued, "As I understand it, the Bubble Up robbery, and the aftermath with Officer Haggerty, was one of the worst things to happen to this department in years. When everything went to hell, who did the department turn to for help in solving the case?"

Diane remained silent. It was obvious that the chief had done her homework. Just as obvious was what she wanted.

"Lieutenant LeRoyer tells me that you

grabbed hold of that case with both hands and made it happen."

"I *had* help."

Lynds continued, ignoring the comment. "You stepped up, supervising your former colleagues in CID, in the middle of a major crisis and got the job done."

Diane studied Lynds's face but remained silent.

"Sounds to me like you've already paid your dues, Sergeant," Lynds said.

Neither woman spoke for a moment, but Lynds held her gaze, making Diane mildly uncomfortable.

"Well, I've taken up enough of your time," Lynds said as she rose and replaced the chair to its former location. "I'll let you get back to it."

Diane stood as well. "Thank you, Chief."

Lynds opened the door to the hallway then stopped and turned. "Just think about it, okay?"

"I will."

After obtaining next-of-kin information from Dustin Tran, Byron directed Nugent to contact the Richmond, Virginia Police Department in whose jurisdiction Faherty's parents resided. Long-distance death notifications were the worst, but having the local authorities make the notification in person was far better than a phone call from some out-of-state cop, from an equally unfamiliar police department. Byron departed from Collins's condo solo while Stevens remained behind to continue the interview in the hopes that they might garner some additional information. It was time to track down Dani Faherty's ex-boyfriend, Morgan Bates.

According to Destiny Collins, Bates now worked full-time for Custom Coastal, a Portland-based construction company known for building high-end homes. Byron was familiar with the builder, although he wasn't sure what constituted high-end. Based solely on the glossy magazine ads that he had seen, high-priced seemed more accurate. Collins had said she believed Bates was currently working on a new subdivision near Falmouth, somewhere off Route 9.

Byron located the fledgling development a quarter mile prior to the Portland/Falmouth town line. The newly paved road wound snakelike through several dozen oversized colonial and Cape Cod style homes, each in various stages of completion. Gravel seemed to be the common landscaping material thus far.

He parked next to a newly installed granite

curbstone in front of two houses that, in addition to having the most activity surrounding them, appeared to be nearly finished. Exiting the car, he noticed an unoccupied city inspector's vehicle parked across the street, a former police cruiser repainted a nauseating shade of purple with a brightly colored City of Portland seal affixed to the driver's door. When it came to fleet automobiles, the Port City had been recycling well before it was fashionable. Experience had taught Byron that wherever the inspector was located, so too would be the site boss, most likely negotiating his position.

The man Byron sought nearly collided with him as he hurried through the left-hand home's breezeway door. The stocky man wearing a red Custom Coastal ball cap was fuming and muttering to himself as he paused in the driveway to light a cigarette.

"Excuse me," Byron said.

"Yeah. Sorry about that."

"I'm looking for the site foreman."

"Well, you found him. Name's Al. Did I fuck up something else?"

"What do you mean?" Byron asked, not understanding the question.

Al inhaled deeply then expelled twin plumes of smoke from his nostrils, reminding Byron of a bull. "With the city, right?

Car gave you away. Let me guess, code enforcement?"

Byron dug the police identification out of his coat pocket. "I *am* with the city. Different department, though. Detective Sergeant John Byron."

"Al Dunn," he said, sticking out a sweaty paw to shake Byron's hand.

Byron suppressed the urge to smile as he wondered how much fun the other contractors had with that name. "I'm trying to locate a guy named Morgan Bates. I was told he works here."

"One of my better framers," Dunn said before taking another long drag off his cigarette. "Tell me you're not about to make my day worse by busting him for something."

Byron wondered what it said when Dunn's first thought was that Byron was there to arrest Bates. "I only want to talk with him."

Dunn cast a wary eye at Byron. "Just talk, huh?" He took one last drag before tossing the butt down on the gravel driveway and crushing it under his boot. "Okay. Give me a minute. I gotta fix the mess your inspector's making, then I'll take you to Bates."

Five minutes later, Byron was following the dust cloud kicked up by Dunn's pickup on the short drive to the other end of the development. They found Danica Faherty's former beau on the second floor of an open structure working with another man. The two men were attaching cripple studs between roof joists with pneumatic framing nailers when the foreman hollered for Bates to take a break.

Dunn turned to Byron. "You good?"

"Yeah, thanks, Al. I'll take it from here."

Dunn returned to his truck and raced off in another cloud of dust.

The two framers strolled out of the building. The bearded one with dark hair, the one who wasn't Bates, headed off toward the side yard with his cell stuck to his ear. Bates approached Byron carrying a large insulated water bottle. He was shirtless, deeply tanned and muscular, dressed in green carpenter pants and tan work boots, with a spattering of sawdust stuck to his sweaty torso. His wavy blond hair, on the longish side of professional, wouldn't have cut it in a police uniform but would have been considered too short for undercover narcotics work.

"Help ya?" Bates said after taking an extra-long swig from the stainless-steel bottle and wiping his mouth with the palm of his hand.

Byron produced his police ID. "My name is Detective Sergeant John Byron. Are you Morgan Bates?"

"That's what it says on my driver's license."

Byron studied him, wondering if his fellow construction workers found his witty banter as cute as the Old Port crowd most likely had when he was still tending bar at Alessandro's.

"Do you know a woman named Danica Faherty?"

"Sure, I know her. She's my girlfriend."

"How long have you been seeing her?" Byron asked, playing along with the lie.

"Not sure that's any of your business, Slick." Bates leaned forward and poured a small amount of water over his overheated head. He stood upright and took another drink then spit it out on the ground between them. He grinned at Byron.

Byron returned the grin but there was no humor behind it. "Reason I ask is because I heard the two of you split months ago."

"Where'd you hear that? Let me guess, Destiny."

Byron said nothing.

"She's got a big mouth."

"Is it true?" Byron asked without confirming the source. "Had the two of you broken up?"

"I guess. Dani said she wanted some space. I think she's coming around, though."

"Meaning back to you?"

"Hard to say no to this," Bates said, cocking a thumb in his own direction.

Byron's disdain for the arrogant young man was growing by the second. "You still haven't asked me."

"Asked you what?"

"Why I'm here. Why I asked about Danica. I would think, being her ex-boyfriend and all, you might be concerned that something bad had happened to her."

Something almost imperceptible shifted in Bates's arrogant expression. "Did something bad happen to her? That why you're here?"

"She's dead, Morgan. We found her body this morning."

Bates stood slack-jawed for a moment. Byron tried to gauge the reaction. If the ex-boyfriend was acting, and he wouldn't be the first, he was damn good at it.

"How?" Bates asked at last.

"We believe she was murdered." Byron waited a tick while the news sunk in. "When did you last see her?"

Bates opened his mouth to speak then closed it, eyes narrowing. "You think *I* killed her, don't you? That's why you're here, isn't it?"

"I don't know whether you did or didn't have anything to do with her death, Morgan. But, assuming you didn't, I would think you'd want to do everything you could to help us find the person or persons responsible. So, let's try this again. When did you last see Dani Faherty?"

"Can't remember."

"Okay, then where were you Sunday morning?"

"I was with Steve, a buddy of mine."

"Steve?"

"Holcolm. We were hanging out Saturday night till about noon on Sunday."

"Great. I'll need a statement from both of you."

Bates took another swig of water, this time swallowing it. The arrogant smirk returned. "Ya know what? Think I want to talk to a lawyer."

CHAPTER 8

Wednesday, 4:30 P.M.,
July 12, 2017

Diane was on her office phone in the process of leaving yet another voicemail message for *Portland Herald* reporter Davis Billingslea when her cellphone lit up with an incoming call from him. She disconnected the call mid-message and grabbed her cell off the desk.

"I've been trying to reach you for hours," she snapped. "Why didn't you call me back?"

"Wasn't aware that I worked for you," Billingslea said.

Diane bit her tongue. She needed this conversation to go well and telling Billingslea off, although pleasurable, would not help her cause. "Tell me you haven't released the information you think you have about the condition of the body we recovered this morning."

"Hmm, that sounds an awful lot like confirmation, Sergeant Joyner. Are you saying that the victim *was* decapitated?"

"I'm not saying any such thing, Davis. We recovered a body, period. What I am telling you is if you put that out there you may well screw up another case."

"My source is solid. Said they saw the body."

Diane considered what Billingslea was saying. So far as she knew, only a handful of investigators had been privy to the condition of Faherty's body. "Who's your source?"

"You know it doesn't work like that. If I'm right, and this is connected to the Horseman murders, it could be the biggest story I'll ever cover. Might even get a book deal out of it from one of the Big Five. Give me one good reason why I shouldn't run with what I already have."

Diane scrambled to think of something that would be too tempting not to consider. "What if you are right?" she said at last.

"What do you mean?" Billingslea asked. His suspicion was obvious.

"Just what I said. What if you're right and the body we found this morning *is* connected to those other murders? Would you rather report the connection or be the one who gets first crack at the story when we solve the case?"

"You're promising me an exclusive on the Horseman case?"

"I'm not saying that our case is related to those others, Davis. What I am promising is to give you the exclusive when we solve this one. *If* you hold back now."

"How do I know you guys will even be able to solve it? Christ, Boston Homicide hasn't been able to."

"Have you met John Byron?"

Billingslea was quiet for a moment. "Point taken. How long then?"

"Until *we* release the details."

"You're asking a lot."

"Maybe. But if you're right about the cases being linked, and we do solve it, you'll be getting a lot."

She held her breath while waiting for him to bite into the sharp hook she was dangling.

"I'll think about it," he said at last.

Byron left his business card with Bates after instructing him to have his attorney call. Byron wasn't holding his breath. Frustrated, he drove back to 109 with a plan to crawl up into the ex-boyfriend's business. Way up.

"Hey, Sarge," Nugent said before Byron even made it into his office. "Dustin found some stuff from last weekend."

"What kind of stuff?"

"About our victim. There was a 911 call made from the restaurant she works at, Alessandro's, about having a customer removed for harassing an employee. Some guy named Gene Wagner."

"Who was the employee?"

"Danica Faherty."

Byron tossed his briefcase in the chair beside his desk. Nugent handed him the printout. "What happened?" Byron asked.

"Nothing. Wagner was gone by the time patrol officers got there. It's not the first time with this guy, though."

"Meaning?"

"Apparently, Wagner has a thing for her. He's a regular at the bar."

"Criminal record?"

"Other than a couple of OUI convictions, nothing interesting. I was gonna go talk to him, unless you'd like a shot."

Byron thought about Destiny Collins's comment about a prior violent encounter between Bates and Faherty. "No, have at him. I've got something else I want to follow up on."

Byron descended the overly warm rear stairwell to 109's second floor and its air-conditioned Records Division. After a quick but stern admonishment by the office manager, who was on her way out the door, about detectives misfiling reports, he found what he was looking for. Faherty's report against Bates was tucked in among the 2015 case files which were still occupying one of the shelves inside the Lektriever, a gigantic floor-to-ceiling vertical file carousel. He made a copy of the entire report, replaced the original, then headed up to the computer crimes lab on the third floor.

Detective Dustin Tran, the PPD's computer guru, was fond of saying if there was something that he couldn't do on a computer, then it couldn't be done. Tran's office was situated across the hall from the Regional Crime Lab. The tiny space was both too small and too warm, due to a myriad of computer towers and high-definition screens that occupied every horizontal surface and were always powered on. They gave the place an oily, mechanical smell.

"Hey, Striped Dude," Tran greeted as Byron entered the office. "Think I found some stuff you might want."

Byron stood waiting as Tran shuffled through the mess of papers stacked on a side table.

"Here you go," Tran said, handing Byron

a short stack.

"What's this?" Byron asked.

"I did a global search on Faherty, looking for prior and current addresses, family, friends, employment, criminal history, everything. It's all in there."

"Anything stand out?"

"Nothing recent. She had a motor vehicle accident in South Portland about three weeks ago, a speeding ticket last August, and she's been listed as a witness to a couple of bad checks passed at the restaurant she works at. The only thing of note I could find happened near the end of 2015. It looks like a DV involving her boyfriend at the time. Some guy named —"

"Morgan Bates."

Tran's eyes widened in surprise. "How'd you do that so fast?"

Included in the domestic violence report were Bates's arrest sheet, a supplemental report from the assigned detective, and a signed statement from Danica Faherty stating that she no longer wished to pursue assault charges against Morgan Bates.

With Bates having lawyered up prematurely, Byron decided that his next stop should be Alessandro's, the restaurant where both Faherty and Bates had been employed. Perhaps the owners would be able to shed some additional light on the relationship.

Located on Fore Street, just east of Exchange, Alessandro's was a swanky Mediterranean offshoot of its New York City predecessor. Both restaurants were owned by the Stavros family. Byron had never dined there, but he knew of the restaurant's popularity and their month-plus waiting list. A self-proclaimed connoisseur of Thai takeout and burgers, Byron had never made a reservation more than two hours in advance.

He stepped inside the restaurant and found two dozen or so employees buzzing about like insects, setting up for the dinner crowd. The change in temperature was dramatic. The Fore St. sidewalk had been sweltering, but the air inside Alessandro's was cool and dry. The space was open and airy, decorated in what Byron guessed was supposed to be an eclectic European style.

The ceiling of the former industrial space, with its massive wooden beams and metal air ducts, had been painted flat black. Strands of clear white lightbulbs hung in rows about twelve feet above the gleaming hardwood floor. Long high tables surrounded by black wooden stools, along with dark leather couches and exposed brick walls, dominated the lower dining area. A wrought iron staircase led to an upper loft. The kitchen space, featuring a thirty-foot-long arched pass-through, was open to the dining room, allowing customers to observe the food preparation. Having spent his youth watching his mother prepare every meal in the Byron kitchen, he couldn't understand the public's fascination with this trend.

"Can I help you?"

Byron turned to see an attractive young woman with dark hair pulled back into a long perfectly braided ponytail. She wore a white short-sleeved V-neck blouse, black skirt, and turquoise-colored waist sash. Her plastic name tag read: Sheila.

"I'm looking for the manager," he said.

Sheila gave him a polite smile. "May I ask who's looking?"

Byron produced his credentials. "Detective Sergeant John Byron. I'm here about one of the restaurant employees."

"I'll go find him for you."

Byron returned the badge case to his jacket pocket and continued his visual tour of the restaurant while he waited. All the waitstaff were attired in the same white-and-black uniform that Sheila was wearing. The one variation was that the men wore white collared shirts and black slacks.

Several minutes later the young woman returned. She was accompanied by a handsome olive-skinned male. The man was drying his hands with a dish towel. "May I help you?" he asked.

"I hope so," Byron said. "I'm looking for the manager."

"Well then, I can definitely help you," he said, extending a hand. "Petri Stavros, I am the manager. Sorry, still a little damp but clean."

"Detective Sergeant John Byron," he said, returning the gesture.

"Pleased to meet you, Detective Sergeant," Stavros said. "What can I do for the police?"

Byron noticed the prying eyes of several members of the waitstaff. "Is there someplace we can speak privately?"

"Certainly. Follow me."

Stavros led Byron through the kitchen, past a handful of employees dressed in chef garb, toward the rear of the building. The office was more luxurious than Byron had imagined. In fact, the furnishings were far better than even Chief Lynds's office at 109. On the wall were dozens of framed black-and-white photos, each depicting the same woman. Some of the pictures were publicity shots while others, depicting her in costume, were obviously from various movie roles.

"Your mother?" Byron asked as he pointed to one of the photographs.

"Angelina," Stavros said. "Lina for short. Glamorous, isn't she?"

"She is. Does she ever come in?"

Stavros laughed. "Nearly every night. In addition to being the owner, she's the star power that packs this place. They come to see her."

Byron noticed a framed color photo sitting atop the desk of two young children and a very attractive woman. "Yours?"

"My sister-in-law, Deborah, and her children. Lina spoils them rotten."

"I'll bet. Your niece and nephew?"

"Correct. Kaia and Leander. Deborah is married to my brother Alessandro, Alex for short. He's the head chef here. You may have heard of him. Had his own cooking show."

"I don't watch much television."

"Sit, please."

Byron sat.

"So, what can I help you with?"

"I'm here to ask you about a couple of your employees."

"Which ones?"

"Morgan Bates and Danica Faherty."

Stavros grimaced. "Morgan no longer

works here. I fired him about six months ago."

"Mind if I ask why?"

"Not at all. We caught him stealing. I believe he may have had a drug habit."

Byron nodded and made an entry in his notepad. "And Faherty?"

"Dani is our maître d'. Works evenings."

"Can you tell me when she worked last, Mr. Stavros?"

"Call me Petri, please. Sure, Dani last worked Saturday night. She was scheduled to work Sunday night, too, but she didn't show."

"That unusual?"

"Very. She's one of my most dependable employees. Why are you asking about her?"

"Have you spoken with her since Saturday?" Byron said.

Before Petri could answer, a man wearing chef's garb walked into the office.

"Petri, I thought I told you to order — oh, sorry. I didn't know you were meeting with anyone."

"Not a problem," Petri said. "Detective Sergeant Byron, this is my brother Alex."

"Pleased to meet you, Sergeant Byron. Detective, huh? What's up?"

"Sergeant Byron was just asking some questions about Morgan Bates," Petri said.

Alex's face twisted up in disgust. "I suppose Petri told you that Morgan was stealing from us."

"He did," Byron said. "I was also asking about the last time either of you spoke to Danica Faherty."

Petri and Alex exchanged a glance that Byron couldn't quite interpret.

Petri spoke up first. "As I told you, Dani didn't show up for her Sunday night shift."

"So, the last time you spoke with her was when?" Byron asked.

"Early Sunday morning. We walked out together after closing up."

"And you?" Byron asked, addressing Alex. "When did you last see or speak to Ms. Faherty?"

"Not since Friday. I was out of town attending a conference over the weekend."

Byron returned his attention to Petri. "Did you try to call her when she didn't show Sunday night?"

"I did. I left several messages on her cellphone, but she never returned my calls. She's due to work tonight. Would you like me to have her contact you when she gets in?"

"We recovered Danica Faherty's body this morning," Byron said matter-of-factly, looking for a reaction from either brother.

"Her body?" Alex looked genuinely surprised. "Then she's . . ."

"She's dead."

"Jesus," Petri said. "What happened?"

"We're still investigating that," Byron said. "We believe she was murdered."

"Murdered?" Petri said.

"We believe so."

"Where did you find her — her body?" Alex asked.

"Not too far from here."

"I can't believe someone would kill Dani," Petri said.

Byron watched as both Stavros brothers stared into the distance as if dazed.

"Petri, you worked with Dani Saturday night, do you remember anything usual happening that evening?" Byron asked.

"Actually, yes," Petri said. "Something did happen. I wouldn't exactly call it unusual, but we did have to call the police."

"What happened?" Byron asked.

"Gene Wagner, one of our regular customers, he kind of has a thing for Dani. He comes in all the time throwing money around. He's really harmless, but sometimes he drinks too much."

"Is that what happened Saturday night?" Byron asked.

Petri looked to Alex as if for approval. Alex

nodded.

"Yes," Petri said. "Gene came in around nine o'clock and sat in the bar lounge. He chatted up Dani every time she passed by. Around ten-thirty he began to get grabby."

"Grabby?" Byron asked.

"I guess he put his hands on her."

"Did you confront him?"

"I started to, but I didn't get the chance. Lina — that's Mom's nickname, was already headed over. Lina told him to leave."

"And did he?" Byron asked.

"Not immediately, no. I took it upon myself to call the police, but Gene left before the officers got here."

"It really wasn't necessary to involve the police," Alex said. "Gene is an old friend of the family, Sergeant Byron."

Petri shrugged. "Well, it was my call. I thought it was necessary."

"Has Wagner been in since?" Byron asked.

"No," Petri said. "He didn't come in Sunday night, and we're closed on Mondays."

"What about last night?"

"He wasn't in last night either. You don't think Gene had anything to do with Dani's murder, do you?"

"We'll be looking at everyone," Byron said as he made a note to pass on Wagner's name to Tran. "So, Lina is the only one who confronted Gene Wagner?"

"That's right," Petri said.

Byron looked to both men. "I don't suppose Lina is here now?"

Alex shook his head. "No, she's at home in Scarborough with my children. Would you like me to get her on the phone?"

"I'd rather speak with her in person."

CHAPTER 9

Wednesday, 5:45 P.M.,
July 12, 2017

Byron departed Alessandro's en route to the nearby town of Scarborough. The address Alex and Petri had provided for their mother was located southwest of Portland in the affluent Greater Portland community of Prouts Neck. Connected to the mainland by a narrow stretch of land and bordered on both sides by sandy beaches, the Neck was a large, heavily forested, rocky promontory jutting out into the Atlantic, facing Saco Bay. It was a locale perfectly suited to someone of Angelina's stature.

The GPS on Byron's cellphone led him along Black Point Road, past the Prouts Neck Country Club, and onto Winslow Homer Road, where the celebrated artist's studio still stands alongside the rugged Maine coastline that made him famous.

Byron slowed as he neared the address

then turned left onto an unmarked paved way. Fifty feet in from the roadway two large fieldstone pillars stood sentry on either side of the drive. Spanning the distance between them was a formidable-looking wrought iron gate replete with piked finials and a large decorative letter *S* that had been incorporated into the ironwork at the gate's center. A stainless-steel pole-mounted electronic keypad stood to the left of the drive. Byron pulled up alongside it, lowered his window, and pressed the call button. His eyes were drawn to the security cameras mounted atop each of the pillars.

A woman's voice emanated clearly from the speaker. "May I help you?"

"My name is John Byron. I'm a detective sergeant from the Portland Police Department here to see Angelina Stavros."

"Oh yes, Sergeant. Petri called to say you'd be stopping by. Please, drive right in."

Byron heard a loud electronic buzz, then watched as the iron gate parted in the center, splitting the *S* as each side rolled away behind the pillars.

He drove on.

Several hundred feet past the gate the driveway turned sharply to the left before re-emerging from the heavily wooded area into a large sunlit clearing. A vast and well-maintained emerald-green lawn sloped upward toward the main house, which sat prominently atop a knoll facing a large pond. As Byron continued up the drive, he could see a woman and small child seated in white Adirondack chairs, facing the pond. A second child, a boy with curly blond hair, was playing at the water's edge, although his idea of playing seemed to include throwing things toward a flock of ducks.

Byron pulled the unmarked into the broad cobblestone turnaround and parked. As he exited the car, he caught sight of a large man approaching on foot from behind a shingled outbuilding. Byron waved but the man neither returned the greeting nor broke stride as he quickly closed the distance.

"Help you with something?" the man growled from beneath his bushy black mustache.

Byron's eyes were drawn to a long angry looking scar on the side of the man's neck, poking up from the collar of his T-shirt. "I'm here to —"

"It's okay, Dennis," Angelina Stavros said from behind Byron. "He's a police detective."

Byron turned as Stavros approached, both children at her heels.

"Good afternoon, Sergeant Byron," she said.

"Mrs. Stavros."

"Lina, please."

Byron turned back toward Dennis, but the burly man was already retracing his steps, quickly returning the way he'd come.

Byron and Lina met at the center of the drive and shook hands.

Dressed in white capris, a navy top, and a straw sun hat, Lina was every bit as glamorous in person as she had appeared on the walls of Petri's office.

"I am sorry about that," she said. "Dennis is my late husband's brother. He wasn't expecting company. I think you surprised him."

"Is he always so guarded?" Byron asked.

"It's a pleasure to make your acquaintance, Sergeant," she said, ignoring his question. "These are my grandbabies, Kaia and Leander," Lina said, her face beaming with pride. "Say hello to the sergeant, children."

The dark-haired Kaia gave Byron a sheepish grin before retreating behind her grandmother's legs.

"Hello, Sergeant!" Leander screeched in falsetto before sprinting back toward the pond, where Byron imagined the duck

tormenting would resume.

"Come," Lina said. "Let's get out of the sun."

She led Byron to a granite patio situated beneath a vine-covered cedar pergola. They sat in white rattan chairs, facing the pond and the ocean beyond. The granddaughter stood pressed against Lina like epoxy.

As soon as they were seated a young woman with a distinctly British accent materialized from the direction of the main house. "Yes, Mrs. Stavros," she said.

"Dorothy, would you please look after the children for me. Sergeant Byron and I need to speak privately."

"Yes, ma'am," Dorothy said as she clasped one of Kaia's hands in her own.

"Kaia, why don't you run along now with Dorothy," Lina said.

Hello Sergeant!" Kaia yelled as she ran off to join her brother, with Dorothy doing her best to keep up.

"Adorable, aren't they?" Lina said as she gazed longingly after the children.

It wasn't the first word that came to Byron's mind as he watched Leander the Adorable hurl another rock toward the unsuspecting fowl. Thing One and Thing Two seemed a better fit.

"Dorothy is?" Byron asked.

"My au pair. She's from London. While I do love my grandbabies, I don't know how I would manage without Dorothy's help. Would you care for some iced tea? Or lemonade? I'll have my assistant bring some."

"No thanks," Byron said, making a note to hire an assistant.

"So, Alex informs me that you're investigating the murder of one of our employees."

"That's right. Danica Faherty."

"So tragic. I heard something on the news about a body being recovered. I had no idea it was our Danica. Such a sweet girl."

"I wanted to ask you about Saturday night," Byron said. "I understand there was a problem with one of the customers at Alessandro's."

"Yes. Most unfortunate. Gene Wagner. He's a regular. Has a bit of a drinking problem, I'm afraid."

"And an infatuation with Faherty," Byron said.

Lina sighed. "Yes, it's true. He was quite taken with Danica, a lovely girl. He really is harmless, though. Lonely, I think. I had the situation well in hand, but my son Petri overreacted, as he's prone to, and phoned the police. I dealt with Gene directly after he refused to leave voluntarily."

"What led up to that?" Byron asked. "Specifically."

"As I said, he drinks a bit too much. Evidently, he may have inadvertently put his hand on Danica, and she took exception."

Byron couldn't help noticing the way she both minimized the accusation and redirected blame. "In what way did he put his hand on her?"

"I don't know exactly. I didn't witness it. I was told that's what happened. Danica was quite upset about it."

"Was this the first time?" Byron asked.

Lina cocked her head slightly. "First time?"

"Yes. Was this the first time Gene assaulted Danica or any of your other employees?"

Her eyes narrowed, forming tiny lines on either side of her face, as she struggled to maintain her composure. It was enough of a tell that Byron knew she'd taken offense to his question. Before she could answer, Byron heard a vehicle approaching. He turned to see a white BMW X5 rolling up the drive.

"Mom!" both children screeched at the top of their lungs. The SUV came to a stop nearby and the Adorables sprinted toward it, leaving Dorothy the au pair in the dust.

"My daughter-in-law, Deborah," Lina said, her pleasant demeanor returning, answering the question before Byron could ask. "She's an attorney."

Byron rose as a tall blonde woman wearing sunglasses walked toward them, the children swarming around her legs, vying for her attention.

"Sergeant Byron," Lina said. "This is my daughter-in-law, Deborah."

"Byron?" Deborah said, removing her glasses. "Oh, my God, John Byron. It's Debbie Strickland. Well, Strickland-Stavros now," she corrected, flashing a rather large diamond solitaire ring.

"You two know each other?" Lina said, sounding perplexed.

"John and I went to Saint Joseph's together, before I changed universities and moved out of state."

"Great to see you, Deb," Byron said as he extended a hand.

"A handshake?" Deborah said. "Not on your life. You don't get out of it that easily." She moved in and hugged him. "John and I dated while we were at St. Joe's."

"Is that so?" Lina said, sounding amused. "This is a small world."

"Do you all live here?" Byron asked.

"My son Alex and his family are staying with me until their new home is ready," Lina said.

"Well, if we decide to stay," Deborah corrected.

"Not exactly roughing it," Byron said.

"Not exactly," Deborah said, giving him a sly smile.

"I'm afraid Sergeant Byron came with some tragic news about one of the restaurant employees," Lina said.

"Oh?" Deborah said with a look of concern on her face.

"Yes," Byron said. "Danica Faherty was found murdered. Did you know Ms. Faherty?"

"I don't think so," Deborah said.

"She was one of our hostesses," Lina added. "Deborah is a corporate attorney, Sergeant Byron. And about the only one in the family not involved in the restaurant business."

"And not affiliated with Hollywood either," Deborah said with a wink.

"Mom, can we go out back and play with Uncle Dennis?" the tow-headed Thing One asked.

"Why don't you go inside with Dorothy and get washed up for dinner," Deborah said, drawing groans of disapproval from both children. "It's so great to see you, John. We should catch up while I'm in town."

"I'd like that," Byron said.

Deborah handed him a business card after scribbling her number on the back. "That's my personal cell. Call me."

"I will," Byron said, looking on as she herded her brood toward the mansion.

"My apologies for the interruption," Lina said as she and Byron resumed their seats in the shade of the pergola. "Where were we?"

"I asked you if this was the first time Wagner had assaulted Danica, or any other member of your staff?" Byron watched as her expression changed again from doting grandmother to protective matriarch.

"Gene Wagner is a well-to-do businessman, close friend, and frequent customer in my restaurant. He has even produced several of my films."

"He financed them?"

"Yes. Now to your question. Gene's attraction to Danica was well-known by the staff. To my knowledge, this was the first time Danica ever took offense to his advances. Truthfully, she was a bit of a flirt. That probably sounds horrible of me, given the circumstances of your visit, but I think she rather enjoyed the attention."

"Until Saturday night," Byron said, continuing to hold eye contact with her, letting the awkwardness of the moment hang between them.

"It's all in the past now, Sergeant."

"Just the same, I will need to speak with Gene Wagner."

"Is that absolutely necessary?"

"Mrs. Stavros," Byron said, intentionally reverting to the formal use of her surname. "I am investigating a murder, and as such I will be speaking with everyone who may have had contact with Danica Faherty prior to her death."

Lina studied him before speaking again. "Surely you don't believe Gene had anything to do with Danica's death."

"I don't make it my practice to rule out anyone until the facts say otherwise. At this point everyone is a suspect."

Byron was turning onto Winslow Homer Road from Angelina Stavros's driveway when his cell rang with an incoming call from Stevens. He answered it.

"Got some interesting news on our security guard," Stevens said.

"Hopkins?"

"Yup. Looks like he lied about when he was last in the lumberyard."

"How do we know that?" Byron said. "I thought there weren't any surveillance cameras."

"There aren't. But I just spoke with David Merrill, the manager of Secure Incorporated. Merrill told me that the company's been getting killed on their insurance premiums. S.I. installed tracking devices in the trunks of each patrol vehicle as a big brotherly way of controlling costs."

"And?"

"And, according to the tracking data, the vehicle assigned to Craig Hopkins was inside Forest City Lumber's fenced-in lot early Tuesday morning."

"This past Tuesday?"

"Yup. For nearly an hour. I've got a printout of the log and a screen shot from Merrill's computer."

"And you're positive it was *inside* the enclosure?" Byron asked, wondering if he dared allow himself the glimmer of hope that the case might be narrowing in scope.

"One hundred percent. Merrill told me the manufacturer of those GPS units guarantees the location accuracy to within three feet in any direction."

"Nice catch, Mel."

"But wait," Stevens said, amping up her tone to mimic a game show host. "There's more. Ten years ago, Craig Hopkins had a charge of unlawful sexual contact filed against him in Massachusetts."

"S.I. had to have done a background check on him, right?" Byron said. "How would they miss something as serious as a sexual assault?"

"Hopkins's history doesn't appear in NCIC. Massachusetts is one of the states that doesn't always report to the feds. Besides, he was only a juvie at the time. Seventeen."

"How did you get it?" Byron asked.

"Oh, I have connections, Sarge. One of my ex-girlfriends works intel for the Mass State Police."

"What happened to the case?"

"Evidently, the victim's family decided not to follow through. Maybe they were trying to avoid embarrassment for their child. What do you want to do about Hopkins?"

"Bring him in."

Byron had just pocketed the phone when it rang again. Thinking it was Stevens calling back, he accepted the call without checking the ID.

"Byron," he said.

"John, it's Kay."

His gaze slid down to his ringless left hand.

Kay Byron was John's ex-wife. Even though they'd been divorced for nearly two years, and contact between them had been infrequent, hearing her voice still affected him. Kay had wanted the divorce, deciding after two decades of matrimony not to compete with John's full-time mistress, police work.

"Are you in the middle of something?" she asked.

"No. Well, actually yeah, but it's all right. I'm in the car right now. What's up?"

"I know how busy you get, so I thought I'd remind you Katherine's nineteenth birthday is coming up, in case you forgot."

"Of course I didn't forget," he lied.

"I'm sure she'd love to hear from her uncle John."

Katherine, too old to be called Katie anymore, was John's favorite niece. One of three children belonging to Kay's stuck-up sister and snobbish husband, Janice and Thurston Whitehill, Katherine was the only one who'd ever given John the time of day.

"I should probably buy her a gift," Byron said. "Any ideas?"

"Actually, yes. I think she'd love to go to a Portland Sea Dogs game with you. And they are playing at home in a couple of weeks."

"Sea Dogs? I didn't know she was into

baseball."

Kay laughed. "Well, she is now."

"Am I supposed to know what that means?"

"Just take her to a game for her birthday and let her tell you."

Byron returned to 109, delivering to Dustin Tran the information Angelina Stavros had provided on Gene Wagner. Additionally, he asked Tran to see if he could locate anything on a Steve Holcolm, the man Bates claimed was his alibi. Given the time of day, Byron sent Tran and Robbins home. They were all running on fumes at this point anyway, and Byron knew it wouldn't be long before Le-Royer started bitching about the overtime budget.

It took another hour before Stevens was able to coax Hopkins into police headquarters, using the pretext that she needed him to read and sign his typed statement. Hopkins was escorted directly into Interview Room Three.

Byron and Stevens sat across from the S.I. security guard, while Nugent monitored from the closed-circuit recorder located in the CID conference room.

"I already told you," Hopkins said. "I

hadn't checked that property in over a week."

"Really?" Byron said. "See, now that's interesting, Craig."

"What is?"

"Well, according to your employer, the patrol vehicle that you were using during your Monday night shift was inside that fenced-in property for nearly an hour." Byron turned to Stevens. "What time did they say that was, Mel?"

Stevens made a show out of checking her notebook. "Um, 1:17 A.M. Tuesday morning until 2:10."

"But I wasn't. I don't know who is telling you this, but it isn't true."

"Really?" Byron said. Keeping his eyes fixed on Hopkins, Byron addressed his next question to Stevens. "When did David Merrill say they installed those tracking devices in each of the patrol vehicles?"

"Um, about three months ago," Stevens said, playing along.

Byron watched as the color drained from Hopkins's face. The guard looked like he was about to be sick to his stomach.

"Care to explain why you've been lying to us, Craig?" Byron asked.

Hopkins looked back and forth at each detective, then hung his head in defeat.

■ ■ ■ ■

"What do you think?" Nugent asked as the three detectives stood in the conference room watching Hopkins on the monitor.

Byron rolled his neck until it gave an audible pop. "I think he's screwed either way and he knows it."

"You think he was with another under-aged girl?" Nugent said.

"I'd take that bet," Stevens said. "His criminal record shows a proclivity toward young girls. And it would explain his reason for not coming clean about why he was inside the fence."

"Proclivity," Nugent mocked. "Big word for such a lowly detective."

"I'll show you how lowly I am," Stevens said, holding up a fist for effect.

"Of course, the other possibility is that he was there disposing of Dani Faherty's body," Byron said, bringing them back on point. The two detectives nodded in silent agreement. "Ellis thinks she was killed early Sunday and placed in the lumberyard sometime later. If Hopkins is our killer, he could have murdered her Sunday morning after she left work."

"Then waited until Tuesday morning

when he was working, and knew he wouldn't be noticed, to dump the body," Nugent said.

"And on his days off he drives to Boston to take heads," Stevens said, poking fun at her former partner.

"Hey, I'm just spitballing, Mel," Nugent said. "I don't have a crystal ball."

"What do you want to do with him, Sarge?" Stevens asked.

"Well, he hasn't lawyered up yet," Byron said as his cell began to vibrate. He removed it from the inside pocket of his suit jacket and checked the ID. The call was from Le-Royer.

"Let me guess," Nugent said. "The LT wants an update?"

Byron hadn't been keeping LeRoyer in the loop, nor had he returned his prior call. He knew he had to give the lieutenant something.

"Hey, Marty," Byron said, answering the call.

"Don't 'hey' me. Don't you return calls?"

Byron got up and walked from the room. "Been a little busy."

"Are you trying to piss off the new chief? Or is it just me you like dicking around?"

Byron said nothing. He'd learned to let LeRoyer get it out of his system. After the lieutenant had finished berating him, Byron filled him in on the latest developments.

"Sounds like you checked off a lot of boxes today," LeRoyer said. "That's good. Lynds will like that."

"Great. Exactly what I was hoping for."

LeRoyer ignored the comment. "What about the car the security guard was using?"

"S.I. agreed to pull it out of service for us. I'll have Gabe process it tomorrow."

"What do you think this Hopkins's angle is? Think he's our guy?"

Byron was well aware that suspects were sometimes known to sound the alarm. It was the equivalent of an arsonist calling in a fire after setting it. Hiding within plain sight.

"Who knows what Hopkins is up to," Byron said. "I only know he lied about being in there on Tuesday morning."

"Well, keep an eye on him. By the way, Chief Lynds wants to hold a presser tomorrow, late morning. You can help me write up some talking points."

"I can't wait."

After he'd finished with LeRoyer, Byron returned to the conference room where the detectives were waiting on him. He addressed Stevens. "Mel, go back at Hopkins. Solo. We still need to establish a link between Hopkins and Faherty. Try and sweet-talk him into coming clean."

"Yeah, you always have a way with the creeps," Nugent teased.

Stevens, who had already reached the conference room door, stopped and turned back. "Must be why we've been partners for so long."

Byron and Nugent spent the next forty-five minutes seated in the CID conference room watching Stevens throw everything she had at Hopkins, but the security guard didn't budge. Hopkins no longer denied being inside the property, but he remained steadfast in his denials of having anything to do with killing Faherty, dumping her body, or even knowing her. And still he refused to explain his reason for being there.

Stevens returned to the conference room. "He's not cracking, Sarge," Stevens said. "And, honestly, I'm running out of gas."

"Me, too," Nugent said, yawning and echoing Byron's own thoughts.

Byron checked the clock on the wall. It was nearly nine-thirty. They'd been going at this nonstop for close to sixteen hours, and he'd need them fresh in the coming days. Exhausted detectives were prone to making mistakes.

"He's agreed to give us prints, though,

right?" Byron asked.

"Yes," Stevens said. "And, short of a confession, anything else we need."

"Okay," Byron said. "Let's get Gabe up here for prints, photos, a hair sample, and a DNA swab. Make sure Hopkins signs consent forms for all of it."

"And then?" Stevens asked.

"We kick him loose, call it a night, and regroup in the morning."

Diane Joyner appeared in the conference room doorway.

"Hey, Sarge," Stevens said.

"What are you still doing here?" Byron asked.

"Had some things to do. But I wanted to give you guys a heads-up before I left."

"I'm almost afraid to ask," Byron said.

"Billingslea ran the headless story," Diane said.

"Fuck," Nugent said, speaking for all of them.

Byron turned to Nugent. "What time did you say Danica's parents are due in tomorrow morning?"

"First thing. I gave them directions to 109 and told them to ask for you."

"They know about the condition of her body?" Diane said.

"No," Byron said. "They don't."

133

It was nearly eleven by the time Byron departed from 109. He hadn't realized how worn out he was until he slid behind the wheel of his unmarked. He was still fuming about Billingslea's story in the *Portland Herald*. Byron wasn't sure which thing pissed him off the most, having the information out before he could break the news gently to Danica Faherty's parents, in person, or that there might be a leak inside their investigation.

He was reaching for his seat belt when his cell rang. He answered without bothering to see who it was. "Byron."

"Hey, cuz," Murray said. "Thought you'd forgotten about me."

"Hardly," Byron said. "Long day."

"I hear ya. So, tell me about your case and I'll tell you what we've got in common."

Byron pulled out of the rear garage then ran down the details including the location, the posing, and what they knew about Danica Faherty. Murray listened without interrupting.

"Any indication of prostitution?" Murray asked when Byron had finished.

"Not that we know of," Byron said. "By

all accounts Faherty was clean. College grad, good employee. And according to the M.E., no indication of illegal drug use."

"Bullshit. Not even weed? Shit, everyone hits the ganja these days, Johnny. Christ, the millennials think it's a friggin' vitamin."

"Not this girl. Why did you ask about prostitution?"

"Both our vics were pros. One really was a pro, at it for at least a couple of years, the other only recently. A few months as best we can tell."

"Didn't see anything about that on the news," Byron said.

"Nope, and you won't. Managed to keep that little detail off the radar. Still pissed that the other stuff leaked out."

"It always does," Byron said as he gripped the steering wheel a little tighter, allowing himself the fantasy that it was Davis Billingslea's neck.

"Not to tell you how to do your job, cuz," Murray said, clearly indicating he was about to do just that.

"But?" Byron said.

"But you might want to double-check on that prostitution thing. Our most recent vic was connected through Back Page. You familiar?"

"Not personally, but yeah I know of it.

Kinda like the sex internet, right? The way some of them advertise now."

"Exactly. World's oldest profession meets the latest social media ad tech. Victim number two, going by the name of Krystal, with a K, had been plying her trade for about three or four months."

"Motive?"

"Who knows. Pissed-off ex-client they had in common, maybe. Some asshole with mommy issues. Religious zealot working out some Whore of Babylon thing. Maybe just a twisted fuck. Your guess is as good as mine."

Byron considered how little they still knew about Danica Faherty. He wanted to get another look inside her apartment. "Okay, we'll look hard at the prostitution angle."

"Bet you find something. My two cents."

"This thing is still developing up here," Byron said. "I'd like to drive down and take a look at what you guys have on your end, but it might not be for a few days."

"I'm not going anywhere. Let me know when you're ready, and I'll roll out the official BPD welcome mat."

Byron was turning onto his road in North Deering as he ended the call with Murray. He pulled the unmarked Ford into the driveway directly in front of his condo's garage door and was sliding the transmission lever into park when his cell rang again. Diane. He answered it.

"You sound beat," she said.

He leaned back against the headrest and sighed. "I am."

"Still at 109?"

"Just pulled into my driveway."

"Want some company?"

He checked the time displayed on the dash. 11:15. "Aren't you home in bed?"

"Couldn't sleep. Besides your bed's so much more comfortable," she cooed.

"But we never sleep when you're here."

"Exactly."

"How soon can you get here?"

Diane laughed.

"What?" The interior of Byron's car was suddenly bathed in the glow of headlights as a car pulled in behind him.

"That was fast," he said.

Forty-five minutes later Byron and Diane lay atop Byron's bed breathless and satiated. Their nude bodies were slick with perspiration, the bedcovers kicked to the carpet. A trail of abandoned clothing marked their progress up the stairs to the dimly lit second-floor bedroom.

The sexual attraction between them had been obvious from the start. Byron knew it was their communication skills, or maybe lack thereof, and a mutual love of independence that was preventing them from having a real relationship. Thoughts that he had been mulling over a lot recently.

Byron had just begun to drift off when she spoke.

"You asleep?" she asked.

"Yup," he said, keeping his eyelids closed.

"Liar." She tweaked one of his nipples.

"Ouch."

"Oh good, you're awake." She lifted her head from his chest and softly kissed the side of his neck.

"Something on your mind?" he asked.

"What makes you say that?"

A smile unfurled. "Because I know you."

"Can't a girl just pay a surprise visit to her boyfriend?"

Boyfriend. He had to admit he liked the sound of that. "I thought the guy was supposed to be the one to initiate a booty call?"

"Where's that written?" she asked, tweaking his other nipple.

"Aah. Okay, okay. But seriously, I've got to get some sleep."

"All right."

A short time later, just as sleep had begun to overtake him, she spoke up again.

"Lynds cornered me today."

Byron forced one eye open. "What'd she want?"

"She's considering realigning CID, now that George is retiring. No more property side people side. One bureau, one lieutenant, two sergeants."

Byron sighed and closed his eye. "That's gonna ruffle some feathers."

"What about yours?"

"My what?"

"Feathers?"

He thought for a moment before answering. "Not sure it's gonna affect me all that much."

Neither of them spoke for several moments before Byron broke the silence. "I don't get it. Why was Lynds sharing any of this with you?"

"She wants me to consider putting in for the vacant CID sergeant position."

Both of Byron's eyes flew open.

CHAPTER 10

Thursday, 4:30 A.M.,
July 13, 2017

Byron awoke to find Diane's half of the bed abandoned. He hadn't slept well. The Faherty murder might have had something to do with it, but more likely was the prospect of Diane's returning to CID. The news had caught him off guard. Diane had read his reaction as negative, and if he was being honest with himself, it had been. He had seen the disappointment etched on her face. She'd expected him to be enthusiastic and supportive, but he had been neither.

It wasn't that he didn't look forward to working cases with her again, because he did. He knew Diane's keen investigative talents were wasted as the face of public relations for the Portland Police Department. And Byron didn't see her return to the bureau as his equal as any kind of threat. He wasn't that shallow. The real problem was that they were finally falling into more of a normal relationship, as normal as two cops can have anyway, and he was beginning to imagine them taking it to the next level. Perhaps even moving in together. But now he worried that Chief Lynds's scheme might well kill that plan before it even began. His failed twenty-year marriage to Kay was proof enough just how hard being wed to someone who was married to their career could be. Byron didn't imagine a relationship between two people married to their careers stood a chance in hell.

He showered, dressed, and was out the door with coffee in hand before the sun appeared above the horizon. What was already slated to be a long day, containing far more questions than answers, had just become infinitely more complicated thanks to his rusty — no, nonexistent — relationship skills.

He arrived at 109 expecting to find CID deserted. Instead he found Detective Melissa Stevens in the conference room updating the whiteboard.

"Hey," he said. "Didn't expect to see anyone here so early."

"Couldn't sleep," she said.

"Tough to shut it off, huh?"

"Impossible. Besides, Christine was snoring her ass off."

Byron, who had yet to meet Christine, wondered how Mel's live-in would react to the sharing of her nocturnal habits with strangers.

Stevens returned to writing on the whiteboard. "Seen the paper yet?"

"How bad?" Byron said, having temporarily forgotten about Billingslea's article.

Stevens pulled up the news story on her cell and handed it to him.

Headless Body Found in Portland May Be Connected to Boston's Horseman Cases, was the headline. Then in smaller print below, *Inside Sources Confirm Portland Detectives Working with Boston Homicide.*

"Fuck," Byron said, knowing that Danica Faherty's parents were flying in to see him in a few hours. He'd been planning to break the news to them as gently as possible, not hit them in the face with what amounted to an editorial sledgehammer.

"Keep going," Stevens said. "It gets worse."

"What could be worse?"

Byron scrolled farther down the page.

"Victim positively identified as 22-year-old Danica Faherty from Portland."

"Fuck," Byron said again. While grinding his teeth together he reread the words *inside sources. Was this Lynds?* he wondered. Meet the new chief, same as the old?

"Let's just hope Faherty's parents haven't seen it," she said.

But of course, they had.

Byron sat stewing in LeRoyer's office, watching as the lieutenant performed the two-finger shuffle across the computer keyboard. The lieutenant was typing up talking points for Chief Lynds to use at the press conference.

"Marty, I really don't have time for this," Byron said.

"Hey, this press conference is for you, too, muchacho. Who knows, it just might help your case."

Byron wondered if the lieutenant really believed that, or if he was just trying to impress Lynds.

"Anything you'd rather I not include?" LeRoyer asked.

"Yeah, everything that got leaked out to Davis-Fucking-Billingslea."

"Look, I can't control that, John."

"That's just the problem, Marty."

"Check yourself, Sergeant. I'm not the enemy. I didn't leak the headless stuff, so don't take it out on me."

Byron was confident that LeRoyer's assurances wouldn't mean a damn thing to the Fahertys.

"By the way, I do have some good news," LeRoyer continued. "Chief Lynds spoke with Angelina Stavros this morning. Stavros has offered up a reward of ten grand for information leading to the arrest and conviction of the killer. Lynds is planning to announce that at the presser. Isn't that great?"

Byron wasn't as excited about this latest development as LeRoyer seemed to be. The telephone calls and front desk drop-ins from attention seekers had already started. He wondered whether Lina Stavros was sincere in her effort to help the investigation or was simply trying to get out in front of the negative press that would undoubtedly find its way back to her beloved restaurants.

He always felt conflicted whenever a reward for information was offered. It usually ended up being a double-edged sword. While on rare occasions a legitimate tip had come in, more often the reward only managed to summon the crazies, wasting valuable time and investigative resources. And he hated that a bounty was needed to entice people to do the right thing.

LeRoyer's desk phone rang with an in-house call. It was CID's office assistant, Shirley Grant. LeRoyer punched the speaker button. "I'm a little busy right now, Shirley. What is it?"

"Sorry to bother you, *Lieutenant,* but there's an Elmer Faherty here to see Sergeant Byron. I don't suppose he's in there with you?"

Elmer Faherty was livid, so much so that he was visibly shaking. Byron led him into his office and closed the door. Faherty was holding the Thursday edition of the *Portland Herald* tight in his hand. Billingslea's story was plastered all over the front page. Above the fold. Faherty was angry and had every right to be. Byron gestured for the man to take a seat in one of the visitor's chairs located in front of Byron's desk. Byron also settled into a chair directly across from him, effectively removing the barrier of the desk.

Although Faherty was several years Byron's junior, the exhaustion displayed upon the man's face made him appear significantly older. Dark circles beneath his eyes and the wrinkled clothing told the story. Elmer Faherty was in mourning.

"Mr. Faherty, let me begin by offering my most sincere condolences for the loss of your daughter."

"Thanks," Faherty grunted.

"Also, I want to apologize for the news

getting to you the way it did."

Faherty's jaw clenched. "Why weren't we told about this when the police came to our home in Virginia?" he barked. "Or when I spoke to your Detective Nugent?"

Byron didn't have a good answer. "I wanted to wait until I could speak to you, and your wife, face-to-face."

Faherty held up the paper and shook it. "Looks like someone in your department didn't want to wait."

He was right, of course. Byron couldn't argue the point. "Again, I am so very sorry."

Faherty lowered the newspaper onto his lap but said nothing.

"Will Mrs. Faherty be joining us?" Byron asked.

"She's not in a good way at the moment," Faherty said. "I thought it might be better if it was just you and me."

"I understand."

"What can you tell me about my daughter's death? Is Dani's murder connected to the Boston cases like they're saying?"

"It's too early in the investigation for me to give you a definitive answer, Mr. Faherty."

"Elmer. It's Elmer. Dammit all to hell, if we're gonna sit here and discuss my baby's murder, I guess we should at least be on a first-name basis."

"Okay, Elmer. As I was saying, there are some similarities to the Boston cases. I'll be meeting with Boston homicide detectives soon. I should know more after —"

"Was she really — ? Did he — ? You know. Did he cut off — ?"

Byron nodded. "Yes."

"Did my Dani — ?" Faherty's voice cracked before he could finish.

Byron could see the aggrieved man wrestling to maintain control over his emotions.

"Did she suffer?"

"There's no indication of that," Byron said. In truth, he had no actual way of knowing that until Ellis provided them with a cause of death. Gabriel Pelligrosso hadn't found anything to indicate a struggle, and Byron wasn't about to cause the man additional pain by speculating.

"Had you spoken with Dani recently?" Byron asked, attempting to change the subject to something a bit less painful.

"Denise did. Her mother. Last week I believe. Dani called home pretty regular. About once or twice a week. Sometimes more frequently if something was happening in her life."

"Was there something happening? Any-

147

thing unusual Dani might have mentioned to her mother? Or to you?"

"I don't think so. I spoke with her a couple of weeks ago. She seemed happy."

Byron made a note to follow up with Denise Faherty when he got the chance. If there had been something noteworthy happening in Dani's personal life, Byron guessed she would have been far more likely to share it with her mother.

"Do you mind if I ask why she moved to Maine?" Byron asked.

"Wanted her independence. She had a friend here. Destiny. A nurse."

"Destiny Collins?"

Faherty nodded. "Dani's old roommate at the university in Orono. After graduation Dani followed Destiny to Portland. They'd been sharing an apartment until recently, when Destiny bought her own place."

"Was Dani seeing anyone?"

"I don't think so. She'd been dating a guy named Morgan Bates, but she broke it off with him a while ago. Few months back, I think."

"Did you ever meet him?"

"No. I guess he is or was a bartender at the restaurant where she worked, Alessandro's. I don't know if he's still there or not."

"Do you know if Dani and Morgan ever had any problems?"

Faherty's eyes narrowed. "What do you mean? What kind of problems?"

Byron knew he had to tread carefully on the off chance that Faherty was unaware of the domestic violence incident.

"Domestic trouble? Arguing? Fighting? Anything like that?"

"Not that I know of. I hope not. Why would you ask that?"

"We always focus on people closest to the victim first, then work our way out."

"I guess Denise would probably know," Faherty said. "If there was any trouble between them."

"How was Dani's relationship with you and Mrs. Faherty?"

"Okay, I guess. Same as most parents." Faherty paused, then broke eye contact, fixating on the floor. "That's not entirely true."

Byron remained silent, waiting to see where Faherty would take the conversation.

"Truth is, neither of us were very happy when Dani made the decision to move away. Guess I felt like she was too young, you know? Not ready. I worried if she moved to the city something bad might hap— Oh, Jesus."

Faherty broke down completely. He hid his face with one hand, his body racked by grief. Byron walked over to him and placed a hand on his shoulder.

It took several moments before Faherty regained some semblance of composure. He looked up at Byron with wet pleading eyes. "Promise me you'll get the son of a bitch who did this to my little girl, Sergeant."

Time and again Byron had been asked to provide the very same assurance to surviving family members of other homicide victims. The truth was that making such a promise was at best foolhardy, and at worst pure arrogance. In the end, all any dedicated cop can offer is to do their absolute best.

"I have some very talented and dedicated people working with me, Elmer. I promise you that we will do everything within our power to try and locate those responsible for killing your daughter and bring them to justice."

"Try?"

"I'll do my best."

Fifteen minutes later, Byron accompanied Faherty in the elevator down to the lobby, then walked with him out to the plaza. The two men parted with a handshake. Byron stood at the top of the concrete steps that led down to Middle Street, watching as the broken man climbed into a rust-colored Ford Fusion and drove away. He couldn't begin to imagine the pain Elmer and Denise Faherty were suffering. And while he didn't have children of his own, Byron could only guess at what he might be capable of if anyone ever harmed Katherine, his niece.

Sea Dogs tickets, he thought. *Shit, I've gotta reach out to her.*

Byron pulled out his cell and dialed Katherine's number. As he listened to her greeting, he couldn't help but notice how mature she sounded. No longer the little girl in pigtails who would drop everything to go fishing with her uncle John.

"Hey, kiddo, it's John. How have you been? Can't believe how quickly summer's going by. Pretty soon you'll be back at school again." He paused a moment, thinking how lame that sounded. "Listen, I know your birthday is coming right up and I want to take you out someplace special. I know you're probably busy, too. Throw me some dates and we'll figure out someplace cool to go. Anywhere you want, okay? I gotta run. Miss you."

Byron ended the call and returned to CID. Melissa Stevens was waiting for him in the conference room.

"How'd it go with the Fahertys?" she asked. "Had he seen the news?"

"He was carrying the paper when he walked in."

"Damn."

"And it was only Dani's father, Elmer. Denise stayed behind at their hotel. She was too distraught."

"I can't even imagine. Fuck Billingslea. What a heartless prick. Did Elmer know anything that might help us?"

"He didn't know about the domestic assault," Byron said matter-of-factly.

"Did you tell him?"

"I didn't think it wise given his current state."

"Why wouldn't Dani tell her parents about that?"

"Maybe she did, just not Elmer." Byron flipped open the notebook and wrote himself a reminder to follow up with Denise Faherty.

"I got your text, but you were already in with Faherty," Stevens said. "Did you need me for something?"

"I did, but Murph was going up to Augusta anyway. I had him deliver the DNA swab that Gabe took from Hopkins last night to the lab. How's Gabe coming on vehicle processing?"

"He's finished with Faherty's car. Found keys in the glove box and several sets of prints on the driver's door handles, inside and out, and the rearview mirror."

"Great. Do we know who they belong to?"

"Several of the prints are Dani's."

"And the rest?"

"No matches on file."

Byron knew that only meant the perpetrator likely didn't have a criminal record. "What about the security vehicle Hopkins was using?"

"Gabe's still working on it. Speaking of which, S.I. placed Hopkins on administrative leave for lying to us," Stevens said. "He called here to complain about it already."

"Called you?" Byron asked.

"No, he called the main number for CID and got Shirley. Sounds like he was really pissed."

"Bet he wishes he'd called someone else."

They both knew that Shirley Grant, the CID office assistant, could handle herself just fine. Over the years they had witnessed her joust with unsatisfied citizens countless times. Grant gave as good as she got. Byron wondered if this move by Security Incorporated might force Hopkins to come clean. Hopkins may not have had anything to do with Dani's murder, but until he could explain his lie he would remain on their list of suspects.

"How goes the crime scene canvass?" Byron asked.

"Slow," Stevens said. "Nuge and Bernie compiled a list of employees and guests from the Marriott. We collected the names and contact information for everyone who rented a room at the hotel between Saturday night and Wednesday morning and we're cross-referencing them against the registered owners of the nearby cars. We're still playing phone tag with most of them. Dustin is still running the names. And of course, there's still the fifty-odd registered owners of the cars parked nearby."

"Great," Byron said absently as he continued checking each box on his mental to-do list. "What about the hotel security? Anything on camera?"

"Nothing from their security system. We are going to check their inside cameras, though, for early Sunday morning, on the off chance that Dani met up with someone at the hotel after she left Alessandro's."

"Good thinking."

Just then Mike Nugent strolled in with a coffee. He was as disheveled and unshaven as Elmer Faherty had been, and looked like he, too, might have slept in his clothing.

"Morning," Nugent grumbled.

"Tough night?" Byron asked.

"Another false alarm with Dee Dee's contractions."

"Hospital?" Byron said.

Nugent nodded. "Yup. Then home again, home again, jiggity jig."

"Shouldn't you be at home with her, Nuge?" Stevens asked.

"Oh sure, and leave you guys to get all of the glory when we solve this thing? No thanks. I'm here until the baby comes. Besides, Dee Dee's sister is staying with us for a couple weeks, helping out." Nugent looked around the room "Where's Robbins?"

"You mean your new partner?" Stevens teased.

Nugent looked at Byron and rolled his eyes.

"He's down with Dustin checking the names from the Marriott," Stevens said.

"Good place for him," Nugent growled.

"Any luck with the canvass around Faherty's apartment?" Byron asked.

"Yeah, actually," Nugent said, reaching for his notebook and flipping it open. "I returned a call on the way in from a woman named Christine Micucci. She's the elderly neighborhood busybody. Doesn't sleep;

entertains herself by monitoring everything that happens in the area."

Byron knew the type and how valuable they could be.

Nugent continued. "She knew Dani. In fact, she lives right across the street from her apartment. Anyway, Micucci says she saw a man driving Dani's car midafternoon on Monday. Says he parked the car in the driveway, then walked back to a pickup truck that was waiting for him, and they drove off."

"Did she get a look at the guy?" Stevens asked as she added Micucci's name to the whiteboard.

Nugent shook his head and checked his notes. "Nah, said he was wearing a ball cap and sunglasses, so she didn't get a good look at him. Definitely a white male, though. Doesn't remember his clothing beyond the hat."

"And the truck? Or driver?" Byron asked.

"Nope. Said she couldn't see the driver from where she was watching, and the truck was just a pickup. She couldn't tell me the make or color."

Byron paused to process what Nugent was telling them. If Dr. Ellis was right about the time of death and Dani had been killed early on Sunday morning, then Micucci may have witnessed the killer, or killers, returning Dani's car to her apartment less than forty-eight hours after she'd been killed.

"We need to interview her in person," Byron said.

"I'm meeting her at eleven to get her statement," Nugent said.

"Good. Did we check Brackett Street for video?"

"Yup. Nothing so far. Bernie and I left business cards at all the addresses where we couldn't make contact. Who knows, maybe some weirdo tech geek like Dustin has a camera aimed at the street."

Byron's cell chimed. He answered it. "Byron."

"Hey, Sarge," a raspy male voice said. "It's Breslin. You in the building?"

Officer Mark Breslin might have been the laziest cop Byron had ever worked with. Maybe the laziest Portland had ever seen, although Bernie Robbins could give him a run for his money. Breslin had been assigned to light duty status, manning the front desk, or "riding the pine" as the assignment was more commonly referred to, following a work-related injury. As was his habit, Breslin paid an annual visit to Dr. Summer Off, but this time the brass had outsmarted the wily old veteran, sticking him on the information desk, as far from the poolside utopia Breslin most likely envisioned as possible.

"What do you need, Mark?" Byron said.

"Got a girl down here who wishes to speak with you, Sergeant."

"Girl got a name?" Byron asked, making no attempt to hide his annoyance.

"Um, Sheila — Vickers. Says she works at some restaurant called Alexanders. Something like that."

"Alessandro's," Byron said, rising to his feet.

"That's the one."

"Be right down."

CHAPTER 11

Sheila Vickers sat alone on the long padded wooden bench abutting 109's tinted lobby windows. She was dressed in a knee-length tan skirt, sleeveless top, and sandals. Backlit by the sun, her shadow fell across the tile floor. Byron studied her for a moment through the one-way glass of the inner lobby. She looked vaguely familiar, but he couldn't recall whether they had met, or if he'd just seen her somewhere in passing. Portland is a small city.

"Ms. Vickers?" Byron asked as he pushed open the security door and stepped out into the main lobby.

"Sergeant Byron?" she said, rising from the bench.

They met in the middle and shook hands.

"What can I do for you?" he asked.

Her eyes flicked about nervously, as if

159

someone she knew might see her talking to the police. "I saw you at the restaurant yesterday. I need to talk to you — about Dani."

"Dani?"

"Dani Faherty. The woman who was murdered."

Byron looked toward the IO desk waiting for Breslin to buzz them inside. Officer Injured on Duty was engaged in a telephone call, oblivious. Byron punched in the security code to the inner lobby door, then led Vickers inside the station along the hallway to the elevators. They rode the lift to the fourth floor, to CID, where he could videotape the interview.

Detective Stevens was standing behind her desk, talking on the phone as Byron and Vickers walked through the detective bureau. Byron made eye contact with Stevens and gestured toward the conference room, signaling for her to monitor the interview. Stevens nodded her understanding.

He opened the door to Interview Room Two, flipped on the light, then stepped to one side. "Have a seat."

Vickers entered the room and sat down in the chair farthest from the door, setting her purse on the floor beside her.

"Can I get you anything?" Byron asked.

"Water?"

"I'm fine. Thank you."

Byron stepped in and closed the door. He sat down across the table from her, then removed a notepad and pen from the inside pocket of his suit coat. "Mind if I take some notes?"

Vickers shook her head. "Not at all."

Byron didn't know what information she might possess that would cause her to show up unannounced at 109, but he'd learned long ago never to assume anything. The most important leads often came from the unlikeliest of sources.

Vickers fidgeted absently with a thin gold bracelet as she waited for him to begin.

"So, you've got some information about Danica Faherty?"

Vickers said nothing, continuing to fidget.

"Something about her murder?"

"I don't know," she said. "Maybe."

"Do you know anyone who might have wanted to hurt Dani?"

Vickers let out a loud sigh. "I really don't want to get anyone in trouble."

During his years as a detective, Byron had observed literally hundreds, perhaps thousands, of people wrestle with the exact same dilemma. For some people doing the right thing often proved difficult when measured against maintaining some imagined loyalty to a possible murderer. Vickers had already taken the first step by walking into 109, and it was now Byron's job to help her take the next. He placed his pen on the table and sat back in the chair.

"Sheila. May I call you Sheila?"

Vickers nodded.

"I'm investigating Dani's murder. I'm not interested in anything else that someone may have done. Catching her murderer is all I'm concerned with. Do you understand?"

She nodded again.

"I know this is difficult, Sheila, but I can tell you from experience that until you get whatever this is off your chest, it will continue to eat at you. What did you come here to tell me?"

She hesitated for another moment before blurting it out. "Dani was having an affair with someone at the restaurant."

"Who?"

"Do I have to say? Couldn't you just talk to everyone who worked with her and find out that way?"

"And what if nobody wants to tell us?"

Vickers maintained eye contact with Byron but didn't respond.

"Sheila, you obviously thought this was

important, or you wouldn't be here. Who was Dani having an affair with?"

"Alex," she said at last.

"Alex Stavros?" Byron asked.

"Yes."

"Do you know that for a fact, or did you just hear about it?"

"Dani talked to me about it."

"How long had they been seeing each other?" Byron asked.

"A few months, I think."

"Did Mrs. Stavros know?" Byron asked, meaning Alex's wife, Deborah.

"I don't know, but I think Lina might have."

"Lina? What makes you say that?"

"Because Lina and Alex had a big fight about it."

"A fight?" Byron said.

Vickers nodded. "A really loud argument. In the kitchen at Alessandro's."

"When was this?"

"A few days before Dani went missing."

Diane stood off to the right of Chief Lynds at the podium in 109's first-floor interview room. Despite the building's air-conditioning, the room was uncomfortably warm, due largely to the lighting set up in advance by several television crews. Among the crowd of reporters, Diane recognized the usual suspects from the local network affiliates of NBC, CBS, and ABC. Additionally, front and center, was the *Portland Herald*'s own Snoop Dog Davis Billingslea. Diane gave the young reporter the coldest glare she could muster. He seemed unfazed.

"Good morning," Chief Lynds began. "Thank you all for coming out this morning. As you are all aware by now, the Portland Police Department is currently investigating the suspicious death of a young woman whose body was recovered yesterday morning in a vacant lot off Commercial Street. As I'm sure you can all appreciate, this is an ongoing investigation and as such I am not at liberty to discuss many aspects of the case.

"The victim, Danica Faherty, was found by a security guard while conducting a routine check on the property early yesterday morning. Ms. Faherty was a Portland resident, employed at Alessandro's Restaurant. She was last seen leaving work early Sunday morning. We are working to piece together her last hours. The owner of Alessandro's, Angelina Stavros, has graciously offered up a reward of ten thousand dollars for information leading to the arrest and conviction of the person or persons responsible for Ms. Faherty's death. We are asking anyone with information about this case to contact the Portland Police Department's Criminal Investigation Division directly. That's all I am prepared to say at this point."

"Chief! Chief Lynds," a chorus of voices shouted. It sounded to Diane as if the entire room was vying for attention.

The first question was barked from the back of the room. Diane couldn't see the reporter's face due to the blinding lights. "Chief, there has been some reporting that would tend to indicate that this murder may be connected to the Horseman cases in Boston. Can you confirm the condition of Ms. Faherty's body? Was she in fact decapitated?"

"As I have already said, this is an active investigation, and I am not able to discuss certain aspects of the case," Lynds responded.

The chief took several more questions, dodging specifics as necessary. Diane wondered if it was as obvious to everyone else in the room as it was to her that Lynds was intentionally avoiding calling on Billingslea.

"That's all I have at this time," Lynds said. "Sergeant Joyner will continue to update all of you with information as it becomes available. Thank you."

As Diane and Lynds were stepping into the elevator Billingslea stuck his foot in the door to keep it from closing. "Chief, is there some reason you wouldn't let me ask a question?"

"I'm glad you asked me that," Lynds said. "Truthfully, I wanted to give some of the other reporters a chance. From what I've seen, you already have all the answers."

Diane fought to suppress a grin.

"No disrespect to you, Chief," Billingslea said, meaning that he was about to do exactly that. "But the public has a right to know."

"I'm sure Ms. Faherty's parents will be delighted to learn of your passionate ideals. It's unfortunate that you didn't give any thought to their rights before running your little story. Good day, Mr. Billingslea."

The doors to the elevator closed, effectively shutting Davis Billingslea out for the second time in a matter of minutes.

Sergeant Kenny Crosby sat in his unmarked Charger parked in the Back Cove lot off Preble Street Extension. The engine's custom-tuned exhaust was rumbling, and the air conditioner was cranked. The battleship-gray muscle car had been seized in a drug raid. The hapless previous owner, having paid cash, hadn't had the foresight to jump on the latest drug dealer bandwagon of simply leasing the car to avoid the inevitable government seizure. Crosby loved the tinted windows. Made him feel important. He had strategically backed up to the rear of the lot so that he was facing Hannaford Plaza, allowing him to observe every vehicle entering or leaving the parking lot popular with Portland's outdoor exercise crowd. And with the Back Cove jogging path passing directly behind him, he had an excellent view of the scantily clad women passing by in the field of his rearview mirror.

Crosby had been sitting there for all of ten minutes when Portland Police Commander Ed Jennings drove up beside him.

"What's up?" Crosby said as he lowered the window on the driver's door.

"I see you put it out there already."

"Why Commander Jennings, I don't know what you're talking about," Crosby said in a high-pitched falsetto.

"Good. Here's something else you need to know. Joyner had a little private time with Chief Lynds yesterday."

"You mean Sergeant All That and a Bag of Chips left Byron and switched to the other team?"

Jennings grinned. "No, I mean Lynds is maneuvering to have Diane submit her name for consideration for Sergeant Peterson's CID spot."

"Fuck that," Crosby snapped. "I've been a detective sergeant longer than Joyner's been here. That job is mine. Everyone knows it. If she wasn't banging Lord Byron, she'd still be pushing a cruiser. Exactly where she should be anyway."

"Well, be that as it may, Lynds is pushing for her to throw her hat in the ring before Monday's deadline."

Crosby mulled it over for a minute. "What the hell can I do about it? You're the commander."

"Christ, Kenny, I can only do so much. I thought derailing Byron was your goal."

"It is."

"Oh, and Lynds is talking about pulling you back from MDEA sooner rather than later."

Crosby hammered the top of the dashboard with his fist. "Fuck. What's this chick's problem?"

"I don't know. But, unless you want to be pushing a cruiser yourself, you'd better think of something."

An hour later, after Byron had finished with Vickers, he and Stevens drove directly to Alessandro's in search of Alex, only to learn that he wasn't due in until later in the afternoon. While speaking with one of the kitchen staff, Byron observed Sheila Vickers scurry by. She appeared to be intentionally avoiding his gaze. He wondered how long it would be before she spilled the beans to a coworker about her visit to 109.

"We could interview him at home," Stevens said as they returned to their unmarked.

"I'd like to avoid that if possible," Byron said.

"Because of Deborah Stavros?"

"That's one reason."

"And the other?"

"Alex and Deborah are temporarily living with Lina."

"No kidding? Oh man, I'd love to see her place. It's beautiful, right? I'll bet she's got a butler like Mr. Carson."

"Who?" Byron said.

"Oh, come on. *Downton Abbey.* Mr. Carson."

"Let me guess, Netflix?"

"No, silly. Amazon Prime."

Byron cast a glance at his star-struck detective and grinned. "I'll take you with me the next time I go, okay?"

"Deal. How about lunch? I'm starving."

Byron and Stevens had to wait nearly twenty minutes before they were able to be seated at Becky's Diner. Some establishments have a very narrow window when it comes to their lunch crowd. Becky's wasn't one of those. They were seated in a booth on the right-hand side of the restaurant all the way in the back and quickly placed their orders. As the waitress was departing, Byron's cell vibrated with an incoming call from Ellis.

"Greetings and salutations, Sergeant," Ellis said. "Catch you at a bad time?"

"Not at all," Byron said. "Whaddya got?"

"I'm afraid I don't have anything more than I had yesterday."

"The tox was negative?" Byron said. Stevens's expression mirrored the dejection Byron heard in his own voice.

"Indeed, it was. I still can't tell you what caused this girl's death, but something external caused her heart to stop beating."

"Best guess?"

"That's all it would be, I'm afraid. Head

trauma. Bludgeoned, maybe. Or shot."

Byron considered this for a moment. "In which case the missing head might be nothing more than an attempt to cover up the manner of death."

"Might just be that simple, my boy. Who was it that said the simplest explanation is usually the right one? Was that Inspector Holmes?"

"Actually, that was William of Ockham," Byron said.

"Ah, the razor guy. I always get those logical types confused. Anyway, as I told you previously, the appendage was removed postmortem. It certainly wasn't to prevent identification, nor was it the cause of death. So, unless our boy is a collector, I can't see any other reason."

Byron ended the call just as the waitress arrived with their food.

"Well, that sucks," Stevens said before heavily salting then shoving a handful of fries into her mouth.

Byron nodded his agreement.

They both ate in silence while dissecting the information. Assuming the killer wasn't Boston's serial murderer, the Horseman, and if Ellis was right about Faherty having been bludgeoned to death, perhaps there was something unique about the weapon they'd used that would connect the killer to the crime. And if she'd been shot, the bullet might not have exited. The killer would have been forced to remove the head to thwart any possibility of a ballistics match coming back on them. Of course, coming to either conclusion involved a great many assumptions. Still, the word *collector* hung out there in front of Byron like a red neon sign. Could it be the Horseman? According to Murray, there were more similarities connecting the three cases than differences. Did the use of a different tool to remove the head signify that the killer was evolving, or had he or she simply been forced to improvise? Perhaps an equipment malfunction? Byron didn't know. And why come to Maine? Had they hunted a specific victim, or moved for some other reason and the opportunity simply presented itself? Had Danica Faherty simply been in the wrong place at the wrong time? And who had Dani's neighbor seen dropping off Dani's car?

There were still too many loose threads for Byron's liking. Too many unresolved possibilities.

"You gonna eat your fries?" Stevens asked, pulling Byron out of his thoughts.

He slid the basket across the table. "Have at it. Lost my appetite."

"Well, if Ellis is right about our guy being a collector, this might be the Horseman after all."

He closed his eyes and gently rubbed his temples. It was exactly what he was afraid of.

It was nearly one-thirty before Byron and Stevens caught up with Alex Stavros. Gone was the self-confidence and air of superiority that the young restaurateur had exuded only the day before. They were seated in Petri's office at the back of the restaurant, and Byron could read the nervousness in the man's dark eyes.

"Have you made any progress toward identifying Dani's killer?" Alex asked.

"Inching forward," Byron said, giving nothing away.

"Glad to hear it. So, what can I do for the two of you?"

"We were hoping that you could clear a few things up," Stevens said.

"If I can. What would you like to know?"

"For starters, we'd like to know why you didn't mention that you'd been having an affair with Danica Faherty," Byron said.

Stavros hesitated a long moment before answering. Avoiding eye contact, he appeared to be focused on an imaginary spot between the detectives. A safety zone. Byron could tell the question had caught him by surprise.

"How did you find out?" Stavros said at last, confirming that he had.

"Doesn't really matter how, does it?" Byron said. "What is important is why you didn't mention it to us earlier."

"I didn't think it was any of your business. Besides, as I told you before, I was out of town all weekend."

"That's right," Byron said. "A conference, wasn't it?"

"Northeast Restaurant Association Conference in Boston. It's an annual event."

"Anyone vouch for you being at this conference?" Stevens asked.

"George Martin. He owns a restaurant in Wellesley." As he spoke, Stavros scribbled a name and number onto a notepad then tore the sheet off and handed it to Byron. "We shared a room at the hotel. You can check with him."

"We will," Byron said, pocketing the contact information. He would have Murray follow up with Martin in person.

Stavros slouched back in his chair. "I'm married, okay? I have two kids at home."

"And a beautiful wife," Stevens added.

Stavros ignored her comment. His attention remained fixed on Byron. "I'm not proud of it, okay? It just happened."

"Do you own a gun, Alex?" Byron asked.

"What? No, I don't own a gun. What do you want from me?"

"The truth," Byron said. "Did you murder Danica Faherty?"

"Don't be ridiculous. Of course not. Why would I?"

"Maybe she threatened to tell your wife about the affair," Stevens said.

Stavros jumped up from the chair. "Look, I've been more than cooperative with your investigation, Detectives. I've answered all your questions. If you think I killed Dani, then charge me. Otherwise, get the hell out. I've got a business to run here."

"Alex, we have a few more questions we'd like you to answer," Byron said, remaining seated.

A female voice floated in from the hall. "Alex is finished answering any more of your questions, Sergeant Byron."

The detectives turned to see a middle-aged woman in a dark-colored pantsuit standing behind them in the office doorway. She held a briefcase in one hand and the look of determination on her face.

"Who are you?" Byron said.

"That's Courtney Levine," Alex said.

"She's Lina's personal attorney."

"I am now representing Alex," Levine said as she approached Byron and handed him a business card. "I am hereby informing you that this interview is over. If you wish to question Alex further, you will have to contact my office."

Byron and Stevens retreated to the car. Byron was quietly fuming.

"That was interesting," Stevens said. "I didn't see that coming. Did you?"

"No," Byron said. "I didn't."

"You think Lina knows something and is covering for Alex?"

"Or perhaps she doesn't know but she's circling the family wagons just to be safe."

"What do you mean?"

"If Alex was screwing around with the help, and Lina discovered it, she has motive in the killing of Danica Faherty. Lina knows she'll be added to our list of suspects. So, is she bringing in an attorney for Alex to keep us from questioning him or to keep us from questioning her?"

"I hadn't considered that," Stevens said. "Can she do that? Doesn't that become like a conflict of interest?"

They were wading into muddy water and Byron didn't have all the answers. But he knew someone who would. Assistant Attorney General Jim Ferguson.

CHAPTER 12

Thursday, 2:30 P.M.,
July 13, 2017

Byron carefully wove his way along the uneven cobblestone surface of Wharf Street, searching for the restaurant. He'd dropped Stevens off at 109 then circled the Old Port searching in vain for a parking spot, even an illegal one. Tourist season was in full swing, which meant there was zero street parking near Portland's waterfront. Finally relenting, Byron parked in the lot at DiMillo's on the Water and walked. Pausing slightly west of Dana Street, he pulled the cell from his pocket and rechecked the text from Ferguson.

Mash Tun on Wharf 2:30.

He scanned both sides of the street looking for a sign before his eyes finally settled on a series of small crowded picnic tables in front of a building to his right. The sidewalk sign read: Outdoor seating for Mash Tun only.

Byron entered the establishment, pausing in the doorway to give his eyes a moment to adjust to the dimly lit interior.

"John. Over here!"

He peered to the far wall where Ferguson sat at yet another wooden picnic table directly under a large wall mounted chalkboard. Byron crossed the room, passing a long bar that appeared to have been constructed from a piece of a reclaimed bowling alley, and approached the AAG.

"I was afraid you got called away," Ferguson said, speaking loudly to be heard above the Led Zeppelin track emanating from ceiling speakers.

Byron slid onto the bench seat across from him.

Ferguson wore a big dopey grin. "Well, what do you think?"

Byron frowned. "What the hell, Jim?"

Ferguson's face reddened slightly. "What? You don't like it?"

"Why would you meet me in a bar?"

"This isn't just any old bar, my cranky friend. I come here for lunch whenever I'm in Portland. Or as Paul Doiron likes to call it, 'Maine's big little city'."

179

"Who?" Byron asked.

"He's a mystery writer. Anyway, I love the blues music they play and the smells."

"The smells?"

"Yeah." Ferguson inhaled through his nose, deep and loud. "Beer still smells great even if I can't imbibe. And the grill. Oh man. Have you ever tried Parmesan Ranch Fries?"

"Can't say that I have." Byron turned and looked across the bar top to where a middle-aged man was dropping a basket into the Fryolator. He turned back to Ferguson. "I thought your doc told you to avoid greasy food?"

"You gonna rat me out to Betty?" Ferguson asked.

"Hey, they're your arteries."

Ferguson tilted his head back to look at the chalkboard hanging on the wall behind him. The beer offerings were written in neat columns, each designated by a different colored chalk. "Nearly thirty beers on tap. I like to pretend I'm sampling each one."

"This some kind of test?" Byron said, wondering why Ferguson, also a recovering alcoholic, would subject himself to the temptation.

Ferguson cocked his head to one side, reminding Byron of a German shepherd.

"Do you need one?"

"Not really."

"Good. Me neither. Besides, I didn't think bars were your trigger."

"They're not," Byron said. "But I think 109 might be."

Ferguson held up his glass of soda water, a slice of lime perched on its brim. "Cheers." He took several large gulps before returning the glass to the table. "Ahh. That really quenches my thirst."

"Are you done?" Byron said, wanting to move on to the case.

"Okay. Okay. Must be the heat. Tell me what you've got?"

Byron ran down the most recent developments while Ferguson listened in silence.

"So?" Byron said after he had finished. "What do you think?"

"What I think is, you don't need any more suspects in this case. Jesus. You could make a case for damn near all of them. Is there anyone who hasn't lawyered up yet?"

"And you wonder why lawyers get a bad rap."

Ferguson lifted his glass. "Touché."

"So, what about Lina Stavros?" Byron asked.

"The movie star?"

"Yeah. Can this Courtney Levine represent her son?"

"Jesus, is that who she sent after you?" Ferguson asked.

"You're familiar?"

"Levine is a pit bull of the highest order."

"Great."

"Technically, Lina Stavros can hire anyone she wants to represent her son."

"Yeah, but it sounds like Lina's got her on a permanent retainer. Doesn't that present a conflict?"

"Depends. Do you consider Lina a suspect?"

"Maybe. If Sheila Vickers is right, and Lina Stavros knew about Alex's affair with Dani, she, too, would have motive."

Before Ferguson could render an opinion, the cook slid a basket of heavily spiced hot fries in front of him.

"Enjoy," the cook said.

"Oh, don't worry," Ferguson said as he dug in. "I will."

Byron departed Mash Tun with more questions than answers. Assistant Attorney General or not, Jim Ferguson was still an attorney. Ambiguity, it seemed, was the legal profession's middle name.

He was on his way back to retrieve his car from the DiMillo's lot when his cell rang with a call from Stevens.

"You're never gonna believe what Gabe found in the Security Incorporated car," Stevens said.

"Blood in the trunk?"

"Nope. Try semen on the back seat."

Byron paused to consider what that might mean for their investigation. Had Hopkins used the lumberyard for sex as they suspected? And if so, who had he been with? "Let's get a list of employees from S.I. who regularly used that vehicle in case the semen isn't from Hopkins."

"I'm on it."

"Also, tell Dustin to look for any connection between Dani Faherty and Hopkins while he's looking through her computer. Hopkins told us he didn't know Dani. Let's see if he's telling the truth."

"You got it, Sarge. So, what did Ferguson say?"

"He said it depends."

"Of course he did," Stevens said. "Friggin' attorneys. Everything is a gray area."

"If it turns out that Danica's murder was connected to her affair with Alex, and any other Stavros family members move into our crosshairs as suspects, it will be up to Lina's attorney how to parse out representation."

"And in the meantime?" Stevens asked.

"In the meantime, we need to take a closer look at Lina and see if she has an alibi."

"Good. I'll get with Dustin and see what I can find out about her beforehand. You headed back?"

"Not yet. I'm gonna pay a visit to Gene Wagner."

Byron's frustration was increasing. The ever-growing list of suspects was keeping pace with the roadblocks being erected. He felt like a tourist caught in some evil summertime repaving project in which every possible route to his destination was blocked off.

He locked up his unmarked in a no-parking zone on Federal Street near the rear of Central Fire Station, as close as he was likely to get to One City Center, then walked several blocks to Gene Wagner's office. The waves of heat radiating up off the sidewalk left him coated in a thin layer of sweat by the time he entered the air-conditioned building.

Wagner Enterprises was located one floor down from the top of the Bank of America building. Evidently, the well-to-do entrepreneur hadn't yet managed to unseat the banking industry, Byron thought. The elevator doors opened directly into the lobby, a bright and cheery sunlit space. A long counter manned by two young receptionists, one male and one female, sat across from him. Both were speaking into Bluetooth headsets which, combined with their youthfulness, made them resemble a pair of stage performers, as if they might suddenly leap up and start singing and dancing.

Byron approached the reception desk. The pale-skinned male, sporting spiky heavily gelled dark hair, made eye contact and nodded, acknowledging Byron without breaking stride in his phone conversation. Byron turned and wandered through the air-conditioned lobby. A bright, nearly full, waiting area positioned next to a twenty-foot span of floor-to-ceiling windows afforded an unobstructed view of Monument Square and Congress Street running westerly toward High. He gazed down at the crowd of pedestrians moving ant-like around the square. Some walked briskly, appearing to have clear destinations, while others meandered about toting shopping bags and searching for the next store. The remaining group, camped out on the grass around the base of the monument, were people-watching or sunbathing.

"Sorry to keep you waiting, sir," the male

receptionist called out from behind him. "May I help you?"

Byron turned away from the window and re-approached the counter. He removed the ID and badge case from his jacket pocket. "Detective Sergeant Byron. I'm here to see Gene Wagner."

The young man studied Byron's credentials for a moment as if he might know a genuine police ID from a fake. "Is Mr. Wagner expecting you, Detective? Or is it Sergeant?"

Byron had never been able to figure out why that rank was so difficult for people to comprehend. Surely it wasn't more confounding than say sergeant major or lieutenant colonel. "Either is fine," he said, returning the wallet to his pocket. "And no, I don't have an appointment."

"Well, he *is* a very busy man."

"Makes two of us," Byron said, admiring the young receptionist's attempt at running interference for his employer. "You might mention that I'm here investigating a homicide." Byron hadn't thought it possible, but at the mention of murder Hair Gel's face became a whiter shade of pale. *Here's to Procol Harum,* he thought.

"He's in the middle of a conference call. If you wouldn't mind taking a seat in our waiting area. I'll check and see if he'll make time for you as soon as he's finished with the call."

Byron glanced at the receptionist's gold magnetic name tag. "Thanks, *Chip,*" he said, accentuating the name as if it was a derogatory term.

Only two of the half dozen identical and uncomfortable-looking retro waiting area chairs were unoccupied. Hoping to keep the pressure on, he chose the one facing Chip. Eventually, Byron grew bored with staring at the receptionist. He grabbed a periodical from the glass table and began to leaf through it.

"Sergeant Byron?" a masculine voice boomed from the far end of the lobby.

Byron stood as Wagner approached, tossing the *Men's Health* magazine back onto the table.

"Gene Wagner," he said, giving Byron a large, predatory smile along with a hearty handshake-elbow grab combination, a subtle power play used by business types and political figures to establish dominance. "Hope I didn't keep you."

"Not at all," Byron said, retrieving his arm. "I just finished five-minute abs and was moving on to how to improve my sex life."

Wagner's smile faltered. "What can I do for you, Sergeant?"

"I'm conducting a murder investigation and need to ask you a few questions."

Wagner checked his watch, a garish metallic appendage that probably cost more than Byron made in two months. Maybe three. "I only have about ten minutes before my next appointment."

"The victim is Danica Faherty," Byron said, speaking a bit louder than necessary. "Worked as a maître d' at Alessandro's. I believe you knew her."

Wagner glanced nervously toward those seated around the waiting area and then at the counter. Both receptionists were listening intently.

Wagner wasted no time in hustling Byron into his office, away from the lobby. Byron took a quick glance around the room trying to get a feel for this man. Every square inch of the wall behind Wagner was hung with professionally framed and matted photographs, depicting various pairings of Wagner and every conceivable celebrity, a veritable who's who of Hollywood. It was his own "wall of me" and exactly what Byron had expected from Wagner.

Byron was offered a chair in front, while Wagner retreated to the safety afforded by the barrier of his large chrome and beveled glass desk.

"I assume you saw the story in the paper," Byron said after they were seated.

"About the body being recovered. Yes. Dreadful business."

It's a living, Byron thought. "And you knew the victim, correct?"

"Of course. I am a regular at Alessandro's. The owner is an old friend of mine."

"Angelina Stavros," Byron said.

"Yes. I've known Lina for decades." He turned and pointed to an autographed movie still hanging on the wall behind him. "I financed several of her films."

Byron imagined that Wagner never missed an opportunity to point that out to anyone who would listen.

"Tell me about Danica Faherty," Byron said.

"Not much to tell, really. As you said, she works — worked at Alessandro's as the maître d'. I would see her from time to time when I came in."

"See her or engage her in conversation?"

"Both. As I did with all of the restaurant employees."

Byron nodded and made a notation in his notebook.

"Am I missing something?" Wagner said,

craning his neck to try and get a look at what Byron had written. "Why are you asking all these questions?"

"Because, Gene, you were asked to leave Alessandro's Saturday night after making a scene. My understanding is that you laid your hands on Ms. Faherty."

"I don't remember much about Saturday night. I was somewhat inebriated." Wagner leaned forward as if sharing a secret. "The truth is, I may have been over-served."

It wasn't the truth, and both men knew it. Byron noted how quickly Wagner shifted the blame to someone else. He wondered how long it would be before the overbearing ass blamed Danica Faherty for what had happened to her.

Wagner continued. "I can assure you that whatever may have happened, and I'm not saying anything did, was not instigated by me."

"You're telling me that Danica Faherty made advances toward you?" Byron said, raising his brows, making no attempt to hide his disbelief.

"Is that so difficult to imagine, Sergeant?"

It was incredibly difficult to imagine. Despite the three-piece suit, expensive jewelry, and dyed hair, the bloated middle-aged boor of a man couldn't hide the bad skin, or the road map of veins tattooed across his bulbous nose. Byron knew all the telltale signs of long-term alcoholism, having only recently admitted to his own addiction.

"It's no secret that I am a very financially well-to-do man," Wagner continued, holding up his ringless left hand. "And single. Many young women are taken with me."

As disgusting and unlikely as that idea was, Byron pressed on.

"According to Lina Stavros it was you who was fixated on Danica Faherty, not the other way around. An obsession that had evidently gone on for some time and was widely known by the restaurant employees."

Byron watched as Wagner leaned back in his chair. Calculating his next move. "So what? I murdered her. Is that what you're accusing me of?"

"No one is accusing you of anything, Gene. I'm only trying to get to the bottom of what occurred Saturday night. What happened after you left the restaurant?"

"I told you, I don't remember."

"How did you get home?"

Wagner opened his mouth as if to answer then closed it. He leaned over and punched a button on his desktop phone. After a moment Byron heard Hair Gel's voice on the

191

other end of the intercom.

"Yes, Mr. Wagner."

"Chip, would you instruct Mr. Paulson to join us."

Several moments later the door to Wagner's office opened and a burly dark-haired man in a gray Armani suit stepped in. His eyes immediately fell on Byron. "Chip said you wanted to see me, sir?"

"Yes, Joe. Sergeant Byron would like to know how I got home from Alessandro's last Saturday night. Evidently, I need an alibi."

"I drove you," Paulson said.

"You see, I don't drive, Sergeant. I decided, after a couple of unfortunate operating while intoxicated charges, that I should probably give up driving."

Byron stopped himself from asking whether it might have been easier to quit drinking, already knowing the answer to that question.

Wagner continued, "Joe is my full-time driver."

Byron couldn't help but notice the telltale bulge beneath Paulson's tailored suit coat. Paulson was armed.

"Driver or bodyguard?" Byron asked.

Paulson took another step toward Byron.

"Whichever is required. I'm versatile like that."

Paulson's New York accent was unmistakable. "You from New York?" Byron asked.

"Here, there, everywhere. I've been all over."

"Were you inside the bar with Gene on Saturday night?"

"Earlier in the evening, then I went out to the car to wait for him."

Wagner inserted himself back into the conversation. "I'm afraid Joe missed all the alleged excitement inside the bar, Sergeant."

"That's right," Paulson said. "I must have missed it."

"And what did you do after you dropped your employer at his house?"

"I drove directly home. Got there about 11:30, I'd guess."

"Anyone verify that?"

Paulson fixed Byron with a knowing grin. "I live alone."

Byron pointed to the bulge under Paulson's coat. "I assume you have a permit for that?"

"Of course. All registered and legal, Officer."

Wagner stood up and checked his watch again. "Well, I'm afraid I am out of time, Sergeant Byron. If you'd like, I can write up

193

a statement for you."

Byron looked back at Paulson. "I'll need one from both of you, if you don't mind."

"Not at all, Sergeant," Wagner said. "Happy to help. Paulson will show you out."

"Thanks, but I think I can manage," Byron said.

CHAPTER 13

Byron was upset at himself for not having foreseen the possibility that Wagner would have had a driver. Angelina Stavros hadn't mentioned it, had no reason to. But still, Byron couldn't help feeling that he'd been played. Now Wagner had an alibi. But Paulson didn't. Joseph Paulson from all over. Byron needed to do some checking up on the slick driver/bodyguard. He didn't like the man, not one bit. Too confident, too aggressive, too pricy. Exactly the kind of troubleshooter that someone of Wagner's means could afford to hire to clean up any spill or misstep. Was that what Faherty had been? A misstep? Had Wagner's infatuation gone too far? Had being rebuffed in public embarrassed the man to the point where he'd want to do something to her? Teach her a lesson? Could he have returned to the restaurant and waited for Faherty to leave? Followed her?

Byron pulled out his phone as he walked back to his car and dialed Dustin Tran. 109's computer virtuoso answered on the second ring.

"Hey, Striped Dude."

"Dustin. You still at 109?"

"I am. What do you need?"

"I want you to check out a guy named Joseph Paulson. He's Gene Wagner's driver and bodyguard. Might be from New York."

"I was just working on Wagner. I'll add Paulson to the mix and let you know what I find. Also, there's like four different people named Steve Holcolm in the Greater Portland area. Any idea which one you're looking for?"

"The one with a connection to Morgan Bates. Anything useful from Dani Faherty's laptop?"

"I'm still sifting through it using some of my special software."

"Anything that might indicate she was involved in prostitution?"

"Nothing yet. But I'll keep looking."

LeRoyer caught Byron as he was exiting the back stairwell onto the fourth floor of 109.

"How's it going, John? Making any head-way?"

"Fabulous," Byron said. "Already got a confession."

"Seriously?" LeRoyer asked excitedly.

"No," Byron said. "Actually, we're stacking up suspects like they were firewood and they're lawyering up so fast you might think they knew each other."

"So, you're not close?" LeRoyer said, looking dejected.

"Gee, Marty. Sorry to ruin your day."

LeRoyer followed Byron straight to his office. "Do you have to be such a dick all the time?"

"I don't *have* to," Byron said after pausing a moment to reflect. He tossed his briefcase into one of the visitor chairs then plopped down behind the desk. "Is this the part where you tell me that the Queen Mum is looking for another update?"

"That's Chief Lynds to you, Sergeant. And maybe I just want to know what's going on."

Byron twisted up his face in disbelief.

"Okay, yeah," LeRoyer said. "Lynds wants an update."

"Tell her we're working on it. When I have something worth sharing, I'll share it."

"Is this really the way you want to start

off your relationship with a brand-new chief?"

"Relationship?"

"You know what I mean, John."

Byron sighed. "I'm just tired, Marty. I've got a dead girl, mutilated and dumped like garbage. A pompous prick who thinks he can do whatever he wants because he has money. And who has an errand boy that looks like a psychopath. An ex-boyfriend who liked to beat up on our victim and took exception to her breaking up with him. A married television star who was getting it on with our victim and is now represented by his mother's paid legal Rottweiler. A lying security guard who may have been using the lumberyard as a sex pad. Um, let's see, am I forgetting anything? Oh yeah, I almost forgot, an overzealous newspaper reporter who thinks he's Jimmy Fucking Olsen and couldn't wait to tell the world that our victim was decapitated by the Horseman even before her parents knew. Guess that just about covers it."

"This a bad time?" Nugent said from the doorway.

Byron needed a reality check. The stress of the investigation was building to a dangerous level, that and the guilt he was feeling about his last encounter with Diane. Having already skipped one meeting this week, the first he'd missed since becoming sober, Byron knew missing another would be unwise. Bad habits and all that. He sat in his usual spot at the back of the room, located in the basement of a church, thumbing through his text messages while waiting for the meeting to begin and for his sponsor to arrive. Shaun Miller was never late. Byron was looking forward to their post-meeting conversation. In need of it. It felt like he got more from his discussions with Miller than he did from the actual group meet-up.

The speaker walked past the rows of folding metal chairs to the front of the room to signal the start of the meeting just as Miller strolled through the doorway and took the empty seat next to Byron.

"Missed you Wednesday," Miller said, leaning in and speaking softly so as not to interrupt the proceedings. "Glad you made it tonight."

Byron watched from across the table while Shaun Miller poured what seemed a ridiculous amount of sugar into his coffee. One packet after another, the old man concentrated on his task as if there were some science to it. Miller was Byron's sponsor, and they met twice a week, usually immediately following a meeting.

A former Boston police chaplain, Miller was a shade over seventy, making him a generation Byron's senior. Miller's close-cropped white beard and the twinkle in his eyes only added to his distinguished, sage-like appearance. Despite the age difference, the two men had bonded in a way Byron had never experienced. A bond of faith. Unusual, given that Byron was miserly with his trust, his faith was shaky at best, and he had only known Miller a mere six months. Although their occupations differed, their life experiences certainly overlapped. But beyond the call to serve, they shared something even more elemental. Addiction. Both had known the sharp sting and unyielding pull of the bottle, as if alcohol was a baited hook waiting for some unsuspecting soul to come along and bite down. And both men had bitten. Hard.

"Thought the meeting went well tonight, John," Miller said matter-of-factly as he tore open another packet. "What'd you think?"

Byron nodded. "Yeah. Good meeting." He knew what Miller was doing of course, trying to get him to open up, but Byron played along anyway.

"How's your week been?" Miller asked.

Byron shrugged.

"Based solely on the newspaper reporting, I'd guess it's been rather stressful."

Byron took a sip of the hot black coffee as he pondered his answer. He regretted not waiting for decaf. The waitress had said she'd be happy to brew another pot, but Byron had declined her offer. The caffeine would likely keep him up all night, and even if it didn't the Faherty case would. "I haven't slipped if that's what you're asking."

Miller gave his trademark deep throaty laugh. "You know, I think that's one of the reasons I like you. John. Your directness."

"You weren't direct as a chaplain?"

"You were raised Catholic. Ever met a man of the cloth who comes right out and says what he means?"

Byron hadn't.

Miller finished stirring the hot liquid in his mug then took a sip. He closed his eyes and loudly smacked his lips together. "Ah, that's good."

"How can you stand that much sweetener?" Byron asked, looking at the pile of empty sugar packets on the table. "It's gotta be pure syrup."

Miller lowered his mug and fixed Byron with an impish grin. "A man's got to have some vices, doesn't he? Besides, isn't substitution the name of the game?"

Byron supposed that it was.

Miller produced a dark blue coin seemingly out of thin air and placed it gently on the table in front of Byron.

"What's this?" Byron asked.

"The next step. Your six-month sobriety coin. Congratulations, my friend."

Byron studied the coin for a moment without touching it. Apart from its color, it looked the same as the others he'd earned. Inscribed around the coin's circumference was the phrase: To Thine Own Self Be True, and at its center was the number 6 surrounded by a triangle bearing the words: *unity service recovery.*

"It's not going to bite you, John. The group wanted me to present it to you at tonight's meeting, but since I know you're not one for making a fuss, I saved it until now."

Byron picked it up then flipped it over to look at the other side. Just a coin. No more, no less. It meant nothing really, no more than the others had, and yet he knew it meant everything. The shiny piece of metal signified six months of fighting the urges, the habit, the craving, the demon. His demon. Half a year of sleepless nights without that reliable elixir to dull the pain within him. And yet it was only a medallion. Byron noticed Miller eyeing the coin. The former chaplain regarded it with a kind of reverence, as if it were a talisman. Perhaps it was, Byron thought. Not all that different from the torn scrap of paper bearing the policeman's prayer that Byron's father, Reece, had worn, tucked behind the Miranda card inside the clear plastic sleeve on the underside of his uniform cap. The same sweat-stained prayer bearing the watercolor image of Saint Michael, patron saint of police officers, that Byron once wore inside his own uniform cap and now carried in his badge holder. Nothing and everything.

"Thanks," Byron said as he pocketed the coin.

"You're most welcome, young man," Miller said before taking another swig of the syrup masquerading as coffee inside his mug. "You know you can ask me anything, right? I have, after all, been at this far longer than you."

After a moment Byron asked, "What's the trick?"

"To sobriety? There really isn't one. It's different for everyone. I have a system that works for me."

"And that is?"

"Addiction is a monster, John. In your line of work, you should know that better than anyone. Some of the monsters you meet weren't born that way, they were created by addiction. I wake up every morning, put both feet on the floor, and begin my day by making a choice."

"A choice?"

"Yup."

"And that is?"

"I can either start the day committed to sobriety, or I can succumb to that monster, hightail it down to the local watering hole, and get drunk off my ass. Thus far I've managed to choose commitment."

"That's it?" Byron said. "That's your secret?"

"Hey, don't knock it," Miller said with a wink.

Byron picked up his own mug and held it in his hands, relishing the warmth radiating through the ceramic. He'd hoped there might be more to it than that. Six months. Jesus, he couldn't imagine starting over.

"Tell me about the case you're working," Miller said. "What's the girl's name again?"

"Faherty," Byron said. "Danica Faherty."

"Any good suspects?"

Byron sighed heavily. "More than I know what to do with. This is a bad one, Shaun."

"Saw more than my share of those when I was chaplain."

"You ever see someone decapitated?"

Miller grimaced. "No, I never saw that. Not during my watch." He shook his head and took another sip from his mug. "Feels like people are becoming angrier."

Byron was too wired after meeting with Miller to go directly home. The coffee hadn't helped. He turned the radio to 96.3 FM, hoping to catch the Red Sox game. He hadn't followed the Sox since his father, Reece, had died. But Shaun Miller was a big fan, and it gave them something to talk about. According to Joe Castiglione, the Sox were up on the Phillies three runs to two in the fourth.

Byron stopped at a traffic light and pulled out his cell to check for new voicemail messages, but there weren't any. He hadn't managed to catch up with Diane during the day, and she hadn't returned the single message he had left. The light changed to green and he pocketed his phone.

The Red Sox broadcast faded into the background while his mind returned to the case. He knew it was important to give equal weight to all of the possibilities. Every suspect and every angle deserved a hard look. Anything short of that was the equivalent of tunnel vision, the same myopic tendency that could get an officer killed on the street. Looking one way while the real threat, or a secondary threat, lurked in an entirely different direction, took another good cop down. An open mind was the key to solving homicides. Allowing the facts to create the narrative, not the other way around. Suspects are ruled out, not ignored. If Faherty really had fallen prey to the Horseman, the facts would eventually bear that out. And if not, then she likely knew her killer. Which meant that everyone in the growing list of possible suspects had to be looked at closely.

Only vaguely aware of his destination, Byron drove toward Portland's waterfront. He threaded the unmarked through the traffic on Fore Street, which at this hour was mainly comprised of pedestrians, local taxis, and Uber drivers. And the pedestrians mostly seemed to be drunk. He drove west past the fray onto the quieter York Street. The car seemed to be leading the way, and he wasn't surprised in the least to find himself turning left onto Maple. He pulled to the side of the road beside the abandoned lumberyard and parked.

Byron killed the ignition, and the radio,

then sat for a while inside the car enjoying the solitude. Running down the case details in his head, he stared through the windows listening to the tick of the engine as it cooled. After several minutes, he exited the car and approached the cyclone fence surrounding the property. He walked along its length toward Commercial Street until he reached the section that had been cut by trespassers. As he had guessed, the previously damaged section was gaping open once again. The wire repair hadn't lasted twenty-four hours. He stepped through the opening and into the darkened yard.

The streetlights didn't penetrate much beyond the fence and it took Byron's eyes several moments to acclimate to the gloom. Unsure of his footing, he stepped forward slowly and deliberately. The crumbling asphalt and plentiful scrub were both equally capable of wrenching an ankle. When at last he reached the drying shed that had served as Danica Faherty's final resting place, he stopped and stood perfectly still. He wanted to see what the killer had seen, to feel what they had felt as they abandoned the young woman's body like so much trash. Had they driven a vehicle into the lot, or simply carried her body in and laid it on the ground? The mystery padlock suggested the former. An image of Katherine, his niece, suddenly appeared in his mind. Instead of Faherty, what if it had been Katherine's torso left on the ground to rot? He closed his eyes tightly, pushing the horrible vision away. When he opened them again there was only darkness inside the shed. Darkness and bare ground.

Only vaguely aware of the occasional passing car and the thundering exhaust of one particularly loud motorcycle headed outbound on West Commercial toward the Veteran's Bridge, Byron's focus was elsewhere. A cacophony of crickets shrilled nearby, like tinnitus effectively drowning out most of the other night sounds. He turned and looked across the street toward the Courtyard Portland Marriott. Many of the rooms were alight, affording him a view inside through undrawn shades. He saw the flicker of flat-screen televisions and hotel guests moving about, each completely unaware of his presence.

This is what it must have been like, he thought. *This is what the killer would have seen once inside the yard.* A deadly voyeur, hidden within plain sight. Had the killer been searching for his next victim? Or had he, or she, been all business, thinking only of the job at hand. Ridding themselves of a decaying body and positioning it as yet another cryptic message to the police. Giving them yet another riddle to solve.

Byron felt an electric chill run up his back. Was this like the excitement the killer felt as they stood here watching the city pass by? The city and its inhabitants all oblivious to the danger lurking within? He was nearly overcome by a sudden urge to take a drink. Just one to settle his nerves. But he knew he couldn't. In his world there was no such thing as just one. *Can't have just one.* Hadn't there been a potato chip company who had used that as their marketing catch phrase? He slid his hand inside his pants pocket and closed his fingers around the coin Shaun Miller had given him. The coolness and weight of the medallion was oddly comforting, providing a much-needed anchor.

Byron turned away from the hotel. Slowly he surveyed the remaining area. Things always appeared different shrouded in the darkness of night. Senses were easily fooled. A dry leaf skittering across the pavement might just as easily be a rat. What had seemed an ill-contrived location to discard a body during daylight hours now seemed far better suited to the killer's modus operandi. Better suited to whatever statement he, or she, was trying to make. That they could live and kill and walk among us, and no one would ever see them. Never suspect them. Never recognize them for what they really were. A thing born of mist in the shape of a human. Soulless, cunning, and deadly, wearing a human mask. Toying with the police, daring them to catch him. Daring Byron to catch him. The Horseman? Maybe.

Byron caught the subtle whiff of marijuana burning nearby but couldn't identify its source. So very different than the familiar burning leaf scent of his college days, this odor was about as pleasurable as a dead skunk. He scanned the area again until he caught the faintest silhouette of a person. Someone was standing just outside the rear of one of the commercial buildings on York Street, holding a joint, perhaps. He continued to watch as the figure tossed something large into one of the dumpsters then closed the lid with a loud bang. *A cleaner,* Byron thought. And another potential witness to the dumping of Danica Faherty's body. He wondered which of the detectives had interviewed them. He would check with Mel. Evidentially finished with the smoke break, Doobie re-entered the building.

Byron's cell vibrated with an incoming

call, startling him. He removed it from his pocket and pressed Accept. "Byron."

"John, it's Pepin."

Patrol Sergeant Andy Pepin worked the early out shift. 4:00 P.M. to 2:00 A.M., the craziest time of day for policing. As such, Pepin and Byron frequently crossed paths. Pepin was one of the good ones. Dedicated.

"What's up, Andy?"

"I'm in the booking room at the county jail with an arrest. A guy drunk off his ass."

"And?"

"He's adamant that he needs to speak with you."

"Adamant?"

"Yeah. So much so that I think he intentionally got himself arrested. He was raving in the middle of Congress Street. When I told him to get his ass back onto the sidewalk, he started pounding on the hood of my cruiser, so I hooked him up."

"Who is he?"

"Name's Erwin Glantz. Says he knows you."

Winn. Byron started toward the car. "Give me five minutes, Andy. I'll meet you in the booking room."

Byron had a long history with Erwin Glantz, a homeless army veteran who went by the

211

nickname Winn. Winn had served his country honorably during the first Gulf War but, like many combat soldiers, he had returned to the States unable to cope with everyday life. Alienated from his family in California, Winn had moved to Maine and taken to the bottle to ward off his own demons. Byron first met him years before while working uniformed patrol on the late out which, before the department went to four ten-hour shifts, had been midnight to 8:00 A.M. Winn had been preparing to commit a burglary at a local business. Instead of busting him, Byron drove him to a nearby restaurant and bought him a hot meal. Winn had gone on to become one of Byron's best informants during his years as a junior detective in CID. Byron knew that Winn wouldn't intentionally get himself arrested unless something was very wrong.

Byron pulled the Taurus into the Cumberland County Jail's sally port just as the Phillies tied it up at three in the sixth on a fielder's choice. He parked in one of the diagonal spaces on the right. Byron had already exited the car and was in the process of securing his sidearm in a locker when the heavy corrugated steel entry door finished trundling down on its tracks.

Sergeant Pepin met Byron in booking, just

inside the second set of security doors.

"Where's Winn?" Byron asked.

"They tossed his ass in the drunk tank," Pepin said.

"How bad is he?"

"Blistered."

Byron and Pepin followed one of the turnkeys to the holding tank in which Winn was being held. Even through the unbreakable glass viewing window Byron could see the state his friend was in. Pepin hadn't exaggerated.

"What do you want to do?" the jail guard asked.

"Nothing for now," Byron said. "Whatever he wanted to tell me will keep until morning." He turned to Pepin. "What did you charge him with?"

"Obstructing a public way, disorderly conduct."

"Criminal mischief?"

"Nah. No damage to the cruiser, he was just being a nuisance."

Byron knew that two misdemeanor charges most likely meant a fine and or time served for Winn, assuming the magistrate didn't just dismiss the charges outright. The bail he would need to post would be low but, unless his homeless friend had a rain day fund that Byron was unaware of, and with tomorrow being a court holiday, Winn wouldn't be getting out until Monday at the earliest. He addressed the guard again. "What time do visiting hours begin on Friday?"

"For you? Assuming he's sober enough to finish processing, you'll be able to sit down with him by nine o'clock."

"I'll be here by 8:45."

CHAPTER 14

Friday, 9:15 A.M.,
July 14, 2017
Byron sat at a scuffed steel table in one of the stark concrete block interview rooms at the Cumberland County Jail. He was reviewing his case notes while trying to choke down coffee that tasted as if it had been brewed using laundry rinse water. An opaque film floating across the top of the dark liquid caught his eye, and he couldn't help wondering if the trustee who'd made it had known it was for him. Deciding to err on the side of caution, he pushed the Styrofoam cup aside and returned to his notes.

Winn was late. According to the jail shift supervisor, they'd been on their way to the interview room with him but had to divert for a shower and clean clothing after Winn vomited all over himself. Byron heard the loud clank of the security lock followed by the sound of the heavy steel door being opened at the far end of the hallway. A moment later Erwin Glantz shuffled into view. Freshly showered and dressed in clean inmate garb, matching bright orange shirt and pants, Winn looked as haggard as Byron had ever seen him. The guard waited until Winn was seated directly across the table from Byron before departing.

"Tough night?" Byron said.

Winn ignored the question and eyed the coffee. "You mind?"

"Knock yourself out," Byron said, sliding the beverage toward him.

Winn grabbed the cup and took several sips before gingerly placing it back on the table. "Jesus, that's horrible."

"Why am I here, Winn?" Byron asked without fanfare. "According to Sergeant Pepin, you went and got yourself arrested just so you could talk to me."

Winn stared back at him from the dark hollows of his bloodshot eyes. "You gotta get me out of here, Sarge."

"Why would I do that?"

" 'Cause, I got something to show ya. Something important."

Byron studied Winn's face. There was no humor in it. Winn looked scared.

It was nearly ten-thirty by the time Byron finally sprung Winn from CCJ. After signing all the appropriate forms and posting bail, Byron waited while Winn changed back into his street clothes. Neither man had eaten breakfast, so Byron drove directly to the Dunkin' Donuts drive-thru on St. John Street. He slid the unmarked into the drive-thru lane then ordered two large coffees and three sausage, egg, and cheese croissant sandwiches, one for himself and two for his charge. As an afterthought Byron had the clerk add an order of hash browns for Winn. Byron looked on with concern as Winn gobbled his first sandwich in what appeared to be two bites.

"You'd better not get sick inside this car," Byron cautioned. "I swear to God. I'll take you right back to jail."

Winn managed a weak smile, crumbs stuck to his beard like Velcro.

"I'm serious," Byron said. "And I don't have all day. I'm in the middle of a case. Where is this thing you need to show me?"

Winn's smile vanished. "Drive down to Commercial. I'll show you where to go."

Twenty minutes later Byron stood on the

side of an overgrown hill, not far from the Casco Bay Bridge, watching Winn, who was down on all fours vomiting up the breakfast sandwich he had just eaten. During a lull in the action, Byron carefully surveyed the area. The dark green garbage bag was right where Winn said it would be, but it appeared to have been ripped open. Or perhaps clawed open was a more accurate description, Byron thought. The bag had been shredded into pieces; its contents, including a woman's purse and clothing, were strewn about in the dirt.

"This is what you got yourself arrested for and dragged me out here to see?" Byron said. "Stolen property?"

"That ain't it," Winn said. He stood up and wiped his mouth with the back of his hand as he scanned the area. "Something's missing."

Byron waited while Winn looked around for whatever it was.

"Oh, shit," Winn said. He was visibly shaking. Byron had never seen the man like this.

"What?"

Winn pointed to an item lying in the weeds about twenty or so feet from where they stood. "That."

Byron stood staring at the object Winn had pointed to. Lying in among the detritus was a badly decomposed human skull. The skull was positioned on its side partially hidden by weeds. Only one glaring eye socket was visible. It was obvious from the claw marks and denuded bone that an animal, or perhaps more than one, had been at it. Any hope at making a visual identification of Faherty, if it was Faherty, would be impossible. Byron removed his cellphone from the inside pocket of his blazer and began dialing the medical examiner's office. Winn vomited again.

Byron remained at the scene making sure all the necessary players were in place. He contacted Police Dispatch by radio and requested two uniformed officers, one to guard the scene and another to transport his sickly witness to 109 for further questioning. Following that, he spent the next twenty minutes making phone calls to Pelligrosso, Stevens, Nugent, LeRoyer, and Ellis. As soon as he had a team en route, Byron retrieved a bright yellow roll of crime scene tape from the trunk of his Taurus and strung a crude but wide border around the evidence. Paying particular attention to where he stepped, Byron included a much larger area than he probably needed, but experience had taught him it was better to preserve a scene that went well beyond what was required. The area to be searched could always be consolidated, but overlooking evidence because the scene had been made too small was unforgivable.

Forty-five minutes later, Byron stood beside Nugent, looking on as Dr. Ellis and Evidence Technician Pelligrosso both knelt beside the remains.

"What do you think, Doc?" Byron asked.

Ellis slapped loudly at the mosquito feeding on the back of his neck. "I think I don't ever remember Portland being quite so tropical."

Byron frowned. "About the body."

"Well, Sergeant, that's another subject entirely," Ellis said as he stood upright and mopped his brow with his forearm.

Byron noted the way the M.E.'s belly stretched tightly at the black fabric of his *Highway to Hell* concert T-shirt. Sweat stains were already forming under his arms.

"At first glance, I'd say that both the remains and the saw marks on the vertebra look similar enough that this is probably the missing piece of the Faherty woman puzzle. Of course, it goes without saying that we won't know for sure until we compare her dental records."

"Beats the alternative," Nugent said.

"I'll bite," Pelligrosso said for all of them. "What's the alternative?"

"That there's another body out here, missing its head."

Byron glared at Nugent. He was tired and hot, as they all were, and in no mood for his senior detective's comedy routine, nor the possibility he was raising, however unlikely.

"How exactly did this Glantz fellow happen upon this site?" Ellis asked. "This wouldn't seem to be a normal travel route."

"It isn't," Byron said. "Hiding the bag and its contents here was his handiwork. Says he was passed out in a dumpster a few nights ago when someone tossed in a garbage bag and drove away."

"Do you know where the dumpster is located?" Ellis asked.

"Somewhere in the Old Port is all we know. I've got uniforms looking for it now. Why?"

"After nothing more than a cursory look, I'd say it's highly likely that the murder weapon was either the claw end of a hammer or a pry tool of some sort."

"So, the gun theory is off the table?" Byron asked.

"Yes," Ellis said. "And unless you manage to locate the tool or the saw around here, you'll want to check the dumpster."

Byron turned to Pelligrosso. "You finished with photos?"

"Almost. Then I need to measure this out. After that I'll start collecting and searching further."

Byron turned to Ellis. "How soon can you post?"

Ellis checked his watch. "It's almost noon now. How's five o'clock?"

"This afternoon?" Byron asked, surprised at the doctor's generous offer.

"Well, I figure you'll need answers sooner than later, and I can't do it tomorrow. If I don't do it now, you'll have to wait until Monday."

Byron looked at Pelligrosso. "That good for you?"

"Sure, if you call in Murph to assist me."

"This afternoon it is," Byron said. He turned to Nugent. "You good to assist Gabe with this until I can get Murphy in here?"

"I'll be right here, assuming the bugs don't eat all of me," Nugent said. "You going somewhere?"

"109. It's time to get the rest of Winn's story."

Byron and Stevens sat across from Erwin "Winn" Glantz in CID Interview Room

One. Winn squirmed uncomfortably. Byron had intentionally given him a chair that was missing a leg caster, an old interrogator's trick designed to keep the witness off balance and uncomfortable. It appeared to be working.

"Why didn't you come to me right away, Winn?" Byron said. "I thought you and I had a history."

"I don't know," Winn said. "I was scared, I guess. Not thinking straight."

"Kinda like last night, huh?" Byron said.

Winn traced a filthy fingernail along a split in the round oak tabletop. "I panicked, okay? I mean, my prints were all over the bag by the time I realized what was inside it."

"And?" Byron asked, knowing Winn was still holding back.

Winn looked sheepishly at Stevens before continuing. "And I had already gone through her purse."

Melissa Stevens fixed him with a look of disgust.

"I was strapped for cash, okay? I swear, I didn't know there was a — what else was in the bag."

"Tell us again what you remember about the person or persons who discarded the bag," Byron said.

Winn shook his head in frustration. "I didn't get a good look. I told you, just a shadow. I think it was only one person."

"Male, female, tall, short?" Byron asked.

"It happened too quick, and I was drunk."

Byron wondered if it really was intoxication hampering Winn's recall, or perhaps it was something else.

"Tell us what you heard," Stevens said.

"About what?"

"That night, Winn. What exactly did you hear?"

Winn exhaled loudly in exasperation. "I don't know."

Byron jumped in again. "You said the shadowy figure who tossed the bag into the dumpster drove up. How do you know that? Was it the sound of the vehicle that woke you? What did it sound like? Was it a quiet car or loud? Engine noise? Exhaust? Footsteps? Come on, Winn. This is important. Focus."

"Okay, okay. Give me a minute to think." Winn closed his eyes.

Byron exchanged a wordless glance with Stevens.

After a moment Winn said, "It sounded big."

"Big?" Byron asked.

"Yeah. Not a car. Like maybe a van, or a

truck. Something with some horsepower under the hood."

"Hell, that could be a sports car," Byron said.

"No. I'm sure it was a truck. It was big and heavy. It's hard to describe, but I know it was a truck. Even by the door."

"The door?" Stevens said.

"Yeah. When whoever it was slammed it, it sounded like a truck door. Like the metallic bang of sheet metal against metal, not all padded like a car." Winn looked to Byron. "Like the transports we had in the army, Sarge. No-frills."

Byron immediately thought of Faherty's ex-boyfriend, Morgan. Bates drove a pickup, a black 1977 GMC Scottsdale. Byron had heard the big rumbling engine and the way it sounded when Bates slammed the door. Could that have been the vehicle Winn heard? Faherty's neighbor Christine Micucci claimed to have seen a male drop Faherty's car off in the driveway on Monday afternoon before climbing into a waiting pickup truck. Could Bates's truck have been the vehicle that Micucci saw? Byron needed to pin down Bates's location for Saturday night into Sunday morning, even if he had to do it through his attorney.

"What else should we know that you're

not telling us?" Stevens asked.

"This wasn't the first time I've seen a decapitated head," Winn said, blurting it out.

Both detectives remained silent, knowing that they had finally arrived at the heart of the matter.

"It was during the ground campaign in Iraq, one of my buddies got separated from our unit during the fighting. Teddy Archibald. We called him Archie after the comic strip, because he was always cracking wise." Winn grew quiet and began tracing the cracks in the tabletop again.

"What happened?" Byron said.

"It took a couple of days, but eventually we found him. They'd left Archie's body lying in the street under the hot sun. He'd been shot twice. Then beheaded. I'm pretty sure he was still alive when they did it."

"I'm sorry," Byron said.

Winn looked up at him. "When I first realized what was in the bag it was like I was back in Iraq again."

For several moments all three of them sat in silence.

"I know I should have gotten a hold of you as soon as it happened," Winn said. "I just panicked. I guess I never thought I'd have to see anything like that again."

Byron's cell vibrated with a text from Pelligrosso. It read: confirmed-purse belonged 2 V.

Byron held the phone out to allow Stevens to read the text. She nodded.

Byron looked back at Winn. "Think you can show us the dumpster where all this happened?"

"I can try."

Byron and Stevens chauffeured Winn through the Old Port in search of the dumpster. All four windows of the Taurus were lowered. Even though Winn had showered at the jail, twice, his ratty street clothes were still overpoweringly pungent. They searched Exchange, Market, Wharf, Dana, Silver, and Pearl, literally every street, alley, and driveway imaginable. Several times Winn made Byron stop so he could get out for a closer look, but then he'd find something that wasn't right, and they'd continue on.

"Winn, how certain are you this happened in the Old Port?" Stevens asked. "We're running out of places to look."

"I know," Winn said. "I'm really trying."

"What time of day was it?" Stevens asked.

"I told you already. I don't know. It could have been late at night — no, wait. That's not right. It was right before sunrise. It was still dark, but I could see the sky starting to brighten in the east. I remember thinking I had to get the bag out of there before people started showing up in the Old Port."

"And this was which morning?" Byron said.

"Couple of days back. Tuesday, maybe. I don't know. Every day is kinda the same for me, Sarge. I'm either drinking or I'm not."

Byron could relate more than he cared to admit.

"I remember there was one of those hydrant thingies sticking out of the back of the building."

"A standpipe?" Stevens said.

"Yeah, a stand — wait. Stop!"

Byron hit the brakes.

"That's it!" Winn said.

"You're sure?" Byron asked.

"Yeah, yeah. Let me out. I gotta check something."

Byron and Stevens exited the car and followed Winn over to the dumpster.

"There's the standpipe thingy," Winn said, pointing to the building's freshly painted silver appendage. He turned and looked at the ground. "And that's where I puked. Right there."

Byron first looked at the building then

228

back toward Stevens. "Alessandro's."

An hour later Byron was standing upwind from his Tyvek-clad evidence techs, surveying the trash that had been laid out on the previously clean white tarp.

"I got nothing, Sarge," Pelligrosso said to Byron. "Manager says the dumpster was emptied yesterday. Whatever may have been in here is long gone."

"It's possible that Winn is telling the truth," Stevens said. "Maybe he kept everything in the bag."

"Or at the very least everything there was to take," Byron said. "We still don't have the saw that was used to remove her head."

"Or the murder weapon," Stevens added.

Pelligrosso and Murphy began picking up the trash that they had laid out on the tarp and tossing it back in the dumpster.

"What do you want to do with him?" Stevens asked, nodding in Winn's direction.

Byron turned to look at Winn through the rear window of the unmarked as he considered it. "Let's get him back to 109, Mel." He turned his attention to Murphy. "Murph, I need you to photograph and fingerprint Winn. And seize his clothing."

"Didn't they print him at the jail last night, Sarge?" Murphy asked.

"You're looking for full set, right?" Pelligrosso asked.

"Yes," Byron said. "Palm prints, too."

"And then?" Stevens asked.

Byron considered it for a moment before answering. "We'll find him some suitable clothing and kick him loose."

CHAPTER 15

Byron stood with arms folded leaning against the counter directly across from the CID conference room watching LeRoyer with amusement as the lieutenant made a nervous swipe back through his hair, using his fingers as a comb. Byron had never met anyone easier to read than Martin LeRoyer. The lieutenant was studying the snack box assortment contained in the two boxes sitting atop the file cabinets to the left of the conference room doorway while Byron briefed him on the latest.

"Tough decision?" Byron asked, attempting to break the tension between them.

"Yeah. Well, kind of. I saw the snack guy come in yesterday afternoon, but I was busy."

"So, there should be a good selection, right? Both boxes."

LeRoyer turned around to face him.

"You'd think so. Except some heartless prick took both Skybars."

At that moment, Melissa Stevens walked past them on her way into the conference room. She was grinning. "How do you know the culprit was a prick?"

Byron and LeRoyer followed her into the room and sat down. The detectives finished bringing LeRoyer up to speed on the latest developments.

"And the killer just happens to pick Alessandro's dumpster to dispose of her head?" LeRoyer said. "Jesus, what are the odds?"

"Well, most of the dumpsters we checked are kept locked by the business owners," Stevens said. "But, yeah, it is a huge coincidence."

"Someone sending a message, do you think?" LeRoyer asked.

"Maybe," Byron said.

"And you're both one hundred percent sure that this Ed Winn guy isn't responsible?" LeRoyer asked, making another finger pass for good measure.

Stevens glanced at Byron for guidance.

"His name is Erwin," Byron said. "Erwin Glantz. Winn for short. And yes, I am one hundred percent sure."

"He was going to take the money from

232

the purse, though, right, Mel?" LeRoyer said. "We should charge him with theft by receiving."

"He returned the money to her purse after he saw what else was in the bag," Stevens said. "We found just over eighty dollars and some loose change."

"Yeah, but he admitted that he was going to steal it, right?"

Byron knew what LeRoyer was struggling with. The lieutenant was dreading having to inform Chief Lynds that they were letting Winn go.

"Look, Marty, I know Winn. He's provided me with solid information for years. And he's one of the reasons we were able to solve the Ramsey homicide. He's also the only reason we even have what we have on this case. I'm not booking him on some bullshit misdemeanor." Byron was also worried about the fact that Winn was currently out on bail for two other misdemeanors. Locking him up again might well mean the end of his cooperation.

"You think it's possible he saw the Horseman?" LeRoyer asked.

"He saw someone discard the garbage bag, but I'm not ready to concede it was the Horseman, Marty."

"Either way, aren't you at all worried that

whoever it was will come after him?"

"Fuck, Marty. I wasn't." Truthfully, although he'd never admit it to the lieutenant, Byron had been kicking that very thought around in the back of his mind, but now LeRoyer had dragged it out into the open. Byron would never forgive himself if something happened to Winn.

"What time is the post?" LeRoyer asked.

"Five," Byron said. "Gabe is grabbing a shower before we head up."

LeRoyer looked at Stevens. "You going with them?"

"No," Stevens said. "I'm gonna pay another visit to Destiny Collins, see if I can't get more out of her about Dani's ex-boyfriend."

All three detectives looked up at the sound of knuckles rapping on the open door.

"Sorry to interrupt," Nugent said as he stuck his hairless dome through the doorway.

"Thought I sent you home, Nuge?" Byron said.

"Yeah," Stevens said. "Go home and be with your wife."

"I'm heading out now."

"What's up?" Byron asked.

"The IO just called, Sarge. You have a visitor."

234

Murder is the ultimate aggravated theft. The one thing every homicide victim shares is that each has had a portion of their lives stolen from them. Dani Faherty's parents had also become victims of the unknown killer and Byron wasn't at all surprised when one of them showed up unannounced at 109 looking to speak with him. The only surprise was which parent it was.

After offering his condolences, Byron led Denise Faherty into his office and closed the door.

"I've come here to tell you something I think you should know," Faherty said. "I knew about the domestic assault. Dani phoned me wanting to talk about it the day it happened."

"What did she tell you?" Byron asked.

"She said that she and Morgan had an argument. He was drunk and he punched her. Gave her a black eye."

"Why didn't she pursue charges against him?" Byron asked. "She went to the trouble to contact the police. Why didn't she follow through?" Byron watched as she wrestled with her emotions for several moments.

"Because I wasn't strong enough," Faherty said at last.

Byron said nothing, waiting for her to explain.

"My daughter asked me what she should do. She said that Morgan told her he was sorry."

Byron had lost count of the number of abusers who tossed around words like *sorry* and *never again* as if they'd just spilled milk on the carpet.

Faherty continued, "I said she didn't have to do anything that she wasn't comfortable with. I told her to listen to her heart." Faherty began to weep.

Byron handed her several tissues from a box atop his desk then sat down to wait.

After composing herself again, Faherty asked, "Did Morgan kill my daughter, Sergeant Byron?"

"I don't know," Byron said, and he didn't. Morgan Bates was only one name on a growing list of people they were looking at. "Did you ever mention the domestic incident to your husband?"

She shook her head. "No, I didn't. At least — not until today. That's why I'm here. I'm worried he'll do something rash."

"Like?"

"Like go after Morgan."

"Why would he do that?"

"I know my husband, Sergeant Byron. He is very protective. If he believes Morgan is responsible, there's no telling what he might do."

"Where is Elmer right now, Mrs. Faherty?"

"Honestly? I don't know."

It wasn't the answer Byron had hoped for. The last thing any of them needed was an aggrieved father going off like some half-crazed vigilante. "Does he have access to weapons?"

She nodded. "We have a camp on Ambajejus Lake, near Millinocket. He keeps his hunting guns there."

Byron had never heard of Ambajejus Lake, but he knew where Millinocket was located, approximately two hundred miles north of Portland. Right smack dab in the middle of Maine. Byron had no way of knowing if Elmer Faherty would really drive that far and back just to lay his hands on a shotgun or a hunting rifle, the only firearms known to his wife, but he wasn't about to ignore the possibility.

After instructing Dispatch to put out a regional attempt to locate, ATL, citing Faherty as despondent over the loss of his daughter, Byron wrote up a quick summary for patrol, attaching a photo from Elmer's driver's license and a description of his rental vehicle. He also requested that the uniformed officers give special attention to Morgan Bates's address, the location of which Faherty was familiar with, but beyond those two things there was little Byron could do. Faherty had neither committed a crime nor threatened to, but that didn't mean he wouldn't. Byron had learned to trust his gut instincts. Better safe than sorry.

Byron tasked Bernie Robbins with transporting Denise Faherty back to her hotel. Before handing her off, he told her the best thing she could do was to stay put and wait for her husband to return. Byron provided her with his cell number and a promise to contact her as soon as they located Elmer.

Byron was hurrying down the back stairwell of 109 while leaving a voicemail for Lucinda Phillips when he nearly collided with LeRoyer on the second-floor landing.

"I thought you were headed up to the post?" LeRoyer said.

Byron held up an index finger signaling the lieutenant to wait until he finished the message to the former Maine State Police detective sergeant.

"Hey, Luce, John Byron. Need a quick favor. I'm looking for someone who may be headed up to the Millinocket area. Guy's name is Elmer Faherty, and I have reason to believe he may be going to his camp on Ambajejus Lake. Hoping you might be able to connect me with one of the troopers assigned to that area. I'm on my way to Augusta for an autopsy, call me on my cell, okay? Thanks."

"How's she doing?" LeRoyer asked as Byron pocketed the phone.

"Lucinda?"

"Mrs. Faherty."

"Not sure what's holding her together right now," Byron said.

"What's up with Elmer? Why are you looking for him?"

Detective Melissa Stevens pressed the doorbell to Destiny Collins's condo, then rapped on the storm door for good measure. Years of working patrol had taught her never to make assumptions. Several moments passed. She was about to knock again when the inside door opened. Collins stood there looking embarrassed, dressed in a white tank top and pink pajama bottoms. Her hair was in disarray and her eyes puffy as if she might have been napping.

"I'm sorry to show up unannounced like this," Stevens said. "I just thought I'd take a chance on finding you at home."

"Detective Stevens, right?" Collins asked.

"Let's make it Mel."

"Forgive my appearance, Mel. I wasn't expecting company."

"Not a problem. May I come in?"

Collins unlatched then pushed open the outer door. "Please do," she said.

After closing the door, Collins asked if she'd like some coffee.

"Don't go to any trouble on my account," Stevens said.

"I'm making it for myself anyway."

"Then coffee would be great."

Stevens followed her into the kitchen and the two women made small talk until the coffee was ready. Stevens wanted to take it slow, not knowing how fragile Collins might be. Destiny handed her a mug and sat down at the end of the table perpendicular to Stevens.

"How are you doing, Destiny?" Stevens asked after taking a sip and setting the mug on the table.

Collins gave her a long appraising look. "Is that really why you stopped by? To ask how I'm doing?"

"That's one of the reasons."

"And the others?"

"Tell me more about Morgan Bates."

■ ■ ■ ■

After more than two decades as a cop, Byron knew that investigating a murder is all about patience. Case detectives simply keep pushing the rock forward, hoping for a break. Ray Humphrey, Byron's old mentor, had been fond of saying that working homicides was a lot like fishing. "Sometimes all you can do is set your lines in the water and wait," he'd say. Byron, who had spent considerable time during his youth fishing on the docks off Commercial Street, understood Humphrey's analogy. Still, it never made the waiting any easier.

Byron stood beside Pelligrosso watching as Dr. Ellis painstakingly went over every inch of what was believed to be Danica Faherty's decapitated head. Silky strands of auburn hair still clung to the scalp. Pelligrosso had photographed the skull from every conceivable angle, and Ellis had taken x-rays of the teeth for the purposes of comparison. Denise Faherty had provided the contact information for Danica's childhood dentist in Virginia. Byron had left a message for the doctor with the emergency call service, but he didn't really expect a call back before Monday.

Ellis fired up the bone saw and proceeded to access the inside of Faherty's cranium. Removing the cap revealed an excessive amount of damage to the brain tissue. If Ellis was right about the murder weapon being the claw end of a hammer, someone had wielded it with deadly intent.

"Just as I suspected," Ellis said. "If you look closely, we have two very clear points of penetration into the brain tissue."

Pelligrosso snapped several close-up shots of the injury while Ellis retrieved a long pair of surgical tweezers from the stainless-steel tray. He waited until the evidence tech was finished before probing into one of the wounds. After several moments Ellis withdrew the instrument and held it up for all to see.

"What is that?" Byron asked.

"A piece of Faherty's skull. The force of the blow broke off a tiny piece and forced it several inches into the brain."

"What kind of hammer should we be looking for, Doc?" Pelligrosso asked.

"The most common type has a pair of rounded claws, for pulling out relatively short or small gauge nails. But these wounds look like they were made with claws that were nearly straight."

"Framing hammer?" Byron asked, thinking again about Morgan Bates.

"Precisely," Ellis said. "But the depth of the wounds isn't the same."

"Meaning?" Pelligrosso asked.

"Meaning one of the claws was likely broken, leaving it shorter than the other, about an inch shorter."

Byron made a notation in his notebook.

"These wounds were inflicted by the hammer being swung downward, striking the victim from behind and slightly right of center." Ellis pantomimed the action as he described it.

"So, the person we're looking for was taller than Faherty?" Pelligrosso asked.

"Not necessarily, my boy. Framing hammers tend to have a longer handle than a regular hammer. Those extra inches could give the appearance of a taller person, but it might only be due to the extended handle length."

"How quickly would she have been incapacitated?" Byron asked after making a note about the suspect most likely being right-handed.

"Instantly. She would have dropped like a stone. Her brain may have kept firing electrical impulses to the body for several minutes after the blow, but given the depth of penetration and the damage to the cerebellum it's unlikely that any of those signals would have been received. Danica Faherty would have simply laid there helpless until the life ran out of her."

"And just the single blow?" Byron said.

Ellis turned back to the skull. "Just the one. But a devastating blow."

CHAPTER 16

July 14, 2017
Seeing is everything, yet Byron knew no two people ever see or interpret what they are seeing in exactly the same way. The gruesome discovery of Danica Faherty's decapitated corpse had been viewed quite differently by everyone involved in the case. LeRoyer saw a body without its head, and the stress that always accompanies a high-profile homicide. Dr. Ellis saw an unusual and fascinating case. Chief Lynds and Davis Billingslea saw opportunity. Byron, however, saw something entirely different. He saw tragedy, and another mystery to be solved.

But even more concerning to Byron was the presence of a taunting and arrogant killer roaming the streets of Portland. A killer so twisted and cruel that their mere existence was a personal affront to him. A murderer who had posed the body where it would be found, before tossing the severed head into a dumpster.

As he drove southbound on the Maine Turnpike, back toward Portland, the hum of the unmarked's tires on the pavement provided a soundtrack to the threads of the case swirling about inside his head. Alone again, his mind was free to wander. Seemingly detached and barely formed thoughts came together then drifted apart, thoughts that thirsted for information. The missing bits and pieces which, once known, would complete the puzzle. Too many suspects. Too many possibilities. As with every murder case, suspects appeared then, once alibied, disappeared from the radar. Then it was on to the next possibility. Morgan Bates, Alex Stavros, Lina, Winn, the Horseman, or by random bad luck, some nameless person who Faherty had the misfortune to cross paths with. The possibilities were endless. Murder cases with too many tentacles are the ones that drive investigators crazy, and, as Byron was aware, often become the cold cases that detectives take with them to their graves.

Byron's cell vibrated inside his suit coat, pulling him from his thoughts, back to the road before him. He slipped the phone from his pocket and checked the ID, expecting it to be Stevens. The number wasn't one he recognized. He answered, "Byron."

"Sergeant Byron, Jeff Kent calling. Lucinda Phillips gave me your number, asked me to give you a call. I'm the trooper assigned to the Millinocket area."

Lucinda had forwarded Byron's request directly to the area trooper without calling him back. Byron couldn't help but wonder if she was still embarrassed about coming on to him during the Haggerty investigation. It was one of the last times they had spoken with each other.

"Thanks for getting back to me so quickly, Trooper," Byron said. "Did she happen to pass along the information on Elmer Faherty?"

"She did. I'm standing on the front porch of the Fahertys' camp now."

"Any sign that he's been there?"

"Hard to tell. There's no one here now and the place is locked up tight. I can ask around at a couple of nearby camps if you'd like."

Byron wasn't sure of his next move. If Faherty hadn't yet made it up to the camp, assuming he even intended to, finding Trooper Kent camped out on his doorstep might scare him off. Or at the very least tip him that the police were onto him. He hadn't thought to ask Mrs. Faherty about neighbors.

"Happy to do it, unless you're worried about spooking him," the trooper said, echoing Byron's own thoughts.

"Let's hold off for now," Byron said. "I'm assuming you got the ATL we put out on his vehicle?"

"I did. And I'll keep an eye out for it."

Byron ended the call. He was about to pocket the phone again when it rang with another incoming call. This time it was Stevens.

"How'd the autopsy go?" she asked.

"It's still gonna take a few days to match Faherty's dental records, but it looks like we know the cause of death."

"Do tell."

"One blow to the back of the head with a framing hammer." As he spoke the words it was hard not to focus on the ex-boyfriend. Carpentry tools had been used both during the murder and afterwards. Morgan Bates was looking better by the minute. "Anything new on your end?"

"Found out some more stuff on Bates."

"Like?"

"Like Bates and his alibi are more than just friends. According to Destiny Collins,

248

Bates and Stephen Holcolm are partners in a house-flipping business right here in Portland."

Stevens had provided the address for the house purchased by Bates and Holcolm. It was located on Longwood Drive in North Deering, Portland's version of the suburbs. Mel had asked if he wanted her to join him, but Byron had declined. He wasn't exactly sure what would even come of his visit to the home, or for that matter what he was hoping to find.

He drove past the address intentionally, wanting to get a glimpse of the property without being seen in case someone was there. The house was a dark green clapboard-sided '70s ranch with an attached two-car. Several of the front windows had been replaced but the surrounding trim had not. There were no signs of life nor cars in the drive, but of course that meant nothing. The garage doors were closed, meaning Bates or his partner could have parked inside. After looping around the neighborhood twice, Byron parked in front of a home with a For Sale sign on its lawn that just happened to be next door to the Bates supreme home makeover.

Byron walked up the drive, pretending to

examine everything as he went. He wanted to give the appearance of a prospective buyer should anyone challenge him.

Apart from its brown shingled siding, and the absence of a garage, the ranch was the dimensional twin of the Bates house. Most likely built by the same contractor, he wagered. Maintaining his pretense, Byron made a show of checking the well-maintained lawn, the flower beds, even the painted trim around the front door. Experience had taught him that the best way to look like you belong somewhere is to act like it. He finished with the front then walked around the left side of the house, toward the back.

The rear yards were divided by a five-foot-tall decorative white fence, the kind made from PVC sold at every big box store, most likely erected to hide the eyesore of the work in progress next door. The fence partially blocked both his view and access to the adjoining lot. He climbed several steps up onto the deck, pretending to inspect the railings for rot. The height of the structure provided a perfect vantage point for looking over the fencing directly into the rear yard of the Bates place.

Morgan Bates's rear yard was overgrown with weeds. What little grass there was had gone to seed and was dotted by saplings. Leaning up against the back of the garage were several pieces of rusted metal staging. The Bates house also had a deck, or at least half of one. Byron could see that much of the decking had been removed but had not yet been replaced. The work had a shoddy half-assed look about it. According to Stevens the house had been purchased by Bates and Holcolm four months earlier. Byron didn't know much about the house-flipping business, but he was pretty sure that the faster the work was done, the sooner one might get out from under the lender who was slowly chipping away at the profits. He scanned the area and seeing no one he stepped off the deck. It was time to have a closer look at the Bates place.

The fence didn't completely surround the yard of the listed home but acted as more of a visual divider, extending to the rear edge of the lawn where it abruptly ended. Byron walked along the fence, periodically stopping and turning to take pretend photos of the house for sale with his cellphone. When he reached the end of the barrier, he took another quick look around then skirted the property line into the Bates backyard.

The first thing he checked was the garage. He wanted to be sure there weren't any vehicles parked inside. There weren't. In fact, there wasn't room for a vehicle. Shielding his eyes as he peered through a dusty window, Byron could just make out the contents of the space. It appeared they were using the garage as a makeshift workshop. A table, constructed from sawhorses and plywood, stood in the center of the left-hand bay. Littered atop the table were an assortment of what appeared to be hand and power tools, but it was too dark to identify specifically what he was seeing. Finished with the garage, Byron moved to the home itself.

He climbed up onto the partial deck and peered through a window into the kitchen. The inside of the house was in total disarray. The kitchen countertop had been torn out along with most of the cabinetry. The remaining cabinets were missing doors. A sheet of plywood capped the island. It was littered with pizza boxes and Budweiser cans, suggesting that more than just home improvement was taking place here.

He was moving to the next window when he was startled by the ringing of his cell. He quickly switched the ringer off then checked the caller ID. It was Diane. After taking a moment to get his heartbeat under control, while wondering if she was still pissed at him, he answered it.

"Hello," he said. "You've reached the world's biggest asshole."

"That your new greeting?" Diane asked.

"Could be," he said.

"I like it. Suits you."

Was she letting him off the hook? "I only use it during special occasions," he said.

"Like after being one?"

"Can't think of a more prudent time, can you?"

Byron waited a long moment for her to respond with something witty. When she didn't, he continued. "Look, about the other night, I owe you an apology. I guess I didn't handle the news very well."

"Figured that out, huh?" Diane said.

"Waking up alone was sort of a tip-off. I'm sorry, Di."

"Where are you now?" she said.

"At the moment? I'm actually sneaking around in a murder suspect's backyard."

"And to think, I could've had a normal boyfriend."

Boyfriend. "You'd have hated it."

"Want to meet for dinner?"

She was already seated at a table as Byron entered the restaurant. The dining room on the upper floor of RíRá Irish Pub was one of the places that they loved to meet because it tended to be quiet enough to allow for conversation and afforded a view of the channel between Maine Wharf and the State Pier, where the bright yellow-and-white Casco Bay Line ferries were lined up like parked cars on a city street. Byron recalled the first time they'd dined there; Diane had spotted a harbor seal while they were seated at that very table. She considered it a good omen. Byron wasn't sure he bought into the whole good omen bad omen thing, but he hoped that the fact that she was sitting there now was a good sign.

The waiter appeared even before Byron had removed his suit coat and sat down.

"May I bring you something to drink, sir?" the broad-shouldered young man asked with just the faintest Irish lilt.

"Diet."

"Pepsi okay?"

"Pepsi's fine, thanks."

The waiter departed, leaving them alone.

Byron glanced around at the nearby tables. Only one was unoccupied.

"What are you looking for?" Diane asked.

"Witnesses," he said. "In case you try and off me."

She laughed. It was an easy laugh, not forced. It was good to hear.

"I've been thinking," she said. "You might consider changing your voicemail greeting to Portland's biggest asshole."

"You think world's biggest is too pretentious?"

"Perhaps a bit. It does have a nice ring to it, though."

Now it was his turn to laugh. "Truce?" he said.

She held his gaze for a moment. "Truce."

The waiter returned with Byron's soda and took their orders. While awaiting their meals they made casual conversation while intentionally avoiding the subject of the CID opening.

"I heard about your visit from Denise Faherty," Diane said. "You think her husband will really go after Dani's ex-boyfriend?"

"Who knows. I can only imagine how Elmer's feeling right now. Fucking Billingslea hasn't helped matters." Byron caught a glance from a nearby table and realized he'd spoken somewhat louder than he'd intended. Raising a hand in contrition, he lowered his voice and continued. "Elmer has every right to be upset."

"True, but he doesn't have the right to take matters into his own hands, John."

"Hopefully it won't come to that," Byron said. Though, if Bates really was responsible,

Byron could almost cheer the aggrieved father on.

"So, what's next?" she asked.

"I'm heading to Boston first thing in the morning. My cousin, Murray, is the lead on the Horseman case. He's agreed to show me their files. I want to compare notes on what we have."

"You really think Dani Faherty was killed by the same guy they're looking for?"

Byron shrugged. "Who knows. Seems like that's what some people are hoping."

Byron, who hadn't realized how hungry he was, made quick work of his shepherd's pie. After finishing, he slid the empty bowl away and sat back in his chair. It was time to tackle the ten-ton elephant in the room, the CID opening.

"I really am sorry for reacting the way I did the other night," he said.

She nodded but said nothing, pushing her own plate away and dabbing at her mouth with the napkin. Byron noticed the faint trace of lipstick she left behind.

"I guess the news took me by surprise," he continued. "But that's no excuse for my not having been supportive."

She reached across the table and slid a hand over his. "Thank you, John. But in all honesty, I'm still trying the idea on."

"You don't want the job?" Byron asked, confused by her response. "But I thought —"

"Of course I want it. I'm just not sure that now is the right time."

"I don't get it. What's holding you back?"

She pulled her hand away and picked up her wineglass. "Truthfully? I'm not sure how well my promotion back to CID would be received. Let's face it, this public relations sergeant's job is BS. Window dressing so they could promote the city's first black sergeant."

"First black female sergeant," Byron teased.

"That, too," Diane said with a grin.

"Whatever their ulterior motives may have been, you *are* a sergeant and would make a damned good detective sergeant, Di."

"Is that your considered opinion, Detective Sergeant Byron?"

"That's the considered opinion of one stubborn SID."

"SID?"

"Yeah. Second-generation Irish-American dick."

She grinned. "Surely you mean SSIAHD."

"I'm almost afraid to ask," he said.

"Stubborn second-generation Irish-American homicide dick," she said.

"That's quite a mouthful."

"You can say that again."

The waiter appeared as they clinked glasses. "May I interest either of you in something from our dessert menu?" he said.

"I was thinking we might have our dessert at home," Diane said, giving Byron a seductive look over the top of her glass.

"You heard the lady," Byron said, addressing the red-faced waiter.

"I'll bring your check, sir."

CHAPTER 17

Byron departed his condo before 6:00 A.M., hoping to make it to Boston PD by 9:00, but his plan was thwarted by the rain-soaked snarl of traffic on Route 1 in Chelsea, Massachusetts. His original thought had been to partner up with Melissa Stevens, but Nugent's most recent late-night trip to the hospital maternity ward had changed that, forcing Mel to stay behind. There was still too much to do in Portland on the Faherty case.

Byron was pleased to see Diane still curled up and sleeping soundly as he snuck out of the condo. The fact that she had stayed through the night meant that he was out of the proverbial doghouse. They had officially made up.

While at a standstill in southbound traffic near the Tobin Bridge, Byron dialed in and remotely accessed his voicemail. The feminine-sounding electronic keeper of the messages informed him that he had fourteen new ones. A handful of the calls were from news agencies looking for updates on the case; not surprisingly none of them were from Davis Billingslea, who after preempting Byron's notification to the Fahertys, wasn't getting any information from Diane or, for that matter, Chief Lynds. All Billingslea would be getting was the cold shoulder he deserved. One of the messages was from a psychic out of San Diego, California offering up her services. Byron deep-sixed that message without a second thought.

It was nearly 10:00 by the time he reached Boston Police Headquarters.

One Schroeder Plaza, the building where Murray worked, was named in honor of a pair of brothers, John and Walter Schroeder, both of whom had been killed in the line of duty in the 1970s. The structure was a long four-story concrete and glass affair with a recessed first-floor entryway. Industrial functional was the architectural description that popped into Byron's head. The building had a depressing fortress quality about it, reminding him of the FBI headquarters in DC. After parking on Tremont, adjacent to the police parking lot at the corner of

Prentiss Street, he grabbed his briefcase off the passenger seat then hurried toward the main entrance.

Byron was drenched by the time he reached the front doors. He stood in line dripping on the tiled lobby floor while waiting to speak to the officer manning the information desk. When it was finally his turn, Byron reached inside his overcoat and produced his credentials. "I'm here to see Sergeant Murray."

"He expecting you?" the desk officer said as he examined Byron's badge and ID.

"Yes," Byron said.

He returned Byron's credentials. "Grab a seat over there, Sarge. I'll have him come down and get you."

He hadn't been seated for more than a couple of minutes before Murray shouted to him from the elevators at the far end of the lobby. "Johnny B!"

Cringing slightly at the nickname, Byron did his best to hide his displeasure as he rose from the chair and walked over to meet him. "Hey, cuz."

Ignoring Byron's outstretched hand, his cousin embraced him in an awkward hug. "Jeez, it's great to see you, Johnny." Murray stepped back and looked at him appraisingly. "Damn, it's been too long."

"That it has," Byron said, forcing a smile.

"Come on up. Stow that wet gear, and I'll fix you up with some coffee."

They got off the elevator on the second floor. Byron followed his cousin to the right along a carpeted common hallway. They passed numerous offices as they went. It being Saturday, most were empty. At the far end of the hall, they entered a room not much bigger than the CID conference room at 109. Occupying the space were five mismatched desks, each with its own computer monitor, two long wall-mounted whiteboards, and a small kitchenette, which was nothing more than a laminate counter with a built-in stainless-steel sink shoved into one corner. Rounding out the space, which appeared to have been recently thrown together, was an antiquated-looking black plastic coffee maker with a stained carafe. A flat-panel television had been mounted to one wall. The TV was set to a twenty-four-seven news broadcast and muted.

"Welcome to the home of the Horseman Task Force," his cousin said. "Or as we like to call it, how the fuck?"

"How the fuck?"

"Yeah, HTF. How the fuck we gonna

catch him?" Murray chuckled. "Catchy, huh?"

"Very," Byron said as he removed his coat and hung it over the back of a chair. "You've already set up a task force. I'm impressed."

"Don't be. There's only two of us assigned right now, Tommy and me. Most of this furniture was appropriated from other precincts. 'Budget crisis looms at City Hall, news at eleven.' "

Byron nodded his understanding. "In Maine we use the more common vernacular when absconding with needed equipment from another unit."

"And that is?"

"Acquired."

Murray laughed. "Works for me. The good news is the powers that be are telling us we may acquire a couple of warm bodies from the drug unit very soon."

"Window dressing?"

"You got it. But when it comes to dressing, my preference has always been blue cheese."

Hoping to avoid encouraging him, Byron ignored the bad joke.

"Anyway, as I mentioned to you on the phone, both of our vics were pros. Evidently, sex workers aren't afforded the same investigative resources as they might if they'd hailed from — say — Boston's elite. Can you imagine how many dicks we'd have at our disposal if the lopped ones were from Beacon Hill?"

Sad but true, Byron thought. He suspected that the same would probably hold true most anywhere.

"You get the statement I took from that George Martin guy okay? The guy sharing the hotel room with Stavros."

"I did, thanks for doing that."

"No problemo. Guy comped me a meal while I was there, too."

Byron wasn't sure he approved of that idea, but kept the thought to himself.

"My partner should be back in a minute," Murray said. "I'll introduce the two of you, then we can get started. Grab an empty desk, cuz. I'll go get you that coffee. You still take it black?"

"Black's good. Aren't you using that one?" Byron said, pointing to the coffee maker on the counter.

"Screw that. It's Saturday."

"Meaning?"

Murray grinned. "Meaning I scored me a key to one of the DC's offices. That two-star prick has a Keurig."

Byron had removed the file from his portfolio and was studying the crime scene photos of the victims taped to one of the whiteboards when Murray returned with the other detective.

"Hey, Johnny," Murray said, breezing through the doorway with a mug of coffee in each hand. "Like you to meet my partner, Tommy Reggetti. Tommy, this is my cousin from another mother, John Byron. John's a DS in Portland, Maine."

Reggetti, who held a file folder in one hand, stuck out the other in greeting. "Pleased to meet you, John. Pete tells me our boy may have paid you guys a visit."

"That's what I'm hoping to find out."

The three men dragged chairs into a circle and sat down. Byron sipped the hot coffee from a white BPD Homicide mug bearing the reaper insignia. After a bit of small talk, they dug into the cases. Murray went first.

"So, what do you know about your vic, John? Any luck making a prostitution link?"

Byron shook his head. "No, and I don't think one exists. We scoured her apartment. Even my Computer Crimes Unit couldn't unearth anything." Byron meant Tran of course, but thought Computer Crimes Unit might sound better to the away team. "Doesn't fit with what we know about her anyway."

Reggetti spoke up. "And you're one hundred percent on that? As I'm sure Pete told you, both of our vics were."

"He did, and I am."

"All right," Murray said. "Well, if it is our perp of the equine persuasion, that's a big departure from his known MO."

"What exactly is his modus operandi?" Byron asked.

"We've been operating on the premise that he's targeting them because they're pros," Reggetti said.

Byron made a notation in his notebook.

"But short of that, he doesn't have a clear-cut MO."

Murray jumped in. "One of our vics was beaten and strangled, one was restrained with zip ties then shot up with a fatal dose of heroin. Both had a history of drug abuse. How about yours?"

"No," Byron said. "Medical examiner said she showed no signs of having been a user. Tox confirmed she was clean also."

Reggetti turned to Murray. "Maybe he's right about Faherty. You know how rare it is in Boston to find a pro who doesn't use?"

"Assuming we're right about Faherty not being a prostitute and assuming we're dealing with the same perp, you think it's possible your guy just might be evolving?" Byron asked. "Maybe his hatred is spreading to all women."

The Boston detectives exchanged a knowing glance. Byron understood that they were holding something back. Reggetti nodded to his partner.

"As far as MO goes, we've only been able to link these two local cases," Murray said. "If he's done others, we haven't found them, at least not yet. We've been in contact with a profiler who says our target has most likely been at this awhile, and that taking heads might just be the latest trick. Maybe they weren't getting enough attention just killing them. Who knows? But contrary to what you've read in the papers, our guy isn't as discriminating as you've been led to believe."

Byron glanced back and forth between both men. "Your victims weren't both women?"

Murray shook his head. "Nope."

"But I thought —"

"Both vics had female names but one of them was trans. Only a few of us know the truth. And now you."

"And the Horseman, of course," Reggetti added.

"Of course," Byron said.

They spent the better part of four and a half hours exchanging notes and details of each case; positioning, dumping grounds, time of death, known personal habits, everything. When they'd finished Murray and Reggetti offered to treat Byron to lunch, but he politely declined. He was anxious to get back to his own team and case.

It was after 3:00 by the time Byron was back on the road and headed north. The rain had let up slightly, increasing visibility and allowing for intermittent wipers. As he drove back toward Maine, Byron mulled over what he had learned from the Boston cases. Aside from the Faherty murder having been committed in Maine, there were other distinct differences between Faherty's murder and the two Boston murders, the lack of a connection to prostitution being the most glaring. Both bodies in the Boston cases had also been abandoned in unused industrial areas of the city, but, unlike the Portland case, neither of the sites chosen in the Boston murders was destined to be anything more than abandoned property for the foreseeable future. The former lumberyard in Portland was about to be developed into a high-end hotel and function center. Finding Faherty's body there had put serious reservations into the heads of the folks financing the project and rumors were already circulating of a possible pull-out. Byron couldn't imagine anything more negative than recovering the body of a decapitated young woman on the grounds. Had the dump site been chosen specifically for that purpose? And if so, who would stand to benefit if the investors withdrew their money for the project?

Byron's cell rang as he crossed the Tobin Bridge, pulling him from his thoughts. He answered without checking the caller ID. "Byron."

"Sergeant Byron, it's Trooper Kent again."

"Hey, Jeff. Any luck locating Elmer Faherty?"

"That's why I'm calling. After we spoke last, I left a message with one of his neighbors on Ambajejus. I didn't want to tip Faherty off, so I told the neighbor that I thought he might be headed up to camp and that I needed to speak with him, to pass along some information. They promised to call me if he showed up. Well, they called. Said they saw a car in the driveway about ten-thirty this morning. When they got back from the store about an hour later it was gone."

"They get a look at what he was driving? Was it the rust-colored Ford we put out in the ATL?"

"No, actually, it wasn't. Not according to the neighbor anyway. Said they didn't get a good look, but they did say it was a dark-colored sedan. Full-sized. Maybe blue. If they're right, and it was Faherty, he may have switched vehicles."

Faherty could have leased another car to try and throw them off his trail, Byron thought. A bad sign. It meant Faherty knew they were looking for him, and that he was up to no good. Byron would need to see if Denise Faherty could check with the credit card company to find out which rental company he'd used.

"Thought you'd want to know," Kent said.

"Thanks for the help, Jeff."

Byron ended the call and dialed Detective Stevens.

"Hey, Sarge," Mel said. "You headed back?"

"I am. Any word from Nuge?"

"Dee Dee's still in labor."

Byron hoped there wouldn't be any complications.

"What's up?" Stevens asked.

"I think we may have caught a break. I need you to check something."

It took Byron until 5:30 before he arrived back at 109. When he finally caught up with

Melissa Stevens in the CID conference room her excitement was obvious.

"Welcome back," Stevens greeted him.

"Thanks," he said as he removed his coat and laid it over the back of a chair. He took a seat across from her. "I assume you found out something?"

She nodded and handed him a file folder. "I had Denise Faherty phone the credit card company. You were right. He went to a different rental company."

Byron opened the folder and began to read. The rental agency had sent a copy of the agreement Elmer had signed as well as a description of a dark blue Taurus.

"Did we update the ATL on Faherty?" Byron asked.

"Already done," Stevens said.

"What about the Fusion he rented from Avis?"

"We still haven't found it and he hasn't turned it in yet."

"Then he could be driving either one."

"Yup. What do you want to do about Morgan Bates?"

Byron sat back and thought for a moment. They still had every reason to think that Faherty would target Bates. And if Byron had been able to locate the property that Bates was flipping, Faherty might, too.

Byron called LeRoyer at home. "I want two plainclothes details set up to watch Danica Faherty's ex-boyfriend."

"Oh sure, John. Money being so plentiful and all. Anything else, Your Highness?"

"Christ, Marty, it's only July. The fiscal year just started. Don't tell me you're out of CID money already. Let me guess, you're trying to impress Chief Lynds with your budgetary skills."

"Don't be a dick, John," LeRoyer snapped back. "Why do we need a detail to watch Bates? You think he's our guy?"

"I don't know if he is or isn't, but if we don't intervene, he may well be our next victim."

Byron proceeded to fill LeRoyer in on the latest developments regarding Elmer Faherty. He also gave him a brief overview of his visit to Boston.

"So, we still don't know if this case is connected to the Horseman murders?" LeRoyer said.

Byron knew to tread carefully with LeRoyer when it came to sharing information gleaned from Murray. The lieutenant would undoubtedly be tempted to share what he'd learned with Chief Lynds.

"Impossible to say at this point," Byron said. "There are some major differences in the cases, though. Are you gonna approve the overtime detail on Bates or not?"

"Do I have a choice?"

It was after eight o'clock by the time Byron departed from 109. He was tired and hungry. On the way home, he stopped by the Eastern Thai Restaurant at the top of Munjoy Hill on Congress Street and picked up an order of spicy pad thai to go. It was still warm by the time he arrived at his condo. He grabbed a pomegranate Polar seltzer from the fridge, the surrogate beverage to replace his alcohol addiction, and sat down to eat.

He'd just lifted the first forkful to his mouth when his cell rang. He got up and retrieved it from the counter. It was Diane.

"Lady Di."

"Whatcha doing?" she said.

"I just got home, actually. Grabbed some Thai."

"I'm shocked."

"Call me predictable."

"How did it go in Boston?"

Byron proceeded to fill her in on his visit with Murray.

"They have a Horseman task force?" she asked.

"It's not quite as glamorous as it sounds.

At the moment there are only two detectives working it."

"Do you think Dani Faherty is connected?"

"I really don't know what to think. There are as many differences in the cases as there are similarities. Any update on Dee Dee?" Byron asked before shoveling another mouthful of noodles into his mouth.

"Nothing yet. I swung by the hospital today. She's had so many false alarms they just decided it would be easier to keep her there. Nuge is driving everyone crazy."

"He wouldn't be Nuge if he wasn't." Byron took a swig of the seltzer, then changed the subject. "Have you made a decision yet? Monday's the deadline, right?"

"Nine o'clock, Monday morning. I've typed up my letter of intent, but I haven't done anything with it yet."

"What's stopping you?"

"I'm not sure," she said. "Guess I'm just worried."

"About?"

"About what happens to us if I get the job?"

It was the first time Diane had verbalized what he himself had been thinking. Was she asking him what he thought? Or was she simply thinking out loud? He didn't know

274

and he didn't dare hazard a guess.

"Cat got your tongue, John?" she asked after a moment.

"I guess I am just trying to be mindful of what I say. I didn't handle the news too well the last time, remember?"

"You're too cute."

CHAPTER 18

Sunday, 8:00 A.M.,
July 16, 2017

Byron was filled with foreboding. He couldn't shake the feeling that he was beginning to lose control of the case. It was bad enough that media had already concluded Faherty was killed by the Horseman; now it appeared that her father was hell-bent on revenge against her ex-boyfriend, who may have had nothing to do with her murder.

The previous evening LeRoyer had obtained limited approval for two plainclothes surveillance officers. Limited in the sense that the overtime details would only run from 6:00 to 11:00 P.M. for the next several evenings. One officer would sit on Bates's apartment while the other kept watch over the flip house on Longwood. It wasn't ideal, certainly not what Byron had hoped for, but it was better than nothing. Byron figured if Elmer Faherty was going to make a move on Bates, it would likely be at one of those two locations.

Saturday night had been uneventful. Elmer Faherty hadn't made an appearance at either of the Bates addresses. Despite the early hour, Byron had already checked in with Denise Faherty, but she'd had no further contact with her husband.

Byron, Nugent, and Stevens sat crammed into a booth at the back of Becky's Diner on Commercial Street. It was a working breakfast. Robbins had asked for the day off to attend some family thing. Byron, figuring Robbins would just mope about all day if he didn't get the time, had readily agreed.

"How's Dee Dee?" Stevens asked Nugent.

"Still pregnant," Nugent growled. "Christ, after having been down this road twice already you'd think I'd be used to it by now."

"I'm surprised you aren't up at the hospital with her," Byron said.

"I had to get out of there. I was going stir crazy."

Stevens jumped in. "Um, Dee Dee's the one who should be going nuts right now. She's the one doing all the work, partner."

Byron was only half listening to the banter as he ran down case scenarios in his head.

"I can see the wheels turning, Sarge," Nugent said. "What's going on up there?"

"If you were going to decapitate someone, what would you use?"

Stevens grimaced. "Not exactly breakfast conversation."

"I know, sorry," Byron said. "I'm serious, though. Would you use a reciprocating saw?"

Stevens thought for a moment. "If I had planned the killing? No, I guess I wouldn't. A rotary saw, like the one Dr. Ellis uses, would be far easier."

Nugent piped up. "If I was going to go to all the trouble to cut a victim's head off, I'd probably keep going."

"At the risk of looking too deep into that warped mind of yours, what do you mean?" Stevens asked.

"Might as well remove the arms and legs, too, right? Smaller pieces would make it easier to dispose of the body."

The three of them sat silently for a moment, contemplating what Nugent had said.

Stevens spoke up first, shoving her half-finished bacon and tomato omelet to one side. "Well, I just lost my appetite. Thanks, partner."

"He has a point, though," Byron said.

Nugent smiled proudly. "See?"

"You mean in addition to the one on top of his head?" Stevens asked.

"Hey," Nugent said, pretending to be offended.

"What are you thinking, Sarge?" Stevens asked. "The copycat angle?"

"Sort of. Except I don't think it's an actual copycat killing. My gut tells me that this was either a planned killing designed to look like the Horseman or only an afterthought designed to throw us off."

Nugent took a swig of his coffee to wash down the food in his mouth. "What do you mean an afterthought, boss?"

"What if the killing was just a spur-of-the-moment thing? Not planned. The killer snaps, kills Faherty, then needs to find a way to dispose of the body without it coming back on them."

"Someone close to Faherty," Stevens said.

"Someone we would obviously suspect," Nugent said.

"Or perhaps not so obvious," Byron said. "An unplanned murder could explain the delay that Ellis described."

"What do you mean?" Stevens asked.

"Ellis said that the body wasn't immediately dumped at the outdoor site. There was a delay. Possibly a couple of days."

Nugent piped up again. "So, the killer commits the murder then says, 'Shit, I gotta cover this up to cast suspicion on someone else.' "

"Right," Byron said. "They go to the news reports covering the Horseman, glean as much information as they can, then prepare and stage the body to match the MO."

"Or at least as much of the MO as they are aware of," Nugent said.

"Or it actually is the Horseman," Stevens said.

"We can't rule it out," Byron said.

"Aren't there still some differences between our case and the Boston cases?" Nugent said.

"There are," Byron said. "But there are also subtle differences even in their cases."

"Maybe the killer's still honing their craft," Stevens said. "Maybe they haven't settled on an MO yet."

"Maybe," Byron said. Troubling him the most, however, was the lack of a connection between the three victims. Neither Boston Homicide nor PPD's own wizard of the Net, Dustin Tran, had been able to connect the cases. Either this was a single killer toying with them, or it was distinct murderers.

Following breakfast, each of the detectives paid their bill at the front counter before heading out. As Byron was fumbling with the bills in his wallet a business card fell onto the floor. It was Deborah Stavros's, with her personal cell number on the back.

"Whatcha got there?" Nugent asked.

"Maybe nothing," Byron said. "But maybe another shot at Alex Stavros."

To Byron's surprise Deborah readily agreed to meet up, raising two possibilities: either Alex hadn't told her about his visits from Byron, nor about his lawyering up, for fear of betraying his infidelity; or he had, and Deborah was fishing for information.

Byron, who wasn't sure he could ingest any more caffeine, had already scored a table at the back of the Arabica Coffee House on the lower end of Commercial when Deborah walked in. She gave a friendly wave upon spotting him.

After ordering, they returned to the table and began to catch up.

"You don't look any different," Byron said, trying to break the ice with a compliment.

Deborah laughed. "You're still full of it, John Byron."

"So, what's it like to be part of such a famous family?" Byron asked.

"Ha. It's hardly as glamorous as it sounds. Seems like all I do is run back and forth between Maine and New York."

"But you'll be moving here eventually, right?"

"Well, that's the plan. Lina is planning to gift us her old house on Bowdoin. It needs some serious updating, though, before we can even think of moving in. I think she just wants her grandbabies within arm's reach."

Byron nodded his understanding.

"What about you?" she asked. "Married? Kids?"

He held up his ringless left hand. "Nope, on both counts. Was married, almost twenty years."

"What happened? That is, if you don't mind my asking."

"Not at all. It didn't take."

"Police work?"

"That's part of it."

"Anyone on the horizon?"

"Maybe."

"You're blushing, John."

"It's complicated."

"Usually is."

Byron figured it was as good a time as any to get to the point. "Things good with you and Alex?"

Deborah grimaced slightly as if she'd gotten a sip of bitter coffee.

"I'm sorry," Byron said. "I shouldn't pry."

"No, it's okay. I started this line of inquiry,

right?" Deborah took another sip of coffee. "Truthfully, we've had our difficulties. That's one of the reasons our children spend so much time with their grandma. I guess it shouldn't be a surprise. My career requires a lot of travel, and Alex, being a television personality, has women throwing themselves at him all the time."

"That doesn't happen to you in the legal profession?" Byron asked.

She smiled. "Hardly. It's corporate law after all. Dry as a bone. Truth is, Alex and I split for a while. Part of the reason for opening the Portland restaurant was to give us some time apart." She paused to look out the window. "Sometimes I feel like I married the wrong brother. Petri is so sweet. I can always talk to him." She turned back to face Byron. "What is it they say about the bad boys?"

"Don't ask me. I made it a point to only date good girls."

Deborah paused and gave him a look he couldn't quite read.

"So, where do you and Alex stand now?" he asked, trying to break the awkward silence.

"We've both been to counseling and decided to give it another go. For the sake of our children anyway. Who knows? Maybe it will be different when we're all living under one roof again."

Unlikely, Byron thought.

After meeting with Deborah, Byron drove directly to Hadlock Field. He parked across the street from the Sea Dogs stadium on Park Avenue and headed to the ticket window.

"Help you?" the teenaged boy said from behind the glass.

"Yeah, I need two tickets for a Sea Dogs game."

"What date?"

"Um, hang on," Byron said as he pulled up his ongoing text thread with Katherine. "August 6th is the game, I guess."

"Okay, that's a Sunday afternoon home game against the Bowie Baysox. One o'clock start."

"Perfect," Byron said.

"Where would you like to sit?"

"I don't know. Where are your best seats?"

"Probably the box seats right behind home plate. Section 105."

"Okay, I'll take two of those. Can these tickets be picked up the day of the game?"

"Sure, the Will Call window. You want your name on the envelope?"

"No, not mine. Katie — I mean — Ms.

Katherine Whitehill. And can you write happy birthday on there, too."

"Of course. They'll be waiting for her on game day."

Byron paid for the tickets then drove to 109 where another batch of reports awaited his attention.

"Must be nice to spend a leisurely Sunday morning flitting about from coffeehouse to coffeehouse, huh?" LeRoyer said as he marched into Byron's office and plopped down in one of the visitor's chairs.

"Actually, I hung out at the ballpark, too."

"That's hilarious. Where are we on this case?"

Byron's cell buzzed in his pocket. He pulled it out without checking the caller ID. "Byron," he answered.

"Sergeant Byron? It's Denise Faherty."

Byron felt the hair stand up on the back of his neck. Something in her voice sounded different. "Yes, Mrs. Faherty." He exchanged a look with LeRoyer. "Have you had any contact with Elmer?"

"That's why I'm calling. He's come back."

"To the hotel?"

"Yes, he's standing right here. Would you like to speak with him?"

"Please." Byron heard the phone being passed from one person to another.

"Faherty?" LeRoyer mouthed the word. Byron nodded.

"Sergeant Byron, Elmer Faherty here."

"Elmer, it's good to hear from you. Your wife was worried about you. She said you left without telling her where you were going."

"I did, and I'm sorry about that. I didn't mean to cause anyone trouble. I just needed some time to think, you know?"

"I do. Are you planning to stay in Portland for a while?"

"No, we have to get back. We're scheduled to fly home tomorrow evening. Dani's remains will be transported to Virginia. We'll be finalizing those details with the funeral home today."

"Well, I'm glad you're all right. I'll keep you informed of any developments in the case. Please let me know if either of you need anything from us."

"I will. We appreciate all your help, Sergeant. Again, I apologize if I made more work for you."

Byron had barely ended the call from Faherty before LeRoyer was up and out of his seat.

"We can stand down then?" LeRoyer said. "False alarm?"

"Yeah. Guess he just needed to sort

himself out."

"That's great news, John. I'm glad he came to his senses."

Byron knew what LeRoyer really meant was that he was glad there wouldn't be any more overtime expended.

"What's next?" LeRoyer asked.

Stevens appeared in the doorway to Byron's office. "Sarge, they just called up from the front desk. We have a visitor. Asked for us specifically. Told the IO that they had information pertaining to the Faherty homicide."

Byron turned back to LeRoyer. "I guess that's next."

Stevens went downstairs to fetch the walk-in while Byron set up Interview Room Two. The visitor identified himself as Graham Serfes, a forty-five-year-old stockbrokerage manager and Portland resident.

After the three of them were seated in Interview Room Two, Byron began the questioning. "So, what can we do for you, Mr. Serfes?"

"Before I speak with you, I need certain assurances," Serfes said.

Byron studied the man seated across the table. Serfes was neatly dressed in a tan suit, white dress shirt, and light blue tie. Clean shaven. His hair was parted on one side. He appeared nervous but determined.

"Mr. Serfes, I've been at this job for more than two decades," Byron began. "Normally, we like to hear what people have to say before we discuss assurances. Over the last week we've received more information, allegedly pertaining to this murder case, than you can possibly imagine. And most of what we have been given has been of little to no value. Why don't you tell us what you came here to say?"

Serfes was absently spinning the gold wedding band on his ring finger. His gaze shifted between Byron and Stevens. "It's about Craig Hopkins."

"You're shitting me," LeRoyer said. "That's the reason Hopkins wouldn't tell you what he was doing inside the lumberyard?"

"Hopkins is gay," Stevens said. "He didn't want us to find out because his lover, Graham Serfes, is married."

"Evidently, they were meeting up regularly during Hopkins's overnight shift," Byron said. "Serfes would tell his wife that he was working late or that he had to go in during the overnight to oversee some issue at the firm."

"So, Hopkins has nothing to do with

Faherty's body being dumped in the lot?" LeRoyer said.

"No," Byron said.

"But what about the underage girl thing you found, Mel? I thought a complaint had been filed against Hopkins before he went into the service?"

"I checked again with the prosecutor's office," Stevens said. "The complaint was withdrawn after it was discovered that the victim had lied about the sexual contact. The truth was that the girl found out Hopkins wasn't into her because he was gay. She was pissed about being shunned and wanted to get even."

"This case is gonna give me an ulcer," LeRoyer said as he made another finger pass through his hair, causing it to stand up worse than it had been. Byron knew the lieutenant would be full-blown Einstein if they didn't catch a break soon.

"Well, it is good news, Lieu," Stevens said.

"How do you figure that?"

"We can cross one of our suspects off the board."

"Great. What's that leave us with, an even dozen?"

It was after five and Byron had sent Stevens and Nugent home to salvage at least one weekend evening with their families. He sat alone in the CID conference room contemplating Marty LeRoyer's earlier question, "What's next?" Byron didn't know what was next. If Ellis was right and Faherty had been killed on Sunday morning, seven days had now passed since the murder and they were no closer to catching the person, or persons, responsible.

A feeling was manifesting itself within Byron, one that he was all too familiar with, an uneasy feeling that always came at a certain point in every homicide investigation. It was the lowest point. The point at which darkness nearly overtook all of their investigative effort. Doubt would come creeping in. The feeling that perhaps he would fail. That he wouldn't be able to solve the case and provide closure for the victim or their family. Humphrey had called it the deepest part of the forest.

"We're a long way from the beginning," he would say. "But nowhere near the end of this thing. This is the time when we should redouble our efforts. Push even harder to get at the truth. Go back and examine everything if you need to. Trust that nothing is as it appears."

The last part of Humphrey's advice had always stuck with Byron. He knew from experience that as soon as any investigator allowed themselves to fall into the trap of trusting that things were the way they appeared, they began to go astray. At that point, the path to the truth falls by the wayside and the investigator stumbles. The investigation falters. It was also true that if the wrong path is trod long enough, the way back can become impossible to find.

He stared at the whiteboard hanging on the wall. To anyone unfamiliar with the case it might have appeared to be nothing but a jumble of words, dates, names, times, and pictures. But to Byron, and the others working the case, it was a flowchart leading to the truth. Or at least it would eventually. The problem was that they didn't know how it flowed together yet.

As he looked at the pictures Pelligrosso had taken at the dump site he remembered smelling marijuana the other night while standing in the dark. He pulled out his cell and sent a quick text to Stevens. Hey Mel, do you know if we ever spoke with any overnight cleaners? Specifically, York Street businesses?

Several minutes later Stevens replied. Not sure. I'll check w Nuge and Bernie 2morrow.

Thanks, he texted back.

"Sarge, you got a sec?" a voice asked from

the doorway.

Byron looked up and saw Detective Gardiner, one of Sergeant Peterson's property crime detectives, standing there. Gardiner had been the detective Byron had wanted assigned in the first place, before he — before they — had gotten stuck with Bernie Robbins.

"Certainly, Luke," Byron said.

Gardiner entered the room tentatively, as if he had done something wrong, something that Byron might not approve of.

"What's up?" Byron said.

"Well, I stopped by 109 yesterday trying to get a handle on my safe burglary cases."

"I heard you had another one last week."

Gardiner frowned. "Yeah. That makes five."

"How's it going?"

"Not great. I'm hoping that they'll screw something up, maybe leave some evidence behind, but nothing yet. Anyway, yesterday I was walking around CID thinking, you know? Do you ever do that?"

Byron grinned. "*Dwelling* is the word I believe you're searching for. And yes, I do."

"Well, I brought my leftovers in here so I could eat at the table instead of my desk. Maybe watch the news."

Byron saw where this going.

"I wasn't being nosy, honest. But someone had forgotten to cover up the whiteboard and I couldn't help but see it."

Gardiner was referring to the detective's practice of covering the case intelligence board at the end of the day so that some civilian, or even another cop not associated with the investigation, wouldn't accidentally get a look at something they shouldn't see. Gruesome crime scene photos and suspect information were frequently part of the intel. They covered the board with heavy brown packing paper from a roll that stood on the floor in the corner of the room.

"It's not a big deal, Luke," Byron said, wanting to add that he should have been working the case with them anyway. He held the thought back. "Was there some reason you're telling me this?"

"I recognized one of the names on the board."

"Which?"

They both turned to look at the whiteboard. Gardiner approached the board and pointed. "This one. Stephen Holcolm."

"How do you know Holcolm?" Byron asked.

"His name came up on my burglary cases. All the homes that have been burglarized have alarm systems."

"The same company?"

"No, two different companies. But Holcolm has worked for both. He left Home Secure six months ago. Since then he's been working installations for Residential One Detection Services."

Byron knew that former security employees were routinely looked at whenever their prior employment gave them insider knowledge into the homes or businesses targeted in burglaries.

"History?" Byron asked.

"No. Both companies say he's a great employee. Hardworking, polite. Other than a couple of driving infractions, I couldn't find anything criminal. Do you mind if I ask how he's connected to this case?"

"He's a friend and business partner of the victim's ex-boyfriend. You like him for the burglaries?"

"Yes and no. He certainly would know the layout of the homes, how to bypass the alarms, and what the owners were trying to protect, but he has an alibi for each of the jobs."

Interesting coincidence that Holcolm had supplied an alibi for Bates in the Faherty case, Byron thought. He mulled it over for a moment. "Maybe he isn't doing the jobs himself. Could be he's telling someone else which houses to hit."

"I thought about that, but if he is, I have yet to figure out who."

"Who were his alibis for the burglaries?" Byron asked.

"The same guy alibied him for all the break-ins."

"Who?" Byron asked.

Gardiner pointed to another name on the board. "This guy. Morgan Bates."

Byron's eyes widened.

Byron picked up the phone and called down to the shift commander.

"Patrol, Lieutenant Price."

"LT, it's John Byron."

"Hey, John. You still burning both ends of the candle?"

"Always. Listen. Lieutenant LeRoyer said he was going to contact you guys to cancel the surveillance details. Did he follow through yet?"

"I think so, but hold on a sec. I'll check and see if the officers who were assigned have actually been called."

Byron waited impatiently. The connection between the men was already known, but the connection to both cases couldn't be a coincidence. Something was wrong here. Could Danica have found out something

295

that got her killed? Something about the safe jobs?

Price was back on the line clearing the nicotine from his lungs directly into Byron's ear. Byron held the phone away from himself, in disgust. "You still there, John?"

"Right here," Byron said, returning the handset to his ear. "What'd you find out?"

"According to Dispatch they were both called and informed that the jobs had been canceled about two o'clock."

"Okay, thanks."

Byron ended the call and looked at Gardiner. "Wanna take a ride?"

"Sure."

Byron and Detective Gardiner were outbound on Franklin Arterial crossing Cumberland when Byron's cell rang.

"Byron," he answered.

"Sarge, it's Gostkowski up in Dispatch."

"Hey, Dale. What's up?"

"You know that Elmer Faherty guy you were looking for?"

"Yeah, we found him already, thanks. He's no longer a problem."

"Well, I hate to differ, but we just received a 911 call from some guy named Holcolm. Says Elmer Faherty's holding his friend at gunpoint on Longwood."

CHAPTER 19

Sunday, 6:00 P.M.,
July 16, 2017

Byron disconnected the call and activated the Ford's emergency lights and siren.

"What is it?" Gardiner asked.

"Faherty's on Longwood. He's holding Morgan Bates at gunpoint."

"Shit," Gardiner said.

Realizing that the unmarked's base radio had been inadvertently turned down, Byron reached down and cranked the volume. He punched the speed dial on his cell for Melissa Stevens.

Forty-five minutes later Byron and Gardiner were seated inside the mobile command post next to the Special Reaction Team commander, Lt. Price. Given that it was the early out shift, 4:00 p.m. to 2:00 a.m., and half of the SRT was already working, it only took minutes to set up a containment perimeter around the Bates house on

Longwood. Regardless of the outcome inside the home, nobody would be fleeing this scene.

Price, wearing a Bluetooth headset, was engaged in a heated exchange. Byron guessed the assistant chief was on the line; Price was having a hard time getting a word in edgewise. Seated next to Price was the SRT communications specialist, Officer Damon Roberts. Roberts was awaiting instructions on how best to proceed with Faherty.

"Goddammit," Price said as he removed the headset and tossed it on the counter.

"Rumsfeld?" Byron asked.

"Yeah," Price said. "He's fucking unhinged."

And on borrowed time, Byron thought.

"You want me to call him, Lieu?" Roberts asked.

Price stared at him a moment without speaking. Byron knew the SRT commander was weighing his options. Price turned to Byron. "How well do you know this Faherty guy?"

"Not very well. I've only spoken to him a couple of times. He was pissed at me the first time and lied to me the second."

"Yeah? That's still two more times than Damon has spoken with him. You think you can talk him out of killing this Bates guy?"

Byron wasn't sure if he even wanted to. If Morgan Bates had murdered Dani Faherty, and mutilated her corpse, maybe he deserved to be put down by her father. Except Byron couldn't allow Elmer Faherty to fuck up his own life any more than it already was, and although Bates was on their radar Byron still didn't know for sure who had killed Dani.

"I'll try," Byron said at last.

A uniformed officer banged on the door to the CP. "LT, Chief Lynds just pulled up. Along with a news van."

"Great," Price said as he stood and headed for the door. "Hold that thought, John. I gotta go brief Her Excellence."

Byron caught Gardiner grinning at the comment.

After the door had closed, Roberts turned to Byron. "What's the deal between Faherty and the guy he's holding hostage?"

"The hostage is Morgan Bates," Byron said. "Faherty believes Bates is responsible for his daughter's murder."

"Is he?" Roberts asked.

"I don't know. He lawyered up before I could ask."

"Well, he's gonna need more than a lawyer now," Roberts said.

Byron's cell chimed with an incoming call. It was Stevens. He answered. "Did you find her?"

"I did," Stevens said. "Denise Faherty is in the car with me now. I'm taking her to 109."

"Okay, good. Keep an eye on her and I'll get back to you as soon as I can."

"Understood."

Byron hung up. He turned his attention to Roberts, pointing at the electronic communication board. "Show me how you work this thing."

Diane Joyner and Chief Lynds stood beside the chief's black SUV, listening as Price ran down the scenario. Both women were dressed in jeans and lightweight PD windbreakers. News crews were gathering at a designated point about a hundred feet away. Diane caught the light of a video camera in her periphery.

"Faherty's holding his daughter's ex-boyfriend, Morgan Bates, at gunpoint and threatening to shoot him," Price said.

"Where are they?" Lynds asked.

Price turned and pointed. "Next street up on the left. About a hundred yards from here."

"You have eyes on?"

"We can't see the hostage, but Faherty is pacing back and forth in front of the garage doors."

"Have we positively identified the hostage?" Diane asked.

"Not visually," Price said. "But his business partner, Stephen Holcomb, confirmed it's Bates. Said Faherty showed up at the house with a shotgun and told him to get the hell out."

"Are we talking to him?" Lynds asked.

"Faherty?" Price said. "We were about to make contact when you showed up."

"Don't let me keep you then, Lieutenant." Lynds turned to Diane. "Ready to face the enemy, Sergeant Joyner?"

Lt. Martin LeRoyer splayed the fingers of his right hand and made a nervous sweep back through his hair, his trademark tic. He'd sent Gardiner packing despite Byron's protests, citing unnecessary overtime. Byron listened on speakerphone as Roberts tried reasoning with a distraught Elmer Faherty.

Byron held his hand up next to his ear, thumb and pinky, extending a signal to Roberts that he'd like a shot at Faherty.

Roberts looked to Lt. Price for guidance. Price nodded. Roberts muted the call and handed the headset to Byron. "Have at it.

301

You can't do any worse than I've done with this guy."

Byron positioned the headset on his own head then waited for Roberts to unmute the call.

"Elmer. It's Sergeant Byron."

"Why haven't you charged this son of a bitch?" Faherty roared.

"Morgan Bates?" Byron asked, intentionally using his name in an attempt to humanize the hostage.

"Yeah, him."

"Because I don't know that he killed your daughter."

There was a momentary pause as Faherty tried to process what Byron had said. "He beat Dani before. My wife told me. You guys took a report but didn't do anything. The district attorney dropped all the charges against this piece of shit."

"The charges were dropped because Dani chose not to go forward with the case, Elmer. Dani asked the DA to dismiss the charges, saying it was all a misunderstanding."

"That's bullshit! My Dani had a split lip from where this piece of shit hit her. He abused my daughter, and now he's gone and killed her."

Byron could hear the desperation in

Faherty's voice. He scrambled to think of something that might defuse the situation. "Elmer, I'm having a hard time hearing you. You're breaking up. I'm only getting about every other word. I'm going to come talk with you in person, okay?"

LeRoyer shook his head violently. "Absolutely not, John," he whispered loudly, causing spittle to fly from his mouth.

Byron ignored the lieutenant while awaiting Faherty's response.

"No tricks?" Faherty said, breaking the silence at last. "Just you?"

"No tricks. Just me. You have my word, Elmer. I just want to talk."

"Okay." Faherty disconnected the call.

"Goddammit, John," LeRoyer yelled. "Why do you have to make everything more difficult?"

"Nothing to do with me, Marty. Things get difficult all on their own."

LeRoyer kept his glare fixed on Byron as he addressed Price. "Got any ideas on how to fix this?"

"Actually, I have a couple."

Byron adjusted the Velcro on the ballistic vest, while Lieutenant Price went through the plan again.

"You're gonna have to get him to come

outside, John," Price said. "Tell him you're having trouble hearing him clearly. Might as well use the same ruse, it worked the last time. Maybe talk low, so he has trouble, too."

"Okay," Byron said. "And if that doesn't work?"

"Tell him you need to see Bates," Roberts said. "You need to make sure he's still alive."

"A show of good faith," Byron said.

"Exactly," Price said.

LeRoyer had stepped outside to use the phone but left the trailer door open. Byron could hear the lieutenant attempting to convince Chief Lynds that this was both his idea and a good one. Based solely on LeRoyer's half of the conversation, Lynds wasn't buying it, on either count.

Roberts finished securing the remote microphone to Byron's vest then stood up. "The mic will allow us to hear everything you and Faherty say to each other, Sarge."

Byron nodded.

"Here, stick this in your ear," Price said, handing Byron a tan object the size and shape of a chocolate chip. "This is the only way that you and I will be able to communicate. When you hear me give the code green, you will need to get the fuck down on the ground. It will mean my guys are at

Faherty's back and you will officially be in the line of fire should they need to shoot him. *Capisce?*"

"Got it."

"The structure isn't finished," Price continued. "There are some window openings that may allow me to sneak a couple of officers in through the first-floor rear to come at Faherty from his weak side. You either need to get him to the front door or a window opening at the front of the house."

LeRoyer stepped back inside the trailer looking like a beaten man.

"Did she buy it?" Price asked.

"Not a single word," LeRoyer said as he glared at Byron.

Slowly, Byron approached Bates's house from the front. As he crossed the lawn, his shoes quickly became coated with dew. His dress shirt had been damp with perspiration before he'd donned the vest. Now sweat rolled freely down his back. There were no lights burning inside the home and the only lit streetlights were located too far away to provide more than a faint glow. The trees and shrubbery were nothing more than random shapes and shadows in the gloom. Byron couldn't see the snipers, but he knew they were there. He could feel their eyes on him.

"Elmer," Byron said as he scanned the darkened windows for movement. "I'm here."

"You alone?" Faherty asked.

"As I promised," Byron said, careful to keep his voice low. Faherty was nowhere in sight. "I want to talk."

"So, talk."

"I need to see that Morgan is all right."

Faherty didn't respond right away. Byron began to wonder if Faherty had heard him.

"Elmer?"

Just then Morgan Bates partially appeared in the breezeway door next to the garage. He was bleeding from the head; his hands were pulled behind his back. Byron took some satisfaction as he noticed the missing arrogance previously displayed by Bates. The young man was bloodied and bound, but he was alive.

Bates was pulled roughly from the doorway and back into the darkness.

"There," Faherty said. "You've seen him."

"I thought maybe we could discuss this face-to-face, like men," Byron said, pushing a bit to see how Faherty would react.

"Is that right? You know what I thought? I thought this piece of shit wouldn't kill my daughter."

"And you don't know that he did."

Faherty didn't reply.

Price's voice came through loud and clear on Byron's earpiece. "Jesus, John. Are you trying to get him to shoot you?"

Byron frowned at the comment. Although, he had to admit things weren't exactly going as he had hoped. He wondered if he might get further by trying to connect on a personal level with the man whose demons seemed to be on the verge of overtaking him.

"Elmer, I know what you're feeling right now," Byron said.

"Really? You ever had someone murder your baby girl?"

"No," Byron said. "No, I haven't. But I have lost people I cared for at the hands of others. I know that pain, Elmer. And I know it makes you feel like you're going crazy. You want to do something, anything to try and fix it."

"Exactly. Like ending this miserable piece of crap's life."

"But that won't fix it. You know if you do this it's not going to bring Dani back. Even if you're right and Morgan is responsible, killing him won't do anything but make it worse. Worse for you, worse for Denise.

You've both suffered a tremendous loss, something no parent should ever have to deal with. But don't make it worse, Elmer. If you end this now, nobody gets hurt. We can still fix this. Let me do my job. Let me get justice for Dani."

Byron could hear the faint sound of sobbing in the darkness.

"John, we've made entry from the rear," Roberts's voice said from the earpiece. "Everyone stand by."

Faherty and Bates stepped out into the entryway. Faherty was pressing the shotgun barrel into Bates's side.

"I could get justice for my baby right now," Faherty said.

"Unless you're wrong," Byron said. "If you're wrong, you'll have to live with that pain for the rest of your life. Can you do that? Can you do that to your wife? To Dani's memory?"

Faherty's shoulders sagged. Byron could see he was beaten.

"Put the gun down, Elmer. Let me get justice for Dani the right way. When we're sure we've got the person responsible."

Faherty lowered the gun barrel slightly. Byron heard Roberts's voice again. "Get down, John!"

As Byron dove to the ground he heard the

deafening boom of a shotgun. He only
hoped it wasn't Faherty's.

CHAPTER 20

Sunday, 9:05 P.M.,
July 16, 2017

Elmer Faherty was in custody and on his way to the Maine Medical Center to be treated for the minor injury he'd suffered after being shot with a bean bag round. Morgan Bates was also en route to the hospital after being checked out by MedCu. Byron made sure that uniformed officers were assigned to guard both men.

As Byron stood inside the Longwood garage looking down at the bloodstained concrete floor, two thoughts ran simultaneously through his mind. The first was whether the blood belonged to Danica Faherty. Could this be where she had been decapitated? There were several different types of power tools strewn about the garage, many of which were saws, several reciprocating. Byron's second thought was how lucky they were that Elmer Faherty

310

hadn't found the stain first.

"What do you want to do, Sarge?" Stevens asked.

"Let's get a search warrant started so we can get Gabe out here to process this scene. We'll work our way through the rest of the house."

"What about Holcolm?"

"Let's get him back to 109 and into an interview room. Holcolm's the one who called us out here. Maybe he can explain this."

As Stevens worked quickly to prepare the warrant, Byron pulled out a chair in CID Interview Room Two and sat down across from a very nervous looking Stephen Holcolm. Using that nervousness to his full advantage, Byron took his time wordlessly preparing for the interview by writing on a fresh yellow pad the date, time, and Holcolm's name. When he had finished, Byron pulled out his cell and checked it as if checking for messages. He gave a slight grin and nodded before sliding the phone back into his pocket and turning his full attention to Holcolm.

"Quite a night, huh?" Byron said.

"Y-yeah," Holcolm stammered. "Quite a night. I could really go for a smoke, you

311

know, to calm my nerves."

"Sorry, my bosses don't allow that inside the building. But I'll tell you what, why don't we go over a few things first, then we can take a smoke break outside? How's that sound?" Byron meant neither statement as a question, but it sounded better for the tape if anyone ever questioned the voluntariness of Holcolm's statement.

"Okay."

"So, why don't you tell me again how it went down tonight?"

"There's nothing to tell really," Holcolm said. "Me and Morg were just doing some work on the house, like always, and this guy comes barging in like he owns the place, waving a shotgun around."

"Did you know who the guy was?"

"Not at first. Not until he started yelling at Morg and talking about Dani."

"Did you know Dani?"

"Sure, I knew her. Morg and I have been friends for a long time."

"So, what did Dani's father say to you?"

"To me? He said it was between him and Morgan and that unless I wanted to get shot, I should get the fuck out of there."

"What did you do?"

"I got the fuck out of there. I'm not stupid."

Byron wasn't convinced on Holcolm's second point, but it was hard to argue with the first.

"Did you hear anything that Dani's dad said to Morgan?"

"Yeah. He accused him of murdering Dani. Said he'd hurt her before."

"And Morgan, what did he say?"

"Said he didn't do it."

"Which?"

"I don't know. Neither."

Byron took the interview slow and steady, asking many easy questions to try and acclimate Holcolm to the softballs he was tossing. He wanted what they'd found in the garage to come as a complete surprise when he finally confronted Holcolm with it.

"Listen," Holcolm said. "We been going like this for a while. How about that smoke break you promised?"

Byron lowered the pen to the table and sat back in his chair. "You're right. We should go grab some air."

Holcolm started to rise from the chair.

"Just one more thing. Where did all the blood come from on the garage floor?"

Holcolm froze halfway between standing and sitting. Byron had caught him off guard exactly as he'd hoped. Holcolm returned to a seated position. Byron watched the man's eyes dart all over the place as he searched for an answer to an unexpected question.

"Well?" Byron asked after a moment.

"We — uh, I mean, I — cut myself the other night."

"We, meaning you and Morgan cut yourselves, or just you?"

Holcolm licked his lips. "Um, just me."

"How'd you manage that?"

"We were working with some aluminum and I cut myself." Holcolm pulled up his shirt and showed Byron the bandage covering his chest.

"Did you seek medical attention?"

"Yeah, Morg drove me to a Quick Care, and they closed up the cut with superglue, or something like that."

"Which one?"

"Which Quick Care?"

"Yeah."

"Um, the one in Westbrook on 25. Out near Mast Landing Brewing."

"That's all the way out on the other side of Westbrook," Byron said, toying with him. "Why not go to one of the closer ones, in Portland?"

"I don't know. I wasn't driving."

Byron nodded his understanding. "What was the metal you were working with?"

"Um, rain gutters for the house."

Holcolm was lying and they both knew it. Byron hadn't seen any indication of gutter work being done when he'd previously poked around the property.

"So, if we went back and checked the garage, we'd find rain gutters?" Byron asked.

Holcolm said nothing.

"What happened?" LeRoyer asked as Byron walked out of the interview room and closed the door.

"He is sticking with his story," Byron said.

"Almost done with the paperwork, Sarge," Stevens called out from her desk.

"Good. And, Mel, we're gonna need to subpoena Holcolm's medical records from the Westbrook Quick Care, too."

"You think that's really his blood in the garage?" LeRoyer asked.

"We'll know soon enough. I got a feeling it wasn't gutters they were working on, though."

Byron retreated outside to 109's plaza. He realized that Stevens's work on the warrant wouldn't go any faster with him standing around bothering her. The air had cooled significantly; it was refreshing. He stood leaning against the warmth of the station's brick façade and closed his eyes for a moment.

"I guess they'll let anyone loiter about these days."

He grinned and opened his eyes. "Lady Di."

"You okay?" Diane asked.

"I'm fine."

"You're lucky. What the hell were you thinking?"

"I was thinking that I didn't want to see a desperate man destroy his life on a piece of shit like Bates."

"You think the DA will go easy on Faherty?"

"I think it all depends on Holcolm and Bates, and what we find at the house. You heading out?"

"Yup. Walk me to my car?"

"Of course."

They were mounting the steps to the rear garage when Byron broached the subject. "So?"

"So what?" she said.

"You never said. Did you throw your hat into the ring?"

"I just slid the envelope under the chief's door."

"Nothing like waiting until the last minute, Joyner."

"Right?"

"I'm happy for you," Byron said.

Diane stopped walking as she reached her car. "Are you? Really?"

"Of course."

"You're not at all worried that this will screw up what we have? You said it yourself. CID is crazy stressful. A relationship killer."

"I'm not worried at all," he said, but he was.

She studied him and he could read the doubt in her expression. "Well, who knows, I might not end up getting the job anyway."

Byron wasn't so sure about that. Given that it was Lynds who had approached Diane about submitting her name, it might well be Diane's position to lose.

She leaned in close and kissed him. "Good night, John."

It was nearly midnight by the time the search warrant had been signed and the detectives reconvened at the Bates house on Longwood. Byron was overseeing the recovery of evidence when Stevens called to Byron from inside the garage.

"Hey, Sarge. You got a sec?"

Byron departed the kitchen and entered the garage. "What's up?"

"Take a look at this," Stevens said as she

removed the tarp covering of a stack of junk in the corner.

Byron saw the remains of several peeled safes partially hidden beneath a stack of building materials and scrap. Visible on the jagged metal casing of one of the safes was a dark crimson-colored stain. Holcolm had cut himself on metal all right, but it hadn't been rain gutters.

Byron pulled out his cell and searched for Detective Gardiner's number.

"Who are you calling?" LeRoyer asked.

"The guy who should have been working on this case with us from the start. The guy you sent home."

Gardiner picked up on the third ring. The sound of sleep was still thick in his voice. "Hello."

"Luke, Sergeant Byron. Get dressed. It's time to go to work."

Byron had Stevens prepare an addendum to the original warrant, attaching information from all five safe burglaries to the affidavit. It complicated the process when cases that seemingly weren't connected suddenly became so, but it wasn't unusual for criminals to cross lines into multiple illegal activities. They woke the judge again but this time obtaining her approval was far easier, as she had already reviewed the original probable cause statement that got them into the house.

Whatever cobwebs of sleep Gardiner may have been fighting when Byron woke him were long gone as the young detective stood eyeing the recovery of all five of his burgled safes, including the one stolen the previous week.

"Probably won't be as easy to locate the missing items," Byron said.

"That's okay, Sarge. We'll figure out where everything went as soon as one of these idiots starts trying to cut a deal."

Byron planned to use that leverage to get Bates and Holcolm to back off on the charges facing Elmer Faherty.

While the others continued to work the scene, Byron and Gardiner returned to 109. Holcolm, who was still being held in Interview Room Two, had fallen asleep with his head down on the wooden table.

"Rise and shine, sleepyhead," Byron said as he and Gardiner entered the room.

"When can I go home?" a groggy Holcolm asked as he eyed Gardiner.

"Probably not as soon as you'd planned," Gardiner said.

Holcolm ignored the comment. "I don't see why you're holding me here. I didn't do anything. It's Dani's dad who should be charged. I'm a victim."

"That's only partially true," Byron said as he scrolled through the photographs on his cellphone. After finding the image he wanted, he held the phone up for Holcolm to see. "Rain gutters?"

The color drained from Holcolm's cheeks, and he hung his head in defeat. "I want to talk to an attorney."

"I don't blame you," Gardiner said.

CHAPTER 21

Byron had driven home hoping to get several hours of sleep before they were back at it. He had set the alarm for seven, then laid down thinking sleep would come easy. It hadn't. His window-mounted air-conditioner wasn't keeping pace with the prolonged period of heat in which Portland was mired. It was beginning to make those strange noises of demonic possession that a refrigerator makes just before it dies. He was wide awake and staring at the ceiling.

Not helping his cause was the fact that the bedding was wrinkled and damp with perspiration. Lying there, Byron realized there was more than the heat behind his insomnia. The close call with Elmer Faherty and the boom of the shotgun played over and over in his head. Thoughts of how differently that incident might have gone had

Elmer not trusted him, the same way he had trusted Byron to keep the gruesome details out of the press. Dani Faherty, and the gruesome way she'd met her end. They occupied a significant portion of his gray matter, ate at him.

If the blood in Morgan Bates's garage really was from Stephen Holcolm, as it appeared, and the two idiots were only using the flip house as a place to strip the safes, then neither of them were likely involved in Dani's murder. Normally it would have been a good thing to rule out one of their potential suspects, but, in this case, there remained far too many possibilities and not nearly enough cooperation from anyone. He couldn't remember a case in which the person offering up a reward was also hiding behind a lawyer. And that was exactly what Lina Stavros was doing. Like an expert chess player, she'd moved her attack dog into position to protect Alex from further scrutiny, while publicly pretending to assist the police.

Defeated, Byron threw back the sheet. Lying there wouldn't accomplish anything. He grabbed his cellphone off the nightstand, checked the time, slid into a pair of faded blue PPD gym shorts, then padded downstairs to the kitchen. The Keurig wasn't set to activate until six o'clock. He pressed the power button, overriding the timer, then sat down at the table to wait. The room was dark except for the streetlight spilling in through the front windows. The clunking and bubbling sounds emanating from the coffee maker as it warmed only served to further remind him of his failing air conditioner. He closed his eyes and tried to imagine what Dani Faherty's last moments had been like.

They already knew the blood found on the floor of the garage was not Faherty's. They still needed to match the DNA profile, but they'd already confirmed that it was the wrong blood type. It was type O, the same as Holcolm's. The patient treatment forms acquired from the Quick Care confirmed that Holcolm and Bates had come in seeking treatment for Holcolm's wound on Sunday morning when Dani most likely was killed. Holcolm, brain surgeon that he was, who hadn't even been bright enough to dispose of the burgled safes, had gouged himself badly trying to peel the latest one. Bates may have been a stalking, abusive ex-boyfriend, but Byron didn't believe he was bright enough to do what had been done, no matter how much Elmer Faherty had wanted him to be responsible.

Had Dani even known her killer or was this truly some random encounter? Simply happenstance for the perpetrator and bad luck for her? The known suspect list was still too long. What were they missing? Was there really a connection to the Horseman cases, or was this someone's attempt to throw them off? Assuming it was the Horseman, had this sick bastard sojourned to Portland for another reason? Business perhaps? Had Faherty just wandered into his path, or had the killer been hunting? Were the cops in Boston mistaken in their assumption that the Horseman was a resident of Massachusetts? What if the Horseman actually hailed from the Pine Tree State? What was the old saying about not shitting in your own backyard? Maybe he had been traveling down to Massachusetts to hunt, but now he'd screwed up, deviating from his pattern of behavior. Perhaps he'd gotten sloppy.

He opened his eyes and looked toward the counter. The Keurig's three lighted buttons were glowing. It was ready. He'd always wondered why there were three. What kind of person brews a small coffee? Not a cop, certainly.

He got up and grabbed a clean mug from the cupboard. The dark blue mug with white block lettering read: World's Best Sergeant. It had been a joke gift from Diane. Diane, who had sought his approval in returning to CID. No, that wasn't right, he thought. It hadn't been his approval she was seeking. She didn't need his approval. What she had wanted was his support, and he'd failed to give it. He could still recall the disappointment in her eyes as he'd reacted negatively to the news. Byron's first thought had been a selfish one. How would her return to CID affect him? They had made up, but he still felt guilty. He sighed deeply, loaded a Green Mountain cup into the Keurig, then slid the mug into place.

He should have been excited for her, but he hadn't been. What did that say about him? Was he too set in his ways, or was he so used to getting his own way that he couldn't see past himself? Was he still carrying that same selfishness that had cost him his marriage to Kay? His head hurt. It was much too early to be wrestling with such heavy thoughts.

The coffee maker sputtered its last drops, and Byron carried the mug back to the table and sat down. His personal life was important, his relationship with Diane even more so, but he couldn't allow the white noise of his many mistakes to overtake the focus he would need to solve this case. He owed his best to the Fahertys. He owed his best to Dani.

He went upstairs to shower.

At eight o'clock Byron descended 109's back stairwell to the third floor to see Dustin Tran.

"Hey Striped Dude," Tran said, greeting Byron as he entered the computer crimes office. "I discovered something quite interesting regarding the Faherty dump site."

"And that would be?"

"Well, you know how the newspaper has been all over this thing, and how it looks bad having a body found on a development site?"

Byron knew if he didn't rein him in, Tran would drag his find out like Tolstoy. "Any chance you could cut to the point, Dustin?"

"Yeah. Sorry. Okay, so one of the bidders on the project pulled out. The top bidder, actually. Investacorp from California. A company spokesperson cited the negative publicity now surrounding the property. I can't really blame them. I wouldn't want to build where a serial killer dumped a body."

Byron still didn't see the significance. "I don't see how that pertains to our case."

"Guess who the top remaining bidder to

purchase the property is?"

Byron fought the urge to grab Tran and shake the answer out of him. "No idea."

"Wagner Enterprises."

"As in Gene Wagner?" Byron said.

"Yup."

Byron took a moment to process the news. Why hadn't Wagner mentioned his connection to the property when they spoke before? It would be impossible not to see the conflict. If Wagner really had nothing to do with Danica Faherty's murder, why keep it from Byron?

"You said Wagner is now the top bidder for the property —"

"Actually, he's the only bidder now that Investacorp withdrew."

"Is there any way to know how much his company bid?"

"No. But I can tell you he has submitted plans to the city to build a high-end hotel and restaurant on the property. Who do we know that might be interested in that?"

Byron bypassed the front desk, ignoring the protests from both receptionists, and marched directly into Gene Wagner's office.

"What do you want me to say?" Wagner said as he glowered over his desk at Byron. "I didn't mention it because I didn't think it mattered."

"You didn't think it mattered?" Byron said, working hard to control the anger building inside him. "A woman you've got the hots for suddenly turns up murdered, her body dumped in the middle of a property that your company is trying to purchase, and you didn't think it was relevant to share that with the police?"

"Look, Dani was a beautiful young woman. I'm sure I wasn't the only person attracted to her."

"But you *were* the only one harassing her just before she went missing."

"I wasn't harassing her. I was playing around. She enjoyed the attention. You can ask Lina."

"I thought you couldn't remember what happened that night. You were over-served, remember?" Byron stood there waiting for an answer, leaving Wagner to dangle from the end of his own lie.

"You can't honestly think that I killed her," Wagner said.

"Did you?"

"Of course not. Besides, if I were dumb enough to do what you're implying, would I then turn around and leave her body for you to find on the very property I'm trying to acquire?"

"I don't know what you're capable of. I guess it would depend on how much money was at stake. Looks like you're the highest bidder now that Investacorp withdrew their offer."

"Lucky me."

Byron didn't trust Wagner one bit, but even he had to admit dumping a body that would so easily be connected to him would've been a foolhardy move, even for a lecherous old prick.

"Now, unless you're planning to trump up some charge on me, inviting me to sue your ass out of existence, I have more important things to attend to. Have a nice day, Sergeant."

Byron fumed all the way out to the parking lot. The interview hadn't gone at all the way he'd imagined. He'd gone to Wagner's office intending to catch him by surprise, knock him off his high horse maybe, but the calculating businessman didn't appear shaken in the least. Byron unlocked the Taurus and climbed inside. He slid the key into the ignition, fired up the engine, then sat staring through the windshield, allowing the air-conditioning to soothe him.

Wagner was arrogant and way too confident for Byron's liking, but that confidence seemed genuine. Stavros had described

Wagner as intoxicated and belligerent the night she removed him from the restaurant. But it's a long journey between belligerence and murder. Could he have killed Faherty during a blackout? Byron himself had managed to do some pretty messed-up things while blacked out. But this play had two acts. Even if Wagner could have pounced after waiting around for Faherty to leave the restaurant, decapitating a body was so far beyond human decency it was hard to fathom. Byron operated on facts and logic, and the facts were that nothing about this case seemed logical. Why had the killer chosen that spot to dump the body when there were so many other easier locations? The new lock had the appearance of pre-planning. Did Dani have sex with her killer before being murdered or had it been someone else entirely? There were still too many unanswered questions. Maybe they were overlooking something. Maybe the answers they were after were closer to Faherty than they thought.

Byron reached back, grabbed his seat belt, then clicked it into place. It was time to go back to the beginning.

Byron climbed the stairs to Danica Faherty's former apartment and let himself inside. The space possessed that strange emptiness that Byron had experienced so many times when investigating the life of the deceased. Once the spark of life is removed from a living space everything else goes with it. Even his footfalls seemed muted as he walked to the center of the kitchen and turned slowly, surveying the room. Nothing stood out. They'd pored over everything looking for any indication that someone new had entered Dani Faherty's life. Tran had scoured her laptop, but nothing had revealed itself. Not even the prostitution angle that Murray had believed they would find. Faherty's contacts were all known to them. Everyone had been questioned. Byron couldn't link anyone as having been with her the night she was believed to have been killed. Even Alex Stavros, her boyfriend on the down-low, had an alibi. He'd spent the weekend in Boston a hundred and twenty miles away, attending a restaurant conference. Something had happened to her after she left work early Sunday morning, but what? And who were the two people the neighbor saw dropping her car off in the driveway? Had she spent the night at someone else's place?

Byron walked over to the refrigerator, studying the post-its and photos again.

There were photos of Dani and Destiny Collins, some together, back in college, some more recent. His eyes scanned the pictures looking for anyone who stood out. Nothing. He reached out and slid one from beneath a colorful butterfly magnet. The solo shot of Faherty depicted her perched on the arm of a couch, dressed in a sexy white negligee and wearing a come-hither expression on her face. He had viewed the photo numerous times but seen nothing helpful. It was impossible to know even how long ago the picture had been taken. This time he looked past Dani, past the couch, to the wall behind her. Had he seen the wallpaper before? It was unusual. Perhaps a bit dated. He closed his eyes and scanned through the past several days trying to recall if he had seen it and if so where. After several moments he opened them again. Still nothing. He replaced the photo on the fridge and walked into the next room.

Twenty minutes later Byron was beginning to think he was wasting his time. He'd found nothing new, and truth be told was beginning to feel like a creeper. Permission or not, he was snooping around in the apartment where Dani had once lived. It seemed wrong somehow. He was headed back down the stairs to the first floor when his cell buzzed with a call from Tran.

Byron answered. "Hey, Dustin."

"Striped One, I think I might have found something."

Byron could hear the breathless excitement in his detective's voice. "Don't keep me in suspense. What is it?"

"I just got Dani Faherty's cell history from the provider, and I've been going through it."

"Good. Anything helpful?"

"Maybe. I was focusing on the history leading up to her death, then I happened to think, what if something new came in? You know, a voicemail or call after she was killed."

"And?"

"She received a bunch of voicemails over the last few days. The messages are all from the same number. The number comes back to a collision repair company out of South Portland."

Byron had been waiting for something, anything, to come from the subpoena that Tran had sent to Faherty's phone company. The cellular provider hadn't been in any rush since, in their view, there was no immediacy. Byron, who didn't share their opinion, wondered if things might have appeared more urgent had Faherty been related to one of their shareholders.

Scanning the call list on Tran's computer monitor, Byron saw three repeat calls from the same number during the previous week. He didn't recognize the number as belonging to anyone associated with the investigation. "Are these the voicemail numbers?" Byron asked Tran.

"Yes. I ran the number and it comes back to Casco Collision in South Portland. Remember I told you that Danica had been involved in an accident a few weeks back?"

Byron did recall Tran telling him that, but at the time he couldn't see how it might be relevant to their investigation. He looked at the duration of each call. The shortest was the first, lasting only seven seconds. Each subsequent call increased in length, culminating with the last which had gone on a full twenty seconds.

"Can we play the voicemails?" Byron asked.

"They're wave files," Tran said.

"Meaning?"

"It's just a type of formatting. Controls which devices you can listen to them on."

"How about your computer?"

"Oh yeah, they'll play here," Tran said proudly, missing Byron's point completely.

"May I hear them?"

"Oh sure, of course."

The first message came from a gruff-sounding male.

"Danica Faherty, this is Joe Crump at Casco Collision. I'm calling to let you know that your car has been repaired and is ready to pick up. Thanks."

"That one came in at 9:06 Monday morning, July 10th," Tran said.

The subsequent voicemails were also from Crump.

"This is the last one," Tran said. "Came in on Friday."

"Ms. Faherty, Joe Crump again, at Casco Collision. You have your car back now, and I want that loaner car returned today. We have other customers who need it. Please contact me as soon as you get this message. If I don't hear back from you, I'll be forced to contact the police. Call me."

Crump's increasing exasperation at not having his calls returned was obvious. Just as obvious was the fact that Byron had overlooked an important piece of the puzzle. Faherty had been using a loaner car that none of them knew about.

"Can you save all of that information for me?" Byron asked as he hurried from the computer lab.

335

"Consider it done," Tran hollered over his shoulder.

CHAPTER 22

Monday, 11:35 A.M.,
July 17, 2017

Byron and Stevens found a short middle-aged bantam rooster of a man pacing around outside Casco Collision on Western Avenue in South Portland. With a cigar in one hand and a cellphone in the other, the man was talking animatedly to someone at the other end of the phone.

"Are you Joseph Crump?" Byron asked as the man ended the call.

"Yup," Crump said. "Who wants to know?"

Both detectives displayed their identification.

"You guys sure take your time about shit. I filed that bad check report two friggin' weeks ago. You think I can afford to take a hit like that?"

"We're not here about a bad check, Mr.

Crump," Stevens said. "We're from Portland PD."

"Then why are you here?"

"We came to speak with you about a car you loaned to a woman named Danica Faherty," Byron said.

"Goddammit, don't you tell me she smashed up my car," Crump said. "I knew something was wrong. She's been avoiding my calls."

"She isn't avoiding you," Byron said. "She's dead."

Crump paused for a moment, making direct eye contact with Byron as if trying to make sure he was serious. "Jesus, she's not the woman who was found decapitated?"

"Actually, she is," Byron said, pleased to see he now had Crump's full attention.

Crump puffed on the cigar until the tip glowed brightly, then exhaled a long plume of smoke before speaking again. "Any idea where my Camry is?"

"That's why we came to see you," Stevens said. "The car you repaired for her was parked at her apartment in the driveway. Any idea how it got there?"

"Couple of my guys dropped it off at her place on Monday. Left the keys in it per Miss Faherty's instructions. She was supposed to return my loaner the following day." Crump took another puff from his stogie before continuing. "But I guess she couldn't, could she?"

"Can we see the paperwork on the loaner?" Byron asked.

"When do I get my car back?"

"Assuming it wasn't used in the commission of her murder, or some other crime, soon as we can find it," Stevens said.

"At a minimum we will probably want to process the vehicle, Mr. Crump," Byron added.

"I don't suppose the Toyota was equipped with GPS?" Stevens asked hopefully.

Crump let out a laugh and dropped what remained of the cigar, grinding it out beneath his boot. "Yeah, right. That's a good one."

"May we see the paperwork?" Byron asked.

"Sure, sure. Come on inside."

Byron and Stevens spoke with the two employees who had dropped Faherty's car at her apartment, confirming Crump's account. They departed the body shop armed with the description and registration of the loaner. Stevens telephoned PPD Dispatch and relayed the vehicle info along with the plate number for an attempt to locate.

"What do you think, Sarge?" Stevens asked after ending the call to Dispatch. "Maybe the killer used the loaner to transport her body to the dump site?"

"Maybe," he said. "Let's recheck there and the area around Alessandro's. It's possible that she never made it to her car after leaving work Saturday night."

"Jeez, I wonder if it was one of the cars parked near the dump site from the list we made," Stevens said.

Byron was wondering the very same thing. A quick call to Tran confirmed that it wasn't.

They spent the next twenty minutes checking every street and parking lot in the vicinity of those two locations but came up empty.

"This sure would be a whole lot easier if the loaner had GPS," Stevens said. "Any ideas?"

Byron thought about it for a moment. It was entirely possible that Faherty had been grabbed while driving the loaner, but if the killer had used the car to flee, it could be anywhere by now, even out of state. He pulled out his cell and dialed.

"Police Dispatch, Operator Thomas speaking."

"Ben, John Byron."

"Hey, Sarge. What can I do you for?"

"Can you transfer me to Parking Control at city hall?"

"Sure thing. Hang on."

Stevens grinned. "You never miss a trick, do ya?"

Byron knew if there was one department in city government that could always be counted on to get the job done, it was Parking Control.

"Parking Control, Green speaking."

Al Green, parking Nazi extraordinaire, was the one person Byron had hoped wouldn't answer the call. Green was responsible for the lion's share of the parking tickets Byron had received, a number of which remained unpaid and crammed inside the glove box of his unmarked. Byron often wondered whether Green followed him around intentionally trying to catch him, as if he received bonuses for writing up city vehicles or, more specifically, unmarked police cars.

"It's John Byron, Al. I need a favor."

"Sergeant Byron. Let me guess, you've decided to pay off your outstanding violations, and you'd like to know if we'll accept a personal check."

Byron glanced over at Stevens to see if she'd heard Green's half of the conversation. The look on her face confirmed that she had and was enjoying every moment of this.

"Actually, that's not it," Byron said, resisting the urge to say something snarky. He did need Green's help after all.

"I'm shocked," Green said. "So, what is this favor you require from *moi*?"

"I need you to check the scoff computer to see if a vehicle has been recently ticketed."

"No can do."

"What? Why not?"

"The scoff computer has been down all week. I can't check diddly. Don't worry, though, I've been writing as many tickets as I can. Just wait until that system comes back up, baby. Woo boy. I'll be towing or slapping a boot on every car I see. Maybe even yours."

The image of a uniformed and jackbooted Green suddenly popped into Byron's head. "And when might that be?"

"Who knows? Check with the computer geeks over at MIS. Maybe you'll get further with them than we have."

Byron, who'd never written a parking ticket in his life, couldn't understand how it was that the only time the system was down was when he really needed it. With no way to take the new information further, they returned to 109 to regroup.

Byron had been thinking about his late-night visit to the lumberyard where Dani Faherty's remains had been disposed of. Recalling the commercial cleaner he'd seen on a smoke break, he followed up with Detective Robbins and Stevens.

"What do you mean you didn't check?" Byron shouted at Robbins.

"You told Nuge and me to canvass the hotel because you thought someone might have seen something," Robbins said.

"I told you to take a couple of uniforms and canvass the area," Byron said. "The entire area. I never said anything about limiting the canvass to the hotel, Bernie. Did you speak to anyone at the businesses on York Street?"

"I knew they would have been closed on Tuesday night, so I didn't bother."

Byron could feel the rage building inside him. "You didn't bother? What the fuck kind of half-assed canvass is that? Did it ever occur to you that commercial cleaners work at night, Detective?"

Byron wasn't sure who he was more pissed at, Robbins for being lazy and disinterested, LeRoyer for sticking him with the second-rate detective, or himself for trusting that Robbins would follow a simple order.

Stevens stepped in, attempting to save him. "We can go out there now, Sarge. Can't we, Bernie?"

"I guess," Robbins said.

"We'll check with all of them about night-time cleaner schedules, too. Let's go." Stevens grabbed Robbins by the arm, literally dragging him from Byron's office.

Byron was pacing the conference room when LeRoyer stuck his head through the doorway. "Everything okay?"

"Ducky."

"Thought I heard some shouting from your office."

Byron took a deep breath. "Just giving Bernie a pep talk."

"How's he working out?"

"How do you think?"

"Any progress on the case?"

"Yeah, we just found out Danica was driving a different vehicle than we first thought."

"What?" LeRoyer said. "How did we miss that? I thought you said Faherty left her car at her apartment?"

Byron, still fighting the urge to say something he'd later regret, answered calmly. "Her car was at her apartment, Marty. But she wasn't driving it. She'd been using a loaner from the body shop. They returned it and parked it in her dooryard last Monday. The truck that Mrs. Micucci, the neighbor busybody, saw belonged to one of the body shop employees."

Byron watched the lieutenant open his mouth to say something else before closing it.

"Dispatch put out an ATL for the loaner and Mel and I checked several locations but so far nada. Now we wait."

"You think the killer might still be using the loaner car?" LeRoyer asked.

"Anything's possible."

Byron had considered the possibility but found it highly unlikely. The person responsible for killing Dani Faherty would have to be completely inept to hang onto something that the police would inevitably come looking for.

"Did you check with Parking Control?" LeRoyer asked.

"First call I made," Byron said. "The scoff system is down."

"That was pretty stupid," Stevens said to Robbins as they walked across the plaza toward 109's rear garage.

"Screw Byron. He's just taking it out on

me because you guys haven't solved this yet."

Stevens stopped walking as they reached the garage steps and turned to face him. "You guys? What? You're not part of the team, Bernie?"

"Riiight. More like a temporary homicide dick because you don't have enough bodies. He's got me calling up owners of parked cars, canvassing closed businesses, and looking for fucking padlocks. Screw him. I know what this shit is." Robbins walked around her and continued up the steps into the garage. "Come on, Mel. We gotta go beat the bushes again, 'cause Lord Byron's got a stick up his ass."

Stevens followed him to the car, shaking her head as she went.

As Mel was pulling out of the garage onto Newbury St. Robbins got in one last jab. "Don't worry," he said. "Everything will be different when Crosby comes to the bureau."

They spoke with three different York Street businesses before hitting pay dirt. Riley & Sons Accountants owned the building that bordered the abandoned lumberyard. They also occupied one of the suites. Being that it was lunch hour neither Riley nor his offspring were present, but the detectives lucked out with an overly cooperative office assistant named Valerie.

"Do you use a cleaning service, Valerie?" Stevens asked.

"Sure, we do," Valerie said. "In fact, all three businesses in this building use the same service. Mr. Riley makes the tenants agree to it as part of their lease."

"A friend?" Stevens asked.

"Mr. R's nephew, Clayton Newsome."

Stevens, who was recording the information in her notebook, paused long enough to glare at Bernie Robbins who couldn't have appeared more disinterested if he'd tried.

Robbins took the hint. "Don't suppose you'd have Clayton's contact information?"

Newsome lived in Portland's Parkside neighborhood in a Park Avenue flat situated directly across from Deering Oaks Park. His bright orange cleaning service van was parked in the dirt lot behind the building. Stevens stood in the entryway on the wrong side of a glass security door observing as Bernie pressed the call button for Newsome's apartment for the third time.

"Guess he's not home," Robbins said.

Stevens shoved him aside and placed her hands over both rows of call buttons and pushed down on all of them simultaneously. "Of course he's home, Bernie. He works nights."

The buzzer on the security door sounded loudly. Stevens grabbed the handle and pulled it open. She turned to Robbins. "You coming?"

Stevens knocked on the door for a full minute before a sleepy-eyed and disheveled Clayton Newsome answered the door and invited them inside.

"Yeah, I clean those offices on Tuesdays and Fridays," Newsome said.

"Clean them yourself, or one of your employees?" Stevens asked.

"I have a part-time kid that helps out sometimes, but I'm always there."

"Do you remember working Monday night, July 10th?" Stevens asked.

Newsome stared into space, appearing to work the math inside his head. "That was last Monday, right?"

"Right," Robbins said, finally bringing something to the table.

Stevens resisted the urge to shoot eye daggers at her temporary partner again. "That's right, Mr. Newsome. Last Monday night."

"I do remember that night, actually. That part-timer I mentioned called out sick." Newsome grinned at Stevens. "Hungover is more like it. Anyway, I was late getting to York Street because I was solo. I'm pretty sure it was after two o'clock before I finally made it down there."

"So, it was actually early Tuesday morning at that point?" Stevens asked for clarification.

"That's right. Tuesday the 11th."

"That business borders an abandoned property," Stevens said. "You know the one I mean?"

"Yeah. The old Forest City Lumberyard."

"Do you ever have occasion to look into that yard?"

"All the time. The York Street offices all share a common dumpster in the back lot. Whenever I take the trash out, or take a smoke break, I'm looking right at that place. Kids are always sneaking in there to hook up."

"Do you remember anything unusual happening there last Tuesday morning?" Stevens asked.

"This would be easier if I had some coffee," Newsome said as he rubbed the sleep from his eyes.

"Take your time," Stevens said.

The detectives waited while Newsome's sleep-muddled brain worked to recall the events of the previous week.

"I don't remember any — no wait! Yeah, there was something. Most of the time there are only people trespassing in there on foot. The only vehicles I ever see in there belong to the security company. Sometimes they pull in and sit with the lights off for an hour or so." Newsome grinned. "Figure the guards must be catchin' some Zs."

"And did you see the security company vehicle in the lot that night?" Robbins asked.

"No, not last Tuesday. But I did see a truck pull in. Pickup. Whoever it was couldn't have been there for more than ten minutes or so. I was dumping out the mop bucket when they pulled in through the gate. When I went back out with the trash a little while later the truck was gone."

"Can you describe the truck?" Stevens asked.

"It was dark colored, I think."

"Anything else you can remember?"

Newsome shook his head. "Nope, that's about it. That help you?"

Stevens and Robbins were headed back to 109 when he asked her to swing by the Dunkin' Donuts at Congress and Oak.

"Come on, Mel," Robbins said. "I need a fix."

You need more than that, Stevens thought.

Reluctantly she pulled to the curb and parked.

"You coming?" he asked.

"No. I'm fine. Hurry up. We've got stuff to do."

"Whatever," Robbins said as he hoisted himself out of the car. "Maybe I'll grab an éclair, too."

Stevens watched as Robbins slowly walked to the door then disappeared inside. She was fuming about his lack of effort when she heard her cellphone chime with an incoming text. Automatically, she unclipped her phone from her belt before realizing the noise hadn't come from hers. She spotted Robbins's cellphone lying in the floor well on the passenger side of the car. She unlatched her seat belt, struggled to reach over the console, and retrieved it. The text was from K Crosby.

Where are you with the Faherty case?

Stevens was speechless. *Why is he having Robbins keep him up to speed on our case?* she thought. Another message appeared below the first.

I want an update. Call me.

She looked up and saw Robbins heading

351

back toward the car. Quickly she tossed the phone back onto the floor. Robbins opened the door and slid inside.

"I got two éclairs," Robbins said, pulling one of the bags and waving it around. "You sure you don't want one?"

"I'm good," she said coldly. "By the way, I think you dropped your phone. It's been making noises ever since you left."

"Shit. I wondered where it was."

She watched as Robbins retrieved it from the floor and checked the display.

"Anything important?" she asked.

"Nope. All good."

Stevens and Robbins returned to 109. Robbins said he had to return some calls, but Stevens knew he was just trying to avoid Byron and probably had to get back to Crosby. She briefed Byron on the cleaner's account. The entire time she was talking she was also struggling with whether to tell him what had happened. She was no fan of Robbins, or Crosby for that matter, but she didn't want to be a rat.

"The timeline and the vehicle description, what little there was, matches up with what Winn told us," Byron said.

"What I was thinking," Stevens said. "Probably discarded Faherty's body then got rid of the head and clothes immediately afterwards."

"Thanks for handling that, Mel."

She stood there awkwardly, still trying to decide what to do.

"Was there anything else?" he asked.

CHAPTER 23

Monday, 6:35 P.M.,
July 17, 2017

Byron sat alone in what passed for the kitchen/dining room of his North Deering condo. He was reviewing his case notes as well as copies of Gabe Pelligrosso's most recent evidentiary supplements. He was growing frustrated that they hadn't yet located Faherty's loaner car, but he didn't believe in wasting time. Reviewing the case for things they might've overlooked was never a waste. Byron had just finished reading over his notes from their visit to the body shop, with the charming Mr. Crump, when his cell began to dance across the table. The number displayed was from 109.

"Byron," he answered.

"Hey, handsome," a sultry female voice said.

Byron recognized Mary O'Connell's voice instantly. She had been dispatching for the

Portland Police Department going on forty years, providing a lifeline of sorts to every boot and suit who ever kept watch over the Port City. A constant and calming presence at the other end of the radio, she'd let every cop know that someone had their back and that help was only a click away. And despite the massive technological advances that had come to the profession, the true measure of a great dispatcher still came down to one thing. Compassion.

O'Connell had taken Byron under her wing when he was nothing more than a wet-behind-the-ear rookie. She had known and dispatched for Byron's father, Reece, when he had still been on the job. Reece was gone, along with many others that Byron had depended upon, but Mary remained.

"Hey, Mare," Byron said. "What's shaking?"

"Me, if I was about twenty — okay — thirty years younger."

Byron laughed. She could always do that to him. No matter how tightly wound Byron was, Mary found a way through his armor, usually with something racy and inappropriate.

"Hope I'm not interrupting anything," she said.

"Not at all, I'm just catching up on some

homework. What's up?"

"I just got a call from Amy Connolly, the officer working the IO desk. It might be BS, but she says a guy just walked in claiming to be the Horseman."

"Seriously?"

"Yup. Says he wants to turn himself in."

Byron grabbed his gun and badge and drove directly to 109. What had promised to be his first night off in nearly a week, maybe even offering some badly needed rest, had been canceled. Despite the feeling that he was being sent on a fool's errand, Byron decided to summon the team. He made calls to Stevens, Nugent, and Tran. Predictably, his last call, to Robbins, went directly to voicemail.

Byron parked in the rear garage and entered through the first-floor rear entrance hoping to get a look at the self-proclaimed killer before speaking with him. He approached the information desk, where Officer Amy Connolly was speaking to patrol Sergeant Andy Pepin, and looked out through the safety glass. The lobby was empty.

"Where is he?" Byron said.

"Right behind you, Sarge," Connolly said.

"We stashed him in the first-floor interview room."

Sergeant Pepin spoke up. "We searched him for weapons already, John. Didn't want to take a chance with other people coming through the lobby."

"Good call. He give you a name?"

"Yeah, here's his license," Connolly said as she handed it to him.

The driver's license, issued by the State of Maine Bureau of Motor Vehicles, identified the man as Kenneth Harper, 43 years of age. The address listed was Acadia Street in Portland, a neighborhood in East Deering with which Byron was infinitely familiar.

"What did he say, exactly?" Byron asked Connolly.

"He just walked in and said he needed to talk with a detective. I asked why he couldn't talk to me and he smiled and said, 'Because, I'm the Horseman.' I put him in the interview room, so he wouldn't just walk out the door, but it was more than that."

"What do you mean?"

"He was giving me the creeps, just pacing around the lobby and staring at me."

"Why I came in," Pepin said. He cocked a thumb toward the interview room. "Whatever else he is, that is one strange dude."

Byron had Connolly and Pepin keep an eye on Harper while he prepared an interview room in CID. Additionally, he wanted Stevens present before they spoke. He knew the odds that this was the guy everyone was looking for were long, but stranger things had happened. And Byron had learned long ago the damage that assumptions can inflict on a case.

As the other detectives arrived, Byron assigned each a task. Nugent would monitor from the conference room while he and Stevens conducted the interview. He handed Tran the information contained on Harper's license and told him to start digging.

"Use the computer in the conference room, Dustin," Byron said. "I want you to check out every bit of information he provides us."

"You think he's the real deal, Sarge?" Tran asked.

"We'll know soon enough."

Byron's initial assessment of Kenneth Harper was that he was average. Average height, average weight, average-length dark hair, and brown eyes. But following a more critical appraisal, Byron noticed some odd things about him. Harper's hands were larger than normal for a person his size, like a boxer. And there was something strange in his gait as he walked, as if his body needed a realignment. He was courteous, but again slightly off somehow. There was something wrong, but Byron couldn't quite place it.

Harper sat across from Byron and Stevens with his large hands folded atop the table. His expression remained neutral. If he was nervous, he showed no signs of it.

Byron began the interview by making introductions, trying to keep things civil. If Harper did turn out to be Faherty's killer, Byron didn't want to provide any ammunition to the defense.

"So, Mr. Harper," Byron said. "I'm told—"

"Call me Kenny."

Byron hesitated a beat before continuing. Was Harper just being polite or was he attempting to assert himself and control the direction of the interview?

"Okay, Kenny," Byron continued. "I'm told that you've come here to confess to killing someone. Is that correct?"

Harper grinned. "Not just someone, Sergeant. I murdered Danica Faherty."

"If that's true, Kenny, I'm required to read

you your rights."

Harper wasn't technically in custody, having turned up at the station of his own volition, to provide a confession, but Byron and Stevens had decided to err on the side of caution. If Harper could prove his involvement in any of the murders, he would not be walking out of 109.

"I understand," Harper said.

Byron proceeded to read the Miranda warning from a printed piece of paper, line by line, obtaining a verbal acknowledgement from Harper after each section. When he had finished reading, Byron had Harper sign and date the form at the bottom, affirming that he understood his rights.

With the subtle efficiency of a new car dealer, Stevens removed the form from the table, sliding it into a file folder. Out of sight, out of mind.

"What made you come here today, Kenny?" Byron asked.

Nugent was sitting across the room from Dustin Tran, intently watching the monitor, when Lieutenant LeRoyer practically skidded into the CID conference room. The move reminded Nugent of a certain cartoon coyote.

"Hey, Lieu," Nugent said matter-of-factly.

"What's he saying about the murders?" LeRoyer asked breathlessly.

"He's only talking about Faherty at this point," Nugent said.

Tran jumped in. "So far he hasn't given them anything that wasn't in the papers or on televised news reports."

"No meat and potatoes," Nugent added.

"So, he's nuts?" LeRoyer said, sounding disappointed.

"My guess," Nugent said.

"Tell us again how you happened to pick Dani," Byron said. "Was she an acquaintance of yours?"

"No, I didn't know her," Harper said. "But she called to me, like the others."

Byron resisted the urge to roll his eyes in disbelief. He knew without turning to look at Stevens that she was having the exact same reaction.

"Called to you?" Byron said. "How exactly?"

"Danica connected with me. Spiritually."

"And where did you take her from?" Byron said, wishing now that he hadn't brought the rest of the team in on what appeared to be a wild goose chase.

"I followed her from the restaurant back to her West End apartment."

"When was this?"

"Saturday night, after she left work. Well, actually it was Sunday morning at that point."

"And how exactly did you abduct her, Kenny?" Stevens asked.

"My apologies, Sergeant. I can't remember every detail. I told you, I lose time."

"How often does that happen?" Byron said.

"Often enough."

"Rather convenient, wouldn't you say?"

"Not for me."

Byron stared at Harper without speaking. Normally suspects grew more nervous the longer the silence went on. Some people talked just to fill the emptiness. Harper didn't seem bothered in the least.

"What *can* you tell us?" Stevens asked.

"What would you like to know?"

"So?" LeRoyer asked as soon as Byron stepped out of the interview room. "What do you think?"

"I think I want to know more about this guy," Byron said.

"Yeah, but do you think he's really the Horseman?"

Byron walked past the lieutenant and into the conference room where Tran and

Nugent were still watching Stevens and Harper on the monitor.

"God, I can't tell you how much I hate that nickname," Byron said.

"Hey, the news media gave him that moniker, not me," LeRoyer said.

"Not a big fan of them either."

"This guy's a piece of work, Sarge," Nugent said.

"Find anything, Dustin?" Byron asked.

"He has provided a number of details," Tran said.

"Cherry-picked is more like it," Nugent said.

"But has he given us anything he couldn't have plucked from the headlines?" Byron asked.

Tran checked his notes. "Um, he did know about Dani's apartment in the West End."

"I'm pretty sure I remember seeing TV news coverage shot in front of her building," Nugent said. "Besides, wouldn't have been too hard to figure out."

Byron nodded in agreement.

"What do you want to do with him, boss?" Nugent asked.

Byron looked up at the monitor. "Let's keep Mel going at him for a bit. Dustin, I want you to find out everything you can about this guy. Give me the works. Triple I,

NCIC, in-house, BMV history, friends, relatives, everything."

"You got it, Inspector."

Byron retreated to his office to make a call to Murray.

"Solve my case yet, Johnny?" he asked, skipping his normal greeting.

"Why I'm calling. We just had a walk-in claiming to be the Horseman."

"No shit? Nut bag?"

"I'm leaning that way, but it's a tough tell. He's giving us some details then claiming selective amnesia for the rest."

"Typical. What information has he referenced about our cases?"

"He hasn't yet. Our primary focus has been Dani Faherty. Anything you can suggest that he'd have to admit knowing about your victims?" Byron waited while Murray thought about it.

After a moment Murray said, "Ask him why he always targets women?"

Byron returned to the interview room, taking the seat next to Stevens. He waited until Mel had finished her line of questioning before he jumped in.

"Why only women?" Byron asked.

Harper turned toward Byron; the corners of his mouth unfurled into a disturbing grin.

"Who says they were all women?"

Byron and Stevens joined the others in the interview room, taking a brief and badly needed respite from the interview.

"That guy is creeping me the fuck out," Stevens said.

"You think he could be our guy?" LeRoyer asked Byron.

"Can't tell," Byron said as he stared up at the monitor, wondering how many times the lieutenant was going to ask that same question. It was obvious that they weren't dealing with the typical attention-seeker in Harper. "He's either the killer or one hell of a con man."

Tran walked back into the conference room holding a stack of papers. "Want to hear what I've got, boss?"

"Go with it."

"Looks like Mr. Harper moved here from Henderson, Nevada in 2014. No criminal history. One speeding conviction, last year. Works for a telemarketing company called Capital Group."

"Yeah, he said he works from home," Stevens said.

"About right," Nugent said. "Can you imagine that freak sitting next to you in a cubicle?"

"I sit next to *you*," Stevens said.

"Are we gonna hold him?" LeRoyer asked, ignoring the banter.

"We've got nothing to hold him on," Byron said. "Other than his word that he did it." Byron realized one other thing as well. If Harper wasn't Faherty's killer, he was setting up a great alternative suspect for the defense team when they finally charged someone for the crime. Byron turned to Stevens. "What about tolls? If he really is the Horseman, he would have to have traveled back and forth to Massachusetts. He must have an EZ Pass transponder, right?"

"Doesn't everyone?" LeRoyer asked.

Stevens shook her head. "I asked. He pays cash."

"Of course he does," Nugent said. "Don't all serial killers? Look, now he's smiling up at the camera. Jesus, this guy's a piece of work."

"What are we gonna do, John?" LeRoyer asked.

"I've got an idea."

Stevens held the elevator door open, while Byron handed the man's license back to him. Harper hesitated a moment before accepting the ID.

"Thank you for coming in, Kenny," Byron said. "We really appreciate your cooperation. Don't we, Detective Stevens?"

"We sure do."

The confusion on Harper's face was exactly what Byron had hoped to see.

"I don't understand, Sergeant Byron," Harper said. "Aren't you worried that I'll kill again?"

"Call me crazy," Byron said. "But I'm willing to take that chance. Besides, I'm going to put my people on you."

"Surveillance?"

"Yes. Of course, we can't always cover you, obviously. But I promise we will be there watching to make sure you stay on the straight and narrow. You'll just never know when or where. Detective Nugent will walk you out."

Harper turned to look individually at Stevens and Nugent then back to Byron. "You're sure this is a good idea, Sergeant Byron?"

"Trust me."

"You sure you know what you're doing, John?" LeRoyer asked after the elevator had descended with Harper and Nugent aboard.

"Yup," Byron said. "I checked with the police department in Henderson, Nevada.

They were all very familiar with Kenneth Harper. Dustin was right, he has no criminal history, but he's been pulling this crap for years and no charges have ever been filed. According to the detective I spoke with, when Harper lived in their jurisdiction, he'd stop by the PD every six months or so to confess to a crime he didn't commit. He studies the news until he finds a case that interests him and then tries to convince the cops that he was responsible."

"Jesus," LeRoyer said. "How screwed up is that? And they've no reason to believe he's ever hurt anyone?"

"None. There's a clinical name for what he has but I can't pronounce it."

"Bat shit," Stevens said.

"Close enough," Byron said.

CHAPTER 24

Tuesday, 9:05 A.M.,
July 18, 2017
Diane was seated in her office returning phone calls, while simultaneously wondering what questions she was likely to face during the upcoming CID sergeant's interview, when Melissa Stevens stuck her head through the doorway.

"You busy?"

"Hey, Mel. Never too busy for you."

Stevens entered the room and closed the door to the office, piquing Diane's curiosity.

"This can't be good," Diane said.

"I was kinda hoping for some advice," Stevens said.

"About?"

Stevens sighed. "This isn't about me, okay? It's a friend of mine who has this problem."

"Oh, a friend. Okay. Anyone I know?"

"Very unlikely."

369

"Good. I was afraid there might be a conflict. So, what is your friend's problem?"

"Well, they work in a profession where internal secrecy is important."

"Keeping things close to the vest," Diane said.

"Exactly. Except lately there have been some pretty damning leaks coming from within the department where my friend works."

"Okay. I think I'm following. And did your friend by chance find out where these leaks were coming from?"

"They're pretty sure they know."

"Has your friend reported these findings to anyone?"

"Not yet," Stevens said.

"Why not?"

"Because they don't want to be that employee. You know. The rat."

Diane pursed her lips as she contemplated her answer. "Well, it's tough to know precisely what your friend should do, Mel, since I don't have the particulars. I guess it comes down to doing what's right. Has your friend given any thought to what people will think of them if it happens again, and they find out that your friend could have prevented it?"

Stevens said nothing.

370

■ ■ ■ ■

Feeling a bit stir crazy while awaiting news on Faherty's loaner car, Byron decided to take a ride around the peninsula to clear his head. He had just settled into the driver's seat of his unmarked when his cell buzzed. He answered the call. "Byron."

"Sergeant, it's Shirley. I tried to catch you before you left the building."

"What's up?"

"There's a woman here in CID asking for you. She's with an attorney."

"Who is she?"

"Janet DiPhillipo. The attorney is a smooth operator, or at least he thinks he is, named Cohen. Jeffrey Cohen."

Byron scanned his memory bank but came up empty. Neither name meant anything.

"I've stuck them in the waiting room," Shirley said.

"Either of them say what it's about?"

"Alex Stavros."

Byron returned to CID. Following brief introductions, he led Ms. DiPhillipo and Attorney Cohen to an interview room.

After they were seated with the door closed, Cohen spoke up. "I'd like to start by establishing the ground rules, Detective Sergeant Byron."

Byron bristled slightly. "The rules are, you and your client came to see me voluntarily. She says whatever it is that's on her mind and I'll listen. How about we start with that?"

Cohen countered, "I think we'd like some assurances that my client isn't in any legal jeopardy *if* she speaks with you."

"Since I have no way of knowing what your client intends to say, I can't make such a promise. But I'm confident that you're more than capable of applying the brakes should we tread into any sticky areas."

"Fair enough." Cohen turned to his client and nodded. "Go ahead, Janet."

DiPhillipo drew a deep breath then spoke calmly. "Alex Stavros wasn't in Boston the entire weekend of the Northeast Restaurant Association Conference."

"How do you know that?" Byron asked.

"Because I attended the same conference."

Byron studied DiPhillipo's demeanor. She seemed confident in what she was saying. There was no bitterness in her tone, as would be expected if she was trying to even some score with Stavros.

"Alex Stavros has an alibi for the night in

question," Byron said. "Specifically, Saturday night July 8th into Sunday morning the 9th. Another gentleman named George Martin has said that he was with Alex most of the night and again first thing in the morning. If what you are saying is true, both of them would have had to be lying."

"They are," DiPhillipo said.

"And what makes you so sure that both men are lying, Ms. DiPhillipo?"

"Because I spent the entire night of the 8th with George Martin, and I think I'd remember if Alex Stavros had been in bed with us."

Byron continued, glancing over at Cohen as he did so. "We've also pulled the EZ Pass records for Mr. Stavros's vehicle. The toll records show that he drove to Boston on Saturday morning and didn't return to Maine until late Sunday afternoon. How do you account for that?"

DiPhillipo spoke up again. "George told me he lent him his car to sneak up to Portland so Alex's wife wouldn't find out, on the off-chance she ever checked the toll records."

"Why would he do that, Ms. DiPhillipo?" Byron asked.

"Alex was planning a rendezvous with another woman."

■ ■ ■ ■

Byron left DiPhillipo and Cohen in the interview room to write out her statement, while he met up with Nugent and Stevens in the interview room.

"Want us to go out and pick up Alex?" Nugent asked. "It will be my pleasure to drag that lying sack of shit in here."

"Let's hold off on that for now," Byron said. He wholeheartedly agreed with his detective, but they were still missing large pieces of the investigation. He wanted to have all his ducks in a row before they were permanently shut down by the high-priced Stavros family attorney, Courtney Levine.

"Sarge is right, Nuge," Stevens said. "We still need the loaner and a legal way inside Lina's former home."

"Can you keep an eye on them?" Byron asked Stevens. "I gotta go make a call."

"Sure thing," Stevens said.

Byron retreated to the solitude of his office to telephone Murray.

"Johnny," Murray said, answering his cell on the first ring. "You solve my cases yet?"

"No, but I may be closer to solving mine. Remember that alibi for Alex Stavros I had you track down?"

"Yeah, the restaurant conference guy. What's his name? George Martin, right?"

"That's him. Think you could do me a favor?"

"Name it."

"Pick his ass up and threaten him with a charge of obstructing a murder investigation."

"I can do that. Let me guess, the alibi was bullshit."

"Looks that way. I've got a woman here named Janet DiPhillipo who says she spent all of Saturday night with George Martin. She's also saying that George lent Alex his car to sneak up to Portland on the night Danica Faherty was killed."

"You want hotel surveillance video pulled, too? They might have some coverage of the parking garage."

"Yeah. And Martin's Speed Pass records, if he has one. Can you get those?"

"Who do you think you're talking to? I'm on the HTF task force, baby."

"Thanks, Pete."

Byron was walking back to the interview room when he nearly collided with a very excited Melissa Stevens.

"Parking Control just called over from city hall," Stevens said. "They found Dani's loaner."

■ ■ ■ ■

Twenty minutes later, after finishing with DiPhillipo and Cohen, Byron and Stevens stood beside Faherty's abandoned loaner parked on Vaughn Street in Portland's West End. They were awaiting the arrival of Gabriel Pelligrosso to process the exterior of the car for evidence and oversee its towing to the basement of 109 where the interior would also be examined. Several overnight parking citations had been shoved beneath the Toyota's wiper blades. The tag at the bottom of the stack had been written nearly a week ago on Tuesday, July 11th. The most recent citation bore yesterday's date, July 17th.

The beige Camry was locked up tight. A visual inspection revealed nothing suspicious on the exterior. Likewise, the passenger compartment appeared unremarkable. No blood on the seats or windows. No signs of a struggle. In short, the car appeared to have been left at the curb exactly as Danica Faherty might have parked it.

"Why here?" Stevens said.

Why indeed? Byron thought as he scanned the area. There was something about this neighborhood that had recently come up in conversation, but what was it?

"Lina said that Alex and his family have been staying with her at the 'new' place on Prouts Neck," Byron said. "She told me that her previous home would eventually be remodeled and gifted to Alex. Her West End home."

"It's gotta be near here," Stevens said just as Pelligrosso pulled up in the black-and-white evidence van.

"One way to find out," Byron said as he retrieved his phone and hit the speed dial.

"Computer Crimes, Detective Tran speaking."

"Dustin, I need you to check the city tax assessor's site for me."

The Stavros mansion was indeed situated in the neighborhood. In fact, according to Tran it was right around the corner, less than four hundred feet from where Faherty's car was parked. Helpful to their cause, but it wouldn't get them the search warrant they needed.

After Pelligrosso had finished the on-site work and departed along with the flatbed wrecker to 109, Byron and Stevens split up, taking opposite sides of the street in hopes that knocking on some doors would lead them to someone who had seen Faherty with Alex, or even entering the Stavros house.

Byron began with the homes on either side of Angelina Stavros's former residence. The home on the right yielded nothing as it appeared that no one was at home. He slid his card under the brass knocker on the front door after jotting his cell number on the back of the card. Not to be deterred, he walked to the home on the left. Standing on the corner of Bowdoin and Vaughn was a two-story Queen Anne styled Victorian, replete with stone lions guarding the driveway entrance. Diane had been pestering him about getting a pet. He wondered how she'd feel about a stone lion.

A maroon Audi was parked in front of a detached brick one car garage at the far end of the drive. The garage door stood open. As Byron walked up the driveway, he noticed a rake leaning up against the house next to a wheelbarrow. He was wondering whether the homeowner did their own landscaping or hired out, when a voice called out.

"May I help you?"

Standing inside the screen entry door to the house stood a middle-aged woman wearing jeans, an untucked white short-sleeved blouse, and gardening gloves. The caution in her voice was unmistakable. Byron reached into the pocket of his suit coat and removed his ID case.

"Sorry to bother you, ma'am. My name is John Byron. I'm a detective sergeant with the police department. I wonder if you might be able to answer a few questions." He waited a moment while she eyed his badge.

She unlatched the door and stepped outside to greet him. "You're not bothering me at all. Giving me a longer break from yard work is all. Portland police?"

"That's right," he said, sliding the ID case back into his pocket.

"Thought you might have been selling bibles or something."

"In my line of work, we never promise redemption."

She chuckled. "What can I do for you, Sergeant Byron?"

"Do you live here?"

"I'm the owner, yes."

"Are you familiar with the people who own the house next door?" He pointed at the home in question.

"No one is living there now, but yes I am aware that the owner is the actress Angelina Stavros."

"Do you know her personally? Are you

friendly with her?"

"No. Just a neighbor."

"Have you seen her there recently?"

"No. No one has been living there for well over a year, I guess."

"Ever see anyone else at the house? Coming or going?"

She shook her head. "No."

Byron detected the slightest pause before she answered. It was barely noticeable, and most people probably wouldn't have picked up on it, but he did. A slight change in her timing. He kept eye contact for an extra beat, looking to see if she'd break away first, but she didn't.

"Is there anyone else living with you who may have seen someone coming or going from the Stavros home? Your husband maybe?"

"I'm divorced," she said, her voice providing a little chill to the otherwise warm afternoon. "And I live here alone."

It was obvious whatever goodwill he had fostered with her had just eroded. "Well, thank you for your time, Miss?"

"Vaughn. Erica Vaughn. Sorry I couldn't be of any help."

He handed her a business card. "If you think of anything that might help, I'd appreciate a call."

Vaughn accepted the card, but Byron wasn't confident he'd hear from her again.

He returned to the unmarked where Stevens was awaiting him.

"How'd you make out?" Stevens asked.

"Zip. No one home at the first, played dumb at the second," Byron said. "You?"

"O-fer. Left cards at the three homes across the street."

"How much money do you think you inherit when you live on a street named after your ancestors?" Byron asked as they climbed into the Ford.

"Don't know. Why?"

" 'Cause I just met a Vaughn."

Byron and Stevens returned to Casco Collision to notify Joe Crump that they had recovered his loaner. Byron informed him that they would need to process and search the interior of the car and asked that he sign a consent to search. Crump told them he'd sign anything if it meant he could have his car back sooner.

Back at 109 Byron headed down to the basement to check on Pelligrosso's progress.

"How goes it, Gabe?" Byron asked.

"Slow. I'm not hopeful that we'll find anything useful."

Byron wasn't hopeful either. The way the

car had been left made it look as though Dani may have parked it there herself, in which case it might not have played a role in either her murder or the disposal of her body. If Janet DiPhillipo was correct, and Alex had snuck up to Maine to rendezvous with a woman, and that woman had been Faherty, then it stood to reason that Dani herself would have driven to the West End directly after leaving the restaurant on Sunday morning to meet Alex. And if she had, then it was very likely that Dani hadn't left Lina's house in the same condition as when she arrived.

"Keep at it, Gabe," Byron said. "Call me if you find anything."

Byron was holed up in his office trying to make a dent in his supplemental case reporting when Diane popped in.

"Hey, sailor," she said.

"Lady Di."

"This a bad time?"

"Not at all." Byron saved his work and exited out of the program. "I'm going cross-eyed anyway."

"Where is the rest of your team?"

"Sent them all home."

"Any progress?"

"Maybe, if I knew which direction we

were supposed to be looking. We did recover Dani's loaner car today."

"I heard. Around the corner from Lina Stavros's old house?"

"Right around the corner."

"What do you think?"

"I think I'd like to get a look inside her house."

Diane sat down in one of the visitor chairs, stretched her legs out in front of her, and let out a long sigh.

"Thinking about tomorrow morning's interview, huh?" he asked.

"What else?"

"Relax. You'll do fine. Just be yourself."

"Easy for you to say. You've already got this cushy office job."

He laughed. "Remember what I always say."

"Be careful what I wish for?"

"Exactly. One day all of this will be yours."

"And where will you be?"

He shrugged. "Wherever dinosaurs go when they're put out to pasture."

"You're hardly a dinosaur, John. Although, I guess you are officially another year older. It is July 18th."

"Yup. It is."

"Did you really think you could sneak your birthday by me?"

"Thought I had."

"Nope. Come on. You need a break. And I need food. I'm taking you out to a birthday dinner at the Pizza Villa."

Byron looked around at the mountain of work that still needed to be done. A case that was now a week old and in dire need of a break. "Sounds perfect."

CHAPTER 25

Portland's West End has a long and storied past. Bordered by Congress, Commercial, and the Western Promenade, the western tip of the downtown peninsula is brimming with nineteenth century mansions erected in the wake of the Great Fire of 1866. Tree-lined streets named after affluent families the likes of Vaughn, Danforth, and Saint John provide a glimpse into the history of the city's former residents.

Byron and Stevens stood on the Vaughn Street sidewalk at the precise location where Faherty's loaner had been parked the previous day. They were still wrestling with how to make a connection between the car and the house owned by Angelina Stavros. Recovering the car in the same neighborhood, while a promising lead, would not get them a search warrant. The fact that

Faherty's friends and family weren't aware of any acquaintances in the neighborhood that she may have been visiting didn't mean there weren't any, it only meant they weren't known.

"Dani's car has likely been here since she went missing," Stevens said. "I mean look at the parking tickets. Wouldn't that give us reason to check the Stavros house?"

"Likely won't do it, Mel," Byron said. "And it's the former house. According to Lina, nobody has lived there since she moved into the home on Prouts Neck over a year ago. We need more."

"This sucks."

Byron couldn't disagree.

"As soon as we get Alex's alibi nullified by your cousin, we go at Stavros again, right?" Stevens said.

"Then what? If Alex did hook up with Dani Sunday morning, and we can get him to admit that he came up here, he'll just say they had sex and that Dani was fine when he left. If he did kill her, and it happened in Angelina's old house, he's certainly not going to let us search it. Besides, according to Dustin the house is still in his mother's name. Alex couldn't give us consent even if he wanted to."

"I'm sure he has access."

"Probably," Byron said. "But he'd have no standing until they officially transfer owner-ship."

"You're right," Stevens said, her exaspera-tion clearly audible.

"Anyway, Alex could simply tell us that they hooked up in a car or somewhere else entirely. We need irrefutable evidence that puts the two of them inside that house on Sunday morning, the day she was killed."

Byron was following the progress of a middle-aged male dog walker on the side-walk on the opposite side of the street. The man wore thick framed glasses, an obnox-iously loud lime green T-shirt, untucked to hide his middle-aged girth, and what the kids called "skinny jeans." Byron couldn't help but be reminded of Elton John. Elton was checking them out while doing a poor job of pretending he wasn't.

"You see what I see, Mel?" Byron asked.

"Yup. Crocodile Rock is hard to miss."

Byron grinned at the reference.

"Think he's just nosy?" Stevens asked.

"Of course he is. And I'm guessing it isn't an anomaly. This is his second pass by here. Wanna bet he knows something?"

The detectives crossed the road then quickened pace in order to catch up to the man.

"Excuse me, sir," Byron said. "Do you have a minute?"

The rock star look-alike turned to face them. "Who, me?"

The dog, looking more like a wharf rat with blond hair, spun around and began yapping furiously.

"Millie, no!" Elton shouted.

Millie's barking transformed instead into a throaty growl. She retreated a couple of paces as if she were planning to flee and the barking had been nothing more than pretense.

"What's the matter, girl?" Stevens asked.

The growling stopped abruptly, and Millie focused her attention solely on Stevens. Millie's tail began to wag as if someone had wound her up. Cautiously the dog approached the detective.

Stevens knelt and extended her hand. "Who's a good girl?"

It was obvious that Millie thought she was, as she placed both front paws on Stevens's knee and began licking her outstretched hand.

"I think she likes you," Elton said.

"Well, I am the police department's version of the dog whisperer," Stevens said.

"Police department? You guys cops?"

"Detectives," Byron said. "Detective

Sergeant Byron and this is Detective Stevens. And you are?"

"Walter. Cleary."

Byron stepped forward to shake the hand that Cleary was offering, and Millie resumed barking at Byron.

"Millie, no," Cleary repeated.

Byron took a step back and Millie returned to the task of hand washing.

"Detectives, huh?" Cleary said. "I couldn't help but notice you weren't from the neighborhood."

Byron grinned. "You keep an eye out do you, Mr. Cleary?"

"Always. Can't be too careful these days."

"That you can't," Byron agreed. "I don't suppose you've noticed anyone strange in the area lately, have you?"

"Aside from you all, no, not recently. Are you looking for someone in particular?"

"How about strange vehicles?"

"Well, yes, now that you mention it. There was a car towed from right here yesterday," Cleary said, pointing to where Faherty's car had been parked. "A tan or beige-colored Toyota sedan."

"Do you know who the car belongs to?" Stevens said as scratched Millie's back.

"I don't know the woman's name, no. But

I see her sometimes when I'm walking Millie."

Byron exchanged a glance with Stevens.

"Can you describe the woman?" Stevens asked.

"Sure. She's young, maybe early twenties, ginger hair, attractive. Kinda bouncy, ya know?"

"Bouncy?" Byron said, not understanding the descriptor.

"Just really enthusiastic and happy all the time. Well, whenever I see her anyway. She just seems very nice. Millie likes her, too. Don't ya girl?" Cleary bent down and scratched Millie behind the ears.

"Have you seen this young woman lately?" Byron asked.

"No. Not for a week or so."

"Have you ever seen her with anyone?" Stevens asked.

"No. Whenever I've seen her, she's always by herself."

"Does she live in the neighborhood?" Byron asked.

"No, but frequently visits."

"How frequently?" Stevens asked.

Cleary considered this. "Once a week. Sometimes twice."

"Does she visit someone in one of these buildings?" Byron asked, gesturing to several nearby homes, hoping she hadn't.

Cleary turned and pointed. "No. Farther up the street. But she usually parks down here."

"That's a little strange isn't it?" Byron asked.

"I guess."

"Have you seen which residence she goes into?" Stevens asked.

"Sure. It's the old Stavros place."

Byron and Stevens exchanged another glance just as his cell rang with a call from Murray.

"Excuse me, Mr. Cleary," Byron said. "I have to take this."

Byron walked away leaving Stevens to continue mining information from Cleary. He answered the call and held the phone to his ear. "Hey, Pete. How'd you make out?"

"You're gonna owe me, Johnny."

"Did Martin recant?"

"He about shit his pants when we threatened to charge him with obstructing a murder inquiry."

"Murder inquiry?"

"Yeah, you know like on all those British mysteries on Amazon. I figured he's probably binging on them like everyone else these days. Besides, inquiry just sounds more official."

Annoyed, Byron couldn't help but think of Tran's recent fascination with the detective shows. "Did he give it up or not?"

"Of course he did. Georgie told us that Alex asked to borrow his car so he could hook up with a girlfriend. Said he thought it was someone in the Boston area; he didn't know Alex was planning to drive all the way up to Maine and back."

Byron felt another piece slip into place. "Good work, Pete. Can you send me a copy of his statement?"

"Sure thing. I'll scan it and email it as soon as I get back to the office. Oh, and there's one other thing you might use to stick it up Mr. TV Star's lying ass."

"I'm all ears."

"George said Alex topped off his tank on the way back, so there should be a transaction record on one of his credit cards. You know, when he was supposed to be at the hotel. Who knows, you might even find video of the dumbass pumping gas."

"Thanks, cuz."

Byron wasted no time in assigning Melissa Stevens to write up the search warrant for Lina Stavros's former residence. Pelligrosso and Murphy were just awaiting the call. Cleary's signed statement made it clear that

Faherty had been meeting Alex Stavros at the family home for several months. Also clear was the fact that Stavros had lied to them about being out of town.

Byron sat next to Stevens at her desk, going over his notes and giving her the occasional prompt as she added in the relevant information to the affidavit.

LeRoyer paced nearby. "Are you both one hundred percent sure about this?"

"Yes, Marty," Byron said. "We are."

Byron knew that the lieutenant was trying to come to grips with the fact that the PD was about to go to war with a prominent family, a family of celebrities, and it would be a public battle. Lina Stavros and heart-throb son Alex were beloved by the locals, and what Byron and his detectives were about to do was sure to have negative repercussions on the department. Right or wrong, they would all take the hit.

Stevens paused her typing. "Blood and other bodily fluids, hairs, fibers, and —"

"Clothing belonging to the victim," Byron added. "Personal effects to include hand-written and electronic communications, electronic devices."

"Like Faherty's missing cellphone."

LeRoyer stopped in front of Stevens's desk. "I mean, this is the home of the woman who put up the reward for God's sake."

"Yup," Byron said. "Former home, actually."

"Who does that, John?" LeRoyer said.

"Maybe a mother looking to protect her son."

LeRoyer returned to wearing out the carpet. "Jesus."

Stevens returned to typing.

Byron waited impatiently as Assistant Attorney General Jim Ferguson perused a hard copy of the affidavit. Stevens sat at her desk tweaking the electronic copy contained in the computer each time Ferguson made a new suggestion.

When he had finished reading the document, Ferguson peered over his reading glasses, addressing both detectives. "You know this is going to create a shit storm of biblical proportions, right?"

"Yeah, but the affidavit is solid?" Byron said, answering for both of them.

"Oh, it'll stand up to any judge's scrutiny. That's not the problem, John. You're about to execute a search warrant on one of Hollywood's elite."

"Yup."

"And, I assume, bring in her restaurateur

son for a formal interview?"

"That's the plan."

Ferguson sighed deeply, removed his glasses, folded them, and placed them in his shirt pocket. "Just know they are going to fight you every step of the way. Whether Alex did this thing or not won't matter to their fans. Stavros has the money to go out and acquire the very best legal team and she will. They will try this case in the media, painting the Portland PD as a bunch of bumbling Keystone Cops. And they will most likely go after you personally. Both of you. You can probably plan on them hiring private investigators to look up both of your skirts." He turned to Stevens. "My apologies on the ill-advised metaphor."

She grinned. "It's okay, I rarely wear one."

"I get it, Jim," Byron said. "And I know you're just trying to caution us, but all the facts point to Alex as the suspect in Dani's murder. I will not be bullied into backing down, no matter how famous or powerful the Stavros family may be."

Ferguson smiled as he stood up. "All right then. That's what I wanted to hear. Let's get this to a judge."

CHAPTER 26

Wednesday, 6:30 P.M.,
July 19, 2017

Alex Stavros was livid. In addition to walking him out of the restaurant just as they were about to open for dinner, Byron had let him stew in the interview room for over an hour giving Nugent and Pelligrosso time to get started on the search of Angelina's West End house.

Byron entered the interview room, placed a bottled water in front of Alex, then sat down.

"Do you have any idea how long you've kept me in here, Sergeant Byron? This is ridiculous. I have been more than accommodating. What's this now, the third time you've questioned me?"

"Seventy-five," Byron said.

"What?"

"How long I've kept you in here. Seventy-five minutes."

"That's funny. Some kind of cop humor, I guess. Well, we'll see how funny you think it is when I sue you, the department, and this whole goddamned city."

"Sounds like we both have the same goal," Byron said.

"And what might that be?"

"Dragging the other into court. Of course, the court I plan on dragging you to is of the criminal variety. Tends to carry more weight."

Alex jumped out of his chair. "I've had enough of your bullshit. I'm out of here."

"Sit down, Mr. Stavros!" Byron commanded.

The surprise on Alex's face gave him away. He sat.

"At the moment, you're not free to go anywhere. You are in custody."

"You haven't read me my rights," Alex said. "I know my rights."

"I haven't asked you any questions. But I can see you're anxious to get started, so why don't we get down to it."

Byron went through the well-rehearsed procedure of Mirandizing Stavros. When he had finished, he slid the typewritten sheet over in front of Alex.

"What am I signing?"

"That you understand your rights as I've

read them to you."

Alex grabbed the pen and scribbled illegibly across the bottom of the page. "There. Happy?"

Byron ignored the question. He slid the Miranda warning into the file folder and removed another document. "You're probably wondering why I brought you in?"

"Quota?" Alex swallowed nervously but his eyes never left the sheet of paper in front of Byron.

"No, it's not because of a quota, Mr. Stavros. I brought you here because I hate being lied to. Fact is, you've been lying to me since we started this investigation. Why did you lie about being in Portland the night Danica Faherty went missing?"

"I didn't. I told you I was at a restaurant owners convention in Boston. Split a hotel room with an old college buddy and I didn't return until Sunday afternoon. Late."

Byron nodded. "That would be George Martin?"

"Correct. You've talked to him then?"

"We have. Twice, in fact. Turns out your old college buddy isn't quite the stand-up guy you imagined. He just finished giving a statement to a Boston homicide detective. Would you like to know what he — well — why don't I just let you read it for yourself."

Byron slid a copy of the statement in front of Alex.

Alex hesitated for a moment.

"Go on," Byron said. "It's a good read. I think *you'll* find it interesting anyway."

Alex picked up the page and began to read.

Byron felt his cell vibrate in his coat pocket. He checked and saw a text from Le-Royer. Alex's attorney in lobby. U should end this.

Byron shot a quick glance up at the camera, knowing that the lieutenant was watching, and gave a slight shake of his head.

Alex finished reading the statement and set it back on the table.

"You probably see now why I found it interesting," Byron said. "Right now, I have a team of detectives and evidence technicians executing a search warrant on your mother's house."

Alex's eyes widened. "You can't do that."

"Actually, I can. It's called probable cause and you've given us a mountain of it."

The team of detectives Byron mentioned consisted of Detectives Stevens, Nugent, Robbins, and Evidence Technicians Pelligrosso and Murphy. They had obtained a key to Angelina Stavros's Bowdoin Street mansion and were now standing in the home's front entry hall.

The two-story hall was ornately decorated in a combination of dark wood trim paneling and expensive-looking wallpaper. Dominating the space was a massive curved hardwood staircase, its center carpeted by an oriental runner secured by brass stair rods, leading up to the second floor. Large framed oil paintings graced the walls.

"Jeez," Nugent said. "This is like an episode of that show with Robin Leach."

"*Lifestyles of the Rich and Famous*?" Robbins asked.

"I was thinking more along the lines of Rich and Shameless," Nugent replied.

"Where do you want to begin?" Stevens asked Pelligrosso.

Pelligrosso scanned the room before speaking. "Let me snap some photos before we start. We'll take it one room at a time. Murph, I want you to be the clearing house. Log every piece of evidence, who found it, where it was located."

"Got it," Murphy said.

Robbins spoke up. "Jeez, we could be here all night. Why don't we start in the most likely place for evidence, the bedroom?"

Nugent gave him a cold glare. "Relax, Bernie. We want to get this right."

He held up his hands in surrender. "Okay, okay."

Stevens turned to Robbins and Gardiner. "By the book. Gabe takes pictures of everything before it gets seized. Glove up, top to bottom, left to right, bag, tag, and log. Nothing gets overlooked. Got it?"

"Got it, Mel," Nugent said.

Robbins grunted.

Alex Stavros stared back at Byron but said nothing. His prior cockiness had departed and left him looking scared.

"We know you met up with Danica Faherty Saturday night," Byron said. "You drove up in your good buddy's car to have sex with her. And we know you met her at your mother's abandoned house on Bowdoin Street. The same place you've been meeting up with her for the past few months."

Byron paused to give Stavros an opportunity to respond. Stavros dropped his gaze to the table. He appeared to be considering his options. After a moment Byron continued.

"I also have a warrant to obtain swabs of your DNA." Byron removed an envelope and vial and set them on the table. "You see

Danica had sex with someone just before she was killed, but when George alibied you we were forced to think it was somebody else. But now —"

"What if I don't want to consent to a DNA thingy?" Alex asked.

"A warrant means that you don't have the right to refuse."

"I want my lawyer."

Much of the furniture in the Stavros house remained. Evidently Lina had other decorating and design ideas for her new Scarborough home on Prouts Neck and they didn't involve sentimentality. The team had been searching for close to an hour and a half when finally Byron arrived.

"Hey, Sarge. How'd it go with Alex?" Murphy asked.

"He lawyered up."

"Did we get his DNA?" Stevens asked.

"Yes, despite his dramatic protests. Should have been an actor himself. Find anything yet?"

"Remember what Doc Ellis said about the body being stored someplace cool before it was dumped?"

"Yeah, why?"

"Lina's got a walk-in cooler," Stevens said "And it's functional."

Byron remembered Dr. Ellis's comment, but a walk-in cooler didn't make Alex guilty of anything except extravagance.

"We find anything incriminating?" Byron asked.

"Not yet, but —"

"I think we just did," Pelligrosso said, causing everyone to look up.

"What did you find, Gabe?" Byron asked.

"Follow me."

They gathered in the ornately decorated kitchen with its ten-foot tin-covered ceiling and oversized stainless Viking range. Byron wasn't much of a gourmand — more of a microwave and takeout man — but even he couldn't help wondering how someone who could afford a top-of-the-line appliance would simply abandon it. He wondered if someone like that was equally capable of discounting the value of a human life. Danica Faherty's life.

Pelligrosso picked up a handheld alternate light source and switched it on. "Someone get the lights."

Murphy reached over and killed the lights.

"Take a look at this," Pelligrosso said as he angled the yellow band of light across the papered wall. Even amid the complex multicolored pattern of the wallpaper, a fine dark spattering showed up clearly.

"Blood?" Byron asked.

"If I had to guess, yes. Looks like spray that was missed during cleanup."

Byron realized that the evidence, if it was Faherty's blood, was consistent with Doc Ellis's theory that someone took a hammer to the back of Dani's skull. The high impact nature of a claw hammer striking and penetrating a live human's skull would undoubtedly result in a fine mist of blood spraying over any surfaces near where the attack occurred.

"And that's not all," Pelligrosso continued. "Look at this." He shifted to the center of the parquet floor causing the other investigators to step back in order to give him room. Switching to a reddish frequency on the ALS, he projected it at the floor. The boards appeared normal but the seams between them glowed brightly in what resembled a circular pattern, previously invisible to them.

"Blood was spilled here," Pelligrosso said. "Someone did an okay job cleaning up the surface of the floor, but as you can see, they missed the blood that seeped down between the boards."

"Jesus," Robbins said. "We don't get much of this on the property crime side of the house. That's nasty."

"You think *that's* nasty?" Nugent said, his voice floating out of the dark and causing them all to jump. "Take a look at this."

They followed Nugent down a flight of creaking wooden steps to the basement. Like most houses its age, and in compete contrast to the elegant home sitting atop it, the foundation was a combination of granite and brick with an earthen floor. Dimly lit by low wattage bulbs the subterranean space was musty and damp. An assortment of cobwebs hung from many of the rafters.

"Watch your step," Nugent said as he led them to a point directly beneath the kitchen and aimed his flashlight at a discolored area in the dirt.

"It seeped through?" Robbins said, surprise evident in his voice.

"You tell me," Nugent said, repositioning the light so that it shone straight up at the boards comprising the subfloor.

There was no need for an alternate light source this time. Byron could clearly see the reddish-brown remnants of blood that had soaked through from above, leaving a dark stain on the subflooring beneath.

"That's sick," Robbins said.

"That's evidence," Nugent corrected.

CHAPTER 27

Thursday, 3:30 A.M.,
July 20, 2017

Byron sat across from AAG Jim Ferguson drinking strong black coffee. The two men occupied a table at Denny's, one of the few remaining bastions of the twenty-four-hour breakfast.

"Give me the rundown," Ferguson said, looking as weary as Byron felt.

"Okay. Assuming the blood we found belongs to Dani Faherty, the Stavros house is definitely our murder scene."

"How long before you'll have definitive confirmation?"

"Two or three days hopefully. The attack happened in the kitchen. Gabe located evidence of blood spatter on several cabinet doors and on the wallpaper, which is consistent with Ellis's finding that she was struck in the head with a single blow from the claw end of a hammer."

"Wouldn't the killer have tried to clean it up?" Ferguson asked.

"Don't think he saw it. The cupboard doors are made from dark wood, mahogany maybe, and the wallpaper is a very similar color to the spatter. Someone did attempt to clean up the blood that pooled on the floor, except it had already worked its way down between the boards and subfloor into the basement before they could get to it."

"And whoever it was didn't notice?"

"Would you?" Byron asked.

"No, probably not. So where was Danica's body between Sunday and Wednesday morning?"

"We think the killer may have moved the body into the walk-in cooler to buy some time before moving it to the lumberyard," Byron said.

"They have a walk-in cooler?"

"Apparently, Angelina used to throw a lot of parties at the old house. I guess they needed a walk-in."

Ferguson shook his head in disbelief. "Sounds like Alex is planning to continue throwing them. If he's not in prison, that is."

Ferguson held his cup up for the waitress who had swung by to refill them. After she departed, he asked, "How did the body get from the house on Bowdoin Street to the lumberyard?"

"I don't know," Byron said. "Obviously, a vehicle of some kind. According to Winn, Erwin Glantz, whoever it was may have used a truck. Although, that's based entirely on his alcohol-muddled recollection of what he heard."

"Glantz is our dumpster guy, right?" Ferguson asked.

"Yeah. Winn said he was awakened by someone driving up in a vehicle with a loud exhaust. Whoever it was tossed the trash bag containing Dani's head into the dumpster, then drove away."

"So, we're still looking for a vehicle with a loud exhaust."

"There was something else he said, though. It sorta stuck with me. Winn said he heard the door slam shut. He described it as sounding like a door on a truck."

Ferguson lifted a brow. "What's a truck door sound like?"

"Older model maybe. Not a lot of padding. Like metal banging against metal."

"Alex have a truck?"

"No."

Both men sat in silence sipping coffee and mulling over case facts.

After a bit Ferguson spoke up again. "So,

are we thinking one or two people to move the body? I guess what I'm asking is, do we have an accomplice we need to locate?"

"I've been thinking about that," Byron said. "I'm not sure. If Alex is the killer, he's certainly strong enough to move Dani's body without help."

"How much did she weigh?"

"Only a hundred and ten pounds, and without her head she would have been closer to a hundred."

Ferguson scratched his graying beard stubble as he considered it. "So, really anyone could have dragged her body into a truck and dragged it back out again, right?"

"Where are you going with this?" Byron asked. "Sounds like you're trying to poke a hole in my case against Alex Stavros."

"Not at all," Ferguson said. "I'm just trying to slide into the shoes of the defense if we charge him."

"All right then, who is your alternate suspect?"

"Why not Alex's wife? Deborah finds out hubby is cheating on her and gets royally pissed off."

"She has an alibi."

"A real alibi?"

"She was in New York City around the time we believe the murder occurred."

"Maybe she enlists the help of a third party, and then she deals with the body dump after she returns to Maine."

"Sounds like a stretch," Byron said.

"Okay, what about Lina? You said she told you that she'd do anything to make sure her grandbabies stay around."

"Yeah, but Jesus. Cutting up a body?"

"Maybe she didn't take part in the disposal," Ferguson opined. "Perhaps she waited until Alex left the house and went in to confront the family's interloper. Warn her off from the son."

"And the hammer claw through the skull?"

"Maybe she hadn't planned on killing her. Maybe they have words and Lina snaps. She grabs the nearest thing she can find and buries it in the back of Dani's skull. You said they were planning to remodel the house. A hammer could have been left lying around."

"And the aftermath?" Byron asked. "Now Lina's got a dead girl bleeding out on her kitchen floor."

"Didn't you say that she got this big scary groundskeeper guy who lives on the Scarborough estate? Kind of protective of her, I believe you said."

"Lina's brother-in-law. Her deceased husband's brother, Dennis Stavros."

"Why wouldn't she reach out for his help?" Ferguson asked.

"Why don't you throw in the butler or the au pair, while you're at it?"

"They have a butler?"

Byron sighed, realizing there was still so much to do.

"More coffee, hon?" the waitress asked, materializing beside Byron.

"Please," he said.

After topping off Ferguson's cup again, too, the waitress departed, leaving the two men in silent contemplation.

"What about the blood and the semen?" Byron asked after a time.

"If both come back a match to our victim and suspect then we'll be a lot closer to tying a bow on this thing."

Byron considered Ferguson's line of reasoning. "If we weren't dealing with Hollywood elite would you be treading so carefully?"

"Honestly?" Ferguson said. "No, I probably wouldn't. But we *are* dealing with Hollywood elite. This family has a lot of money and a lot of clout."

Byron slouched back on the bench. He was physically and emotionally spent.

"Look, John, I agree with you that Alex is a part of this, but that doesn't necessarily mean he had anything to do with her death. I'm just trying to save us both a lot of aggravation later by playing devil's advocate now."

Byron stared silently across the table at his friend.

"What?" Ferguson asked.

"I liked you better as a prosecutor," Byron said.

"Look, John, this case comes down to motive. If Danica had been pregnant that might have risen to the level of providing Alex with a strong motive, but she wasn't. The way I see it, Lina and Deborah had the best motives to want Faherty out of the picture."

"Too bad Alex doesn't have you representing him," Byron said.

"I just call 'em like I sees 'em, my friend." Ferguson raised his mug. *"Slainte."*

Byron paid the check and the two men parted ways. He climbed into his unmarked then checked his cellphone for messages before leaving the lot. There was a text from Diane that had been sent ten minutes prior.

U awake?

He responded with a text of his own, Yup. After a moment Diane responded, Coffee?

Where?

Becky's in ten?

C U there.

Byron wasn't sure he needed more coffee. Despite his exhaustion the caffeine was making him feel jittery, but he was looking forward to sitting down with her. Despite Diane's assurances that she had moved past his callous response to the news that she would be applying to the bureau, it still felt like a chasm had opened between them. Was it only in his head? Or was it because the news had caused him to delay floating the idea of moving in together? He didn't know. What he did know was that he was suddenly hungry. He'd been so preoccupied while tossing around theories with Ferguson that he hadn't eaten.

Byron turned out of the lot and headed inbound on Congress Street.

One of the advantages of arriving at a popular Portland eatery like Becky's Diner at precisely the moment the doors opened was the choice seating that punctuality afforded. Byron and Diane sat at the rear corner of the dining room, well away from the morning crowd spilling in. Most of the early risers preferred to sit at the counter or at a booth near the front of the diner. Byron's preference was sitting anywhere he could have his back to the wall.

"You gonna order food?" he asked.

Diane shook her head. "Just coffee."

Byron's attention returned to the waitress. "I'll have the hash, scrambled eggs, and an English, grilled."

The waitress departed.

"You really nervous about the interview?" Byron asked.

"My stomach is in knots."

He grinned. "It's not like you haven't done detective work before."

"I know. I guess I'm just feeling a little rusty. As the public relations sergeant I don't get to do much sleuthing."

"You'll do fine."

"What's up with the Faherty case?" she asked, an obvious attempt at changing the subject. "Were you working when I texted you?"

"Yeah, we didn't finish the search until late. I just met up with Jim Ferguson. In fact, this is like my fifth cup of coffee since midnight. I may never sleep again."

"How did the search go?"

"It isn't over," Byron said. "Pelligrosso

414

and Murphy are heading back over there in a few hours to finish up. I've got a uniform sitting on the house. We found some pretty damning evidence. Including blood in the kitchen."

"You think Faherty was killed there?"

"I'd be very surprised if she wasn't."

"You still like Alex Stavros for the murder?"

"I did until Jim started floating out alternative theories, now I'm doubting myself again."

It was Diane's turn to grin. "He is an attorney, after all."

"Yeah, well he's good at it."

"What theories was he suggesting?"

"Mostly problems with motive. He suggested that Lina Stavros or even Alex's wife, Deborah, might have had more motive to kill Dani than Alex would have. The jealous wife, the grandmother worried that her son's philandering would drive Deborah away along with the grandkids."

"Good theories." Diane took a sip of coffee as she contemplated it. "You think he's right?"

"Who knows. But it got me to thinking, what if Dani wasn't the target?"

"What do you mean?"

"What if she was just a way to point the

finger at someone else for the murder?"

"To what end?"

"Well, dumping her body at the lumber-yard effectively messed up some big-time business plans."

"Giving Gene Wagner an edge on the bidding," Diane said.

"Yeah, but also making him look like the guy who benefited from it. Not to mention tainting the future of that property as the site of a gruesome discovery. Hey kids, who wants to stay at the hotel where they found the headless woman?"

"You're thinking Dani was killed just to screw with Wagner?"

"Or help him. I guess I'm not sure what I think. I'm just looking at cause and effect."

"Who else was directly affected by Dani's death?" Diane asked.

"Alex."

"Meaning?"

"Meaning if Alex gets charged for the murder, he would be out of the way."

"Of what?" Diane asked.

"I haven't figured that out yet. The restaurant business, maybe. The heir apparent to Lina's fortune. I don't know. I'm just toying with an idea."

The waitress dropped off Byron's order, refilled their coffees, then scurried away to wait other tables.

"What time's your interview?" Byron asked.

"Ten-thirty."

"And there's four of you interviewing?"

"Three. Me, Kenny Crosby, and Andy Pepin. Tom Fitzgerald pulled out."

"Your odds are improving. Who's on the panel?"

"Lynds, Rumsfeld, Commander Jennings, LeRoyer, and Barry Sonnenfeld."

"Sonnenfeld? Why the legal advisor?"

Diane shrugged. "Test our knowledge of case law maybe?"

"Hell, you probably have a better understanding of case law than he does."

Diane sipped her coffee.

"Well, you know Chief Lynds wants you, and by extension so will Marty. No idea about Sonnenfeld."

"And the others?" Diane asked.

"Who knows? Rumpswab might go along to get along, although I don't imagine that Lynds gives a fuck what he thinks at this point. His days are numbered."

"And the commander?"

Byron thought back to the inside information he'd received about Jennings during the Haggerty shooting. "I trust him as far as I can throw him. He'll probably have to

417

roll over and ask Mayor Gilcrest what she thinks."

Diane was unsuccessful at hiding a smile behind her cup.

At precisely eight-thirty Martin LeRoyer breezed into Byron's office and closed the door.

Byron looked up from the stack of reports he was still going though from the previous night.

"Where are we on arresting Alex Stavros?" LeRoyer asked.

"And good morning to you, Lieu," Byron said.

"I'm serious, John. Where are we?"

"What do you mean, where are we? We're nowhere near that yet." Byron's eyes narrowed with suspicion. "Why are you asking?"

"Because there are about five different news media outlets camped out in the lobby looking for confirmation."

"Confirmation on what? We haven't even confirmed that the blood in Lina's house belongs to Faherty yet."

"Well, someone leaked the story that we're looking at Alex Stavros. They are reporting that an arrest is imminent."

Byron could feel the anger burning within

him. "Well, that's just fucking great. Ever get the feeling that someone is trying to sabotage you, Marty?"

"No one's trying to sabotage you, John."

Byron didn't believe that for a second. "Perhaps you forgot about the first leak. You know, the one that led to a standoff between Elmer Faherty and Dani's ex-boyfriend."

"Shit," LeRoyer said as he made a pass with the fingers of his right hand back through his hair. It wasn't even nine in the morning and the lieutenant's hair was already standing at attention in front. "Lynds is gonna have to give them something."

"How about telling them the truth?" Byron said. "Some asshole is talking out of school, and we're still investigating the case. Better yet, why don't I go down and sort them out?"

LeRoyer held up his hand like a crossing guard. "No, John. I'll fix this. The last thing I need is for you to make it worse." The lieutenant flung the office door open and hurried out, nearly running over Mike Nugent in the process.

"Morning, Lieu," Nugent said. He turned to Byron. "What's with him?"

Byron grabbed Nugent, Robbins, and Stevens and headed downstairs to the lab to meet with E.T.'s Pelligrosso and Murphy far away from whatever ears might have been listening in.

"What the hell, boss?" Nugent said. "You think it's someone at 109?"

"Could be one of the court clerks, Sarge," Murphy said. "They've got our affidavit for the search at Angelina's house."

"That affidavit was supposed to be impounded," Stevens said.

"Yeah, for all the good that does," Nugent said.

"Might be the Stavros family," Pelligrosso said. "Get it out in front of the public now and make it look like we're targeting Alex."

"He's right," Nugent said. "Oldest trick in the book when you know you're about to get snatched up."

"It could be anyone," Byron said. "The point is, we've been dogged on this since the start. We need to find a way to lock this down." Byron addressed Pelligrosso. "You guys headed back to Lina's?"

"Yes. Murph and I will spend a little more time with the alternate light source and I still want to dust for prints."

"Prints?" Robbins asked. "Whose prints are you hoping to find?"

"Namely?" Pelligrosso said. "Danica

Faherty's."

Stevens spoke up. "Prints will put her in that house regardless of what the blood shows."

Byron's cell rang. It was Jim Ferguson. He accepted the call. "You heard?"

"I did," Ferguson said. "How soon can you meet me?"

CHAPTER 28

Thursday, 9:30 A.M.,
July 20, 2017

Byron provided marching orders to Nugent and Robbins before departing 109. Byron and Stevens headed to the Woodford's Corner Dunkin' Donuts, grabbed a peace offering for Ferguson then drove by way of Ocean Avenue to Payson Park where the AAG was already waiting.

As they drove up, they found Ferguson leaning against the hood of his car watching two teenagers playing tennis.

"Either of you play?" Ferguson asked as the detectives approached on foot.

"Nope," Byron said.

"Used to," Stevens said.

"Any good?" Ferguson asked.

"I was. You?"

"Yeah, but I wasn't. These kids would've kicked my ass up and down the court."

Byron waited until Ferguson was finished

before handing him a coffee and addressing the proverbial ten-ton elephant. "Here."

"Figured it was the least we could do," Stevens said.

"Thanks," Ferguson said.

The three of them stood in uncomfortable silence for a long moment, listening to the thwap of the ball off the rackets as it was sent hurling back and forth across the net.

"So?" Byron said.

Ferguson lifted the tab and took a sip before answering. "So, we've got a big old leak, huh?"

"Goes without saying," Byron said.

"Any idea where it's coming from?"

"Not yet."

"I can think of a few possibilities," Stevens said.

Ferguson raised a brow. "Only a few." He took another sip, keeping his eyes on the tennis match. "How long did you say it would take to confirm that the blood you found was Faherty's?"

"Two or three days, although it is Thursday. Don't imagine weekends count," Byron said. "Unless you can pull some strings to speed up the process."

"I might be able to," Ferguson said.

"What can we do to help?" Stevens asked.

"It would be nice if we could stop any further leaks. If Alex Stavros is responsible for Faherty's murder this is gonna make it much harder to control. His lawyer will likely go on offense now. We might have to charge Alex anyway just to keep him from leaving the country. Get a judge to grab his passport."

"Can't we do that without charging him?" Byron asked. "I'd rather not jump the gun on this."

Ferguson looked at Stevens and cocked a thumb in Byron's direction. "You angling to get this guy's job someday?"

Stevens grinned. "I'm hoping."

"Well, if you do, you have to promise me two things."

"What's that?"

"Don't be a pain in my ass."

"And the second?"

"If you're gonna be a pain in my ass, at least have the courtesy to bring me a chocolate cruller to go with my coffee."

In addition to everything else going wrong with the investigation, Byron was struggling with motive. If Alex was responsible, why would he kill Danica? The wide variety of motives for murder makes them very different from other crimes. Thefts, burglaries, and robberies are usually committed by perps with a straight-forward motive. Money. Money for drugs, money for booze, or money for whichever orangutan-sized habit had taken up residency on the back of the offending criminal. Homicide motives run the gamut from rage and revenge, to jealousy and betrayal, to every sick and twisted reason in between. Some are spur-of-the-moment actions while others are meticulously planned. Had Alex planned this killing? Would he have gone to the extreme of killing his girlfriend just to keep Deborah from finding out, or was something else happening here?

As they departed from Payson Park, Byron was less sure of where they stood on the case than before their meeting with Ferguson. Byron and Stevens drove directly to Angelina Stavros's old house on Bowdoin Street. While Pelligrosso and Murphy were busy dusting the bedroom and first-floor bathrooms for prints, Byron and Stevens stuck to the kitchen.

"What are we looking for?" Stevens asked.

"I don't know," Byron said. He looked down at the spot on the floor where Pelligrosso had identified the blood, yet again invisible by the light of day. "Let's walk through this."

"All right."

It was a process that Byron had learned from Ray Humphrey, and had performed with Diane countless times. Running through the case facts out loud with another investigator often revealed things that had been overlooked. Two heads and all that.

Byron began, "For the sake of argument, let's say Alex had nothing to do with Dani's murder. He drives up here from Boston for a midnight rendezvous —"

"In his friend's car," Stevens added.

"Right. In his friend's car. He and Dani do the dance, maybe they fall asleep, and then he gets up early to be back in Boston before anyone at the convention notices he's missing. What does Dani do?"

"I don't know."

"What would you do?"

"If I were Dani?"

"Yeah, if you were Dani."

"I'd pick better boyfriends."

"Come on, Mel. I'm serious."

"Sorry, I'm just a little punchy." Stevens took a moment to think it through. "Okay, she probably gets up with Alex and sees him to the door."

Byron nodded. "Good. Then what?"

"They part with a kiss, and he leaves the house."

426

"What is she wearing?"

"How would I know that?"

"Haven't you ever walked a lover to the door?"

Stevens grinned. "Ah, gotcha. Um, she's wearing her new bra and panties. The matched set she was wearing when we recovered her body. Probably purchased in advance of their planned Sunday morning hookup."

"Right." Byron would task Tran with checking Faherty's credit card statements to try and confirm the purchase. If she purchased them either Friday or Saturday it would mean the meeting with Alex had been preplanned.

Stevens continued, "But someone comes in —"

"Or was already in the house waiting," Byron said.

"What makes you say that?" she asked.

"Because of what she's wearing. She wouldn't answer the door to let in someone she wasn't expecting, dressed in only her underwear."

"Or maybe she didn't let them in. Maybe they let themselves in."

"Someone with access," Byron said. "Someone with a key."

"That's assuming one of them locked up

after Alex left. They might not have."

"So, who are we looking at?"

"Someone who may have had access to the house, like a family member."

"Who else?"

"Someone who already knew where they were hooking up."

Byron nodded and looked down at the floor again. "And when."

It was nearly eleven as Diane walked out of the chief's conference room on legs that felt like rubber. The promotional interview had gone badly. At least in her opinion. All her preparation had been for naught. None of the questions she had anticipated were asked. And her answers to the questions that had been posed felt disconnected and vague. And when they got to the part where she was asked if she had any questions, Diane hadn't been able to think of a single one. Her mind had gone completely blank.

Whatever connection Diane may have felt with Chief Lynds appeared nonexistent as she sat across the table from the panel. Even LeRoyer had seemed chilly and distant. She couldn't understand it. Maybe it took a different kind of person to supervise a homicide case. Perhaps she wasn't cut out for this after all.

Maintaining a painted-on smile, in case she passed anyone in the hallway, Diane walked directly to her office and closed the door.

Byron and Stevens compiled two separate lists. The first was Stavros family relatives. The second consisted of restaurant employees. They made a calculated decision to change it up with the family matriarch, hoping to catch Lina with her guard down. This time Stevens would have a go at her. Byron dropped Stevens off at 109 and they split up to work their respective lists.

"May I help you?" A pleasant feminine-sounding voice emanated from the speaker box above the security keypad at the entrance to the Prouts Neck compound.

Stevens recognized the voice immediately. "My name is Detective Melissa Stevens. I'm here to speak with Angelina Stavros."

"I've read the paper, Detective," Stavros said, her tone no longer pleasant. "I know you're targeting my son."

"We aren't targeting anyone, Mrs. Stavros. We only want to find the truth," Stevens said as gently as she could. The goal after all was Lina's cooperation.

Following a short silence Angelina's voice returned through the speaker. "Drive in,

Detective."

Stevens waited for the gate to trundle open, then she drove up to the house.

Byron parked on the street right around the corner from Alessandro's. His list was comprised of Dani's coworkers. Given the day's headlines Byron figured there was zero chance that Alex would be at work, making it the perfect time to poke around.

He walked up the service alley and found one of the employees outside having a smoke. Based on his white pants and shirt, kitchen staff. Byron identified himself and asked the man his name.

"Louis. Louis Violette. Folks call me Louie. I remember seeing you here last week. You had another detective with you. Cute."

Byron grinned. "I'll be sure and pass that along, Louie. Did you know Dani Faherty very well?"

"Sure. We all did. Well, most of the staff."

"Did Dani have any enemies? Someone that might've wished her harm?"

Violette tossed the butt of his cigarette on the pavement then lit another. "Oh, shit," he said, realizing what he had just done. "Sorry about that."

"Relax," Byron said. "I left my littering

citations in the car. So, did she?"

"Nah, I don't think so. Couple of the other women might've been a little jealous of all the attention she got from the boss."

"The boss?"

"Yeah, Alex. The two of them got along pretty well. Maybe a little too well, if you get my meaning."

"You think there was something going on between Alex and Dani?" Byron asked.

"Hey, I don't like to start rumors, but they acted a little different toward each other whenever Lina or Alex's wife, Deborah, was around."

"Thanks, Louie," Byron said. "Manager inside?"

"Petri? Yeah, he's probably overseeing setup in the main dining room."

Angelina's assistant, Ruth, greeted Stevens at the door, then led her to a sitting room located at the back of the estate. Stevens was trying to stay focused on the reason for her visit, but she couldn't help but be taken with the extravagance of her surroundings. The new home made the one on Bowdoin Street seem cheap and outdated.

"Detective Stevens to see you, Mrs. Stavros," Ruth the Assistant announced.

"Thank you, Ruth," Angelina said. After

Ruth had departed, Stavros focused her attention on Stevens. "Detective," she said, nodding her head but making no attempt to stand. She gestured toward a padded antique divan. "Please, have a seat."

"Thank you."

"I'd offer you something to drink but, as it so happens, I'm not feeling all that benevolent. Given that my son is about to be locked up and my daughter-in-law will probably take my grandbabies back to New York."

"I'm sorry, Mrs. Stavros," Stevens said.

If the pained expression on Lina's face was any indication, she would not be consoled.

"Well, you drove all the way out here. I assume you have questions? You may as well ask them."

"Did you know about the affair between Alex and Danica Faherty?" Stevens asked.

"I suspected."

"Did you ever speak to Alex about it?"

"My son is a grown man, Detective. He is completely capable of managing his own life."

Stevens found a fair amount of irony in her answer, given that Lina was about to gift a house to Alex and his family.

"Did Deborah know about the affair?"

Stevens asked.

"If she didn't, she certainly does now. Honestly, I don't know if she was aware or not. You'd have to ask her."

"Had Alex and Deborah experienced any marital problems previous to this?"

Lina hesitated before answering. "They dealt with some issues while still living in New York City. But that's all I can tell you. As I indicated previously, you'll have to ask Deborah if you want to know more."

Byron was seated in Petri's office waiting for the restaurateur to return. Their conversation had been interrupted no less than five times in the short span of time that Byron had been there. Byron looked around the office at the various photos hanging from the walls. One in particular caught his eye. It was an older picture of Alex standing with Deborah and Petri. Deborah looked very much like she had when Byron knew her in college. All three were smiling.

Petri breezed back into the office and sat down. "I'm sorry about this. Lunch rush."

"I totally understand," Byron said. "I only need to ask you a few more questions."

"Fire away."

"Did you know about your brother's affair with one of the staff?"

433

"You're talking about Dani Faherty?"

"Yes. Were you aware that they were seeing each other?"

"No, I wasn't. But Alex has a long history of being unfaithful to his wife and family. This wasn't the first time."

"There had been problems between Alex and Deborah before this?"

Petri nodded. "In New York. They even split for a time. Deborah and I spent a lot of time talking about it." Petri stopped speaking. He appeared to be trying to read Byron's expression. "Sergeant Byron, I know you think my brother did this horrible thing but you're wrong. Alex isn't that kind of person. He doesn't have it in him to commit murder."

Byron wasn't at all surprised by Petri's defense of his brother. They were siblings after all. And most people, at least those outside of law enforcement, have difficulty imagining, much less comprehending, the dark side of human nature. Police work lifted the veil. It had been a long while since Byron had any doubt about what people were capable of. The truth was, regardless of Petri's assurances, not only did Alex Stavros have the opportunity, but he had also planned an elaborate scheme to meet up with Dani and establish an alibi for the night she went missing. As for motive, it might have been as simple as Dani threatening to out him to Deborah. It wouldn't have been the first murder committed to cover up an affair.

"Can you think of anyone on your staff who had a problem with Dani Faherty?" Byron asked.

Petri thought for a moment then shook his head. "No. Our core group gets along quite well. Pretty typical for people in this business. There are always the job jumpers, folks who think it would be neat to work at a high-end restaurant like this one, at least until they find out how much work it really is and move on. But our core group thrives in this environment. Loyalty and attention to detail are very important to me."

"I want to ask you about Lina's former house on Bowdoin Street."

"Sure. What would you like to know?"

"Who, besides Alex, has access to it?"

"Well, Lina, obviously. And me, I actually stayed there for a bit when I first came up to Maine to get the restaurant off the ground, before my house was 'move-in ready'." Petri made quotation marks with his fingers.

"Anyone else?"

"My uncle Dennis. Deborah. Um, I guess

that's about it. It was the family house."

"When was the last time you visited the house?" Byron asked.

"I'm not sure. It's been a while. I guess it must have been about a month after I moved into my house in Cape Elizabeth. You know, getting the last of my things moved."

"And when was that?"

"Six months ago, maybe. Give or take."

One of the waitstaff appeared in the doorway to Petri's office. "You're needed in the kitchen, Mr. Stavros."

"I'm sorry, Sergeant Byron," Petri said as he stood. "Duty calls. Was there anything else?"

Byron closed his notebook and rose, too. "I think I'm all set for now."

There was a knock on the closed door to Diane's fourth-floor office.

"It's open," she said, quickly pulling herself together.

Detective Mike Nugent stuck his bald pate through the doorway. "Hey, Sarge. You busy?"

"Not at all, Nuge. Come in. You can leave the door open."

He hesitated. "You sure?"

"Yeah, I'm good."

Nugent pushed open the door then walked in and sat down directly in front of her desk.

"Well? How'd the interview go?"

She forced a smile. "Not great, actually."

"Really?"

"Let's just say I don't think I wowed anyone."

"Well, for whatever it's worth, I've done a bunch of interviews in my time and I find that whenever I get a chance to review the video they're never quite as bad as I thought."

"Thanks, Nuge."

"Besides, they all know you, Sarge. One crappy interview isn't gonna keep them from giving you a chance, right?"

"I hope not."

"Did they say how soon they'll make a decision?"

"They didn't, but I'm guessing early next week. So, what's the latest on baby Nugent?"

"The word is *stubborn.*"

"Sounds like someone we know."

"Jeez, I hope not. If this pregnancy is any indication, this kid won't move out of the house until they're fifty."

CHAPTER 29

Saturday, 12:05 P.M.,
July 22, 2017

Byron was at home in his North Deering condo emptying the dishwasher. Despite his attempt at housework, his thoughts remained occupied by details of the case. The previous day had felt like a waste. They'd made no noticeable progress aside from Pelligrosso's confirmation that he had recovered a number of Faherty's prints from Lina's Bowdoin Street house. He could tell that his team was nearing the point of exhaustion, so he had given them the weekend off. Having been at it nonstop for a week and a half, he knew they all needed some downtime to be with their families, to try and restore order to their personal lives. The sole exception was the Nugent family, whose order was unlikely to be restored anytime soon. Byron had spoken to Diane several times by phone, but she, too, was

438

wrapped up in her own thoughts of promotion.

He had just shelved the last of the glasses when his cell began to dance across the kitchen counter. The name displayed on the caller ID was none other than Jim Ferguson.

Byron grabbed the phone and answered. "I would think having the Assistant Attorney General call you at your house, on a Saturday no less, might be perceived as a bad thing. Tell me I'm wrong."

"You sitting down?"

"As a matter of fact, I'm not. Does this have anything to do with my request to speed up the results from our tests?"

"As a matter of fact, it does."

"You're worse than Dustin Tran. Tell me already."

"The blood you recovered from Angelina Stavros's kitchen belongs to Dani Faherty."

Byron was pleased but not overly surprised. "And the semen?"

"None other than Alex Stavros, Chef to the Stars."

Chef to the Stars who's lawyered up, Byron thought.

"What do you want to do, John?"

Byron slung the dish towel over his shoulder and sat down at the table, taking a moment to consider what they had. Everything pointed to Alex being the killer, including Alex himself by lying about his affair with Dani. The secret rendezvous and phony alibi, borrowing a car, all of it. Still, Ferguson had brought up too many loose ends and alternate possibilities for Byron's liking.

"Can I interpret your silence as meaning that you're conflicted, *mon ami*?" Ferguson asked.

"Yeah," Byron said. "I guess I am."

"Because of my alternate suspect theories?"

"That's part of it."

"Let me see if I can help you with that. My theories were just that. I was throwing shit at the wall, like any defense attorney worth their salt. But it's still shit, John. We deal in facts, and in this case all the facts still point to Alex Stavros as the killer."

Byron couldn't refute it.

"Let me ask you a question," Ferguson said. "Would you hesitate for even a second if this was just some Joe Shmoe from Podunk, Maine, instead of the well-heeled son of a Hollywood movie icon?"

"Throwing my own words back at me, huh?"

"In your general direction perhaps," Ferguson said.

"No, I guess I wouldn't." It bothered him that Ferguson was right. Maybe he was just being overly cautious, or maybe there was an intimidation factor at play here.

"I know you wouldn't," Ferguson said. "Those cuffs would already be clamped on and we both know it."

"Then you're prepared to charge him?" Byron asked.

"Prepared, willing, and able."

After joining up with Stevens at 109, Byron placed a courtesy call to LeRoyer, giving him the heads-up.

"Does Lynds know?" LeRoyer asked.

"No, Marty, she doesn't. I figured you could tell her. Unlike some around 109, I follow the chain of command."

LeRoyer ignored the comment. "Who's with you?"

"At the moment it's just Mel, but Nuge and Bernie are headed in."

"You guys gonna let the shift commander know?"

"Already have. He's assigned two uniforms to go with us."

"I know I don't have to say this, but go easy, okay? We don't need more negative publicity than we've already had."

Byron bit his tongue. He knew what

LeRoyer was saying was that he didn't want to look bad to the new chief, again. The leaks on this case had been a PR nightmare. It seemed someone had been one step ahead of them at every turn. Byron knew LeRoyer was only worried about keeping his seat when the music stopped. Chief Lynds was evaluating each member of her inherited command staff and Marty LeRoyer wanted to remain in her good graces, unlike Ass. Chief Rumsfeld who seemed to have already begun the process of becoming irrelevant.

It was 1:30 by the time they drove to the restaurant from 109. The plan was simple enough. They would park around the corner, slip in through the service entrance, grab Alex, and slip back out. But as the detectives approached Alessandro's they found the restaurant already surrounded by news vans. Someone had beaten them to it, again.

Byron, Stevens, and two uniformed officers entered the kitchen from the rear of the establishment, while Nugent and Robbins waited in the alley. Whatever food prep the staff had been engaged in abruptly ceased as all eyes turned to look at them. The look on Alex's face upon spotting Byron said it all.

Petri Stavros entered the kitchen from the front of the business. "Sergeant Byron, we're trying to run a business here. What the hell is this?"

"The media wasn't my idea, Petri," Byron said. "I wanted to keep this low-key."

"You failed."

Byron turned his attention to Alex who stood mouth agape between the uniformed officers and Stevens. "Alex Stavros, you're under arrest for the murder of Danica Faherty," Byron said.

"Is this absolutely necessary?" Petri persisted.

Byron paused long enough to recall finding Dani's body abandoned in the lumberyard and the image of her severed head lying among the weeds after having been mauled by God knew what kind of creature. He nodded at Stevens and the uniformed officers and they stepped forward and placed Alex in handcuffs. Byron then turned to face Petri. "Yes, it is."

Word had gotten to the media from inside the restaurant, and they had repositioned their circus. A throng of reporters and cameras were awaiting them in the back alley as the officers escorted Stavros to the waiting black-and-white.

"Alex Stavros, do you have any comment?" one of the reporters shouted.

"Why did you cut her head off?" asked another less cultured vulture.

Byron exchanged a wordless glance with Alex. Defeat was etched on the younger man's handsome face.

As Byron and Stevens were climbing into the unmarked, they spotted Davis Billingslea amid the throng.

"How the fuck did he get word already?" Byron said.

Stevens said nothing.

Byron was still steaming as he and Stevens departed from the jail. Their attempt at a low-key Saturday afternoon arrest had failed miserably. The same media outlets that had stormed Alessandro's as the police took Alex into custody were now camped out in front of 50 County Way, each of them looking to get an exclusive on the charges and the facts that led up to them.

Byron's cellphone was jammed with missed calls, voicemails, and text messages. He didn't have to check them to know what they were all about. As he was about to pocket the phone again it rang with an incoming call, this one from Lieutenant Le-Royer. Against Byron's better judgment he answered.

"What part of go easy didn't you guys understand?" LeRoyer snapped.

Byron looked over at Stevens. She was shaking her head.

"Where are you?" LeRoyer asked.

"With Mel. We're heading to 109 from the jail."

"I'll see you both there." LeRoyer hung up without fanfare.

Thirty minutes later Byron, Stevens, Nugent, Robbins, and LeRoyer were all seated around the CID conference room table. The arrest of Alex Stavros should have been cause for celebration, marking the end of a long and arduous investigation. Instead a dark cloud hung over the case and its investigators. All eyes were fixed on the television where the lead story of the evening news was being broadcast live from the Cumberland County Jail. Byron recognized the WGME reporter as Leslie Thomas.

"In a strange twist of fate Angelina Stavros, beloved star of stage and screen, who just last week put up a reward for information leading to the arrest and conviction of the person responsible for the killing of Danica Faherty, an employee at her restaurant, must now contend with the fact that her son may be responsible for that grisly murder.

"A little over an hour ago, Alex Stavros, best known for his television cooking show and his trendy restaurants in Portland and New York City, was taken into custody, led out of Alessandro's by several Portland police officers and detectives."

Byron cringed as he watched the video footage of Alex doing the perp walk to the black-and-white.

Thomas continued, "A short time ago I spoke with Portland Police Lieutenant Martin LeRoyer. LeRoyer, the commander of the Criminal Investigation Division, declined to go on camera, but he did tell me that the case is still under investigation and that additional information may be released at a later date.

"Viewers may recall we first identified Alex Stavros as a person of interest last week after obtaining a copy of the search warrant affidavit filed by Portland police detectives. The search warrant was executed at the former Bowdoin Street home of Angelina Stavros. Lieutenant LeRoyer refused to provide any detail beyond saying that evidence recovered from the home directly links Alex to the crime."

Robbins turned to Byron. "Well, that

ought to make our jobs a whole lot easier."

Nugent chimed in, "I'd like to strangle the fucker who released that information."

"Dammit, this case has been dogged by a leak since it began," LeRoyer said.

"I don't disagree," Byron said. "But it didn't come from my team."

LeRoyer took a moment to scan the room before speaking again. "I know I don't have to tell you how detrimental this leak has been for Chief Lynds. This is her first time at the helm during a homicide investigation. I had hoped for better for her."

Byron couldn't help but wonder if it was really Lynds that LeRoyer was concerned about or his own chances at promotion under her regime. Wisely, he remained silent.

CHAPTER 30

Monday, 9:35 A.M.,
July 24, 2017

Diane Joyner was busy at her desk sorting through a mountain of emails and voice-mails. She was trying hard to juggle the fourth estate's need to know against her own needs concerning the detective sergeant vacancy.

Her desk phone rang. It was Chief Lynds calling. Diane grabbed it after the first ring. "Sergeant Joyner."

"Diane, do you have a second?"

"Certainly, Chief," Diane said while holding her breath.

"Why don't we meet in my office?" Lynds said.

"I'll be right over."

Diane hung up the phone then exhaled. This was it. The moment of truth. The chief had made her decision. One way or another Diane would know her future. The news would either be good, or it wouldn't, but either way she could move on and cease worrying about it. She stood up, grabbed the gray suit coat off the back of her chair and slid it on.

She paused a moment before exiting the office. *Was the chief having her come to her office a good sign or bad?* It was certainly much more formal than when Lynds had paid a visit to Diane's office several weeks back. *Had the other candidates already been informed of her decision or was she the first?* But she could *what if* herself to death. Drawing a deep breath, she exhaled slowly, steeling herself for whatever was coming, then walked out into the hall.

Byron was seated at his desk going through the murder books, making sure everything was in order. Sunday had been spent updating his own supplemental reports and chasing down others. He'd added the lab results confirming the presence of Dani Faherty's blood in Lina's former residence and the report matching Alex's DNA to the semen recovered from Dani's body. He was about to check in with AAG Jim Ferguson when his desk phone rang. The call originated from an outside line.

"Byron."

"Detective Sergeant Byron, this is Stuart Forsyth. I am the attorney of record representing Alex Stavros."

Byron hesitated a moment before responding. Stuart Forsyth was one of the most well-known and well-respected defense attorneys in all of New England. And in Forsyth's case, well-respected corresponded directly with high-priced. Lina was most definitely footing the bill on this. Byron wasn't sure which was more surprising, direct contact from Forsyth or that it had come so soon after the arrest.

"I thought Courtney Levine was representing Alex Stavros," Byron said.

"Not any longer."

"I see," Byron said. "What can I do for you?"

"My client has requested a sit-down. Alex wishes to converse with you face-to-face."

Byron was momentarily taken aback by the request. "Mr. Forsyth, I don't need to tell you how unusual this is. Your client has been charged with the murder of Danica Faherty. He has had ample opportunity to talk with not only me but my partner, Detective Stevens, as well. Alex was quite clear on the matter of exercising his right to remain silent. What has changed?"

"I wish I knew, Sergeant. Unfortunately,

Alex hasn't seen fit to share that with me. I have advised him against this course of action, obviously, telling him, as you said, that this is highly unusual. I have also told him that anything he does tell you will mean that he runs the risk of further incriminating himself."

"And he still wants to sit down with me?" Byron asked.

"Yes, he does. As soon as possible."

Byron considered his next move. If Alex Stavros wanted to bury himself, Byron certainly wasn't about to stop him, but he did want to talk it over with AAG Ferguson first. "Mr. Forsyth, give me your number and I'll call you back."

"Well that's a first," Jim Ferguson said from across the table, after Byron laid out what Attorney Stuart Forsyth had proposed. The two men decided to meet up at the Miss Portland Diner rather than discuss the matter by telephone. They snagged a table at the far end of the coach.

"You think Stavros and Forsyth are running some kind of game?" Byron asked.

Ferguson raised a brow. "If they are, it's no game I've ever heard of. Forsyth must know that once his client starts talking, even if they've rehearsed what he'll say, it would be very easy to misspeak. A slip-up during questioning might bury Alex for good. Tough to put the proverbial genie back in the bottle once he's popped out."

"And the risk to us?" Byron asked.

"Might make more work for you. Alex might be trying out an alternate suspect theory on you to get you to chase a ghost. Forsyth will likely try to convince the jury that perhaps you had doubts about his client's guilt after all. That's assuming you follow whatever lead they intend on providing you."

"I follow every lead," Byron said. "Why would this be different?"

"The difference is that you've already charged Alex. Anyway, Forsyth is the defense counsel. The snake oil he's peddling doesn't have to be true, he only has to get the jury to buy it."

Byron played with a marmalade packet as he ran through the alternate theories Ferguson had previously mentioned. They were way past probable cause with Alex, for Dani Faherty's murder, but arriving at their intended destination of beyond a reasonable doubt was a long drive yet.

"There's always the possibility that Alex isn't the killer," Byron said. "Part of the reason he's in custody now is because he chose not to cooperate when he had the chance. He forced our hand."

Ferguson nodded. "That and the lies he's already told you. His credibility is pretty much shot at this point."

"I want to do it," Byron said at last.

"It's your case, John. You know I'll back your play."

He knew Ferguson would, the wildcard was Chief Lynds. Would she stake her new command against Byron's reputation?

"You might want to get a handle on this media leak problem you have, though," Ferguson said. "If word leaks out that Alex is talking about alternate suspects, and that you're pursuing those leads, you'll be helping Forsyth try the case in the papers before it ever gets to trial."

Byron went through the motions, parking in the lot near the main entrance to the Cumberland County Jail, signing in at the front desk, and securing his firearm in one of the wall-mounted lockers, but inside he was running the forthcoming interview through his head. Was he being played? Had the high-priced attorney agreed to some scheme with his client? Or was Stuart Forsyth just as in the dark as he claimed?

Following a short wait, Byron was led into

the secure area beyond the lobby to one of the no-frill concrete block interview rooms. He walked in and sat down across from Alex Stavros and his attorney. Forsyth gave Byron a silent nod.

"Why am I here?" Byron asked, cutting through the formalities and looking directly at Stavros.

Alex turned to Forsyth for guidance.

Forsyth cleared his throat and responded for his client. "Sergeant Byron, I want the record to reflect that I strongly advised Alex against this, but he was insistent that he needed to speak with you."

Byron knew Forsyth was simply trying to cover his own ass. Ultimately, if Stavros were found guilty, he might later try and claim ineffective assistance of counsel in order to vacate the verdict. And, if that happened, this very meeting could prove to be the turning point in their case against Alex.

Byron returned his attention to Stavros. "Mr. Stavros, I've been around the block more than a few times and it has been my experience that a man facing a murder charge will say almost anything to get out of it. We have more than enough evidence, all of which points directly at you, to proceed to trial. If your goal is to try and confuse the issue, you should save that for court."

Byron glanced in Forsyth's direction. "I'm sure your attorney is more than capable of confusing a jury."

"I appreciate your candor, Sergeant Byron," Stavros said. "But whether you believe it or not, I cared deeply for Dani, and I did not kill her. I only want to help you get the person responsible."

Forsyth squirmed in his chair.

Byron removed a small digital recorder from his jacket and set it on the table between them. He powered it on and activated the record feature, checking to make sure the red light was illuminated.

"I assume you won't mind if I record this as well," Forsyth said, pulling out his own recorder which Byron saw was already running.

"By all means," Byron said.

Never a fan of anything digital, Byron pulled out his notebook and prepared to take notes. You could never go wrong with redundancy. After taking care of the preliminaries, which included the rereading of Miranda, Byron began the interview. "Alex, take me back to Saturday night, July 8th. Where were you?"

"As I told you before, I was attending the annual Northeast Restaurant Association Conference in Boston, Massachusetts."

"You also told me that you were in Boston for the entire weekend and that you didn't return to Maine until late Sunday, but that's not true, is it?"

"No, it isn't. I didn't tell you the truth because I didn't want my wife, Deborah, to find out that I was having an affair."

"Did you meet up with Danica Faherty during that weekend?"

"Yes, I did."

"When?"

"I drove to Maine Saturday night, before midnight."

"Was this a planned meeting?"

"Yes. Dani and I had already discussed it during the week."

The admission confirmed Byron's suspicion as they had previously checked and found no record of contact or texts from Alex on Faherty's cellphone history obtained from the cell provider.

"Where did the two of you meet?" Byron asked.

"At my mother's former residence on Bowdoin Street in Portland."

"Had the two of you met there before?"

"Yes. We met up at Lina's house because it is vacant."

"How many times?"

"I don't know. Quite a few."

"What's quite a few?" Byron asked. "Half dozen? A dozen?"

"We had been seeing each other for several months."

"When you say seeing each other, by that you mean what?"

"Having sex."

"Did you have sex with Danica Saturday night July 8th?"

"No. Dani didn't arrive until almost two o'clock."

"Sunday morning?"

"Yes."

"Did you have sex with Danica on Sunday morning July 9th?"

"Yes. Twice."

"What happened afterwards?"

"We fell asleep."

Byron maintained eye contact with Alex, pen poised above the notepad, waiting for him to continue.

"I had set the alarm on my cellphone for five o'clock and it woke us up."

"Why so early?"

"Because I wanted to get back to the hotel where the conference was being held before anyone began to look for me."

"You mean before you were missed? You needed to establish an alibi, right?"

Forsyth jumped in. "Alex, I'm afraid I

must advise you not to answer that —"

Alex held his hand up to silence his attorney. "Please, let me finish."

Forsyth punctuated his displeasure with a long sigh and a shake of his head. "Go ahead."

Alex readdressed Byron. "Yes, I was trying to establish an alibi, but not because I killed Dani. I needed an alibi because of my affair. Deborah and I have had problems before, Sergeant. She threatened to divorce me and take the kids away." Stavros paused to look down at the table. The reality of his situation was beginning to sink in. "Now, I guess she probably will."

"Let me get this straight," Byron said. "You were so worried about Deborah finding out that you cheated on her again anyway."

"Look, I know I haven't always been the best husband, but I am not a murderer. Deborah and I haven't really been in love for quite a while now. Honestly, we're really only together because of the children."

"Why did you borrow George Martin's car for the return trip to Maine?"

"Because, if I had used my own car Deborah would've seen the trip on the EZ Pass statement," Stavros said.

"So, you borrowed your friend's vehicle

then asked him to lie for you?"

"Yes. But I never meant for George to get into trouble."

"Where was Danica when you left Bowdoin Street on Sunday morning?"

"I got dressed, and she walked me to the door."

"And?"

"She kissed me goodbye, and I left."

"The last time you saw Danica she was standing by the door?"

"Yes."

"What was she wearing when you left?"

"A bra and underwear."

"Did you see anyone as you were walking to Martin's car or as you were driving away?"

"No. But it was early. I didn't see anybody."

Byron kept his gaze fixed on Alex waiting to see if he'd look away. He didn't.

"Did you kill Danica Faherty, Alex?"

"No. I swear to you, when I left Bowdoin Street on Sunday morning, Dani was alive."

"When did you first learn that something was wrong? That Danica was missing?"

"I tried calling her Tuesday afternoon —"

"Tuesday the 11th?"

"Yes, but her phone went directly to voice-mail."

"Did you leave a message?" Byron asked, already knowing he hadn't.

"No. We had a rule about that."

"Your rule?"

Stavros shrugged.

"When was the last time you saw or spoke to Danica Faherty, Alex?"

"When I left her at Bowdoin Street on Sunday morning, July 9th."

Byron closed his notebook and returned it to his coat pocket. "Alex, you failed to mention that you were having a sexual relationship with Danica Faherty the first time I spoke with you."

Stavros opened his mouth to respond. Byron held up a hand to stop him.

"You were the last person to see her alive. You lied about sneaking up to see her on the morning she was killed. You borrowed a friend's car so there would be no EZ Pass record of your trip. You asked a friend to lie for you if the police asked where you were. We have evidence confirming that Dani was killed in the very house where you had been meeting regularly for sex. And lastly, traces of your semen were collected during her autopsy. In fact, nothing you have told me changes a thing. I'm curious, what exactly did you think meeting with me today would accomplish?"

Stavros glanced nervously at his attorney.

Forsyth held up both hands in surrender. "You've gone this far against my advice. You might as well go all in."

Byron waited for Stavros to show his final card.

"Sergeant Byron, you say you recovered my semen from Dani."

"That's correct. The medical examiner who conducted the autopsy did. There were traces of semen containing your DNA in and around her vaginal area and on the underwear she was wearing when we recovered her body."

"Dani and I had sex numerous times over the past few months, I don't deny it. But I always wore a condom. Trojan brand condoms. Each and every time. She insisted on it."

Byron felt something tighten inside. *Had they missed something?*

"So, how exactly did my semen get into Dani?" Stavros said.

CHAPTER 31

Monday, 12:35 P.M.,
July 24, 2017

Byron departed 50 County Way and drove directly to 109. He parked in the rear garage and was exiting the unmarked when his cell buzzed with an incoming call from Gabriel Pelligrosso.

"Sarge, you in the building?" Pelligrosso asked.

"In about thirty seconds."

"Can you swing by the lab? I've got something to show you."

"Be right there, Gabe."

Pelligrosso led Byron to one of the back rooms inside the regional crime lab. The space housed the cyanoacrylate fuming chamber, a large glass and metal enclosure which might have resembled a fish tank had it not been attached to a direct ventilation system. Byron could see that his evidence tech had constructed a makeshift metal rack, over which a dozen or so pieces of dark-colored high-density polyethylene of various sizes had been stretched.

"What are those?" Byron asked.

"Scraps of the trash bag we recovered on the hill near the Casco Bay Bridge. The bag that contained Faherty's head."

"You're fuming all of them?"

"I wasn't planning to, as I figured the only prints I was likely to find would belong to your buddy Winn."

"But?"

"But I was wrong."

"You mean you didn't find Winn's finger-prints?"

"No, I recovered plenty of evidence left behind by Winn's greasy paws, but I've also recovered a couple of prints that aren't his."

"Were you able to match them to anyone?"

Pelligrosso shook his head. "I ran them through AFIS but got no matches."

"Not even Alex Stavros?"

"First comparison I did. They aren't Alex's."

Byron considered this latest find and what it might mean to the case against Alex. If Forsyth and his client were playing the alternate suspect game, an unidentified set of prints lifted from the garbage bag that had been used to discard Faherty's head and clothing would go a long way toward swaying a jury. It was time to regroup.

"You available to meet with the rest of the team?" Byron checked the time. "Say, twenty minutes, CID conference room?"

"I'll be there, Sarge."

At one o'clock every investigator assigned to the Faherty case had gathered around the long table in the CID conference room listening as Byron relayed the new information.

"You believe him, Sarge?" Nugent asked, referencing Alex's claim of being framed.

"I haven't decided yet. But if he is telling the truth about the condom, it puts a big wrinkle in our case against him. It also means we need to take a harder look at anyone who had access to Lina's old house."

"Like?" Robbins asked.

"Like Lina, Deborah, Petri, Uncle Dennis, and anyone else we can think of."

Stevens stood up and circled the names as Byron listed them.

Byron turned to Pelligrosso. "Gabe, did we find any evidence that someone may have used a condom at Lina's house? Maybe a discarded wrapper?"

"We weren't specifically looking, but I don't recall seeing anything like that."

"Anyone else?" Byron asked as he glanced around the room.

No one else had either.

"Did Alex tell you how he disposed of the rubber?" E.T. Murphy asked.

"Says he discarded it in a wicker bedroom wastebasket," Byron said. "There should have been a liner."

"There wasn't," Robbins said. "Not when we searched."

"Did he provide you with specifics about what he used, Sarge?" Stevens asked. "Brand, where he purchased them, anything like that?"

"Actually, he did," Byron said as he handed photostatic copies of the relevant information from his notes to the other investigators. "According to Alex, Danica purchased the condoms for him and kept some in her purse. We need to check her apartment again to see if she stashed any there."

"I can take care of that," Stevens said.

"Thanks, Mel," Byron said. "Where are we at processing the recovered evidence?"

Pelligrosso spoke up. "Murph and I are still working on the items retrieved from both the house on Bowdoin and the Commercial Street recoveries."

At Byron's urging Pelligrosso brought

them up to speed on the fuming for prints.

"Why?" Nugent asked. "Wouldn't all the prints belong to that Glantz guy? Alex would've at least been smart enough to wear gloves."

"That's what I figured, but in the interest of being thorough I fumed a few pieces of the bag anyway."

"And?" Nugent said. "Tell us already. Jeez, you're as bad as Dustin."

"Hey," Tran said.

Stevens leaned over and punched Nugent in the bicep. "Don't be a dick."

Byron hid a grin.

"And, I lifted a couple of prints that don't belong to Winn," Pelligrosso continued.

"Whose are they?" Stevens asked.

"I don't know. They aren't in AFIS."

"Fuuuck," Nugent said.

Byron knew he needed to consult with Ferguson again.

"Sergeant Byron," a voice said, causing every head to turn toward the doorway where Shirley Grant was standing.

"What is it, Shirley?"

"The front desk just called up. You have a visitor in the lobby."

"They say who?"

"An Erwin Glantz."

Byron and Glantz stood outside in the bright sunshine of 109's plaza, next to the large concrete planter that bordered the rear garage. Given Glantz's propensity to avoid regular personal hygiene, like showering, an out-of-doors meeting seemed the prudent course. The rectangular weed-filled planter, built into the garage and the steps leading up to it, had become PPD's unofficial smoking area. Winn sat down on the edge of the planter, availing himself of that particular bad habit, while Byron patiently waited for him to delve into the specifics of his unannounced visit.

"Been thinking a lot about that night in the dumpster," Winn said.

Byron wondered if there were any other professions, besides law enforcement, where a conversation might begin with those words. It seemed unlikely. He remained silent, allowing Winn to lead the conversation.

"Dreaming about it really," Winn continued. "I seen some really bad shit in Iraq, Sarge. Believe it."

Looking into Winn's haunted eyes, Byron couldn't help but believe it.

"But I never imagined I'd come home to that." Winn paused long enough to finger a bent Marlboro out of the nearly empty pack in his pocket. His weathered hands trembled as he lit the new cigarette using the stub of the last. He inhaled deeply before continuing.

"I remembered something that I hadn't when I spoke to you before."

"What was that?" Byron asked.

"About the truck. Remember I told you it had like a loud rumbling exhaust?"

"I remember."

"Well, there was something else about it that stood out. The engine. Had kind of a hitch in it."

"A hitch?" Byron asked.

"Yeah. The way it idled. Wasn't smooth. You know? Like an old carburetor in need of a screw adjustment to set the idle fuel mixture."

Byron studied his veteran friend. Winn may have carried more than his share of demons, some souvenirs from the Middle East, some of his own creation, but he wasn't stupid. Much like a seasoned cop, Winn saw and heard things to which others paid little or no attention. Being homeless meant people went out of their way to avoid him. It is simply human nature to avoid anything unpleasant. Dressed in filthy secondhand clothing and sporting poor personal hygiene, Winn was definitely unpleasant. He could stand or sit anywhere in Portland, listening to other people's conversations and, as long as he wasn't invading anyone's personal space, they would hardly take any notice. He was literally a surveillance expert without a target. Byron was confident that if Winn believed the vehicle they were looking for was an older truck with a loud exhaust, and a hitch in its engine, then that's exactly what it was.

"You eaten today?" Byron asked.

Winn looked up at him through rheumy eyes. "Not yet."

Byron removed the wallet from his pants pocket and slid out a twenty-dollar bill. "Here," he said handing it to Winn.

"What's this for?" Winn asked. "I didn't tell you all that stuff about the truck for money."

"And that isn't why I'm giving it to you," Byron said. "It's not for the information."

"Then what?"

Byron smiled. "For food. Man's gotta eat, right?"

Winn closed a grubby hand around the bill. "*Gracias,* Sarge."

"*De nada,* my friend."

■ ■ ■ ■

Byron retreated to the now deserted conference room and studied the whiteboard.

He made a notation about the hitch in the truck engine, then added a new column to the board titling it *Unknown.* Under the heading he wrote, *condom, truck,* and *fingerprint.* He stopped to survey the changes to the board and realized that he could have just as easily written *Forsyth* in the new column's heading. Byron was unwillingly constructing a defense for Alex. He thought back to Ferguson's theories. It was beyond ironic. But as in any investigation, every learned fact brought them closer to the truth, much like an optometrist dialing in a lens until everything was in perfect focus. *Is it clearer now, or now?* Was Alex responsible for the death of Danica Faherty? Possibly. There was more evidence to support his guilt than not, but that was only a preponderance of evidence. "More likely than not" would've been great if Alex Stavros had run a red light, but this was murder and anything less than beyond a reasonable doubt would see him walk. And if Alex was responsible, then this was nothing more than a misdirection campaign, likely thought up by

Attorney Forsyth. A way of forcing Byron and his team to chase their tails. All Byron could do was keep checking every fact and detail until a clearer picture began to emerge.

He was placing the black marker in the tray at the base of the whiteboard when his cell rang, startling him. He answered it.

"Byron."

"Jim Ferguson here. You rang?"

After bringing Ferguson up to speed, Byron met up with Melissa Stevens. If Alex and his attorney were right about the planted evidence, then someone was trying to set up Alex for the crime. But to figure out who that might be they'd need to know the motive behind it. Byron and Stevens pulled up in front of Danica Faherty's former Brackett Street residence and parked.

The landlord had allowed them to maintain possession of a key to Faherty's apartment. While Earl Wescott couldn't afford the loss of rental income indefinitely, he agreed to wait for a few weeks if it would help the case. Byron unlocked the door to the apartment and the two detectives stepped inside.

"Where do you want to start?" Stevens asked.

"Let's take it room by room," Byron said. "We're looking for the birth control described by Alex, obviously. But let's search as if we have no idea what we're looking for. There may well be something else we've missed."

They spent the next hour tearing Faherty's apartment apart. Taking care not to destroy anything, they pulled out drawers and checked the undersides, removed wall hangings, and looked under the mattress. They searched anything and everything until they were confident that nothing had been overlooked.

Byron was just finishing up in the bathroom when Stevens appeared in the doorway holding a slip of paper.

"What's that?" Byron asked.

"Found it crammed in behind her desk drawer. It's a CVS Pharmacy receipt from May 3rd. Guess what's listed among her purchases?"

"Trojan brand condoms."

"Yup. Pleasure pack. Box of forty. Guess Dani thought she and Alex had a future."

"Any luck finding the box?"

"Nope. Maybe they used them already."

Byron felt his face redden.

"So, Alex was telling the truth about the

472

condom," LeRoyer said, making a nervous pass through his hair with the fingers of his right hand.

"Possibly," Byron said. "But we still haven't located any condoms. All the receipt proves is that Dani purchased some birth control during the time she was seeing Alex Stavros."

"She may well have been seeing other people, too," Stevens said.

"Still, he did correctly identify the brand," LeRoyer said. "Let's assume for a moment that Alex is telling the truth, and someone planted his semen to point the finger at him. What's the next step?"

"We need to work the lists," Byron said.

"What lists?" LeRoyer said.

Stevens spoke up again. "Access and motive."

Byron and Stevens had compiled two lists. The first was comprised of anyone who had direct access to Lina's West End mansion. The second was anyone who might have wanted Danica dead. The entire list of suspects amounted to Angelina Stavros, Deborah Stavros, Alex Stavros, Petri Stavros, Dennis Stavros, and Dani's former roommate Destiny Collins. Everyone agreed that their best use of resources was to focus on the crossover names.

Shirley Grant appeared in the conference room doorway.

"Hey, Shirl," LeRoyer said. "You need me?"

"No, but Chief Lynds is looking for you."

"Okay."

"And Sergeant Byron, your cousin Peter Murray is on hold. Where do you want to take the call?"

"Switch it to my office."

Byron was sitting at his desk talking to Murray when Detectives Nugent and Stevens appeared in the doorway. He waved both in as he continued his conversation.

"That's great news, cuz," Byron said. "Is he talking?"

"Not yet, and it's way too soon to get excited about it," Murray said. "We've still got a long way to go with our case. This is very preliminary. Just wanted you to know that we made an arrest."

"All right, I'll wait until I hear back from you. Congrats."

Byron hung up and looked at the two detectives seated in his office.

"Who was that?" Nugent asked.

"My cousin in Boston," Byron said.

"They made an arrest?" Stevens asked.

"About an hour ago."

474

"Holy fuck," Nugent said. "That's great. How'd they catch him?"

"Pole cam video. Apparently, DEA was up on a drug case connected to a warehouse near where the last body was recovered. They finally coughed up some footage of the van they think may have been used to dump the body. The guy's got all sorts of cutting equipment. Looks like he's some sort of metal rat. Ripping off these empty businesses and selling the scrap on the black market."

"Makes sense, right?" Stevens said.

"He's talking then?" Nugent asked.

"Not yet," Byron said. "And Murray said it's crazy down there right now. Do me a favor, okay? I need both of you to keep that little nugget to yourselves. I don't want our leak fucking up their cases."

Nugent and Stevens exchanged a glance that Byron couldn't interpret. "What?"

"Go on, Mel," Nugent prodded. "Tell him."

"Tell me what?" Byron said.

"I know who the leak is," Stevens said.

CHAPTER 32

Byron burst into the CID locker room. The heavy wooden door banged against a row of lockers.

"Jesus Christ, Sarge," Robbins said. "You scared the shit out of me."

"I'll ask just once," Byron said. "Why?"

"W-why what?"

Byron took two steps forward, as Robbins stood up from the bench.

"Hey, what are you doing?" Robbins said louder than necessary.

Byron stepped on the toe of one of Robbins's dress shoes then grabbed a handful of his tie just below the collar, twisting it and pushing the detective backward until his head and shoulders were tight against the lockers. "I know you're the leak, Bernie."

"I don't know who you've been talking to,

but I didn't leak anything to the press. I swear."

Byron leaned in close enough that he could smell Robbins's bad breath. "Who said anything about the press?"

"Then, what are you talking about?"

"Why have you been giving case updates to your buddy Kenny Crosby?"

Even in his current state Robbins couldn't suppress a nervous chuckle.

"This funny to you, Bernie? Fucking up our case. Having Dani's parents find out about their daughter being mutilated on the front page of a newspaper?"

"I don't know how the paper got that, Sarge. Honest."

"But you *were* giving regular updates to Kenny, weren't you?"

"J-just a couple of texts. That's all."

"Why?"

"H-he asked me to. Look, I don't want to get in the middle of this. I —"

"Too late," Byron said as he pulled on the tie jerking Robbins's body forward away from the lockers then shoved hard, slamming him into them again. "Why were you texting him?"

"K-Kenny thought if you got jammed up on this investigation, if you screwed it up, Lynds would boot you out, and there would be two CID sergeant vacancies to fill. He wasn't sure he'd get the first one, but he knew Lynds would have to take him if there were two."

"And you volunteered to help him, huh? Good ol' Bernie. No matter who got hurt in the process."

"I — I'm sorry, Sarge. Really. I didn't think anyone w—"

"What exactly have you told him?"

"Not much."

Byron saw the bead of sweat rolling down Robbins's ruddy forehead. "Just a couple of texts, huh?"

"Yeah. That's all."

"Give me your cellphone," Byron said.

Byron located Crosby right where he knew he'd be in the PPD gym on the second floor. The drug sergeant was covered in a sheen of sweat and putting a hurt on the heavy bag when Byron walked in. The two men had the entire gym to themselves.

"Well, well, well, if it isn't the world's most fucked-up detective sergeant," Crosby said as he stepped away from the bag. "Tell me, how many people are you going to lock up for that Faherty murder before you get to the right one?"

"I know what you've been doing, Kenny,"

Byron said.

Crosby hesitated a moment, obviously taken aback by Byron's comment. "I don't know what you're talking about. I haven't been doing anything."

"Oh, no?" Byron said as he held up Robbins's cell.

"What's that?"

"Your stoolie's cellphone. Got some very interesting text messages on here. Lots of back and forth between a certain disgruntled and soon to be returning to the PD drug sergeant and Bernie Robbins, who will be lucky if he still can find a uniform that fits after I get his ass booted back to Patrol for being a rat."

"That stupid fuck," Crosby growled. "I told him to delete those texts after I sent them."

"Yeah, well, he didn't. And I've got the proof that it was you who leaked all our progress to Davis Billingslea. It's all right here."

Kenny circled around to try and get between Byron and the door. He tightened the Velcro wrist straps on his boxing gloves. "You really think I'm just gonna let you walk out of here with that?"

"That's exactly what's gonna happen," Byron said as he slipped off his suit coat and tossed it over a bench.

"You're such a pussy, John. How long before you're fucking the Queen Mum anyway?"

Both men turned at the sound of the gym door closing. Standing there with her arms crossed tightly was Chief Lynds. Standing next to her was an equally pissed-off looking Lieutenant LeRoyer.

"Oh, hey, Chief," Crosby said. "Hey, Lieu. How long have you guys been standing there?"

"Long enough," LeRoyer said.

"My office, Sergeant Crosby," Lynds barked.

"Sure thing. I just gotta —"

"Now!"

Chief Lynds may have directed her wrath at Crosby, but LeRoyer wasn't about to let Byron off the hook for his handling of the issue.

"What the hell am I supposed to do with you? You threaten one of your own detectives. Take his phone. Jesus, John."

"Actually, he's one of George's detectives, Marty. And he voluntarily turned over the phone to me when he realized his mistake."

"Oh, is that what happened?"

"Bernie say different?" Byron asked.

"He's not saying anything. Says he came to you because he felt guilty about what he'd done."

"Well then, there you have it."

LeRoyer tented his fingers above his desk. He was staring Byron down trying to be intimidating. It wasn't working. It never did.

"Look, you wanted the leak stopped. I stopped it. It isn't my fault Kenny tried to throw the contest. By the way, they announce the new CID sergeant yet? I'm assuming it isn't Crosby."

A grin appeared on LeRoyer's face. "Diane got the position. Not sure when Lynds is planning to make the announcement, so don't say anything yet." LeRoyer's manufactured scowl returned. "And don't do that to me, John. I hate it when you do that. I'm still pissed at you, okay?"

Byron held up his hands in surrender. "Okay. So, can I have Luke Gardiner now?"

"Yeah, yeah, he's yours," LeRoyer said. "What about the case? What's the next move?"

As Byron opened his mouth to answer his cell buzzed with a call from Tran.

"Hey, Dustin," Byron said, answering on the second ring.

"Striped Dude, where are you?" Tran said.

"Upstairs with the lieutenant. What's up?"

"Well, you know how we couldn't figure out who might have had a truck as none of our suspects had one registered in the BMV database?"

"Yes, I know. And?"

"And I just tripped over a little factoid of which we were previously unaware. Angelina Stavros has set up an LLC for her various financial interests."

"How does that help us?" Byron asked.

"She has a three-quarter-ton pickup registered under AS Holdings. A GMC Sierra."

Dennis Stavros, Byron thought. "Her handyman probably uses it."

"Alex's uncle, right?"

"Right."

"Because, I just located the military records for Dennis Stavros. And a full set of fingerprints."

"I'll be right down."

Byron took the information Tran had provided directly to Gabriel Pelligrosso in the lab.

"Can you work with these?" Byron asked, not sure if the printer quality was detailed enough for comparison purposes.

Pelligrosso slid the prints under a magnifier and studied them for a moment before answering. "Should be able to."

"Let me know."

"Will do."

Byron immediately grabbed Detectives Nugent and Gardiner. He assigned Gardiner to continue the search that Robbins had previously undertaken trying to locate where the lumberyard padlock had been purchased, while Nugent was tasked with conducting surveillance on Prouts Neck, just down the road from the Stavros family compound. Tran finding a truck no one knew about had the potential to be big. And if Byron's intuition was right, Dennis Stavros might just turn out to be the missing piece to their puzzle.

"You want him pulled over if I make contact?" Nugent asked.

"Not at this point," Byron said. "I just want to keep him in our sights. He may be in a different vehicle than the one we're looking for, and I don't want to tip our hand until we're sure he's involved. If you see him in the truck, let me know."

Byron was pacing the conference room like a caged tiger. He could feel things starting to come together. Some of the answers seemed nearly close enough to grab onto.

Waiting was simply part of the process, but it had never made him comfortable. He wanted to be doing something, anything that would drive the investigation forward. But he had done all he could. Each of his people had been assigned a task. Now all he could do was wait. He reached into his pocket and removed his AA coin. Holding it in his palm he thought about the will-power it had taken to earn it. The patience. After a moment he returned it to his pocket and resumed pacing.

"Do you find that helps?" Diane said from the doorway.

"How long have you been standing there?" Byron asked.

"Long enough. Well, does it?"

"Probably not. But boy if I had a Fitbit, I'd be kicking ass."

"That you would."

"Any word yet?" Byron asked.

"I met with Lynds this morning," Diane said.

"And? Did she make a decision?"

"Yes, but they haven't told all the applicants yet. I promised not to say anything. I'm not sure Kenny knows."

Oh, he knows, Byron thought. "So, did you get it?"

A smile lit her face as she nodded.

"That's great! I'm so proud of you, Di."

"Are you? You're okay with all of this? I mean, it's really —"

Byron leaned in and kissed her, cutting her off in mid-sentence. "I'm more than okay with it."

"Don't say anything, okay? I don't want to get jammed up with Lynds before I even start the job."

Byron held up his hand in the sign of the Boy Scouts. "Scout's honor."

Diane's eyes narrowed, and she placed a hand on her hip. "You were a scout?"

"No, but whenever I do this it always seems to put people at ease."

They sat down at the table and Byron brought her up to speed on the case.

"So, you think it's the uncle?" Diane asked.

"I'm not sure. I'm betting he's involved, but maybe only in discarding Dani's body. I think he's loyal to the family, specifically Lina. Whether he was involved in the murder or not, he'd want to find some way of diverting suspicion away from her and the rest of the family."

"How does that square with Alex's claim that he's being set up? Why would Dennis want to frame his nephew for murdering Faherty?"

"I don't know. I haven't figured that out yet."

Byron and Diane both looked up as E.T. Pelligrosso entered the room with a grin on his face.

"Well?" Byron said impatiently. "Do they match?"

"Oh yeah. The only prints on that bag belong to Erwin Glantz and Dennis Stavros."

CHAPTER 33

It took until five o'clock that afternoon before Nugent caught sight of Dennis Stavros driving inbound on Black Point Road. Stavros was alone behind the wheel of a pine green GMC Sierra pickup; the very same truck Tran had discovered registered to Lina's LLC.

As he was in an unmarked and outside of Portland's jurisdiction, Nugent radioed for a Scarborough unit to make the stop. Stavros nearly made it all the way to Route 1 at Oak Hill before they finally pulled him over. Nugent explained the reasons for the stop and for impounding the truck as he took Dennis into custody. Nugent left the Scarborough officer to oversee towing the vehicle, while he transported Stavros to 109.

Byron and Stevens watched as Nugent escorted a handcuffed and subdued Dennis

487

Stavros through CID and deposited him in Interview Room One.

"What did he have to say when you told him why you were arresting him?" Byron asked.

"Nothing," Nugent said. "Honestly, I think he was waiting for this. Like he knew we'd show up sooner or later."

LeRoyer breezed into the conference room. "That the uncle?" he asked, pointing at the monitor.

"Yes," Byron said. "Dennis Stavros."

"Who's interviewing him?"

"I thought I might," Byron said. "Unless you feel strongly about it, Marty."

"Don't be a dick, John. Does he know about the fingerprints?"

"Not yet. Nuge told him that he was under arrest in connection with our murder investigation into Danica Faherty, but that's it."

"What did he say?"

"Nothing," Nugent said. "But I don't think he was very surprised to see us."

"Where's the truck?"

"Scarborough PD is towing it back here now," Byron said. "I've got Gabe waiting to process it."

"And get this, Lieu," Nugent said. "It's got a loud exhaust and a hitch in its idle."

Byron turned to Stevens. "You ready?"

"Let's do this," she said.

After a brief and somewhat failed attempt at cordiality, Byron read Stavros the Miranda warning. After providing confirmation that he understood his rights, Dennis waived them and agreed to speak with the detectives.

Byron led off the questioning. "I believe Detective Nugent already explained why we stopped you, and why it is that you're in custody. Is that correct?"

"Yes," Stavros said.

"You should know that my evidence technicians are combing over your truck as we speak looking for any evidence that links it to the murder of Danica Faherty."

Stavros indicated his understanding.

"You're probably wondering how we linked you to the crime?" Byron looked over at Stevens and nodded.

"We lifted several of your fingerprints off of a garbage bag that was used to dispose of evidence of the crime," Stevens said.

"How did you get my fingerprints?" Stavros asked. "I've never been arrested."

Byron found it interesting that Dennis's first comment hadn't been a denial, or some excuse that the bag used was probably taken from Lina's old home and that he might have touched them previously before the killer used them.

"Your military record," Byron said. "Care to explain how your fingerprints got on the bag?"

Detective Luke Gardiner stood in the checkout line at Maine Hardware on St. John St. in Portland's West End. He had taken up the search for where the padlock had been purchased following Bernie Robbins's departure from the case. He knew that trying to locate the store from which a single padlock had been purchased nearly two weeks prior was a fool's errand. The lock could have been purchased anywhere, including the internet. He would rather have been working some other more important aspect of the case, but he knew from his limited major case involvement that it was often the smallest details that broke a case wide open.

It was dinnertime and only a single register was open. Gardiner guessed that the other employees were on break. The customer directly in front of him had finally made it to the counter but then the clerk and the customer got into a disagreement over a sale price for one of the items.

Gardiner shook his head. To those on the outside, detective work probably seemed glamorous. It wasn't. Gardiner was beginning to drift off into his own thoughts when a voice called out to him.

"I can take you over here, sir," a slightly built man said from the other register.

Gardiner hurried over to the clerk and produced his ID. "Thanks a lot."

"What can I do for you, Detective?"

"We're checking every store in the area looking to see if you would have a record of someone purchasing a very specific padlock about two weeks ago."

"What kind of lock?"

Gardiner removed his cellphone and scrolled through the images until he located the picture of the padlock taken off the gate at the lumberyard that Pelligrosso had sent him. "This one."

The clerk slid on a pair of black-framed reading glasses and bent to look at the screen. "That's a Shade lock," he said. "Do you happen to have the lock with you?"

"No, it's in evidence. Do you sell them?"

"We certainly do. Is that a picture of a similar lock or the actual lock that was purchased?"

"This is a photo of the actual lock. Why?"

The clerk began tapping the keyboard in

front of a desktop computer sitting atop the counter beside the register. "Because there are several different style Shade padlocks. That one is pretty specific."

Gardiner's excitement was building. He hoped that the clerk's knowledge meant he was getting close.

"Yup," the clerk said. "We did sell one of those a couple of weeks back. Looks like it was on Monday July 10th."

"Cash or credit?"

"Actually, it was purchased on account. There's already a card on file."

"Who is the account holder?"

"Don't you need a subpoena or warrant or something?" the clerk asked.

"Sir, I'm working a homicide. The longer it takes for me to do my job, the more likely the persons responsible will get away with it."

The clerk looked over his glasses at Gardiner, sizing him up.

"Please," Gardiner said. "I just need the name of the account holder."

"I don't know the actual account owner because it's an LLC, but the name on the account is AS Holdings."

Gardiner could feel disappointment creeping in.

"What about the person who used the account?" Gardiner asked. "Do you know him?"

"No, not by name. But he's in here quite frequently."

"Can you describe him?"

"Middle-aged. Rugged. Mustache."

"Do you have in-store surveillance video?"

"Yeah, but we don't keep it that far back. It writes over itself every few days. Storage space and all."

"Did this man make any other purchases, or just the lock?"

The clerk looked back at the screen and tapped a few more keys. "Bought a few things actually."

"Like?"

"Construction grade garbage bags, several large plastic tarps, a box of nitrile gloves, and a pack of saw blades."

"Saw blades?" Gardiner's voice cracked as he fought to hide his growing excitement. "What kind of saw blades?"

"Reciprocating saw blades."

Byron returned to the interview room holding a printout of the purchase invoice that Gardiner had obtained from Maine Hardware. He sat across from Stavros, placing the sheet of paper facedown on the table. Stavros stared at it, unblinking.

Byron pounced before Stavros had a chance to think. "You know the weird thing about police investigations, Dennis? You never know what will be important in making a case. Often, it's the most insignificant things. It's not like the movies where every killer is a brilliant sociopath. Most murderers are everyday people who just snap. Once they realize what they've done they scramble to try and cover their tracks. Problem is, they make a lot of mistakes." Byron tapped his index finger slowly and repeatedly on the paper invoice. "I bet you're wondering what mistakes you made."

Stavros looked up from the table and picked a spot on the wall behind Byron to stare at.

Byron continued. "One of the curiosities of this case was the lock we found securing a gate at the lumberyard. See, the security company had a key that fit every lock on every gate, except the one securing the Maple Street entrance. All I could figure was that the person or persons who had abandoned Danica Faherty's body must have cut the old one off and replaced it."

Byron could see the emotional wall Stavros had erected beginning to slip.

"My detectives have scoured the Greater Portland area trying to find where that lock might have been purchased, and who might have purchased it. See, we figured if we could establish that we could identify Danica's killer."

Stavros's shoulders sagged in defeat and his eyes began to water.

Byron pressed on. "Imagine our surprise when we found out where the lock had been purchased and when. You see, it was the day after Danica was killed and two days before we found her decapitated remains."

Stavros reached for the cup of water and drank. His hand was shaking.

Byron continued. "And the lock wasn't the only thing that the salesman rang up for the customer that day." He paused long enough to flip the Maine Hardware invoice faceup and slide it toward Stavros. Stavros looked away.

"You're not looking at it, Dennis. Don't you want to see what else the customer purchased? Or do you already know?"

Stavros wiped at his eyes with the base of his palm. Byron could see the faint welts on his wrist and the residue of calamine powder. Byron realized that what he had thought was a scar on the side of Stavros's neck, the first time he'd met him at Lina's house in Prouts Neck, was a poison ivy welt.

Byron pointed at Stavros's wrist. "One of

my detectives encountered some poison ivy during the body recovery. Got a nasty rash on his ankles. Looks like you got into something similar. Mind if I ask where that happened?"

"Outside," Stavros said, pulling his sleeves down to cover the marks. "I was working in the yard."

"Where, exactly? Because we could send some detectives out to check."

Stavros said nothing.

Byron waited a beat before continuing. He could see that the pace of his questioning was having the desired effect. Stavros was slowly coming apart as Byron pushed him further into a corner.

"I think the thing about all of this that I have the hardest time wrapping my head around is what kind of a monster could do such a thing to a decent young woman like Danica? Murdering her in cold blood, then trying to cover up the crime by —"

"I didn't kill her," Stavros said at last. "I didn't. That isn't what happened."

Byron let that statement hang there a moment. "Tell me what did happen, Dennis."

Byron could see the wheels turning inside LeRoyer's head as the lieutenant processed what he had been told.

"So, Uncle Dennis has admitted to cutting off Danica's head, then moving and dumping the body, but that's it?" LeRoyer said.

"That's all he'll admit to," Byron said.

"Then who killed her?"

"Says he doesn't know," Byron said. "He told me that Lina had sent him to the Bowdoin Street house on Monday to retrieve a few small items of furniture. Dennis told me he found a woman's body in the kitchen."

"Does Dennis think Lina killed her?"

"He assumed she'd sent him there knowing he'd find the body, and that he'd deal with it. Kind of like don't ask don't tell. I get the distinct impression this wouldn't be the first time that Uncle Dennis has been called upon to clean up a family mess."

"Did he know who Danica Faherty was?"

"Says he didn't, but he did know that Alex had been taking young women to the house and figured that she was one of them."

"How did he know?"

"On several different occasions he had found evidence that someone had been having sex in one of the bedrooms."

"What made him think it was Alex and not Petri?"

Byron gave the lieutenant a "seriously?"

look. "Alex's reputation was well-known within the family. Besides, Petri isn't married. Why would he need to sneak around?"

"Why in hell did he cut her head off?" LeRoyer asked.

"Dennis told me that he'd been reading the news stories about the Horseman and figured copying the killer's signature and relocating the crime scene away from the house would be the perfect way to cast suspicion away from the family."

"Then Alex may still have killed her?"

"The uncle can't say who the killer is, only that he thought it might have been Lina. Or, it's possible that Lina found the body in the kitchen and, knowing who it was, sent the uncle there to deal with it."

"It's also possible that Lina killed her." LeRoyer made a nervous swipe through his hair with the fingers of his right hand. "Jesus, is there anything about this case that's clear?"

"I think that's the whole point with this family," Byron said. "Deniability."

"Now what?"

"I think it's time to take a different approach with the Stavros matriarch."

Byron brought the Taurus to a stop directly in front of the mansion, then stepped out.

Stevens pulled her unmarked in behind his. Lina stood in the open doorway to the home watching them. She was dressed in a dark wool pullover and cream-colored slacks. Clothing better suited to January than a humid July night.

"Good evening, Sergeant Byron," she said. "I've been expecting you." She turned her attention toward the procession of vehicles parking adjacent to the duck pond. "I assume, given the entourage, that you have in your possession a warrant to search my property?"

"I do," Byron said as he climbed the steps toward her.

On the lookout for a weapon, he focused on her hands, but the only thing the elegant woman held was a ceramic mug. Not much of a threat, unless she planned on throwing it at him.

"May I come in?" Byron asked.

"I suppose," she said. "I wouldn't want you to accuse me of being uncivil."

"I'll wait out here," Stevens said.

Lina turned and stepped inside. Byron followed her through the foyer down the hall and into a massive living room.

At the far end of the room she perched on an expensive-looking antique wingback facing the ocean beyond. "Sit, please," she said.

Following her lead, he sat in a matching chair. The room was cold and dry. Byron enjoyed air-conditioning as much as the next person, but this bordered on uncomfortable.

For a moment they sat in silence. Byron waited while she sipped her beverage and stared off into the distance. It was not lost on him that she hadn't offered him anything to drink.

"Dennis has gone missing," Lina said at last as if that was the topic of discussion and the reason for Byron's unannounced visit. "He's not returning my calls. I assume you know where he is." It wasn't a question.

"I do," Byron said. "And I assume you know what it is we're looking for."

She turned to face him. "You assume incorrectly. I have no idea why you are here."

"Your brother-in-law has confessed to removing Dani Faherty's body from your house on Bowdoin Street and dumping it at the lumberyard."

"I'm afraid I don't know anything about that," she said, completely devoid of emotion. "Does this mean you'll be releasing my Alex?"

"Sorry to disappoint you, Lina, but insofar as Alex is concerned nothing has changed.

He's still our best suspect for Danica Faherty's murder. That is, unless you have something to tell me?"

"I'm afraid I don't know what you mean. Are you now implying that I had something to do with Danica's death?"

"Did you?"

"Why would I want Danica dead?"

"You told me when we first met that you would do anything for your grandbabies. They bring you so much joy. Perhaps you were worried that Deborah would make good on her threat to leave Alex if he were caught cheating again. Maybe you figured that if Ms. Faherty were gone, Deborah wouldn't find out that he was still being unfaithful."

"And yet, Deborah is moving back to New York permanently and taking my grandbabies away from me anyway." Lina choked a bit on her last words. She paused to sip some more tea. "You must not think me very intelligent if you really believe that I was responsible for all of this. One of my sons is now facing a murder charge, I'm about to lose my only grandchildren forever, and I assume you'll be charging Dennis with something now."

"As we speak, there are divers searching your duck pond for evidence."

"What evidence?"

"The saw Dennis used to remove Danica's head after you sent him to the Bowdoin Street mansion to retrieve some things."

Byron thought he caught a flash of anger in Lina's eyes, but then it was gone, masked by the skill of one of Hollywood's finest actresses. Could she have successfully contained that same ire she felt toward the young woman who was messing about in her son's life? In Lina's life? Was her rage enough to cause her to lash out and kill Danica Faherty in cold blood? Byron didn't know, but he knew what he had seen.

"Dennis thinks you sent him to Bowdoin Street on purpose, knowing what he would find. Did you?"

Lina said nothing.

Byron's cell vibrated with an incoming call from Stevens.

"Hey, Mel."

"Sarge, sorry to interrupt," Stevens said.

"What is it?" Byron said.

"They've located something in the duck pond."

Byron and Stevens walked up to the edge of the pond and stood beside Lieutenant Jenkins, Scarborough PD's on-duty shift commander. The glow of Jenkins's cigarette stood in contrast to the growing gloom as daylight faded behind the trees. Gabriel Pelligrosso and Dive Master Phil Goodall were floating on the pond in the Zodiac, a small inflatable boat, as they waited on the divers below.

Jenkins turned to greet Byron. "How'd it go? She give up her son?"

"No," Byron said. "She didn't."

They looked on in silence as one of two Portland divers surfaced on the opposite shore, handing a dark bundle to Pelligrosso.

"What are you guys hoping to find?" Jenkins asked. "I mean besides the murder weapon?"

"Something that was used to misdirect us," Stevens said.

Byron observed the camera flash as Pelligrosso photographed the bundle in situ. Several moments later, after removing the contents, the E.T. held it up and illuminated it with a flashlight for them to see.

"What's that?" Jenkins asked.

"Reciprocating saw," Byron said.

"Damn. Is that what they used to —"

"Yeah," Byron said. "It is."

"Well, I guess congratulations are in order. Looks like your case is really starting to come together."

Except Byron wasn't feeling celebratory.

The discovery of the tool used to dismember a young woman wasn't a moment to revel in. Besides, the recovery only meant that Dennis Stavros had told them the truth about where he'd hidden the saw. It didn't mean he was telling the truth about everything. Byron realized that they were still a long way from having all the answers.

Jenkins slid another cigarette between his lips and lit it, then exhaled a large plume of smoke. "This is one fucked-up world we live in, Sarge. One fucked-up world."

Byron couldn't disagree.

CHAPTER 34

Tuesday, 6:35 A.M.,
July 25, 2017

Tuesday morning came shrouded in the gloom of coastal fog, a perfect reflection of Byron's confidence in the case against Alex Stavros. He knew there was something that they were all missing, but he didn't know what it was.

Despite Dennis Stavros's ill-conceived attempt at deflecting suspicion away from Lina and the rest of his late brother's family, it was obvious that the handyman wasn't a criminal mastermind. Certainly not the kind of man who would slaughter a young woman simply because she'd committed a mortal sin. Hell, Byron thought, it wasn't even Danica Faherty's marriage bed, it was Alex and Deborah's.

Byron thought back to his interview with Dennis. The man said he'd thought Lina had sent him to the West End house under false pretenses, knowing that he'd find the murdered girl's body and would know how to deal with it. Byron supposed it was possible, but it was just as likely that Lina hadn't known anything about the murder. Pure coincidence. Byron wasn't a big believer in coincidence, but even he had to admit that it did occasionally stick its nose into murder investigations. Often enough, in fact, to make any good investigator wary. But if Lina hadn't known about the dead woman in her former residence, and Alex had killed her, why leave the body in the kitchen? Surely Alex would've been anxious to hide the evidence of his crime.

As he scanned his mental checklist for suspects, Byron realized that whatever else was driving this case there was an underlying Stavros family matter. Alex was still at the top of the list, obviously, but Lina couldn't be ruled out. Nor could Byron discount Deborah, as much as he might want to. Uncle Dennis had been helpful but, much like Alex himself, only when pressed. And Dennis, by his own admission, had displayed the lengths to which he would go to protect the family. Was killing Danica that much different? Byron didn't know. There was one member of the Stavros family who might still be able to shed some light on the subject, though. Lina's other son, Petri.

It was just after ten o'clock as Byron pulled into the paved drive and parked. The sun had burned through the clouds, promising another hot and humid summer day.

Petri Stavros lived modestly, despite his family's wealth and stature. With its weathered gray shingles and light blue shutters, his New Englander style Cape Cod was expensive only because of the Cape Elizabeth location and proximity to the coastline. A row of freshly planted cedars lined the drive on one side; Byron caught their pleasing aroma as he exited the car. The yard was well-manicured and near enough to the water that Petri was likely afforded an ocean view after the leaves had fallen.

Byron followed the cobblestone walkway around to the front door and mounted the steps. He was reaching for the buzzer when the door opened.

"Sergeant Byron, isn't it?" Petri joked.

Dressed in running sneakers, maroon shorts, and a wicking white tee, Petri was drinking from a plastic bottle of Poland Spring water and sweating profusely.

"Am I interrupting something?" Byron said.

"Not at all. Just went to war with my elliptical. To what do I owe the pleasure? I don't suppose you've come by to drop these bogus charges against Alex?"

"No, I'm afraid not."

"Can't blame a guy for trying." Petri stepped outside, closing the door behind him. "So, what can I do for you?"

"I was hoping we might talk a bit."

Petri gave Byron an appraising look as if he didn't believe him. "You know I have no interest in helping you build a case against my brother, Sergeant."

"That's not why I'm here."

"Okay, now I'm curious. Let's take a walk. I need to cool down anyway."

"Beautiful property."

"Thanks. It's a lot of work."

"You don't have a man for that, like Lina?"

Petri laughed. "Uncle Dennis? No, I don't have that luxury. One of us must live in the real world. Truthfully, I don't know why he stays around her." He paused to check out Byron. "You must do your own yard work, am I right?"

"Condo."

Petri nodded his understanding. "So, what did you want to ask me?"

"When Alex and I spoke at the jail, he seemed to think that someone was setting him up. That he was being framed. I wonder if you might know of someone who would have a grudge against your brother?"

Petri silently considered the question. "What, you think you charged the wrong man now?"

"Not at all. The evidence still points directly to Alex as the person responsible for murdering Danica Faherty."

"But?"

"Alex brought up the idea of being framed by an enemy."

"And you believe he was?" Petri asked.

"I believe in being thorough."

"An admirable trait for a police officer."

Byron bristled, but fought back the urge to respond to Petri's backhanded compliment. "So, does he have any?"

"Enemies?"

"Yes."

"My brother Alex has been very successful. Our mom's a famous movie star, he's had his own television cooking show, and he's the chef at two of the hottest restaurants on the East Coast. I'm sure he has made some enemies, mainly due to jealousy. But I don't know of anyone personally who has a problem with Alex."

"What about you?" Byron asked.

Petri stopped walking. "Me? Sergeant Byron, Alex and I are brothers. Why would

I have a problem with him?"

"Maybe for the very reasons you've mentioned. Alex has been very successful, while you've had to take the back seat. From where I stand, it seems like you do all the work at the restaurants while Alex gets all the credit. That might make me resent him if he were my brother. Might piss me off royally."

"Well, I guess that's where you and I differ, Sergeant. I am quite satisfied with the role I play. And I am very happy for Alex and Deborah. Now, if you have nothing further, I have to get ready for work."

Byron returned to 109. He was sitting in his office listening to voicemails trying to decide his next step when Stevens popped in.

"How'd you make out with Petri?"

"I'm not sure. He said all the right things, but I still wonder if he's as accepting of his role as he says he is."

"You think Alex is still in a cooperative mood?"

"Dunno, why?"

"I was thinking maybe he'll have a different take on Petri."

Byron considered it. "You up for a ride to County?"

■ ■ ■ ■

Byron and Stevens were seated in one of the county interview rooms when Alex was led in by a deputy.

"Alex," Byron said. "You remember Detective Stevens?"

"Did you check out what I told you?" Alex said, ignoring Byron's attempt at civility.

"Alex, it's Stuart Forsyth," a male voice said, emanating from Byron's cellphone which was lying on the table and set to speaker mode.

"Hey, Stu. Why aren't you here?"

"I'm in Boston at a deposition, but I wanted to make sure you're represented properly. I suggested to Sergeant Byron that we do it this way in the interest of expediency. If that's okay with you?"

"If it gets me out of here sooner, I'm okay with anything," Stavros said.

"Have a seat," Byron said.

Alex sat as the deputy departed.

"Well?" Stavros said.

"You do realize that you are still in custody and facing a charge of murder, correct?" Byron asked.

"Of course. And I'm still waiving my rights, I get it. You cool with that, Stu?"

"Do I have a choice?" Forsyth said.

"Stu's good with it," Stavros said. "Go ahead."

"We did check out what you told us, and we found the evidence you mentioned," Stevens said.

"Then you believe me? That I was set up?"

"We're a long way from that," Byron said. "The fact that Dani had a box of condoms doesn't mean she was using them with you."

"Or that you used any on Sunday morning, July 9th," Stevens said. "We checked the wastepaper basket in the bedroom where you claimed to have disposed of the used prophylactic."

"And? You found them, right? You guys can test them and see that they were mine, right?"

"The bedroom wastebasket was empty, Alex," Byron said.

Hope drained from Alex's face. "I don't know what else I can do to convince you. I didn't kill Dani, okay? I swear. Someone is framing me."

"You keep saying that, Alex," Byron said. "But who would benefit from you being charged with Dani's murder?"

"I already told you, I don't know."

"What would you say if I told you that we lifted your uncle's fingerprints from the bag used to dispose of Dani's head?"

"Dennis? No friggin' way, Uncle Dennis would never —"

"Alex, I'm advising you not to say anything more about your family," Forsyth said.

"Dennis wouldn't have anything to do with this, Stu. He's been like a father to me. Even more so since Dad died."

Stevens jumped in. "Really, Alex? Because Saint Dennis admitted to us that he cut Danica's head off then dumped her body."

Stavros turned up his face in disgust. "Jesus Christ. That's sick. Why would he do that?"

"Told us he thought he was protecting your mother."

"Lina? Why would she need protecting?"

"Dennis thought maybe she killed Dani."

"Why would he think that?" Alex said. "What's wrong with you guys? What reason would my mother have for killing a woman who worked for us?"

Byron took lead again. "Perhaps because you were sleeping with that woman. Putting your marriage to Deborah at risk. Increasing the likelihood that Deborah would leave you and file for custody of the children. Lina's grandbabies."

"Bullshit. Lina would never do something like this. Not to me."

513

But the dazed look on Alex's face confirmed that he hadn't given any of this much thought, until now. It was obvious to Byron that the only thing Alex had been concerned with was getting out of jail. The possibility that a family member could be behind his arrest hadn't occurred to him.

"Tell me about your relationship with your brother," Byron said.

"Petri? What about him?"

"How do the two of you get along?" Byron said.

"Okay, I guess. We've had our issues. No different than any other siblings. Brothers fight sometimes, right?"

"What did you and Petri fight about, Alex?" Stevens asked.

Alex looked back and forth between the detectives. "You're not seriously suggesting that it's Petri who's setting me up?"

"Would he have reason to?" Byron asked.

Byron and Stevens walked across the lot of the county jail toward their cars.

"What do you think?" Stevens asked.

"I think he's holding something back."

"Me, too. But what?"

Byron had no idea. Despite all outward appearances to the contrary, the Stavros family had its share of dysfunction. Lina's gifting of a house to Alex while Petri had to fend for himself was evidence of favoritism. Dennis seemed convinced that Lina had sent him to Bowdoin Street to dispose of a body. Byron wondered what other secrets they might be hiding.

"Now what?" Stevens asked.

Byron opened the door to the Taurus and paused. "If this is some feud among family, let's see if we can turn up the heat."

Byron sat impatiently in the unmarked car outside of the gate at the end of the Stavros driveway. It had been close to a minute since he pressed the call button. There was no response. Byron reached through the window and pressed the button again, this time holding it.

"What do you want, Sergeant Byron?" Angelina Stavros's voice barked from the speaker just below the security keypad.

"I need to talk with you, Lina."

Several moments passed and Byron began to wonder if she'd left him hanging.

"Haven't you done enough damage to my family already? How many times must I be subjected to your harassment?"

"That isn't why I'm here."

"Why are you here then?"

"I'm trying to help Alex."

515

There was another long pause, then Byron heard the electronic click and the iron gate began to slide open.

Byron drove the length of the driveway and parked in front of the house. Angelina was standing in the open doorway to the home.

"Thank you for seeing me."

"Did I have a choice?"

Stavros turned and headed inside. Byron followed. She led him to a luxuriously decorated library. Walls lined with built-in cherry bookcases and a French door that opened onto a balcony overlooking the ocean.

"Sit," she said, gesturing to one of two leather wingback chairs facing a large leather-topped desk. Stavros lighted in the chair behind the desk.

Byron glimpsed what appeared to be a movie script sitting atop the desk. He sat in the wingback to the left, affording him an angle on the door through which they had entered the room. He wondered what it would be like to have your own library.

Stavros closed the notebook containing the manuscript and set it aside.

"You said you wanted to help Alex. I'm listening."

"What can you tell me about Petri?"

Angelina's eyes narrowed with suspicion. "Is this your idea of helping? Dragging my other son into this?"

"Petri mentioned a falling-out years ago between the two of you," Byron lied. "Can you tell me what that was about?"

She turned the chair so she was facing the Atlantic. "Petri was upset with me. He blamed me for breaking up his engagement to Deborah."

"Petri and Deborah were engaged?" Byron said, unable to contain his surprise.

"For about five months. It happened during their senior year of college. Alex, Petri, and Deborah were inseparable."

Byron recalled seeing a picture of the three of them on the wall in Petri's office. "What happened?"

Lina turned back to face him. "Just after graduation Alex split up with the girl he'd been seeing, Suzanne Hayman. A short time later, Deborah broke off her engagement to Petri."

"Why?"

"I never knew. All I can tell you is when Alex moved to New York to learn the restaurant business from his father, Deborah followed."

"Why did that cause you and Petri to have a falling-out?"

"He blamed me. He got it into his head that I had convinced Deborah that Alex was the better catch. Petri accused me of always playing favorite to Alex."

Byron had wondered why Alex and his family were staying with Lina while waiting for the old house to be renovated. Petri always seemed to be on the outside looking in.

"Do you have children?" Stavros asked.

Byron shook his head. "No."

"Every parent says that they don't have favorites, but that's a lie we tell ourselves. The truth is, Alex has always been my favorite son."

"Why?"

"Alex and Petri aren't really brothers, Sergeant Byron."

"But I thought —"

"No. I had both of them while I was married to Dimitri, but Petri wasn't his." Angelina stood up and started to pace the room. "Dimitri and I had hit a bad patch, and I strayed. I'm not proud of it, but it happened. I had an affair with Gene Wagner. It only lasted a few months, but as you can see it cost me dearly."

"Petri is Gene's son?" Byron asked. "And that's why Gene is always around?"

She nodded. "Yes." Defeated, Lina walked

back to the desk and slumped into her chair. "Maybe that's the reason I've always loved Alex more than Petri. Petri is a constant reminder of my failings as a mother, and a wife."

"Does Petri know?" Byron asked.

"I don't know. He may have figured it out, I suppose, but he's never said anything if he has. Petri and I agreed to put the past behind us a couple of years ago, but there is still an awkwardness between us. I've thought about telling him the truth, but I'm not sure our shaky détente could survive that." She looked directly at Byron. "And he may end up being the only son I have, now that you've locked Alex away."

"Did Petri ever marry?" Byron asked.

"Once. Esme Panagakos."

"Esme?"

"Short for Esmeralda. A beautiful young woman. Wealthy family friends of Dimitri's. The marriage only lasted a couple of years, though."

"What happened?"

"I only know that Esme left him, citing irreconcilable differences."

"Lina, did Petri ever get over losing Deborah?"

There was a long pause before she answered. "I don't know."

Byron was on the phone to Stevens even before reaching the security gate at the end of Angelina's driveway.

"Hey, Sarge," Stevens answered. "What's up?"

"Two things. I need you to locate a woman by the name of Esmeralda Panagakos. She was briefly married to Petri."

"There can't be too many people with that name. And the second?"

"Did we ever obtain location history for Petri for Sunday morning July 9th?"

"From his cell provider?" Stevens asked.

"Yes."

"No. We had Tran check Alex, Dennis, and Lina, but that's it. You want me to subpoena Petri's?"

"Yes. Like yesterday. Get Dustin to work his magic."

"I'll make the call."

Byron returned to 109. Esmeralda Panagakos's contact information was waiting on his desk in the form of a handwritten note from Melissa Stevens. Byron made the call.

"And what did you say your name was?" Panagakos asked.

"John Byron. I'm a detective sergeant with the police department in Portland, Maine."

"What is this about?"

"I'm calling to ask you about your marriage to Petri Stavros."

There was a long pause in the conversation. Byron was beginning to wonder if Panagakos was still on the line when she finally answered.

"I haven't heard that name in a while. Why are you asking about Petri?"

Byron explained that he was investigating the homicide of a young woman who'd been seeing Petri's brother Alex.

"And you've charged Alex?" Panagakos asked.

"Yes. He is currently in custody, charged with murder."

"That's hard to imagine. The last I knew Alex was married to a woman named Deborah Strickland."

"Alex and Deborah are still married," Byron said, although he didn't imagine they would be for much longer.

"As sad as all of this is, Sergeant Byron, I don't understand what any of it has to do with me."

"It doesn't have anything to do with you. My question is about Petri."

"What about him?"

"I hope you'll forgive me for asking such a personal question, but I couldn't help but wonder why you and Petri divorced after such a brief marriage."

"That *is* a rather personal question, Sergeant."

"I wouldn't ask if it wasn't important," Byron said.

"We divorced because I wouldn't share my husband with another woman."

"He was cheating on you?"

"Not exactly. At least not in the physical sense."

"I'm not sure I follow," Byron said, attempting to draw it out of her.

"Petri was still in love with a girl he had dated in college."

"Who?" Byron asked, already knowing the answer.

"Alex's wife, Deborah."

CHAPTER 35

Tuesday, 12:35 P.M.,
July 25, 2017

Byron could feel things beginning to come together. As so often happens when a murder case seemed to have more questions than answers, suddenly everything was snapping into focus. Turning on the single fact of Petri's continued infatuation with Deborah, Byron believed he may well have found a solid motive for the killing of Danica Faherty.

The Taurus fired up as Byron turned the key in the ignition. He was reaching for his cellphone when it rang with an incoming call.

"Byron."

"Sergeant, it's Shirley. I'm sorry to bother you with this, but I'm not sure it can wait until you get back to 109."

"What is it, Shirley?"

"A man keeps calling here saying that he

needs to talk with you. He's very insistent."

"Who is it?"

"Dennis Stavros."

Byron phoned the jail. After being on hold for the better part of ten minutes, he was finally connected with Dennis Stavros.

"What was Danica Faherty killed with?" Dennis asked.

"What?" Byron said.

"You told me that Danica Faherty, the woman I found in the kitchen on Bowdoin Street, was struck with a weapon. I saw two wounds in the back of her head. What was she hit with?"

"A hammer," Byron said, resisting the urge to expound upon his answer.

"Did you locate it?" Stavros asked. "The hammer?"

"Why? Do you know something, Dennis?"

There was a pause. "I might."

Not wanting to lose a single minute, Byron put Stevens on search warrant duty yet again. This time it was for Petri's residence and vehicle.

Byron paced around CID as Stevens worked. LeRoyer stood behind her looking over her shoulder and quizzing both detectives on the latest.

"You think you know where the hammer is?" LeRoyer asked.

"Petri's uncle asked me if we'd ever identified the murder weapon," Byron said. "I told him she had been killed by a hammer blow to the back of the head. When I asked him why, he asked me if the hammer could have been a framing hammer with a broken claw."

LeRoyer's eyes widened. "How would he know that?"

"Because he loaned Petri a hammer exactly like that a few weeks ago, so that he could frame out his deck."

"Evidently not the only thing he was hoping to frame," Stevens said.

"And Petri still has it?" LeRoyer asked.

"That's just it," Byron said. "Petri returned a framing hammer to him shortly after Danica was murdered. A brand-new framing hammer."

"You think he might still have it? The murder weapon I mean."

"It's a long shot, but with a little luck, he might."

"Why wouldn't Petri just get rid of the evidence?" LeRoyer asked.

"Because he might need it later to bolster the case against Alex. And we're still missing Danica's cellphone."

"What's the cell tower history thingy?" LeRoyer asked as he scanned over the probable cause affidavit for the search warrant on Stevens's computer screen.

"I had Tran query Petri's cell provider for location history," Byron said.

"Why?"

"Because I wanted to know where Petri's cellphone was on Sunday morning," Byron said.

"And?"

"And early Sunday morning, when Petri claims he was at home sleeping, his phone was pinging the towers around Portland's peninsula. Not possible if he was in Cape Elizabeth."

"Alex says he's in Boston, and that turns out to be bullshit," LeRoyer said. "Petri is at home sleeping, also a lie."

"Not to mention the worst cover story ever," Stevens said without looking up from her work.

"Does anyone in this family know how to establish an alibi?" LeRoyer asked.

Apparently not, Byron thought.

"I don't get it," LeRoyer said. "Why would Petri want to frame his own brother?"

"Keep reading," Byron said.

It took another ninety minutes before they

were able to find an available judge to sign off on the warrant. While he and Stevens worked on that, Byron sent Detective Gardiner to watch Petri's home. Gardiner was instructed to tail Petri as soon as he left the house. The plan was to wait until Petri left for Alessandro's before executing the warrant. Things were likely to go much smoother if Petri didn't realize they were searching his residence. As soon as Petri arrived at the restaurant Gardiner phoned Byron.

"He's here, Sarge," Gardiner said. "Parked his Volvo around the corner in the parking garage on Pearl."

"Okay, Luke, sit on that car," Byron said. "Let me know if he moves an inch. It would be just like a nosy neighbor to give him a heads-up."

"You got it."

As soon as they had the signed warrants in hand Byron instructed the search team to rendezvous at Petri's home. Time would be of the essence.

The search team consisted of Byron, Stevens, Nugent, Pelligrosso, and two of Peterson's property crime detectives. Normally, Byron wouldn't have cared about damaging the door to a home that they were searching, but given the high status of the Stavros family he opted for the services of a local locksmith to get them inside.

Methodically, they searched Petri's home from top to bottom. The warrant authorized them to look for the murder weapon, Faherty's missing cellphone, and any evidence linking Petri to the crime. The last piece included any clothing which might contain the victim's blood. It took them the better part of two hours before they found anything significant. It was in a room they'd previously searched.

Byron and Nugent stood next to Pelligrosso with mouths agape. Gabe had removed a panel covering a false wall at the back of Petri's closet. The panel had been held in place by strips of Velcro. Contained within the compartment were hundreds of photographs of Deborah Stavros. Many had been cut from larger photos, effectively removing any other persons from the image. Byron leaned in closer and noticed some of the photos had been digitally altered; Petri had inserted himself into the pictures with Deborah, as if they had been together.

"Think we just established a motive," Gabe said.

"This guy's right off the fucking rails,"

Nugent said.

"Yeah, and we're gonna need an addendum to the warrant," Byron said as he pulled his cell to call Gardiner.

"Hey, Sarge," Gardiner said. "How's the search going?"

"Where are you?" Byron asked.

"Still sitting on Petri's car. He hasn't been back to it. You still want me to sit tight?"

"No, forget the car for now. Grab a couple of uniforms and head directly to Alessandro's. I want you to take Petri into custody for the murder of Danica Faherty."

"Yes, sir!"

Twenty minutes later, Byron was giving LeRoyer an update by telephone when his cell beeped with an incoming call from Gardiner.

"Marty, I got a call coming in from Luke," Byron said. "I'll get back to you."

"Okay, I'll give Lynds the update. Keep me in the loop, John."

Byron switched calls. "You got him?"

"He isn't here," Gardiner said.

"What?" Byron said. "What do you mean he isn't there? Where the hell is he?"

"One of the kitchen staff said he left about ten minutes ago. Told them he accidentally locked his keys in his car. Asked if he could borrow theirs."

Shit. Had Petri figured out they were onto him? Had he made Gardiner's tail?

"Did they say where he was heading?" Byron asked.

"They don't know. Told them he had to pick someone up and that he didn't know when he'd be back."

Byron felt the hairs stand erect on the back of his neck.

"What do you want me to do, Sarge?" Gardiner asked.

"Text me the details on the car he borrowed then have Dispatch put out a statewide ATL. I want him picked up before he hurts anyone else."

"Any idea where he might be headed?"

Byron looked back at the twisted diorama displayed inside Petri's closet. "I'm afraid I do."

Byron ended the call and rushed from the bedroom, nearly running into Nugent as he did.

"We lost Petri," Byron said. "I think he's going to try and grab Deborah."

"You want me to come with you, boss?"

"No. I need you to stay here and oversee the remainder of the search."

"Be careful, Sarge," Nugent said, holding up an empty handgun case. "This sick fuck is probably armed."

Byron hurried to his car. He pulled out his cell again and dialed Deborah's cell. The call went directly to voicemail. Byron hung up and dialed Lina Stavros's number. After several rings it also went to voicemail. "Lina, it's John Byron. Listen, I'm calling because I think Deborah might be in danger. Call me as soon as you get this."

"Fuck," he said, ending the call. They had finally uncovered who Petri truly was only to watch the plan to take him into custody unravel before their eyes.

Byron had activated the strobes on his unmarked and was using the siren intermittently as he navigated his way through traffic, weaving around and passing other vehicles. He grabbed his cell and dialed Portland Police Dispatch.

"Dispatch, Brad speaking."

"Brad, it's John Byron," he said, shouting to be heard above the siren.

"Hey, Sarge, what's up?"

"I'm on my way to Scarborough to try and stop a possible kidnapping in progress."

"What do you need from me?"

"Contact Scarborough PD and tell them I'm en route to Angelina Stavros's on Prouts Neck. If I'm right, Petri is heading there from Portland to pick up Deborah Stavros. I have reason to believe he's planning to kidnap her, or worse."

"This the dark green Camry that Gardiner just called about?"

"Yes. Make sure Scarborough gets that information along with the plate number. Tell them we believe he may be armed with a handgun."

"I'm on it, Sarge."

Byron was making good time, considering the traffic. He had just entered South Portland when his cell rang. He punched the speaker button and shouted, "Byron."

"This is Lina Stavros," the actress said. "Why are you bothering me again?"

"Where is Deborah?"

"What business is it of yours where my daughter-in-law is?"

"She may be in grave danger, Lina. Is she with you?"

"No, she isn't."

"Tell me where she is, Lina!"

"If you must know, she just left here with Petri. He's taking her to the airport."

Byron felt his skin crawl. He didn't know what Petri's intentions were, but he was pretty sure they didn't include taking Deborah to the Portland International Jetport.

Whatever sick game Petri was playing at was nearing its conclusion. "Where are the children?"

"What?"

"Your grandkids, Lina! Where are they?"

"They left yesterday. They're already in New York with their au pair. What is this all about?"

Byron disconnected the call with Lina. It was obvious that she was in complete denial, allowing her anger over the incarceration of Alex to cloud her common sense. He needed to concentrate on driving, or he would never make it to save Deborah. Racing inbound on Ocean House Road, he struggled, trying to outmaneuver Petri. *Where would he go?* Assuming Petri didn't know about the search of his house yet, it was logical to think he might try and take her there. And Highland Avenue would be the most direct route for Petri to take. Byron made the sharp left turn onto Highland Avenue, narrowly avoiding a small SUV, the tires of his unmarked squealing on the pavement in protest.

He had traveled about a half mile beyond Evans Street, racing toward the Scarborough town line, when he noticed a dark green sedan traveling toward him from the other direction. He tensed up inside. Byron knew it was Petri. As they approached Byron clearly saw Deborah silhouetted in the passenger seat. He stomped on the brake and cut the wheel hard to the left as Petri passed by. Byron jammed the shift lever into Reverse and mashed the accelerator to the floor, cutting the steering wheel hard right and causing the Ford's front end to slingshot to the left. He hit the brake to stop the spin then dropped the transmission back into Drive. He could see that Petri had reacted to him by accelerating.

"720 to Dispatch," Byron yelled into the microphone, trying to be heard over the noise of his siren.

"Go ahead 720," Dispatcher Mary O'Connell said.

"I'm in pursuit of the green Camry from the ATL. South Portland traveling inbound on Highland. Petri has Deborah Stavros. Give me a signal."

"Ten-four, 720." O'Connell sounded the emergency radio tone, giving Byron priority. "All units a signal 1000 is now in effect for 720."

A signal 1000 is a priority code put into effect whenever a unit or units are in a life-or-death situation and need the radio airwaves to be kept clear.

"720, what is your location now?" O'Connell asked.

Byron just caught the flash of a street sign as he made the turn. "Nutter Street from Highland, toward Evans."

"Ten-four, 720. South Portland units are en route to intercept."

"200," the shift commander called out. "What does 720 have?"

"Possible kidnapping, Lieutenant. The driver is wanted in connection with a 10-49."

The large commercial oil tanks were a blur as the chase continued. Byron was having a difficult time keeping pace with the much faster Toyota, especially with Petri driving so recklessly. Byron knew, given Petri's infatuation, that losing them might well mean a death sentence for Deborah.

"Right on Evans," Byron said.

"Ten-four, right on Evans."

Traffic was backed up from the intersection where Evans met Broadway. Byron could see the blue lights and flashing headlights coming from the other direction as one of the South Portland cruisers closed in. Petri saw the cruiser, too, and the Camry shot up Hill Street. Byron followed.

"720," Byron said. "Right on Hill."

"Copy, right on Hill Street," O'Connell said.

"Lieutenant," Diane called from the doorway to LeRoyer's office. "Have you been listening to the radio?"

"No, why? What's up?"

"John is involved in a vehicle pursuit in South Portland."

"What? I just talked to him on the phone. He was searching a house in Cape. Who the hell is he chasing?"

"Petri Stavros. He just grabbed Alex's wife, Deborah. He's got her in the car."

LeRoyer jumped out of his chair. "Let's go!"

The six-cylinder roared as Byron pinned the accelerator to the floor, trying to get every ounce of horsepower out of the Taurus.

The Camry's brake lights flashed as it reached Broadway. Petri turned hard left, violently sideswiping a car traveling in the opposite direction before continuing.

Byron keyed the mic again. "10-55 with another motorist. Suspect vehicle fled, now outbound on Broadway, back toward Evans."

"Ten-four, 720."

As the chase continued, traffic was slow to move over for Petri's Camry, allowing Byron to gain on him. Byron watched in horror as Petri recklessly moved into the oncoming travel lane, forcing cars to swerve to the right side of the road to avoid a collision. Byron, who had lost sight of the South Portland unit, was confident that Petri was headed toward the Interstate. He knew that if Petri made it onto the highway, they might lose him, and in the process lose Deborah for good. Byron couldn't let that happen.

Byron guessed that Petri would likely turn right onto Lincoln Street, giving him a direct shot at I-295, but in order to make the sharp turn the Camry would have to slow down. Byron would only get one shot at what he was planning. He prayed that Deborah had her seat belt on. The Camry's brake lights lit up again. Byron, who was right behind them, swerved to the right and stomped on the accelerator, pulling partially up beside them. Petri saw what Byron was attempting and shifted to the right to try and squeeze him off the roadway. Byron felt the passenger side tires of the Taurus briefly contact the curb. Byron matched Petri's speed and position. As both vehicles neared the intersection with Lincoln, Petri slowed and started into the turn. Byron jerked the steering wheel hard left and accelerated, executing a PIT maneuver. The unmarked Taurus collided with the right rear quarter panel of the Camry just as Petri was entering the turn. The Camry's tires squealed loudly as it spun out into the oncoming lane, up and over the sidewalk, striking a utility pole.

Byron stood on the brake pedal, feeling the pulse of the antilock mechanism, but the Taurus was traveling too fast to stop. The front wheels hit the curb, bouncing up and over the sidewalk, and jarring him forward in his seat. The Ford's momentum carried it across the small parking lot toward the cinder block façade of a vacant business. Byron braced for impact and the car passed right through the display window and into an empty showroom, setting off the airbags and filling the passenger compartment with smoke.

Amid the shattered glass and debris and deflated airbags, Byron struggled to free himself from the heavily damaged Taurus. He had to get to Deborah. Byron heard sirens approaching as he hurried out of the building toward the wrecked, smoking Camry, his gun drawn. The driver's door was standing open. Petri was gone. Byron lowered his weapon and looked through the open door. Deborah was bloodied and pinned against the seat back, but she was alive.

"Are you all right?" Byron said.

"I don't — I don't know. I think so."

"Did he hurt you?"

"No. He told me that he killed Dani Faherty to get Alex out of the way, so we could be together. He's got a gun, John. He's crazy."

"Just hang on, okay? Help is coming." He quickly scanned the area, just managing to catch a glimpse of a figure running down Lincoln Street. Byron knew it was Petri and knew exactly where he was headed.

A black South Portland cruiser skidded into the parking lot and a uniformed officer jumped out. "What the hell is going on here?"

Byron flashed his badge. "Get this woman medical help, now! I'm going after the driver. He's on foot and armed with a handgun. Get me some backup."

"You've got it, Sarge."

Byron didn't hear the officer's response; he was already running down Lincoln Street toward the cemetery.

CHAPTER 36

Forest City Cemetery is large, nearly one hundred acres. Bordered by Lincoln Street, Broadway, and the Fore River, it is split down the middle by Clark Road. The cemetery, one of the oldest in Greater Portland, is comprised of thirty thousand monuments, which, combined with the many mausoleums, hedges, and trees, afforded Petri Stavros excellent cover and concealment.

Byron knew the odds were not in his favor. He had some serious disadvantages to overcome, not the least of which was that he was wearing plainclothes and might easily be mistaken for Petri by an overzealous officer, a scenario dreaded by all law enforcement officers. While he certainly did not welcome the prospect of being shot by one of his own, neither did he want to be the reason that an officer hesitated, exposing them to being shot by Petri. Regardless of the outcome, Byron knew that he couldn't risk Petri escaping, not after he had kidnapped Deborah. And after seeing what the psychotic restaurateur had done to Danica Faherty and how he'd set up his own brother for the crime. Byron had witnessed firsthand the consequences of Petri's infatuation with Deborah. The monster either had to be caught or put down.

Byron knew he would be most vulnerable at the cemetery entrance where there was nothing but an expanse of open lawn. If he could reach the gravestones before being seen, Petri's advantage would be mitigated. He stuck close to the row of trees bordering the right side of the cemetery.

It took several minutes but Byron reached the stones without incident. Kneeling behind a large marker, he paused to catch his breath and survey the area ahead of him. There was no movement and no sign of Petri Stavros.

He heard the sirens and rapid acceleration of other police vehicles arriving on the scene, both behind him and on the far side of the cemetery near Broadway. Things were escalating quickly. He knew that South Portland and probably Portland officers were surrounding the entire area. He was also aware that his risk of being misidentified as a threat was increasing exponentially. This was a gun call and adrenaline was coursing through the veins of everyone involved. To the responding uniformed officers Byron was just another civilian waving a gun around. He removed the badge from his belt and clipped it to the outside breast pocket of his suit coat attempting to make himself more identifiable. He prayed it would be enough.

Byron remained in a low crouch as he began moving forward from stone to stone, slowly and carefully making his way toward the center of the cemetery. He looked toward the brook and to his horror saw something he hadn't considered: a small group of people gathered for a graveside service.

Veteran South Portland Officer Dick Moulton had just finished taking a burglary report at a sporting goods store near the Maine Mall when he heard the dispatcher put out a 10-74, officer needs assistance call.

"Any unit in the vicinity of Lincoln Street, please respond. A Portland detective is in foot pursuit of a kidnapping and possible murder suspect in the area of Forest City

Cemetery. The suspect, Petri Stavros, is believed to be armed with a ten thirty-two handgun. Units acknowledge."

"Car 20, responding code 3 from Maine Mall Road," Moulton said, referring to lights and siren.

"Ten-four, unit 20."

By the time Moulton arrived in the area he had received additional information from Dispatch by phone as well as Petri's photo by computer. Moulton took the Broadway side of the cemetery, parking at the end of Latham Street. He unlocked the shotgun from its rack and entered the property on foot.

Compounding Byron's problems was the fact that he had left his portable radio somewhere inside the wrecked Taurus. Carefully, he scanned the graveside service for Stavros. Satisfied that Petri was not standing among them, he moved on, each time repeating the process of taking cover behind a large stone, then slowly scanning everything around him.

"I know you're here, you son of a bitch," Byron whispered. "Show yourself."

Byron began to worry. He hadn't caught sight of Petri since entering the cemetery. *What if he managed to slip out before they cordoned off the area?* He fought to suppress the thought. The police were on top of this. Petri couldn't have escaped undetected.

Byron moved up behind yet another stone.

Moulton was sweating profusely in his dark-colored uniform. He held the shotgun in both hands at the low ready, finger outside the trigger guard, safety off, one round chambered. Slowly and deliberately, he walked toward the Lincoln Street side of the cemetery, eyes scanning left to right and then back again. Moulton was rounding a large oak when he noticed a man kneeling in front of a grave marker. Cautiously, he approached the man. When he got close enough, he whispered, "Hey, you."

The kneeling man turned slightly to his left. "Who, me?" he asked.

"Yeah. You haven't seen a guy running around here with a gun have ya?" Moulton asked as he lowered his weapon slightly.

The man's eyes widened and he shook his head from side to side. "No. No, I haven't." The man stood and turned to face Moulton. "What's he look like?"

"He looks like — Oh, shit." Moulton realized his mistake a split second too late. Petri raised his pistol and fired twice, striking Moulton in the thigh and the stomach.

Moulton squeezed the trigger on the shotgun just as he felt his legs go out from under him.

Byron heard gunshots coming from his left, in the direction of Fore River, two quick pops from what sounded like a handgun immediately followed by the distinctive booming report of a 12-gauge shotgun. The shooters were close. Maybe fifty yards. Byron hurried toward the sounds, gun held at the low ready, staying in a low crouch, moving in a serpentine fashion around the many grave markers.

The first thing Byron saw was the prone body of a uniformed South Portland officer, the second was Petri Stavros. Stavros was bent over and in the process of removing Moulton's sidearm from its holster.

Byron took cover behind a monument and pointed his handgun at Petri. "Freeze," Byron said.

Petri came up firing in Byron's direction, while scrambling for cover.

Byron returned fire and watched as Petri stumbled to the ground then crawled behind a ten-foot hedgerow. Peeking around the stone, Byron quickly scanned the bushes for Petri.

Several rounds were fired in Byron's direction from beyond the hedge. Byron ducked down just as one of the bullets ricocheted off the headstone he was using for cover. Petri continued to fire blindly in Byron's direction, but each of the rounds sailed wide of the mark. Byron knew that there was a big difference between cover and concealment. Byron had the cover and protection afforded by a granite monument while Petri's hedge offered only concealment. As soon as the shooting ceased, Byron popped up into a shooter's stance, took aim and fired into the center of the hedge until his weapon was out of ammo. Byron's heart was racing as he ducked behind the grave marker again, dropped the empty magazine, and slammed in a fresh one.

He turned his head slightly to the sound of footsteps on gravel rapidly approaching from behind.

"Police! Drop it," a male voice commanded from Byron's right.

"Drop the gun," echoed a female voice from somewhere behind him.

"I'm a police officer," he said. "Sergeant John Byron. One of yours has been shot and is down. He needs an ambulance."

"Put your weapon down now," the female officer repeated.

"Okay, okay, I'll put it down," Byron said "But I need one of you to cover that piece of shit behind the hedge. Not sure if I wounded him or not."

Byron tossed his gun onto the grass then placed his hands behind his head.

"I'll cover him, Jimmy, go check the hedge," the female said, clearly outranking the other officer.

"There's nobody here," the officer shouted.

The female officer approached and saw the shield hanging from Byron's jacket.

"Sorry, just needed to be sure," she said, handing him his gun.

"Call for an ambulance," Byron said as he hurried over to where Moulton was lying and checked for a pulse.

The female officer keyed her mic. "10-74, 10-74, officer down. Send a rescue 10-18. Suspect is at large."

The dispatcher's voice broke through the static, "Ten-four, fire rescue en route. 100, copy?"

"100, I'm pulling up to the scene now."

"Fuck," the officer named Jimmy said as he knelt over his fallen comrade. "It's Dick Moulton."

"I've got a weak pulse," Byron said. "Here, put pressure on his leg." He turned to the female officer as he began unbuttoning Moulton's shirt. "Petri Stavros is still out here somewhere, and he's armed. Stay alert. Can you get a K-9 out here?"

Byron and Jimmy assisted the EMS personnel and the South Portland shift commander, Lieutenant Johnston, as they hurriedly prepped Moulton for transport and loaded him into the back of the rescue. The air was thick with the smell of diesel exhaust and Byron's ears were still ringing from the gunfire. They had managed to slow Moulton's external bleeding, but one of the bullets had entered his stomach below the vest. Moulton needed a trauma team if he had any chance of surviving his wounds.

Several more unmarked cars pulled up behind the ambulance, stopping on the side of Clark Road. Byron saw Diane and LeRoyer approaching on foot.

"Christ, John," Diane said. "You okay?"

"Yeah, but Petri got away."

"He won't get far," Lieutenant Johnston said. "Between Portland and South Portland, we've got this whole area saturated."

Byron didn't share the lieutenant's optimism.

LeRoyer looked at Byron. "What the fuck happened here?"

"Long story, Lieu."

The EMS driver cranked up the siren as the rescue unit quickly pulled away toward the cemetery entrance. Two South Portland cruisers assisted in the transport, one led while the other followed.

"Did you hit him?" Diane asked.

"Not sure," Byron said. "I may have. We found blood over there in the grass on the other side of the hedge. Petri has Moulton's shotgun."

"What about his sidearm?" Diane asked.

"No. Couldn't get it out of the holster."

"The AG's office is en route, John," LeRoyer said. "I'm gonna need you to —"

The South Portland lieutenant's portable radio crackled. "Dispatch to 100."

"Go," the lieutenant said, reaching up to the mic clipped to the epaulet on his uniform shirt.

"Can you give me a 10-21, Lieutenant?"

"Ten-four." Lieutenant grabbed his cellphone out of the holder on his gun belt and dialed Dispatch. He put the phone in speaker mode then looked at the others. "Might as well all hear this."

"911, Operator Jennings speaking. What is your emergency?"

"Paula, it's Johnston."

"Hang on, Lieutenant. Let me transfer

you to the other operator."

"Lieu?" the dispatcher said.

"What's up, Robbie?"

"Didn't want to put this out over the air. The K-9 tracked that Stavros guy out toward Broadway and that's where the track ended."

"He got into a vehicle?" the lieutenant asked.

"Looks like he may have stolen Moulton's cruiser, sir. It's missing."

"Fuck," the lieutenant barked. He looked at Byron. "He must have grabbed Dick's keys, too. Any idea where he'd run?"

"Yeah," Byron said. "I do." He turned and pointed at Stevens. "Let's go."

"John, you were just involved in a shooting," LeRoyer said in protest. "You're not going any —"

"Petri just shot a cop, Marty. It's my fault he got away. I'm going after him with or without your permission."

LeRoyer looked at Stevens. "I don't suppose anything I say is gonna matter to you either, is it?"

"Nope," Stevens said as she shook her head and stepped closer to Byron.

"Time's wasting, Marty," Byron said.

LeRoyer sighed deeply. "Go. Just go."

"Where are you going?" the South Portland lieutenant asked.

"Prouts Neck," Byron shouted back. "Petri's going home. Call Scarborough and tell them to meet us at Lina's house."

CHAPTER 37

*Tuesday, 7:45 P.M.,
July 25, 2017*

It was nearing twilight as Byron and Stevens arrived at the entrance to Angelina Stavros's estate. Stevens slowed and turned into the driveway where two Scarborough officers awaited them. Large evergreens blocked what little sunlight there was, enveloping everything in shadow. The stolen South Portland cruiser, now abandoned and stuck between two twisted sections of iron fencing, appeared to have been rammed repeatedly into the gate. It was obvious that they would need to climb over the vehicle to gain entry to the property beyond.

"Wouldn't Petri have known the access code?" Stevens said as they exited her unmarked.

"I'm guessing Lina changed it," Byron said, but he couldn't help wondering if maybe Lina had known about Petri's dangerous infatuation with Deborah all along.

"Hey, guys," the older dark-haired cop carrying the rifle said. He wore the chevrons of a supervisor on his uniform and given his timeworn appearance, Byron imagined that the long-sleeved shirt he donned during cold weather probably carried with it enough hashmarks to connect wrist to elbow. "We found it just like this and called it in to our Dispatch. Hasn't been here that long. Tires are still warm."

"John Byron," he said, extending a hand. "This is Detective Melissa Stevens."

"Tim Pasquale," the sergeant said. "And this is Officer Kinney."

"Anyone go in yet?" Byron asked, reaching into the trunk of Mel's unmarked and removing a spare Kevlar vest, like the one he should have been wearing before he pursued Petri into the cemetery.

"Nope," Pasquale said. "Waiting on you."

"How's Dick Moulton?" Kinney asked.

"No word yet," Stevens said.

"How do you want to do this?" Pasquale asked.

Byron thought for a moment. He knew that in addition to taking the keys Petri had also disarmed Moulton at the graveyard. "Stavros is armed with at least one handgun and Moulton's shotgun," Byron said as he adjusted and secured the last of the Velcro straps on his vest. "We haven't been able to contact Lina, but we have to assume she's home. And given Petri's state of mind, it's a good bet that Lina may well be in danger."

"Petri's wounded, too," Pasquale said.

"How do you know that?" Stevens said.

"There's blood all over the driver's seat," Pasquale said, pointing toward Moulton's cruiser.

"Shouldn't we call out our SWAT guys?" Kinney asked.

"Probably," Byron said. "But I'm not waiting. Petri killed Danica Faherty, kidnapped a friend of mine, put two in Dick Moulton, and fired a half dozen rounds at me. And now he may well have taken his own mother hostage. I want this fucker.

"You guys want to call out the cavalry and wait right here, that's up to you," Byron continued. "But I'm going in."

"Me, too," Stevens said.

Pasquale paused a moment as he thought it through. "Technically this is Scarborough, not your jurisdiction, Sarge. But the way I see it, you and Detective Stevens here are still in fresh pursuit."

"And?" Byron said, hopeful that he'd see it Byron's way.

"And, we're going in with you."

"You two gonna be able to face the consequences for this?" Stevens asked.

Pasquale grinned. "Detective, I've been doing this job for twenty-five years. Trust me, this isn't the first dumb thing I've done. Hopefully it won't be the last."

Byron turned to Kinney. "You good?"

Kinney nodded. "If you think he has a hostage up there, that's good enough for me. I'd rather deal with the fallout for going in than live with Stavros hurting or killing anyone else. You think he knows we're here?"

Byron pointed to the security cameras. "If he's watching those, he does."

"Doesn't matter," Stevens said. "There are four of us and only one of him. Besides, he knew it was a matter of time until we got here."

The mic clipped to Pasquale's epaulet crackled with static. "Car 5, status report." He made eye contact with Byron.

"That you?" Byron asked.

"Yup."

"Well?" Byron said.

Pasquale grinned as he reached down to the portable radio hanging from his gun belt and switched it off. "Damn radio service has always been a bit spotty out this way."

"All right, let's do this," Byron said. He

555

turned and grabbed onto the roof rack of the South Portland SUV and stepped up onto the right rear tire. "Cover me."

LeRoyer had just finished briefing Rumsfeld when he saw Chief Lynds hurrying past the gravestones directly toward them.

"Fuck, here she comes," Rumsfeld said under his breath. "Chief."

Lynds ignored her second in command and focused directly on LeRoyer.

"Lieutenant, I see people from the Attorney General's Office, Portland and South Portland PD are well represented, even the media big top has arrived, but I've noticed that one thing is glaringly absent from my scene."

"What's that, Chief?" LeRoyer asked, trying his best to sound convincing.

"Where the hell is Sergeant Byron?"

Byron jumped down off the heavily damaged SUV, careful to avoid the jagged metal protruding at odd angles from the crumpled hood. Stevens followed, while Pasquale and Kinney continued to provide cover, aiming down the driveway through the fence. After Stevens was safely on the other side of the obstacle, they swapped duties with the detectives providing cover for the

Scarborough officers.

As soon as all four officers had made it over the SUV they continued on. Realizing that Petri might well be lying in wait, they availed themselves of the cover offered by the undergrowth, sticking as close as possible to the trees lining both sides of the darkened drive.

It took them several minutes to traverse the wooded section of the property and arrive at the clearing. Byron stopped then, holding up a hand to signal to the others to do the same. They crouched at the edge of the woods, Byron on the right flanked by Pasquale, while Stevens covered the left side of the drive with Kinney right behind her. Slowly, Byron scanned the expanse. The open space between where they were holed up and the house appeared empty. No Lina sitting by the lake. No grandbabies terrorizing ducks. No au pair. All seemed peaceful. A light breeze coming off the ocean kept the mosquitoes at bay. Small victories, Byron thought. They'd take all the help they could get.

"What do you think?" Pasquale asked.

"Looks clear," Byron said. "But from here on out we'll be totally exposed until we get to the house."

"Darkness should help a little," Pasquale said.

Byron hoped it would be enough.

"Let's spread out as we cross open ground," Byron said. "I don't want to make it easy in case Petri starts shooting. As we get closer, I want you and Kinney to make your way around to the rear of the house. Mel and I will take the front and hopefully make entry from there."

"Do you want to set up some kind of signal?" Pasquale asked. "You know, in case you guys run into trouble."

"If we do run into trouble, I imagine you'll have no trouble identifying our signal."

"Roger that," Pasquale said.

Byron's cell vibrated. He checked the caller ID, saw it was LeRoyer, then pressed Ignore. Better to ask for forgiveness than for permission. He couldn't remember where he'd first heard that, but it'd proved invaluable. He looked at the others. "Ready?"

They each responded accordingly.

"And kill your ringers," Byron said. "I don't want to get shot because of a text message."

LeRoyer navigated his unmarked through the snarl of evening traffic using the lights and siren. He drove as fast as he dared toward Prouts Neck. Chief Lynds, who sat in the passenger seat, cellphone pressed to her ear, was fuming. The chief disconnected the call again.

"Byron's still not answering," Lynds said.

Nothing unusual there, LeRoyer thought.

Rumsfeld, on the phone to Scarborough PD, sat alone in the back seat. "What do you mean you can't reach them?" Rumsfeld hollered. "You've got two officers on the scene and neither one is answering the radio? What kind of department are you running?"

LeRoyer, fighting back the urge to point out the obvious, knew all too well who was probably behind the radio silence. He knew whenever Byron set his sights on something, neither rank, nor chain of command, and certainly not the threat of discipline ever seemed to matter. Byron wanted Petri, period. LeRoyer knew that, one way or another, this thing would play itself out tonight at Angelina Stavros's Scarborough home.

Byron had lost sight of Pasquale and Kinney several minutes before. Darkness was falling quickly as he and Stevens approached the front of the house from opposite corners.

The windows were dark, no visible lights inside, only the lamps on either side of the main entry were illuminated. In the driveway was a white Porsche Macan, a vehicle Byron recognized only from its vanity plate. Wagner 5. It was Gene Wagner's, probably one of many he owned. *Was Wagner part of this?* Byron wondered. *Or had Lina telephoned him when she realized what was happening, that their dirty little secret had gone off the rails? And where was Wagner's errand boy, Paulson? Would Wagner have involved him, or come alone?*

As they mounted the granite steps, Byron observed that the front door to the home was ajar. The damage around the latch was obvious. Someone had forced it. He waited until Stevens arrived at his side before giving the heavy oak a shove. The door swung the rest of the way open, revealing the gloom of the home's interior.

Byron and Stevens stepped inside, moving as slowly as possible to give their eyes a chance to adjust. They crept through the entryway into the main living space.

They skirted either side of the dining room, pausing outside the kitchen door. Byron silently signaled for Stevens to hang back. He wanted her out of harm's way, out of sight as his backup while he faced whatever awaited them in the next room. Stevens nodded and Byron slid into the kitchen. The room was dark except for the pendant lights suspended above a large granite-topped island, reminding Byron of some old-time noir interrogation scene.

In the light, Byron saw fresh blood drops glistening on the tile floor.

Byron's heart was racing as he surveyed the room. He adjusted his breathing, attempting to bring it down a notch.

Cautiously, he skirted the island. The first thing he saw was Gene Wagner's motionless body lying faceup on the floor. Wagner was bleeding from a head wound. Byron checked the other darkened corners of the room, but there was only Wagner. He returned to Wagner and knelt down. Pressing his fingers against the carotid artery on the side of Wagner's neck, Byron felt for a pulse. He found one, but it was weak. Wagner was still alive, but for how long?

"Is he dead?" Stevens whispered from behind him.

"Jesus, Mel," Byron said, startled. "I thought you were still in the dining room."

"Sorry. Got bored."

"No, he's not dead. Looks like someone knocked him a good one, though." Byron looked closely and saw the knot forming on the side of Wagner's head.

"He'll have to wait," Byron said as he stood up and headed back toward the dining room. "Let's go."

They checked the remainder of the first floor, including the library and several bathrooms, but there was no sign of either Lina or Petri.

Byron and Stevens stopped at the base of the stairs. The second-floor landing was faintly illuminated by what looked like a nightlight casting baluster shadows on the wall. As Stevens covered the top of the stairs with her Glock, Byron bent down and checked for blood. The steps and risers were dotted with red. Petri was upstairs. Byron stood up and nodded to Stevens. Slowly, they ascended.

Lieutenant LeRoyer killed the siren. Using emergency lights only, he slalomed his way along Black Point Road. He gave the occasional blast of the unmarked's air horn when they needed to wake up an inattentive driver. None of them had any idea what they were getting themselves into, but there was no advantage to tipping off Petri if Byron and Stevens were in trouble.

"Want me to try Byron's cell again?" Rumsfeld asked from the back seat.

"What's the point?" Lynds said. "He hasn't answered my calls or returned the last two messages."

"Dammit," LeRoyer yelled as he dished out another burst of the electronic horn. "How can you people not see these lights?"

"Try calling Detective Stevens," Lynds said. "Maybe she's still thinking with a clear head."

Rumsfeld dialed. She wasn't.

The second floor of Lina Stavros's house was divided by two perpendicular hallways. Byron signaled for Stevens to take the one on the right while he indicated that he would check the one leading toward the rear of the house.

Sticking close to the left side of the hall, Byron moved slowly and quietly. On every step he placed his heel down first then rolled his foot forward until the shoe was flat on the floor. The first door was open and, after performing a quick peek into the bedroom, he stepped inside.

Byron had just finished clearing the bedroom and the en suite when he heard gunshots coming from Stevens's side of the house. *Shit.* Byron hurried back the way he had come. "Mel, where are you?"

"First door on the left," Stevens said.

As Byron neared the landing, he heard the Scarborough officers forcing entry into the house from the first-floor rear.

"Sarge," Pasquale shouted.

"Second floor," Byron shouted back.

"Drop it, Lina," Stevens said as Byron entered the room.

Angelina Stavros stood in front of a door to a walk-in closet. She was holding a handgun down by her side. Lina was facing away from Stevens toward the far corner of the dimly lit room where a badly wounded Petri sat slumped on the floor. Lina's son had his back to the wall, cradling the shotgun in both arms, its barrel pointed up toward the ceiling.

"Lina, toss the gun on the floor," Stevens commanded.

"Right behind you, Sarge," Pasquale announced from the doorway.

Seeing that Stevens had Lina covered, Byron trained his Glock on Petri.

"Drop it," Stevens said again. "Now."

Lina finally let the gun slip from her grasp. It landed on the carpet with a thud.

Byron moved away from Stevens, his gun still pointed at Petri, finger snug against the trigger. "Put the gun down, Petri," Byron said. "It's over."

"Is it?" Petri said in obvious pain, his lips

forming into a grin. The blood around his mouth made the gesture look ghoulish.

Byron saw Stevens and Officer Kinney move farther into the room in his periphery. Stevens retrieved the gun Lina had tossed while Kinney grabbed Lina and backed her toward the hallway.

"I've got him, Sarge," Stevens said.

"Me, too," Pasquale said from the opposite side of the room.

"Petri, you can still end this without hurting anyone else," Byron said. "Just lower the shotgun to the floor."

"But I have hurt people. Lots of people. Been quite a disappointment around here for years, haven't I, Mother?" Petri raised his voice to be sure Lina heard him.

Byron waited to see if Lina would say something that might help to defuse this situation, but she didn't respond. Byron wasn't sure she could respond. She was in shock.

"Put the gun down, Petri," Byron said.

"Alex is only my half brother, Sergeant Byron. Did you know that? I was the byproduct of Mother's affair with Gene Wagner. A fucking mistake. I wonder, did you ever tell Dad what you had done? Is that what drove him to his accident?"

Byron jumped in again, trying to control

the direction and pace of what was happening. It was obvious that Petri wanted to get some things off his chest once and for all. "Your father died in a boating accident, Petri."

"Is that what Lina told you?" Petri laughed out loud but there was no humor in it. "My father was an expert sailor. He was the best at everything he put his hand to. Do you really think he would have been out on the ocean in those conditions if he hadn't meant to end it? People believe what they want to believe, Sergeant Byron. Whatever makes them feel safe. Isn't that right, Mother?"

Byron could hear Lina sobbing in the hallway.

"That's right," Petri said. "Have a good cry. Want to know what I believed, Sergeant? For years I told myself that Lina loved Alex more because he was better looking, more charming, maybe even because he was smarter. But none of that was true, was it, Mother?"

Lina said nothing.

"No, the truth is that she loves Alex more because she loved his father. Still loves him. I'm nothing more than a reminder that she cheated. Does Alex even know, Mother? Does he? Or was he like me, stupid enough to believe you?"

"I still don't understand why you had to kill Danica Faherty, Petri," Byron said, stalling for time and attempting to build a rapport in the hope that Petri would surrender. "What did Dani have to do with any of this?"

"I killed her because I wanted Alex to pay. Pay for everything. For the years that I had to play second fiddle to him, had to watch as he was given everything while I worked my ass off. I'm a world-class chef, too, but do I get credit for that? No. I'm the one who runs everything. I ran the restaurant in New York then, when Lina wanted to open another one up here, she sent me to make it happen. Then, after it was up and running, she brought little old Alex to take over while Petri got relegated to the fucking back burner. Banished from the limelight once again. Alex gets all the glory while I spend my days hiring and firing snot-nosed undergrads and drop-outs to wait tables. I might as well be scrubbing the pots and pans."

Byron could see that Petri was winded, growing weaker. He was using the barrel of the shotgun to hold himself upright, but his hands kept slipping. The longer this went on the more likely it was that Petri might simply pass out from blood loss.

"I followed Dani that night after she left

the restaurant. I knew she was sneaking off to meet Alex, and I knew where they'd been having their little rendezvous. I knew Alex would find some way to sneak back to Portland to be with her, and he did. I waited all night for Alex to leave our old house. After he did, I snuck in and confronted Dani."

"Is that what you tell yourself?" Byron said.

"What are you talking about?"

"You never had any intention of confronting her, Petri. You snuck up on her from behind and buried that hammer in the back of her skull. You wanted to set your brother up, to make him pay. You were pissed because Deborah married Alex and not you. She was just one more thing that Alex had that you couldn't."

Petri grimaced in pain. "That's right, I love Deborah, and she could love me. She's too good for my philandering half brother. He doesn't give a damn about her. Deborah is just one more thing that Alex takes for granted."

"And you think you'd make a good husband, Petri?" Byron said, intentionally goading him. "She doesn't love you. Deborah's terrified of you."

"And whose fault is that, Sergeant? You're

no better than Lina the Great. You both turned Debbie against me. You ruined my life."

"Oh please," Byron said. "You really think Deborah would have any interest in marrying a cold-blooded killer?"

A crooked grin spread across Petri's face. "You think you're pretty smart, don't you, Sergeant Byron?"

"I don't know about that," Byron said. "My current situation would tend to suggest otherwise, but I figured you out."

"Well, good for you. It took you long enough to figure out that it wasn't me who cut off her head and dumped her body at the lumberyard. Uncle Dennis should have stayed out of it. This was supposed to have been easy. You should have suspected Alex from the start, not that damn Horseman."

"The more we dug into Dani's past, the more we found she didn't fit the profile. She wasn't a prostitute like the Horseman's other victims. Then, I began to wonder who could hate Alex enough to kill his girlfriend? Who could hate him enough to set him up for murder?"

"Me!" Petri shouted. "I could. I still do. I knew if I could just get Alex out of the way, my life would be better. They'd find Dani's body in our old house, and Alex would take the fall. Maybe even drag Lina into it. It was so simple. But then Dennis got involved. I couldn't believe it when you showed up at the restaurant asking about Dani. It wasn't until I found out that she'd been moved that I knew I was in trouble."

"Put the gun down, Petri," Byron repeated. "We can work all of this out."

"There's nothing to work out. I love Debbie, and I thought she loved me. I thought she'd come back to me if Alex was gone." Petri's breathing was coming in loud ragged gasps now as he fought to pull air into his dying lungs.

"Can't seem to do anything right," Petri said. "Even at birth I was nothing more than a mistake. Right Mom? The bastard child."

Lina let out an audible groan.

"Petri," Byron said. "For the last time, lay the gun on the floor."

"You know how I found out, Mom? Gene told me. One night at the restaurant, when he was soused, Gene told me that he was my real father. I wonder if Dad ever knew what a bitch you were?"

"Stop!" Officer Kinney shouted from the hallway.

Byron caught a flash of movement from the corner of his eye. Lina was on the move, charging into the room toward Petri. A scream of anguish was building from some-where deep inside her. As Byron moved to cut her off, he saw Petri's blood-soaked hand slide down the barrel toward the trigger. Petri raised the weapon and lowered the barrel toward Lina.

"Don't do it, Petri!" Stevens yelled.

Byron dove across the room, wrapping his arms around Lina and dragging her backward to the floor where he covered her with his body.

Byron heard Petri scream like a wounded animal as the room erupted in gunfire.

By the time the smoke had cleared, Petri lay dead on the floor. Three rounds from Stevens's Glock and two rounds from Pasquale's rifle had ended the nightmare that had begun two weeks prior.

Byron retreated to the home's rear deck where he found Nugent sitting next to Stevens, keeping her company.

"You okay?" Byron asked Stevens.

"I'm good," she said. "Thanks. Just thinking what a waste that Dani was caught up in this."

"Fucker got what was coming to him anyway," Nugent said.

Byron couldn't argue with that sentiment, but he also didn't imagine the Fahertys' grief would be lessened by the fact that Petri was dead.

"How's it going in there, boss?" Nugent asked.

"About like you'd imagine," Byron said. "Marty's out in the driveway briefing Lynds and Rumsfeld, while all three of them are trying to placate a very disgruntled Scarborough police chief."

"What do you think will happen?" Stevens asked.

"My guess? Same thing that always happens. They'll be more concerned with how it looks than my break in protocol. In the end, they'll most likely decide to hold a joint press conference, giving Scarborough PD kudos for their part in the apprehension of Faherty's killer. And Lynds will talk about the importance of inter-agency cooperation in this time of financial uncertainty."

"Jeez, boss," Nugent said. "That's good. You should be the chief."

"I'll pass, thanks."

"So, all's well that ends well?" Nugent said.

"Something like that," Byron said.

"What happens now with Alex?" Stevens said.

"I just spoke to Jim Ferguson," Byron said. "Based on Petri's confession and the evidence against him, the AG will be dropping the charges against Alex, and he'll be released."

"What about Dennis Stavros?" Stevens said. "Will he still be charged?"

"Probably," Byron said. "But he has no priors. I imagine the court will go easy on him."

"He still tried to cover up a murder," Nugent said. "Man, this is one fucked-up family."

Byron sat down beside Stevens. "You sure you're good, Mel?"

"I heard the shotgun wasn't loaded," Stevens said. "Is that true?"

Byron chose his words carefully before answering. "Not entirely. It was loaded, but the only thing in the chamber was the spent cartridge from the round Moulton fired in the cemetery."

"I don't get it," Stevens said.

"I don't think Petri knew how to operate a pump shotgun," Byron said. "Probably why he bashed Wagner in the head with it instead of shooting him."

"Doesn't matter," Nugent said. "There's no way you could have known that, Mel. Isn't that right, Sarge?"

"Nuge is right. None of us could have known. He was holding and pointing a deadly weapon and ignoring commands. You did what you had to do. Period. I'm proud of you, Mel."

"Yup, my partner is a bad-ass, Sarge," Nugent said, putting an arm around her and giving her an awkward hug.

"Thanks, partner," Stevens said. "Does this mean your bromance with Bernie is off?" Stevens asked.

"Thank Christ."

Nugent's cell chimed with an incoming text message. "Holy shit."

"What?" Stevens asked.

"It's happening," Nugent said, jumping to his feet. "Like right now."

"The baby?" Byron asked.

"Yeah. Jesus, I gotta go."

"Then go," Byron said.

"Hey, Nuge," Stevens said.

Nugent, who was halfway across the deck, stopped. "Yeah?"

A smile spread across her lips. "Congrats, partner."

Epilogue

Sunday, 12:45 P.M.,
August 6, 2017

Sunlight shone down on Portland from a cloudless, cerulean sky. The previous evening's thunderstorms had departed along with the humidity, leaving the air crisp and warm. Byron slid his car into a no-parking zone on Park Avenue directly across from Hadlock Field. He removed the gun and holster from his belt and locked them inside the console. Sporting a new pair of Ray-Bans, he climbed out of the Ford, then fell into step with the crowd of people crossing the street toward the ballpark.

As he passed the uniformed cop working the gravy detail manning the crosswalk, Byron cocked a thumb back over his shoulder in the direction of the unmarked. "Keep an eye on it for me, would you?"

"Worried about vandals?" the cop asked.

"Parking Nazis."

The cop laughed. "Leave it to me, Sarge."

Nearing the stadium, Byron spotted his niece standing on the sidewalk beneath the bronze statue of a family on game day. Katherine's long auburn hair was threaded through the back of the Sea Dogs cap she wore. She was up on her tiptoes peering through the throng of people walking toward her from the east on Park Avenue and hadn't spotted him yet.

He snuck up behind her, resisting the urge to shout out "Katie." She had always been his Katie, but she was a young woman now, preparing for her sophomore year of college. His niece had cast off the childhood moniker.

"Happy birthday, Katherine," he said.

Katherine spun around surprised. "Uncle John!" She embraced him tightly.

Byron released her. "Great to see you, young lady."

"It's great to see you, too. I'm so excited for you to meet Carlos."

"Carlos?"

She rolled her eyes. "My boyfriend. He's the Sea Dogs catcher. Didn't Aunt Kay tell you?"

"Must have slipped her mind," Byron said, realizing that she really had grown up.

"Isn't that totally cool?"

He kept the smile painted on his face. "Totally. Can't wait to meet him. So, you got the tickets okay?"

"Sure. They had them in an envelope at the Will Call window, with my name on them."

"Whoa, you must be pretty important with that kind of clout."

"I know people," she said, handing him his ticket. She turned and headed for the entrance to the ballpark. "Come on. I don't want to miss the first pitch."

As they neared the turnstiles Byron's cell rang. The number was blocked.

Katherine turned and looked at him, the shadow of disappointment clouding her face. "I thought you said you weren't going back to work until tomorrow?"

"I'm not. Diane's still covering for me, but I gotta take this call. You go on ahead and I'll catch up, okay?"

Katherine hesitated. She didn't look convinced.

"Honest," Byron said. "I'll just be a minute."

"Okay," Katherine said, her smile returning as she bounded past the checkpoint and inside the stadium.

He stepped off to one side, so as not to be mowed over by the fans, and answered the call. "Byron."

"Sergeant Byron," a somber male voice said.

There was something vaguely familiar about the voice. "Who is this?"

"Elmer Faherty."

Byron wasn't sure he would ever hear from either of the Fahertys again. "What can I do for you, Elmer?"

"Guess I just wanted to thank you for — that is, Denise and I want to thank you for getting justice for — our Dani."

Byron paused a moment before speaking. *Had he? Is that what killing Stavros had been? Justice for Dani?* Not to Byron it hadn't. To him it had been about saving Lina from her deranged son, saving Alex from a fate he didn't deserve, and it had been to prevent Petri from killing anyone else. But to Elmer Faherty, the aggrieved father who had lost his only daughter to the sick and twisted jealousies of Petri Stavros, maybe justice had been served. Maybe justice, like so many other things, is simply in the eye of the beholder. Perhaps Petri's death at the hands of the police was enough to bring the Fahertys a little peace.

"I'm very sorry for your loss," Byron said.

ACKNOWLEDGMENTS

Within Plain Sight, novel number four in the Detective Byron Mystery Series, is a testament to how incredible you, my readers, are. My first publishing contract was for three novels, a typical series offering in the publishing world. I had, it seemed, at least for the foreseeable future, all that I could handle. *Among the Shadows* was slated to be released in the fall of 2016. I was halfway through the manuscript for *Beneath the Depths.* And novel number three, *Beyond the Truth,* was still swirling about the gray matter inside my head. At that early stage in my novel writing journey, I couldn't imagine anything beyond three Byron novels. But here we are, looking another Byron novel square in the eye. John Byron lives on, and for that both John and I continue to be eternally grateful to all of you.

As always, I must give thanks to the many special folks without whom I might never have gotten this far: Paula Munier and Gina Panettieri at Talcott Notch Literary for continuing to believe in me and my stories; Nick Amphlett, Danielle Bartlett, Gena Lanzi, Guido Caroti, and the rest of the Witness Impulse Team at HarperCollins; fellow bloggers at Maine Crime Writers and Murder Books; and the many great folks at the libraries and bookstores throughout New England.

My beta readers and fact checkers, Mary Simonelli, Darcel Devou, Alice Persons, Sara Coffin, Mary Pearson, and Chris Stearns. Any mistakes were my own.

The Gallant Family for allowing me to keep the memory of a very special young man alive and well. Thank you, Pattie.

My immediate family and friends for their unwavering encouragement and support along the way.

The countless men and women in the field of criminal justice, true professionals, I was fortunate to have served with, as well as those who continue to serve (these are their stories).

John Byron, Diane Joyner, and the rest of the fictional 109 team, who have become as much a part of my life as those with whom I once worked.

Lastly, and most importantly, my wife,

Karen, for her love, inspiration, and infinite patience. Without you in my life, there would be no story.

ABOUT THE AUTHOR

Bruce Robert Coffin is a former detective sergeant with more than twenty-seven years in law enforcement. At the time of his retirement from the Portland, Maine, police department, he supervised all homicide and violent crime investigations for Maine's largest city. Following the terror attacks of September 11, Bruce spent four years working counterterrorism with the FBI, earning the Director's Award, the highest honor a nonagent can receive.

He is the author of *Among the Shadows, Beneath the Depths,* and *Beyond the Truth.* He lives and writes in Maine.